The Pink
Magnolia Club

Today I will do something deliciously wicked. . . .

Just the thought of it gave her the shivers.

She'd deliberated long and hard about just what constituted wickedness for this purpose. Anything illegal was definitely out. She certainly didn't want to act in a way that might cause harm or heartache of any kind to anyone. Holly wanted to do something juicy enough that she would remember it in the years to come. She wanted to do something naughty, not evil.

Eventually, Holly had concluded that her definition of deliciously wicked meant she need not step over to the wild side entirely. She simply had to dip her toes a bit.

She'd painted her toenails Louisiana Hot Sauce red in honor of the occasion.

Justin would love it. He'd love her nail color and the lingerie that matched and even the little henna tattoo she'd had painted on the inside of her thigh. And he'd love it soon. This very afternoon. Because in order to satisfy the requirements of item twenty-one on her list, Holly intended to make love with Dr. Justin Skipworth in a totally inappropriate setting. . . .

SIMMER ALL NIGHT

"Delightfully spicy—perfect to warm up a cold winter's night."

—Christina Dodd, author of *Rules of Surrender*

"A romance buoyed by lively characters and Southern lore. Dawson sustains readers' attention with her humorous dialogue and colorful narration."

—*Publishers Weekly*

"Once again, Geralyn Dawson has come up with a winner."

—*Romantic Times*

THE BAD LUCK WEDDING CAKE

"Fast and captivating from start to finish. This humorous story is as delicious as one of [the heroine's] cakes!"

—*Rendezvous*

"A delicious gourmet delight! A seven-course reading experience."

—*Affaire de Coeur*

"Geralyn Dawson has written a laugh-out-loud tale with a few tears and a big sigh at the end. Another keeper."

—*Romantic Times*

Also by Geralyn Dawson

The Wedding Raffle
The Wedding Ransom
The Bad Luck Wedding Cake
The Kissing Stars
Simmer All Night
Sizzle All Day
The Bad Luck Wedding Night
The Pink Magnolia Club

Published by POCKET BOOKS

GERALYN DAWSON

The Pink Magnolia Club

Pocket Books
New York London Toronto Sydney Singapore

This book is a work of fiction. Names, characters, places and incidents are products of the author's imagination or are used fictitiously. Any resemblance to actual events or locales or persons, living or dead, is entirely coincidental.

An *Original* Publication of POCKET BOOKS

POCKET BOOKS, a division of Simon & Schuster, Inc.
1230 Avenue of the Americas, New York, NY 10020

Copyright © 2002 by Geralyn Dawson Williams

All rights reserved, including the right to reproduce this book or portions thereof in any form whatsoever. For information address Pocket Books, 1230 Avenue of the Americas, New York, NY 10020

ISBN: 0-7434-4265-2

First Pocket Books printing August 2002

10 9 8 7 6 5 4 3 2 1

POCKET BOOKS and colophon are registered trademarks of Simon & Schuster, Inc.

For information regarding special discounts for bulk purchases, please contact Simon & Schuster Special Sales at 1-800-456-6798 or business@simonandschuster.com

Cover design and illustration by Melody Cassen
Photo © David Muench / Corbis

Printed in the U.S.A.

To Fran Hansen

and the men and women of the
Making Memories Breast Cancer Foundation

May all your wishes come true.

❀ holly's life list

1. I will be kind to telemarketers.

2. I will skydive at least once.

3. I will walk barefoot on a beach in Tahiti.

4. ✓ I will own something perfect to wear if the man of my dreams wants to see me in an hour.

5. I will attend a World Series, preferably one where the Texas Rangers represent the American League.

6. I will have a friend who makes me laugh and one who lets me cry.

7. ✓ I will spend New Year's Eve at Times Square.

8. I will save a life.

9. I will catch a fish that weighs over five pounds.

10. I will write a letter to my dad, telling him how much I love him and why.

11. I will make an honest effort to understand why men like the Three Stooges.

12. ✓ I will bungee jump.

13. I will ski a black diamond mountain.

14. I will fly a kite in every month of the year.

15. I will own glasses that match, a good set of wrenches, and a pair of crotchless panties.

16. ✓ I will teach an adult to read.

17. I will learn to play the piano.

18. I will be a man's "Best He Ever Had."

19. I will dive an underwater wreck.

20. I will ride every roller coaster in Texas.

21. I will do something deliciously wicked.

22. I will learn where to go when my soul needs soothing.

23. I will collect each of the state heritage quarters.

24. I will create a piece of art.

25. I will win the Yard of the Month award.

26. I will control my own destiny, at least for a little while.

27. I will read a thousand books simply for pleasure.

28. ✓ I will watch a sunrise from the deck of a windjammer.

29. I will watch a sunset from Mallory Square in Key West.

30. I will keep enough money in a savings account to support myself for six months.

31. I will clean out my closets once a year.

32. I will know how to walk away when the time is right.

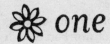 one

holly Weeks kept her dreams tucked inside her wallet.
The list of thirty-two items had been penned in
black ink on white paper, folded into a small rectangle,
and slipped into a special spot between her driver's license and, appropriately enough, her Discover card.
Across its front, bold red ink and loopy handwriting
fashioned the heading: *My Life List.*

Currently her list nestled inside the little red purse
slung over her shoulder. The purse was new, bought to
coordinate with the red polka-dot nothing of a dress purchased specifically for today's special occasion. It was
short, sassy, and unlike anything else in her wardrobe.
Holly loved it.

A seventh-grade math teacher in the Fort Worth ISD,
she ordinarily wore tailored slacks and modest blouses to
work, jeans and tee shirts at home. She chose comfort
over style and kept dry-clean-only purchases to a mini-

mum. The little red dress was an exception. It made her feel exceptional.

Today, Holly's agenda required something extraordinary. Today, she intended to accomplish goal twenty-one: *I will do something deliciously wicked.*

"If I can just get Justin to cooperate," she murmured as she sashayed up Main Street in downtown Fort Worth toward the Greystone Hotel. Holly had met Dr. Justin Skipworth last year while visiting one of her students at Children's Medical Center of Dallas. Since then he'd completed his residency and joined a pediatrics practice in Fort Worth. They'd been lovers for six months.

Justin was smart, handsome, generous, caring—just about everything a woman could want in a man. His only less-than-desirable quality was a tendency toward stuffiness on occasion. Since stuffiness wouldn't get twenty-one checked off her list, Holly had dressed today for battle by adding take-me pumps, Saturday night makeup, and make-him-suffer perfume to the package.

She looked good. A shade trashy, but good. Justin was about to get the stuffy knocked right out of him. This was war and Holly was a determined woman.

She had developed both her attitude and her list three days before her thirteenth birthday, the very evening she and her dad returned to their empty house following her mom's funeral. As time passed, she focused her determination on refining the list—adding, deleting, and checking off each dream that came true. Her attitude remained unchanged.

Holly revamped her list entirely at the age of nineteen. When a collision on the basketball court during a collegiate intramural game resulted in a badly broken leg and extended bed stay, she developed a TV talk-show habit. Under the influence of the daytime divas, she discarded all but three items on her original list, replacing them with goals more adult in both scope and content.

Four years ago on her twenty-first birthday, Holly celebrated by declaring her list complete and in its final form. She would make no more changes or deletions. Only check-offs.

She bought a special twenty-three-karat gold plate pen to use for check-offs, and she had set her thirty-second birthday as her deadline to get the job done.

Considering her circumstances, she thought it best not to drag it out any longer than that.

Today, she intended to use her check-off pen for the sixth time. She chose which goal to pursue at random and now, bright red checks added a splash of color up and down her page. Not enough color, however. She craved more red. Checking off twenty-one today would help. Then, depending on how it went, she might decide she'd met the requirements for number eighteen, too.

Holly grinned at the thought as she jaywalked across the street in front of the hotel. Pausing to snag a ball cap that the strong March breeze had snatched from a teenager's head and sent skittering her way, she caught it midair, earning a thanks from the young man and an admiring once-over from the parking valets. Feeling pretty, and unusually flirtatious, Holly winked at the teenager as she handed him his hat, then blew a kiss to the cute valet who risked his job by letting loose a wolf whistle as she approached the hotel's revolving door. The attention put an extra bounce in her already springy step.

I will do something deliciously wicked. Just the thought of it gave her the shivers.

She'd deliberated long and hard about just what constituted wickedness for this purpose. Anything illegal was definitely out. She certainly didn't want to act in a way that might cause harm or heartache of any kind to anyone. Holly wanted to do something juicy enough that she would remember it in the years to come. She wanted to do something naughty, not evil.

Eventually, Holly had concluded that her definition of deliciously wicked meant she need not step over to the wild side entirely. She simply had to dip her toes a bit.

She'd painted her toenails Louisiana Hot Sauce red in honor of the occasion.

Stuffy or not, Justin would love it. He was a man, after all. He'd love her nail color and the lingerie that matched and even the little henna tattoo she'd had painted on the inside of her thigh. And he'd love it soon. This very afternoon. Because in order to satisfy the requirements of item number twenty-one on her list, Holly intended to make love with Dr. Justin Skipworth in a totally inappropriate setting.

The very thought of it made her tingle. Wasn't it handy she'd managed to think of something that would satisfy both her list requirements and her hormones?

Justin would positively love it.

As she breezed into the hotel, Holly checked her watch. Three-fifteen. Exactly on time. Pretty darn good, considering she'd stayed to the very end of the softball game, where the Texas Ladies, of whom five players were Holly's seventh-grade pre-algebra students, faced off against the Be-Attitudes, a team containing four of Holly's religious ed students from church.

"Good afternoon, ma'am," a bellhop said when she sailed past him.

"Yes it is, isn't it?" Holly's gaze swept the lobby, searching, then settling on the man in jeans and a blue chambray shirt who straddled the grand piano's bench and idly one-handed a melody. She let out a little lovelorn sigh.

At thirty, Justin Skipworth was classically handsome, with sun-bleached hair, a straight blade of a nose, and light brown eyes framed in unfair-to-women lashes. Tanned, tall, and whipcord lean, he was the kind of man who looked comfortable and confident everywhere he went.

So why, she wondered, when he spied her, rose, and walked toward her with a lanky, long-legged stride, *are his eyes shining with a nervous light?*

"Hey, beautiful. That is some dress." He bent and gave her a quick kiss. "Mmm . . . you smell good, too. Who won the game?"

"The Be-Attitudes. Those church girls of mine are mean competitors. What did you do this morning?"

"Slept late. Dreamed about you."

Holly melted. "Oh, Justin. That's so sweet."

"No, not at all." His mouth twisted in a rueful grin. "My dream was a nightmare. I dreamed you jumped out of a plane."

At that, she sighed and made a show of rolling her eyes. Skydiving was number two on her list. While she kept the existence of her Life List private, she had mentioned her interest in a few of the activities, skydiving being one of them. Justin thought she was crazy.

At least she wasn't stuffy.

"Don't start, Skipworth."

"Not today. It'll hold." He gestured toward the lobby sign, which read ANTIQUE FISHING LURE SHOW, BONHAM

BALLROOM, and added, "No sense spoiling a lovely afternoon filled with Musky Lipped Wigglers."

Holly chuckled and rose on her tiptoes to kiss his cheek, then give his earlobe a quick nibble and lowered her voice to a sexy purr. "It's the Bobbin Bass Bait I can't wait to get my hands on."

Justin winced. "I hope you didn't share that particular bit of news with your dad."

She put a theatric hand to her chest. "Tell Daddy I'm after a Husky Plunker today? Are you crazy? I want it to be a surprise."

"Oh, I imagine he'd be plenty surprised to hear you talking that way about Husky Plunkers. Come on. Let's see what we can find." He grabbed her hand and followed the signs toward the Bonham ballroom and the fishing lure show.

Holly did hope to find a fishing lure or two to include with her father's birthday gift. Jim Weeks was a historian by profession and a fisherman by avocation, so his interest in collecting antique bait suited him well. It also gave his daughter handy gift possibilities, so when Justin saw an ad in the paper and suggested they attend the show as part of their Saturday afternoon date, she had jumped at the chance.

Justin had no idea that Holly wanted to add an extra stop to their itinerary at the Greystone.

She had prepared for the event by exploring the hotel and its nooks and crannies in advance of today's adventure. She'd located two areas that fit her requirements: an out-of-the-way stairwell and a small storage room off the ballroom.

The storeroom was her first choice, and she hoped its door remained unlocked. As much as she liked to imagine herself as bold and free-spirited, she feared that when the moment arrived, the stairwell might be too public for her sensibilities.

Glancing at Justin, she again noted the tension that seemed to hover around him. Had one of his patients run into trouble? One of his partners had told Holly that Justin cared too much, that he was too empathetic and would burn himself out before he ever got started if he didn't build some walls. She worried about that, wondered how he could find a balance that would soothe his mind without destroying his heart. Justin had such a big heart.

Just as she opened her mouth to ask if something was wrong, he yanked her to a stop, grabbed her by the shoulders, and planted a searing kiss right on her lips.

Oh, my. Her knees all but buckled. Justin seldom indulged in public displays of affection. What had gotten into him? She smiled dreamily and melted against him. What a positive start to today's proceedings.

"I love you, Holly."

She blinked. He was so handsome, so dear. So *nervous.* "I love you, too, Justin."

He nodded once. Hard. "Remember that."

Then he was pulling her down the red-carpeted corridor once again. For a moment, she worried over her lover's strange behavior, but that concern was quickly overwhelmed by the sheer force of the excitement thrumming in her veins.

This was going to work. She knew it. She, Holly Weeks, proper and demure seventh-grade math teacher, was about to shed her prim-and-proper skin and take a short stroll on the wild side. They'd shop the fishing bait sale, buy some spinners and plugs. She'd tease him and make suggestive jokes about rods and spin-tail kickers. Then she'd lure her lover into the storeroom and have her deliciously wicked way with him, satisfying both herself and number twenty-one.

The idea of it made her feel wonderfully alive.

Holly was so busy fantasizing that at first she didn't realize they'd gone beyond the Bonham ballroom. It wasn't until they'd turned the corner into the hallway that led to the larger, Austin ballroom that her brain caught up with her feet. "Justin, you passed the show."

"I know. That was just a lure."

"A lure. Cute." She pulled from his grasp and stopped in the middle of the hall. Glancing in the direction of the elevators, she asked, "Did you get a room?"

While it wasn't exactly wicked enough for number twenty-one, Holly nevertheless found the idea intriguing.

"No. Not a room," he said, not meeting her gaze. "I want to show you something."

Vaguely aware of a low hum of feminine voices drifting from the ballroom down the corridor, Holly narrowed her stare and studied the man she loved. Hmm. This wasn't like Justin. Something was definitely up. Something he wasn't certain she was going to like. Her stomach took a roll.

Maybe she wouldn't get to use her special gold check-off pen today, after all.

Justin sucked in a deep breath, then exhaled in a rush. He closed his eyes, visibly braced himself, then lifted his chin and met her gaze head-on. His nervous look had disappeared, calm determination taking its place. She had the odd sensation that this was how Dr. Skipworth looked when he prepared to deliver a difficult diagnosis.

"This didn't go quite like I had planned, but . . . " He reached into his back pants pocket and withdrew a folded, tri-fold brochure. Handing it to her, he said, "I thought we could shop for something other than fishing tackle here today."

"O-kay," she replied in a slow, tentative drawl. Paper crackled and Holly's hands trembled as she unfolded the brochure and read: *Making Memories Breast Cancer Foundation. Making a Difference for Today. Leaving Memories for Tomorrow.*

The old, familiar pain struck from out of nowhere and pierced to the marrow, murdering her seductive mood. Angry and hurting, she shook her head and shoved the pamphlet back at Justin. "I don't want this."

Calmly, he turned the brochure over. His voice was soft and gentle as he said, "I thought it would be a nice way to honor your mother."

Her mom?

Sounding pleased with himself, he added, "Your dad told me the two of you were very close."

Holly's throat constricted and she blinked repeatedly in order to read through the sudden tears that swelled in her eyes. Oh, God. What had he done?

Almost against her will, her gaze trailed over the words printed on the leaflet.

Dressed in bridal finery, a woman walks down the aisle to begin a new life. Now, thanks to the Making Memories Breast Cancer Foundation, a bride has the opportunity to help those men and women walking a far different path—that toward the end of life. By donating her wedding gown for resale by the foundation or by purchasing her gown at one of Making Memories' wed-

*ding gown sales, she has the opportunity to help grant a
wish—possibly a last wish—and help make a memory
for the family of a person with metastatic breast cancer.*

Emotion clutched at Holly's heart, sank razor-sharp
talons into tender muscle. The brochure slipped from
her fingers and floated to the floor as Justin tugged her
slowly, inexorably toward the Austin ballroom.

Mama.

Upon reaching the doorway, Holly came to a dead
stop. "Oh, my God."

It was a scene right out of a fairy tale. The glittering
ballroom held rack after rack after rack of wedding
gowns. Thousands of dresses. So much white, in fact,
that Holly felt snow-blinded. Snow-blinded and dizzy
and oh, so afraid.

Time seemed to halt. Holly couldn't breathe. Memories from the past swirled with dreams of a future destined never to be, and it hurt. It hurt so desperately.

Then, to make matters even worse, in front of God and
meandering bait collectors and a ballroom full of brides,
Justin Skipworth, M.D., man of her dreams, dropped to
one knee and offered up a black velvet ring box. "Holly
Weeks, will you marry me?"

She heard gasps of delight from the crowd amid a rushing, roaring noise in her ears. Pain. Fear. Confusion. Spin-
ning wildly within her, a cyclone of emotion with yearning
at its core. Yearning, strong and fierce and foolish.

There was only one thing for her to do.

Holly dashed toward the ladies' room to throw up.

Maggie Prescott addressed the pair of hot pink Keds
in the stall next to her and drawled, "Sugar? This one is

all out of paper. Do you have any over there you can share?"

"Yes, I do," returned a soft, kindly voice. "One moment, please."

Maggie heard the spin of a roller, then a hand appeared beneath the metal divider that separated the two stalls. Always one to take note of jewelry, she eyed both the simple but lovely diamond wedding band on the woman's third finger and the generous supply of toilet tissue she offered.

"Thanks." Maggie divided her cache into two, used half to blow her nose and the rest to wipe the tears from her cheeks. She may have let herself go the last day or so, but she was back on track now. She was ready to face the world standing tall with her chin up. Hang it if she'd let anyone see her at less than her best.

She tossed the used tissue into the commode, then flushed. Lifting her Kate Spade purse from the hook on the door, she exited the stall and crossed to the sink to wash her hands. The lady with the Keds was drying her hands at the next sink.

Their gazes met in the mirror and they shared a smile. The other woman wore her salt-and-pepper hair in a short, flattering bob and her eyes were a summer sky shade of blue. Laugh lines fanned out across her temples, and she looked a little tired. Maggie guessed her to be in her early-to-mid sixties.

Maggie's stare shifted to her own reflection. Her stomach sank and she sighed heavily at the runny-mascara raccoon eyes gazing back at her. She looked beyond tired, at least a decade older than her actual mid-forties and a poor applicator of makeup to boot. "If I don't stop this nonsense, I'll have to go waterproof."

"Pardon me?"

"My mascara. I've been so teary-eyed of late, I might as well just paint my cheeks rather than my lashes. I think it's probably time to switch to waterproof, but I sure do resist it. I hate those oily removers. They make me feel like a fish."

"Oh." The woman's smile turned sympathetic.

Maggie grabbed a rough manila paper towel, dampened one corner, and wiped at the mess beneath her eyes. Attempting to hide her embarrassment, she asked, "Who makes a good waterproof mascara, do you know?"

"As it happens, yes." The other woman's stare flicked over the diamonds on Maggie's hands before she added, "Although I do my cosmetics shopping at Walgreens."

"I'm partial to Eckerd, myself," Maggie returned, flashing an honest grin. "Though I admit to sneaking into Saks for YSL's Radiant Touch. It works miracles on a girl's wrinkles. Next best thing to going under the knife. I'm Maggie Prescott, by the way. Please, tell me about the mascara."

"It's nice to meet you, Ms. Prescott. My name is Grace Hardeman and the brand is Her Secret. Tears will not smudge it, and they also have a non-oily remover you might like. I'm partial to baby oil, myself. A quick swipe with a cotton swab and I'm done."

Baby oil. Maggie had a vivid flash of memory of the scent of baby oil, and once again, her eyes filled with tears and overflowed. "Call me Maggie, please."

Grace clicked her tongue and tugged a packet of tissues from her purse.

Babies. Maggie missed her babies. They were grown up now. All four of them. Even Chase, her youngest. Off to college. Her boys were not babies any longer, but men. Men.

Like their father.

That dog.

A quick, gasping sob joined the waterworks and Maggie yanked two tissues from the packet Grace offered and buried her head in her hands. "I'm sorry . . . I don't know why I'm . . . I just . . ."

Grace gave Maggie's shoulder a comforting pat. "Don't you worry, I understand. That's your wedding gown in the box on the couch in the ladies' sitting room, isn't it?"

Maggie looked up, trying desperately to blink away her tears. "Yes. How did you . . . ?"

She pointed to the logo on her candy-apple pink tee shirt. "I'm the Making Memories volunteer stationed at the donations desk. I noticed your box on my way into the lounge."

"Oh." Maggie thought about the heirloom box, the gown and the memories it contained, and bit her tongue to keep from bawling.

Grace's smile was sympathetic. "Don't feel bad; you're in good company. Nine out of ten women who have donated their gowns today have shed a tear or two."

Maggie glanced toward the outer section of the ladies' room lounge where she'd left the heirloom box on a sofa and knew a sudden surge of anger. Ms. Grace Hardeman had a point. Maybe Maggie should keep her wedding dress, hang it on the wall, and use it for a dart board.

With such a vision churning through her mind, Maggie was shocked to hear herself ask, "Would you like to see my gown?"

"I'd love to."

Grace followed her into the front area of the rest room and took a seat in the chair perpendicular to the sofa. Maggie's hands trembled as she removed the lid from the large rectangular box.

She hadn't looked at her wedding gown in years. This morning when she read the newspaper article about the Making Memories Breast Cancer Foundation wedding gown sale and decided to donate her dress, she'd almost opened the box. But she was still reeling from yesterday's blow to her twenty-five-year marriage. She'd been afraid if she looked at her wedding gown, she might do something really stupid.

Like run after Mike and say everything was all her fault.

Now, though, Maggie felt more in control. Maybe. She believed she could look at the dress without losing it. Then champagne slipper satin and Belgian lace spilled out of the box and she realized she wasn't as strong as she had thought. Her eyes overflowed yet again.

"Poor thing." Grace patted her knee. "Judging by your reaction I think it's better you hang on to your wedding gown. You could always make a cash donation if you want to help Making Memories."

"Mmm . . ." Maggie vaguely replied. Lost in her memories, she gently drew the gown from the box and held it up against herself.

"It's exquisite," said Grace.

"It was my mother's. She got married in May of 1941. The dress was made by a dressmaker in lower Manhattan. The lace all came from Belgium and they didn't have enough to finish the gown. Since the war was on, they worried they wouldn't get any more shipments in time to finish the dress. Then Pearl Harbor happened, and the wedding was postponed. Four years later, she got a package from Europe."

Maggie traced the crisscross of lace on the gown's bodice and added, "From my dad. It was yards and yards and yards of Belgian lace."

"What a lovely story." Grace trailed the back of her hand across the soft slipper satin.

"I always thought so. My mother stored her wedding gown in her cedar chest. As a kid I would always sneak into the chest and try it on. I adored it. When Mike asked me to marry him, I never considered wearing anything else. Mama was smaller in the bust than I and the seamstress worked magic to get it to fit."

Grace fluffed out the gown's long satin train and observed, "You must have been a beautiful bride."

"He always told me I was." Maggie stared at her reflection and tried to mesh memory with the reality of today. If she stripped right then and slipped into the gown, the twenty-six buttons up the back would fasten. The seams might be a little snug, but for the most part, the wedding gown would fit.

It would fit the body, but not the woman.

Maggie swallowed a sob. She had changed. Her life had changed. God, how she hated change.

Her children were grown and didn't need her. Her husband didn't want her.

She hadn't a clue who she was anymore.

The dark, cold cloud of misery that had hovered in her personal sky for months now descended once again. The fog swallowed her, seeped into her bones, and extinguished the lingering embers of the anger that had burned hot since yesterday afternoon.

Maggie had never felt so cold. So alone. "Oh, spit."

She tried to lift her chin, strained to square her shoulders and straighten her spine. She told herself she needed new wishes, new aspirations, new desires. New dreams.

But she didn't believe it.

The fact was Maggie loved her old life. The life that she'd lost. The one that time and circumstance had wrested away from her. The accursed tears returned as she lowered the wedding gown and made a halfhearted attempt to fold it back into the heirloom box.

"Here, let me help," said Grace, handing Maggie yet another tissue.

"I'm sorry. It must be hormones. I think I'm peri-menopausal." Either that or *man*-a-pausal. Mike-a-pausal. *Oh, God. I miss him.*

How, she wondered, did two people share the same house, the same supper table, the same bed, and still be a continent apart?

Suddenly, she knew a fierce urge to wear her wedding gown one last time. Kicking off her leather clogs, she tugged off her emerald green cotton shirt and white jeans, then stepped into the dress and slipped into the sleeves.

"I'm still donating it," she insisted. "I don't want to keep it. Truly, I don't. I don't have any daughters, any reason to keep it. I was barely twenty when I wore it. Can you imagine that? A baby. But I was so in love."

"I understand." Grace stepped behind her and helped with the buttons. "I was a young bride myself."

Emotion buffeted Maggie as she looked at herself in the mirror. She saw so much more than a forty-plus housewife with an empty nest and a marriage in trouble. She saw her mother, standing behind her as she had on Maggie's wedding day. She'd fastened a pearl necklace around her daughter's neck and wept happy tears.

Tears and weddings. *Should have seen the warning in that.*

Maggie still thought of her mama every day. She still missed her every day, especially in times of trouble when she needed a shoulder to cry on. Nobody's shoulder was as comforting as a mother's.

Oh, lordy, she needed her mama today.

Seeing herself in this gown again after so many years was like staring into the past. She saw herself as yesterday's bride, the young woman whose heart had overflowed with love, with hope. She saw the woman she used to be, and also, the woman she had wanted to be. In every bead, every button and bit of lace, she saw her dreams, her aspirations, her wishes and desires. She saw her femininity, her sexual allure, her maternal might.

Where had it all gone?

Why was she so empty now?

But even as she asked herself the questions, a welcome distraction burst into the room as a young woman rushed inside. Seconds later, Maggie heard the unmistakable sound of retching.

"Poor thing," she said, just as the outer door swung in once again. This time, however, the person who swept into the ladies' lounge was a man. A handsome, angry man who clutched a velvet ring box in his right fist. "Holly!"

"Go away, Justin."

Once again, Maggie heard the young woman being sick.

"Oh, that's great," muttered Justin. "That's just freaking great." Viciously, he threw the ring box toward the corner. It thwacked against the hunter green wall, then fell, open, onto the gray Berber carpet as he stalked from the rest room.

Maggie's practiced eye identified a two-carat solitaire on a platinum band just as Justin shoved the door open once again. This time, he didn't stop, but marched straight into the inner section of the lounge.

"My oh my." Maggie met Grace Hardeman's wide-eyed gaze. "Wish I had some popcorn. Something tells me we're fixin' to see a show."

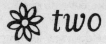 *two*

*G*race Hardeman considered herself one of the luckiest women around. She had a loving husband, an adoring family, truly caring friends. She and her husband Ben lived in a small, but comfortable home in a nice suburban neighborhood. They were active in their church, local politics, and a weekly readers' group that met downtown at the Fort Worth Public Library.

The only thing Grace was missing, so went the saying, was her health. But she was working on that, watching her diet, exercising, following her doctor's orders. Faith and feminine intuition told her she'd continue to do so for years to come.

In the meantime, she lived her life in keeping with a tenet some friends had taught her: *Today is a gift. That's why it's called the present.* Grace vowed never to waste a minute of this precious gift of life.

Keeping such a vow proved difficult at times. At others, all but impossible. Besides, passing her sixty-fifth birthday gave a woman the security within herself to skirt, if not flaunt, convention. So Grace indulged herself upon occasion, using her vow as an excuse to do things she ordinarily wouldn't do. Like eavesdrop on a private conversation.

She and Maggie drifted closer to the doorway leading to the lavatory portion of the ladies' lounge.

"I said go away, Justin," the young woman snapped. "This is the ladies' room."

"I don't care if it's the damned Oval Office. Holly, what the hell just happened out there?"

"You asked me to marry you."

"Yes. That's not an easy thing for a man to do, you know. I worked myself up to it for weeks. And what was your response? Your face went white, then green, and you dash off to the ladies' room like you're about to lose your lunch. Not exactly a boost to a man's ego. A simple no would have sufficed."

"Justin, this isn't . . . I'm not . . . I didn't expect . . . "

"I love you. And unless you've been lying to me, you love me, too."

From beside her, Grace heard a stifled sob, and she automatically searched her handbag for another tissue to give to Maggie. She heard the commode flush once again, then the sound of running water. From the inner room came the young woman's voice. "Oh, man. I wish I had a toothbrush."

Now Maggie dug into her purse and pulled out a cellophane-wrapped travel toothbrush and a small tube of Crest. She pressed them on Grace and made a shooing motion with her hands. Since tears continued to spill from Maggie's eyes, Grace sighed, shook her head, and walked into the rest room's brightly lit lavatory section.

The young woman was bent over a sink splashing water on her face. The man was leaning against the wall watching her, his arms folded, his expression fixed in a scowl. Grace set the offering beside the sink, then turned without a word, intending to leave the ladies' room entirely.

"Thank you," Holly said.

"Ma'am?" Justin asked, his hard, narrow gaze never leaving Holly. "If anyone else comes in, would you please explain that this rest room is closed? My friend and I need to talk."

"Um . . . yes . . . all right." She didn't see what it would hurt to stand outside the door and redirect traffic. There was another ladies' room upstairs.

Then she rounded the corner into the muted light of the sitting area and discovered it wouldn't be quite that easy. Dressed in her wedding finery, Maggie Prescott sat on the lounge's sofa bent over double. She was sobbing, of course. She used the tissue from inside the wedding gown box to blow her nose, then said, "Mike and I were young like those two, a long, long time ago."

"My oh my." Grace sighed and mentally muttered the expression she'd picked up from her granddaughter. What had made the ladies' lounge Drama Trauma Central today?

Reflected in the full-length mirror, Grace could see both the middle-aged bride and the twenty-something lovers. As she watched, Holly wiped her mouth on a brown paper towel and turned toward Justin. "Please don't be angry."

He sighed, then stepped toward her, reached out, and

tucked a stray lock of hair behind her ear. "I'm not angry. I'm just . . . well . . . I guess I am angry. I knew you might be surprised, but I didn't expect . . . well . . . I didn't think I was asking that difficult a question."

"Oh, Justin. It *was* a difficult question. The most difficult of all. I didn't see it coming and I wasn't prepared."

"I don't understand."

She closed her eyes and licked her lips. "Justin, please. You're making this harder than it needs to be."

His arm, still outstretched, abruptly dropped to his side. He cleared his throat. "Are you turning me down?"

"Why do we have to change?" she asked earnestly. "I've been so happy with you. Can't we leave things the way they are?"

"The way they are?"

She offered a tentative smile and a pleading gaze. "We can skip the fishing bait show. We could take a carriage ride through downtown instead. It's a beautiful day. Maybe we could have a picnic in the park, fly kites."

"This isn't about picnics," he snapped. "It's not about today. It's about tomorrow. Our tomorrow."

Holly turned away, grimacing.

Seated in the lounge area of the rest room, staring at the watercolor of pink magnolia blossoms hanging on the wall, Maggie philosophized. "Tomorrow is always the problem. No matter how hard you try, you can't stop it from coming."

Now *that* was a statement Grace easily understood.

"That's just the problem, Justin." Holly wrapped her arms around herself. "We don't have a tomorrow. And I'm not ready to give up today."

"Poor girl," murmured Grace.

"I know just how she feels," added Maggie, stroking

the back of her hand across the shimmering skirt of her wedding gown.

"Dammit, Holly. This makes no sense to me." Justin slammed a hand down on the counter beside the borrowed toothpaste. "We've been together for almost a year. I'm building a practice now, and you've completed work for your master's. Our lives are changing, moving forward. Our relationship needs to grow, too. You know that. You know I'm right."

Grace frowned into the mirror, noting the fear simmering in Holly's voice as she said, "I wasn't going to date you. I turned you down at first, remember? Then you said you didn't want to get married until you were well established in your practice and maybe not even then. You promised me. I have a very clear memory of it."

"I changed my mind." Justin threw out his hands and began pacing the hard green tiles of the lavatory floor. "I fell in love with you. And you love me, too. I have a very clear memory—you telling me you love me over and over and over again every time we make love."

He stormed around the room, raking his fingers through his hair. Once, his pained gaze met Grace's in the mirror, and she found herself wanting to rush into the lavatory and give both young people a hug. She wanted to tell them not to waste a minute, that life is fleeting. She wanted to tell them to treasure every moment with those they love, and to approach life at its fullest and count their blessings every day.

"Oh, dear," Grace said with a sigh. "Now I'm starting to get teary-eyed."

Maggie patted her shoulder, then moved to block the outer door, which had begun to swing open. She grabbed the handle, halted the door's progress, and poked her head outside. "This rest room is closed," Grace heard her say. "Fashion show. You'll have to use the one upstairs."

From the inner room, Holly called out a tremulous "Thank you."

Justin drew a deep breath, then let it out on a sigh. "People in love get married. That's the way it works. What did you think would happen with us?"

"I don't know. I've tried not to think about it."

"That's stupid."

Maggie looked at Grace. "Mike talks that way to me sometimes. I hate it."

Holly lifted her chin and went on the defensive by marching to the sitting room and addressing Grace and Maggie. "What's stupid is that I didn't see this coming. Does love create some sort of misfire in a woman's brain? It must. I sure haven't been thinking right. I should have known to expect this. After all, he told his family we were engaged."

Justin swept into the outer lounge and scowled at Holly. "How did you find out about that?"

"Your mother all but abducted me on Thursday. She showed up on my doorstep and demanded I go shopping with her. I thought it was to buy you something for your birthday, but oh, no. She took me to some little boutique over on Camp Bowie Boulevard. To shop for wedding gowns. Wouldn't listen to a word I said. I had to strip for a man named Randall."

Justin winced. "He's her personal consultant. She's worked with him for years."

"He put me in a six thousand dollar wedding gown. Six thousand dollars for a dress. Like I can afford that."

Now Holly was the one storming around, her arms folded, her lips pursed in a pout.

Grace saw Maggie's lips twitch with a smile. She leaned toward Grace and murmured, "The girl does a good snitty pout. I've had great respect for that particular tool ever since the ninth grade when I watched Cheryl Harris pout her way into a date with Tommy Lee Wilson to the homecoming dance."

Grace nodded. "I can manage a decent pout, but I'm a better sulker. When I do resort to pouting, it usually proves productive."

"Less is best," Maggie agreed.

In this case, it obviously worked. Justin walked over to the lounge chair and took a sprawling seat. Grimacing, he rubbed his forehead. "I shouldn't have mentioned marriage to Mother. It slipped out when she said she'd fixed me up with Puffy Larson's daughter for a Kimball Art Museum fund-raiser."

Maggie perked up. "Puffy Larson's daughter Jenna? I know her. She's a pretty girl, but bubble-headed. Dated one of my sons in high school."

Holly flopped down on the couch beside the empty wedding gown box. "Jenna Larson is a beautiful blonde, thin as a rail with long supermodel legs."

Grace gave the young woman a sympathetic nod. "I despise her on principle."

Staring blindly at the magnolia painting on the wall, Holly asked, "So you have a date with Jenna Larson?"

Justin sighed. "No, Holly. No. I'm thirty years old. I don't let my mother fix me up and I don't want a date with Jenna Larson. You know me better than that. You know me better than anybody."

"Oh," Maggie said with a sigh. "That's so sweet."

Grace simply shook her head. This was getting out of hand. "Maggie, why don't you gather up your things. There's a dressing room in the ballroom. I think we should give these two some privacy."

"Either that or get them a room. I personally believe discussions like this one are better held in close proximity to a bed rather than a toilet."

Justin gave a short, bitter laugh. "I don't think we can solve our problems with sex."

Holly tossed him a hopeful look. "It wouldn't hurt to try, though, would it?"

"Dammit, Holly. You're breaking my heart."

"No!" She whirled around on him, temper flashing in her eyes. "Don't say that. It's not true. I don't break men's hearts. I won't do it. I swore I never would. I promised."

Her outburst shocked the room into silence.

She closed her eyes and rubbed her temples. "I care about you, Justin. Too much. I do love you. But marriage? . . . Please, can't we just keep this simple? Can't we just—"

"Fuck?" he finished bitterly, the look in his eyes as mean as the word. "I'm good enough to fuck, but not to marry?"

Grace wasn't going to listen to language like that. She had no business being in the middle of this argument at all. Gathering up her purse, she stood and motioned for Maggie to join her.

Even as Maggie gathered her billowing skirt to rise, Holly erupted from her seat. She advanced on Justin, her hands clenched at her sides, anger snapping in her eyes. "We don't fuck. We don't even have sex. We make love, and damn you for calling it anything different. Just stop it."

Justin shoved to his feet and squared off in front of Holly. His jaw was tight and he stood with his hands braced on his hips. "Well, maybe I should just stop it. Maybe that's exactly what I should do."

He laughed, then, but the sound was anything but amused. Stalking toward the corner, he scooped up the engagement ring from the floor and said, "It's obvious I'm wasting my time here. It's a beautiful day outside. Think I'll go fishing. Maybe I'll see if Jenna Larson wants to come along. Maybe she'll want to try out my Bobbin Bass Bait."

Holly buried her face in her hands. "Justin . . . please."

At the door, he paused. Without turning around, he said, "I love you, Holly. I want to marry you, to have children with you, to be a family with you. I want to grow old with you. I didn't expect it to happen, but it has, and damned if I understand how you can tell me you love me, show me you love me, and not want to take the next logical step. Hell, you won't even consider it."

"It can't work, Justin. Believe me."

He looked over his shoulder and fired the word like a bullet. "Why?"

She didn't answer him. She wouldn't even look at him. Justin muttered a particularly ugly curse, then said, "All right. Have it your way. Damned if I'll continue to beg."

The door swished shut behind him.

Holly wrapped her arms around herself and shuddered. Below the hem of the darling red dress, her knees began to sag. "Oh, God. What's the matter with me? Why do I have to be such a coward?"

Maggie clucked her tongue and crooned in a soothing tone, "Now, sugar. Calm down. It's all right. Everything's all right. Just don't cry, okay? You'll get me started again and I'm trying hard to give it up. Crying is bad for me. I'm sloppy at it. No matter how much I want to weep like Scarlett O'Hara, I always ended up shedding Lucy Ricardo tears. Just ask Grace here. She's seen me in action. Believe me, you don't want to get me going again. Hush now, sweetie."

Grace saw Holly sway and feared she might collapse. With Maggie's help, she guided the young woman onto the sofa, where she sat stiff and still, staring blindly ahead. She spoke in a tone barely above a whisper. "He doesn't know it, but that's the cruelest thing he's ever said to me."

Grace sat at her right side and took her hand. "Which thing is that?"

"Marriage. Marrying Justin is my most cherished dream."

Grace and Maggie shared a look of surprise. Swishing her train to one side and taking a seat on Holly's left, Maggie asked, "So why did you refuse him?"

"Because I love him."

Again, Grace and Maggie's gazes met. Maggie waggled her eyebrows. "You love him so you can't marry him."

"That's right."

"Are you already married, sugar?"

"Of course not."

In a gesture repeated thousands of times with her daughter, Grace gently tucked an errant strand of hair behind Holly's ear. "What is it, Holly? What's the problem?"

"I can't talk about it. I won't. I try not to even think about it." Holly burrowed against Grace's bosom and finally broke down. Grace held the weeping young woman, absorbing her emotional pain, while Maggie patted her knee and murmured words of comfort.

"I think my heart might explode," Holly sobbed. "Can a person die from crying?"

Maggie wrinkled her nose and shook her head. "I don't think so, sugar. Otherwise, I'd be a goner myself. Although considering the circumstances, I won't swear drowning isn't out of the question."

Though slow off the mark, once Holly let loose, she gave Maggie a run for her money in the bawling department. She went on for what felt to Grace like hours—maybe even days—but turned out to be about ten minutes. When finally the young woman had wrung herself dry, she lapsed into hiccups. Those, too, eventually stilled.

"Mercy." Maggie exhaled a loud sigh of relief, rose, hitched up her wedding gown, and fetched an entire roll of toilet paper from a stall. "Here, sugar. Blow."

Holly blew, then said to Maggie, "That's a beautiful dress. Did you buy it here at the sale?"

"Ac-tu-al-ly," Maggie drawled, drawing the word out into four, very long, Southern syllables, "it's *my* wedding gown. My mama's, too. I brought it to donate to Making Memories." Addressing Grace, she asked, "I'm curious . . . because it's old and all . . . will they even have a use for it? I'm not trying to back out of donating it, mind you. I just wonder if a girl would even want it. Nowadays, strapless gowns are all the fashion."

"Some girl would love it," Grace assured.

"I'd love it," Holly said in a wistful, dreamy tone. "I'd love to wear a vintage gown like yours. If I were going to marry, that is. Which I'm not. Not ever."

Still again, Grace and Maggie's gazes met and held.

Then Maggie spun her gold charm bracelet around her wrist and said, "You know, Miss Holly, my friend Grace and I can't help but be a little curious. Considering how we've become bathroom buddies and all, why don't you tell us why having that handsome fella ask you to marry him sends you into hysterics."

Holly swallowed a hiccup and shrugged.

"Oh, come on, now. We'll keep your confidence, won't we, Grace? A ladies' room is like a confessional when it comes to secrets. Call me Father Maggie, if that will help."

"You want me to pretend you're a male priest while you're wearing a wedding gown?"

"Sugar, this is the Church of the Makeup Mirror. We're very liberal." After a moment's pause, she reached over and squeezed Holly's hand. "Besides, it might help you to talk about it. Talking helps me."

"Who would have guessed?" The glint of amusement in Grace's eyes defused her dry tone.

Holly looked down at her feet and made a vain attempt to change the subject. "Oh, dear. I've scuffed the toes of my shoes something awful. Maybe I'll make a run by the mall this afternoon and buy a new pair. I have an extra fifty dollars in my bank account from tutoring an undergraduate calculus student last week."

Maggie studied her hot pink nail tips. "Well, now. A girl can never do too much shoe shopping."

"That's right. Thank goodness I'm about through buying textbooks. Can you believe what a racket that is? Tell me how they justify charging almost two hundred dollars for a single book. How much does a professor earn for writing a textbook anyway?"

"Sweetheart," Grace said, patting Holly's knee. "We'll leave you alone if you truly don't want to talk about it, but I agree with Maggie. I know firsthand that it helps to have a friend with whom to talk over one's troubles."

"You have troubles, too?"

Grace pursed her lips, considered explaining, but settled for saying, "I'm living with them."

"We all have troubles," Maggie added. "Actually, I wouldn't mind sharing mine with a girlfriend right about now."

"Go ahead," Holly said.

"You first."

Holly grimaced and nibbled at her lower lip. A full two minutes passed before she opened her mouth. Words tumbled out like kittens. "I can't marry Justin and I can't tell him why because he'll argue with me and cajole me and try to make me out to be an irrational fool. I'm not irrational. I have my reasons for feeling like I do. Excellent reasons. And as for my feelings, well, they are my feelings and I own them and . . . and . . . and . . . Oh, God. I can't think."

She threaded her fingers into her dark curls and exclaimed, "He's going to date Jenna Larson and marry her and have two-point-three blond-haired, blue-eyed children who play the piano and go to Montessori school and eat artichokes for lunch."

"Oh, sugar."

"But at least he'll have children. He'll have a wife. A family of his own. That's important to Justin. Justin and Jenna. Justin and Jenna and Jeremy and Janet and . . . how do you name a third of a kid?"

Tears were once again running down her face. Out of tissues and with the toilet paper beyond her reach, Grace wiped the wetness away with her fingers. "Sweetheart, why can't you marry him?"

"I'm so pathetic." Holly swallowed a nervous giggle, then slowly looked up and met first Maggie's gaze and then Grace's. Swaying, she said, "I think I'm going to faint."

Grace frowned. "Do you think we should get a doctor?"

"Either that or take off her bra. That always makes me feel better."

Holly shoved to her feet. "I've got to . . . I'm going to . . . "

"Let's get her to the stall, Grace."

They made it just in time. With Maggie Prescott, dressed in a vintage wedding gown, tenderly supporting her shoulders, Holly lost what little was left in her stomach. Again.

"Sugar? Are you in a family way?"

"No, I'm not. I can't let that happen." Staggering out of the stall, Holly headed for a sink. "I'd love it. I love children. That's why I decided to teach. I teach math. Pre-algebra." She lifted sad, soul-weary eyes and met Grace's gaze. "I still have twenty-seven items on my list."

"What list?" Grace asked, worried by the look.

"My Life List. Goals I want to achieve. I was going to mark one off today, but I blew that. No sex in the storeroom for me now. And I'm afraid I'll run out of time. I wanted to be deliciously wicked today. That's number twenty-one: I will do something deliciously wicked. Oh, God, I don't want to die."

"Die?" Maggie exclaimed. "Sugar, are you sick?"

"No. I'm healthy as a horse. I bungee jump and ski dangerous mountains. I clean out my closets once a year. I plan to skydive and scuba and get politically involved by the next election."

"I hope that's not local politics you're talking about,"

Maggie warned with a smile. "Then I'd think you do have a death wish."

"No, it's the opposite. I have a *no death* wish. Not for ten or twenty or fifty years."

"That sounds like a plan to me." Maggie glanced at Grace, the arch of her brows asking what to do next.

Holly made use of the toothbrush once again, brushing with fast, angry strokes. "I'm so mad at him," she said, through a froth of bubbles. She rinsed, then wiped her mouth with a brown paper towel which she crushed into a ball and threw into the trash can with a hook shot.

"He was supposed to be safe. He said he wasn't looking to get married. I took a chance on him." Her look of despair offset her tone of outrage. "Now he's ruined everything by proposing."

She marched into the lounge and flopped back against the sofa, letting her head rest against the cushion. Her gaze fixed on the painting of pink magnolias. "He did it in honor of my mother, you know. That's why he proposed here, today."

"Your mother?"

"It's all about my mom." Tears filled weary eyes yet again. Her voice cracked. "Everything. My relationship with my dad, with my friends, with men. Especially with men." She grimaced. "She died when I was twelve years old."

"Oh, honey." Grace sat beside her on the left.

"I miss her so much."

"Sure you do." Maggie sat on her right, patted Holly's knee. "Girls never stop needing their mamas."

"My dad is still lost without her, even after all these years. I promised myself I wouldn't do that to a man or child."

Maggie leaned away, angled her head, and stared at Holly. "Do what?"

"I'd never seen Daddy cry before. In the hospital room, afterward, he sobbed. He held her hand and cried so hard it scared me. Finally the nurses made us leave. On the way home, I promised myself I'd never break a man's heart like that."

"And that's the reason why you won't marry Justin?"

"Part of it."

"What's the rest?"

Holly opened her mouth, then shut it abruptly. "Never mind. It doesn't matter. I'm not going to marry him. That's the bottom line. There is nothing anyone can do or say to change my mind."

Grace and Maggie shared a skeptical look. Maggie drawled. "Sugar? Just a small piece of advice. You've used that 'C' word a few times here today."

" 'C' word?" Holly looked almost haggard.

"Change. I've lived a bit longer than you—not all that long, mind you—and I've learned a thing or two about change during that time. Sugar, one thing you can count on, change is gonna happen. Life is just a big old square dance. Just as soon as you think you're getting the swing of it, it's allemande left and do-si-do. Sometimes it's hard to stay on your feet."

Holly sighed heavily. She closed her eyes and let her head fall back against the sofa. "What is your point, Maggie?"

"My point is that it's easier to keep your balance if you let your knees bend. Bend a little, Holly. Be flexible."

Grace smiled her encouragement. "It's good advice, Holly. That way, when the dance ends, you'll still be standing strong. Believe me, standing strong is very important to a woman."

❀ *three*

*i*t took Holly a good twenty minutes, but she eventually pulled herself together. After she washed her face and touched up the little bit of makeup she wore, Grace suggested they all adjourn to the hotel restaurant to indulge themselves in a slice of the Greystone's famous triple chocolate cake.

As they walked toward the restaurant just off the main lobby, a Making Memories volunteer flagged down Grace. "We're getting awfully busy," the harried woman said. "Could you please take another turn at the table? People are stacked up waiting for tax receipts."

Minutes later, Grace chatted sympathetically with a woman donating a wedding gown in memory of her best friend, and Maggie had pitched in to work the floor helping brides find sizes and styles among the rows and rows of gown-filled racks.

Holly dawdled in the doorway. When she realized her

two new acquaintances probably wouldn't be breaking for chocolate cake anytime soon, she decided to wave a good-bye just as soon as she caught their notice. She needed time alone to lick the emotional wound she'd suffered when Justin walked out in anger.

She'd have made it safely away had she not spied the wedding gown lying on the ground, its pristine white satin train now sullied by a dirty footprint. When she stopped to hang it up, a volunteer snagged her and guilted her into helping. Half an hour later as she hung yet another wedding gown on a clothes rack, she tried to figure out just how she'd gone from potential sex in the storage room, to bawling in the bathroom, to dressing-room duty at the Making Memories wedding gown sale. This world of white dresses and bubbling brides was absolutely the last place Holly wanted to be.

Thinking about marriage made her teeth hurt.

"That's what I get for falling for a chocolate bribe," she grumbled through set teeth.

The sense of self-preservation that had kept her hanging back from the hustle and bustle of the ballroom fell in the wake of Grace's tentative request for help clearing the dressing room of stacks of discarded gowns. Knowing better but prodded by her conscience, she grabbed a handful of hangers and dived in.

Working with the wedding gowns proved just as bad as she had feared. Being adrift in this sea of satin and lace took an emotional toll on her psyche. In a perfect world, Holly would be shopping for her own wedding gown right now. But this was far from a perfect world. Holly had learned that hard lesson young. Today had simply reinforced the fact. Four hours after leaving the ladies' room, Holly was still immersed in wedding dresses and a pity party.

From overheard remarks, she had gathered that the Making Memories Foundation transported the gowns from sale to sale, city to city, by way of a truck and gooseneck trailer donated by a radio personality from Arizona. In order to make the loading and unloading go as smoothly as possible, a rushed woman in a pink tee had said, it helped to have all the gowns hanging in the same direction on the racks.

Holly worked her way through the dresses turning hangers, hooking trains up off the floor, and wistfully mooning over the beauty of some of the gowns. All the while, she tried desperately, and in vain, to put Justin out of her mind.

He wanted to marry her. Have a family with her.

He'd brought her here today to buy a wedding gown in tribute to her mother.

Did a finer man exist on this earth? Holly blinked rapidly, willing away another bout of stupid tears. Fighting herself.

"Oh, spit," Maggie said as she stopped beside Holly and tugged a froth of satin and lace from the rack. "Look at this. It's a size twenty and it was hidden in with the sixes. I'll bet that nasty-spirited girl from Plano stuck it here so no one else would see it. Oh, I'd like to wring her neck."

Holly remembered the bride-to-be to whom Maggie referred. She'd been a loud, obnoxious, demanding woman with an equally loud, obnoxious, and demanding mother.

"This gown would have been perfect for that sweet Sarah Jones I tried to help about an hour ago," Maggie continued. "Look, Holly. Isn't it beautiful? A classic style. The bride who wears this dress will be drop dead gorgeous."

Holly eyed Maggie's Christie Brinkley body and liked her all the more for thinking a size twenty woman could be "drop-dead gorgeous." She smiled. "It's a lovely dress."

Maggie hung the gown on the end of the rack, folded her arms and studied it, then nodded decisively. "I don't care if I have to buy it myself, that Plano girl isn't getting this dress. Sarah Jones mentioned her wedding was going to be at First Methodist. I wonder if I could get her address from the church. It's worth a try, don't you think?"

Holly didn't respond. She couldn't. The candlelight silk gown she'd just lifted from the floor to replace on its empty hanger was a close duplicate of the one her mother wore in the photo her father kept on his nightstand.

Oh, God. If she didn't do something quick the tears were going to start all over again.

"Now that's a pretty one," Maggie said, stroking a hand across the fabric. "Old-fashioned. Reminds me of a lace-trimmed valentine."

A sudden fierce need to share replaced Holly's desire to cry. "My mama wore a wedding gown similar to this."

"Did she?" Maggie gave the dress a closer look. "Do you still have it?"

"No. I don't think so, anyway. I haven't seen it. Daddy didn't keep many of her things."

"Oh, sugar." Maggie reached over and gave her a hug.

The emotion clogging her throat told Holly to change the subject quick or she'd be back in the ladies' lounge bawling again. She gestured toward another gown and attempted to redirect the conversation. "Look, that one is lovely, too. Although I still think your gown is the prettiest one I've seen here today. And I must have looked at a thousand gowns by now."

"You really like mine best?" Maggie asked.

"I do."

"Better than your mama's gown?"

Holly's hand trembled slightly as she looped the train around the hanger. "This is not my mother's wedding gown. It's similar, but not the same one."

"But it makes you think of her. I think you should try it on."

Holly lost her grip on the dress and it floated to the floor. She ignored it, glaring at Miss Meddling Maggie Prescott.

"I'm not trying on any wedding gown."

"Why not?"

"I'm not getting married. Surely you didn't miss that little fact."

Maggie picked up the fallen gown, held it up, and studied the design from top to bottom. She fiddled with a loose hook here and the hint of a stain there, then turned a speculative, measuring gaze toward Holly.

"Stop it," Holly insisted, grabbing the gown from Maggie. "I don't like it. I wouldn't buy it even if I were going to ruin Justin's life and marry him. Look at it." She held it up against herself. "It's at least four inches too short."

"You're right." Maggie tapped her lips with her index finger. "I bet that doesn't happen often, tiny thing like you are. You could add—"

"No." Holly hung the dress back on the rack. "It's not that pretty. Just because my mother wore one like it doesn't mean I would have to wear it. Sentiment doesn't mean stupidity. A bride can honor her mother other ways than by wearing her gown. If my mother were alive, she'd be the first to tell me to buy a dress I adored. If my mother were alive, I'd be looking for a gown like yours."

"So buy my dress. It would be perfect for you."

"I'm not buying any dress. I'm not getting married."

Maggie shrugged, her mouth twisting in a sad smile. "And I never thought I'd give away my wedding gown, but there you go."

Hearing the pain in Maggie's voice, the fight drained out of Holly. She tilted her head to one side and watched the other woman closely as she asked, "So why are you doing it? You obviously still have an emotional tie to it. Why give it away?"

Maggie glanced away and avoided the question. "Well, well, look at that."

Holly followed the path of Maggie's gaze toward the check-out table, where a silver-haired gentleman leaned over to kiss Grace's cheek. The smile Grace beamed up at him was filled with such tenderness and love that it took Holly's breath away and brought Maggie to tears. But then, judging by their short acquaintance, just about everything brought Maggie to tears.

Maggie wiped her eyes and sighed. "That's got to be her husband. Do you know what she told me? She collects angels and he—his name is Ben—e-mails her an angel picture every day from work."

"How sweet." Holly fell instantly in love with Grace's Ben.

"When Mike and I were first married, he used to call me at lunchtime every day." Now Maggie's expression hung between wistful and another waterfall. "It didn't matter whether he was in his office or eating out with a client, he always took a moment to call. I haven't thought of that in years. I don't quite know when it stopped."

Then she squared her shoulders and added, "I don't guess it matters anymore."

Maggie had shared a brief synopsis of her marital troubles in the ladies' lounge, promising to add further detail once she had chocolate within reach. The sadness in her voice now tore at Holly's heart and caused her to reach for a distraction.

"Look at this dress." Holly grabbed blindly from the rack. "Isn't it just . . . uh. . . ."

Awful. It was truly ugly. The gown was a shimmery material with poofy, Jane Jetson wings at the seams of the sleeves.

"Oh, sugar," Maggie said, clucking her tongue. "When I see a fashion accident like that, I always try to remind myself that I once wore a dress made from the Yellow Pages to a job interview."

"You wore what?"

Maggie waved her question away, saying, "Something good must have happened to Grace."

Holly glanced across the ballroom to see Grace stand and hug a woman wearing a pink Making Memories tee shirt, then go up on her tiptoes to give her husband a loud smooch right on the mouth. He looked bashful; Grace glowed. Then, catching sight of Holly and Maggie, she waved them over.

"I want to introduce you to a couple of people. Maggie Prescott and Holly Weeks, this wonderful angel is Fran Hansen, the founder of the Making Memories Breast Cancer Foundation."

The women exchanged greetings and a few sentences of small talk, then Grace linked her arm through the gentleman's and added, "And this is my darling, Ben."

"Hello, Darling Ben," Maggie said with a teasing smile.

"Gracie," he protested gruffly. Turning to Maggie and Holly, he added, "I'm Ben Hardeman and I'm pleased to meet you, ladies. Gracie tells me she's coerced the two of you into joining her as she feeds her chocolate cravings."

Holly grinned. "I don't know that I'd call it coercion, exactly."

"Sure it is," Maggie interjected. "I'd never indulge in something as decadent as triple chocolate cake if I weren't forced. Will you join us, Ben?"

"No, thank you. I'd love to visit with you ladies more, but I have an important appointment soon and I can't be late. I just stopped by to check on Gracie on my way."

Grace shook her head. "He and our two sons have tickets to the Ranger baseball game."

"That's almost as good as chocolate," Holly said.

"Much better," Ben insisted.

He and Holly discussed the home team's chances for the season, then Ben excused himself and prepared to take his leave. He turned to his wife. "Promise me you won't overdo, honey."

"Be-en," Grace protested, drawing his name out.

He shrugged, gave her hand a squeeze, then sauntered away whistling "Take Me Out to the Ball Game."

"He is a darling, Grace," Maggie said, a hint of envy in her tone.

"For the most part, he is." Grace smiled after her husband, then continued, "Our fiftieth wedding anniversary is three months from Tuesday."

"Your golden anniversary," Holly said. "That's wonderful. Congratulations. How do you plan to mark such an auspicious occasion?"

"We're going to have a party. A wonderful party. All the family will be there. I intend for it to be a completely happy occasion. I'm very excited about it."

"Of course you are," Maggie said. "Fifty years. Imagine that. If that's not the most beautiful thing I've heard all day. I think we should adjourn to the restaurant and lift our forks full of triple-fudge decadence in toast to the Hardemans' accomplishment, don't you, Holly?"

"Either that or go buy stock in the Kleenex corporation," Holly replied in a dry tone as Maggie wiped her eyes with the back of her hand.

"Kimberly-Clark," Maggie offered. "Mike's been buying it for years because of me. I tend to tear up rather easily."

"No," Holly replied with patent disbelief. Both Grace and Maggie chuckled at that, and the mood among them brightened. Ten minutes later, the three women sat at a small round table in the hotel restaurant as a waitress placed three plates, three forks, and a huge slab of chocolate cake in front of them. Without exchanging a word, each woman took a bite. Flavor exploded on Holly's tongue and she groaned with delight.

Maggie moaned. "That's the closest thing to an orgasm I've had in months."

"And just who the hell's fault is that?" came a man's furious voice from behind her.

Holly's jaw gaped and Grace murmured, "Oh, my."

Maggie's fork slipped from her hand and clattered to the floor. "Mike!"

He held her note in his hand as if it were something rank. With exaggerated care, Maggie lifted her napkin and wiped her lips. Though outwardly calm, inwardly Maggie trembled like a tree in a gale. "I didn't expect to see you here."

"I kinda gathered that when I found the note you left on our bed." He made a show of lifting the note up to read. "'I've gone to the Greystone Hotel to give away my wedding gown. Perhaps while I'm there I'll find a man and give away something else, something you don't seem to want anymore. I understand there is an antique fishing bait show at the hotel. What do you want to bet I can do a little luring myself?'"

Blood thrummed in Maggie's veins and her every muscle went taut. A dozen different emotions buffeted her heart, including fury and embarrassment and a little bit of shame.

Bracing herself, she looked at her husband—really looked at him—for the first time in weeks, maybe even months. At forty-seven, Mike Prescott continued to get better-looking every year, curse the man. He had a golf pro's good looks: light brown hair going gracefully gray at the temples, a square jaw, and a thin straight nose.

The fury in his ice blue eyes took her breath away.

At a nearby table, someone smothered a laugh. At them? She shot a look to her left. Well, spit. Mike had made them a public spectacle.

Maggie's own wrath flared in response. How dare he track her down like this, filled with righteous anger and accusations when *he* was the one who'd ignored her all day yesterday. Yesterday. Their twenty-fifth wedding anniversary.

Jerk.

She drew a deep, controlling breath and exhaled it just

as carefully. "A public restaurant is not an appropriate place to have this conversation, Mike. If you'll wait until I'm through visiting with my friends I'll be happy—"

"Dammit, Maggie," he exploded. "All I've done is wait. I've been waiting for months now and I'm sick to death of it. But guess what? I'm done with it. I'm through waiting." He tossed the note onto the table. "Since I'm already downtown, maybe I should stop by the lawyer's office."

With an abrupt about-face, Mike marched out of the restaurant and toward the front door. Maggie sat straight as a board in her velvet upholstered chair, frozen inside and out.

As if through a haze, she saw Grace and Holly exchange a concerned glance. Holly whispered, "Maggie should be crying. Why isn't she crying?"

Maggie wondered that herself. The waterworks had hardly stopped since yesterday when she realized Mike had either forgotten or, more likely, decided to totally ignore their silver wedding anniversary. She couldn't have cried right now if she wanted to. In fact, she couldn't work up a spit to save her life. Mike's cruelty had sucked all the moisture right out of her.

Grace snapped open her purse and removed a pair of bills from her wallet. She folded them and stuck them beneath her plate, then stood and said to Holly, "Let's get her somewhere private."

They guided her toward the logical spot—the ladies' lounge. Halfway there, as if from a far distance, Maggie heard Holly say, "He's come back inside. He sees us."

Maggie suddenly found her running feet, and she dashed for the bathroom, Grace and Holly following closely. Inside, she leaned against the door, breathing as if she'd just run a mile rather than twenty feet.

Grace led her over to the sofa, sat her down, then took a seat beside her. Holly glared at the two women drying their hands at the sinks, silently demanding they leave. When finally they did, Holly checked the rest of the stalls and observed. "Thank goodness for low-traffic ladies' rooms."

Maggie began to shake as Holly sat in the chair beside the sofa. She accepted the box of tissues the younger woman offered—the lounge had been supplied since their last visit—and instead of using the tissue to wipe away tears, she shredded it into paper snow.

"We have a little tradition for our wedding anniversaries." Her voice sounded dead to herself. "It began on our first—we were young and too poor for gifts. We wrote love letters. They were our gifts to one another. Later when we had money, we'd buy a little something, but we continued to exchange letters, too. I have a special box I keep them in. Twenty-four of them. Once or twice a year, I'll read through them."

Maggie tugged at the collar of her cotton shirt, even though it wasn't close to binding. The constriction in her throat come from within. "Yesterday was our twenty-fifth anniversary. Mike didn't leave me a letter. He was already gone when I got up. His secretary called and passed along the message that he was going straight from work to the baseball game with clients. I waited up for him until after midnight. By then, our anniversary was over. Twenty-five. Silver. Tarnished silver." Her voice broke around the harsh words. "I don't know if he forgot or if he simply didn't care."

"I didn't forget, Maggie," Mike said softly from the doorway. "I cared. I wrote a letter, but I couldn't . . . it's not . . . a letter isn't the right way this time."

Maggie closed her eyes. "Oh, God."

Grace stood and grabbed Holly's hand, tugging her to her feet. "I'm beginning to think this must be National Ladies' Room Invasion Day."

"No," Maggie said, pleaded. "Don't go."

Holly hesitated, but Grace was determined. The two women slipped past Mike and disappeared out the door.

Maggie stared blindly at the magnolia painting on the wall. For a long moment, the only sound to be heard was a drip from a faucet in the lavatory. Maggie thought about making a dash for a stall and locking herself in, but she couldn't quite make herself move.

She breathed deeply, almost choked on the rose scent wafting from the bowl of potpourri. "All right, Mike. What was in the letter?"

Wordlessly, he reached into his pocket. Instead of pulling out an envelope or even a folded sheet of paper, he removed a TV remote. *His* TV remote.

The one she'd hidden a month ago.

As her stomach dropped, Maggie did her best to innocently ask, "What's that?"

"I think you know." He tossed it onto the sofa. "You've watched me tear the house apart for a month looking for it. Didn't say a word. *Pretended* to help me look."

Oh, spit. Busted.

"Why did you bring it here? Now?"

He didn't answer.

Maggie decided she didn't feel the least bit guilty. Instead, she looked at him and worked up a fume. In her mind, the TV remote control symbolized the trouble at the heart of their marriage. It made her sadly furious that it had taken him this long to locate it, so she lifted her chin and said, "It started out as a joke. I expected you to find it sooner."

He looked at her as if she'd grown two heads. "So you admit it? You hid the remote?"

He said it in the same tone as he might have had he asked, *You murdered the paper boy?*

Maggie straightened her spine. "Yes, I did."

"What the hell for?"

"To make a point."

"What point?"

She gave her head a toss that sent her long blond hair whipping across her shoulder. "You should figure that out based on where I hid the fu—"

Shocked at herself, Maggie broke off abruptly. She never used the "F" word. Why had she almost used the "F" word? Her lack of control frightened her. But then, her lack of control was part of the problem, wasn't it? She swallowed hard, then finished more calmly. "On where I hid the stupid thing."

Temper snapped in his eyes. "You hid it in our bed."

"Actually, I hid it on *your side* of the bed. The side of the bed where you haven't been sleeping for the past month."

"Dammit, Maggie." He braced his hands on his hips and glared at her. "That's exactly the problem. It's not a month. I haven't slept in our bed since *Valentine's Day*. We haven't made love since Christmas! And you didn't even notice. You've hardly noticed a damned thing since Chase left for college in January."

"That's not true." Chase was the youngest of their four sons and while Maggie admitted she hadn't dealt well with the emptying of her nest, she hadn't been totally oblivious. "I noticed you started working late."

"Yeah, and why shouldn't I?" he fired back. "It's not like I have anything better to do in the evenings around home."

She blinked and reared back against the flowered sofa seat, taking it like a blow. *He's so angry.*

How could she not have known?

As silence stretched between them her light-headedness worsened. A nervous snicker bubbled up inside her, and before she quite knew what was happening, she was giggling. Hysterically. Her vision blurred, her stomach churned, and she began to gasp for air.

Mike cursed beneath his breath, stalked across the room, and firmly guided her head down between her knees. "Breathe. You're hyperventilating."

No, her heart was breaking.

After a few minutes, Maggie managed to regain control of herself, if not her life. She slumped back against the sofa and closed her eyes.

Mike stood against the wall looking almost as sick as she felt. Her gaze met his, and for a second, she saw in his brilliant blue eyes a pain so sharp and strong that it stabbed her heart.

What happened? How did we get here? What have I done to him?

Mike cleared his throat. "What about you? Did you write a letter?"

Maggie recalled the twenty-four-page manifesto she'd begun when she realized he'd left for work yesterday without so much as a "Good morning" and finished after getting his secretary's message last night. It had been the ugliest collection of thoughts put down on paper since her treatise about Marti Sue Reynolds, boyfriend stealer, in the seventh grade.

She'd torn it to pieces and flushed it.

"I wrote one. It's . . . I threw it out."

Mike sighed heavily. "I can't do this anymore, Maggie. It's tearing me apart. I've . . . um . . . found a place . . . to stay."

Maggie's stomach clinched. A place?

She went cold to the marrow of her bones. *Another woman?*

Oh, God. No. Please Mike, no.

She should ask. She didn't want to ask. She didn't want to know. She should say something. She should protest his leaving. She should beg. She should promise him anything he wanted.

But she couldn't manage it. She was numb inside and it took everything she had to force a single word through her constricted throat. "Where?"

She simply couldn't bear to ask who.

"Actually . . ." He dragged his hand along his jaw and she noticed for the first time he hadn't shaved. He dropped his chin to his chest, waited a beat, then looked up and boldly met her gaze. "I'll be at the lake for a little while, then I'm going to the Caribbean."

The Caribbean! She had a sudden vision of a twenty-something bimbo in a string bikini crooking her finger while casting Mike a come hither look. Feeling nauseous, Maggie rose and headed for the inner section of the rest room.

He stopped her with a sentence. "I bought a boat."

She blinked. "Excuse me?"

He drew himself up, squared his shoulders, and in a voice brimming with defiance said, "I bought a fifty-foot Viking and I'm taking her on a cruise. I have her moored up at Lake Texoma while I get her seaworthy. Then I'm shipping her to the coast and heading out. I need some time, Maggie. I need to settle some things in my mind. I'll be gone a couple of months, three at the most. If you want to contact a lawyer and make it a legal separation, I won't object. I think anything more involved than that should wait until I get back."

The door swished closed behind him.

Maggie lifted the lotion dispenser from the counter and hurled it against the wall.

When Holly turned thirteen, her father began a new family tradition for Saturday afternoons. Sometime around noon, he would fire up the engine of his fifty-seven Chevy convertible named the White Swan and back it out of the garage. While he spent the next half hour doing guy stuff under the hood, Holly filled a cooler with sandwiches, drinks, and snacks. Then they'd load up the picnic fixings and the dog and go for a Sunday drive—on Saturday afternoon, which was all part of the fun.

They took their drives in every kind of weather, bundling up in blankets when necessary, lowering the rag top to let the wind blow whenever conditions allowed. They never had an itinerary, just followed their noses, as her dad liked to say. Sometimes they stayed in town, cruising through residential areas, stopping for their picnics in parks or schoolyard playgrounds. Usually, though, they left the city and explored the dozens of narrow farm roads that crisscrossed north-central Texas. Holly remembered one Sunday drive in particular when her dad only made right turns. It took them forever to get back home, but that didn't matter. Their drives always lasted at least two hours and they often didn't come home before dark.

Holly loved their Saturday-Sunday drives, and she wanted desperately to believe her father did, too. That's why she always pretended to fall asleep during the last ten minutes of the trip. If her eyes were closed, she wouldn't see the tears that slipped from his eyes and slid silently down his cheeks each time they made their way back home.

She always knew he was missing her mother at those times, but it wasn't until she was older that she made the connection between the drives and the "naps" her parents had taken in their bedroom every Saturday afternoon. It was the first time Holly had cried just for her dad, and not for herself.

To this day, her dad never spent Saturday afternoons at home. If he'd found someone else with whom to "nap," he'd kept it private from Holly, and she bet it never happened on Saturday afternoons. Because thirteen years after her mother's death, he still took his Sunday drives in the White Swan, now renamed the Gray Swan due to mileage in excess of two hundred thousand. Holly joined him whenever her schedule allowed. Once a month, at least. And every time, every single time, as he turned The Swan onto his street, a tear or two would slip down his cheek. Holly's dad had never gotten over losing her mother.

It was a lesson Holly took to heart.

It was a lesson that broke her heart.

Because Justin was so much like her dad.

Justin.

Tears stung her eyes as she gunned the engine of her three-year-old Mustang, taking the blind curve faster than she should. She was driving on a farm road leading north out of Weatherford. After the emotional upheaval of the afternoon, she hadn't wanted to face an empty, lonely apartment, so she'd decided to take a Saturday-Sunday drive of her own.

She'd invited her new friends Grace and Maggie to come along, which was a sure sign of just how off-kilter she truly was.

As a rule, it took Holly time to warm up to people, and usually she got along better with men than with women. She was comfortable around guys. They weren't as nosy as her girlfriends. They weren't as complicated. They weren't as mean. As long as everyone kept sex out of the mix, they proved to be more loyal than the women she'd counted as friends.

So what wild hare had possessed her to ask Grace and Maggie to join her? Was it simply a case of her not wanting to be alone? Maybe she felt some cosmic connection to them because they'd inadvertently become part of one of the worst experiences of her life.

Then there was the question of why they'd come along. Maggie, she could understand. Her day hadn't been any better than Holly's. Grace was another matter. Her life wasn't out of control. Her man hadn't left her crying. He'd kissed her and gone away whistling. But why would Grace want to spend her time with two women? In her place, Holly would have run screaming in the opposite direction.

Maybe it had something to do with security. Any woman who'd managed to stay married to the same man for fifty years probably felt pretty good about herself. Holly figured she certainly would.

Whatever the reason, the two women were with her now. Grace sat in the front passenger seat. Maggie rode in back. She hadn't joined the get-to-know-you chitchat

Grace and Holly exchanged as they'd left downtown, but when they breezed past the city limits sign on I-20 West, Maggie started to mutter.

"He bought a boat. A yacht. To cruise the Caribbean without me. Didn't even ask me to run away with him. Just up and leaves me." She paused, then grumbled, "I'll show him a legal separation."

"That's probably not a bad idea," Holly cautioned, glancing in the rearview mirror toward Maggie. "It's better that you protect yourself financially."

Maggie wrinkled her nose. "Oh, Mike wouldn't take advantage of me that way. No, he'll just run over me with twin screws."

"Twin screws?" Grace asked.

"Boat propellers," Holly said.

"I don't ordinarily use foul language, but I am compelled to say that the man is a sorry boat-buying bastard." Maggie flicked open her compact and reapplied her lipstick with angry slashes. "I can't believe he's doing this. How dare he even think of doing this to me?"

She slammed her compact closed. "I'll tell you this much, ladies. I've cried my last tear over Mike He-Can-Cruise-to-Pluto-for-All-I-Care Prescott. He can swab his deck and polish his brass from now until kingdom come. I have better things to do. More important things to do."

She fell silent for two mile markers, then said, "Good heavens. What am I going to do?"

Holly handed back the box of tissues she kept under her seat, then exited off the interstate onto one of the farm roads leading north through the rolling countryside.

Grace adjusted her seat belt and twisted around to

look at Maggie. "I have a friend—one of my doctors, in fact—who always responds to that particular question by asking, 'What do you want to do?'"

"Oh, I know what I want to do," Maggie said with a sad laugh. "I want to keep doing what I've been doing for the past twenty years, but that's not possible. My children are grown and gone, and my husband's running off to St. Somewhere. I don't know who or what I am anymore, but right now, I'm tired of worrying about it. Let's talk about something else. Holly? Any ideas? Do you want to talk about Justin?"

"Absolutely not. I want something cheery to think about."

"I know what we can do," Grace said. "It's something we did when I was a Girl Scout leader with my daughter. How about we all pretend we're Maria in *The Sound of Music* and sing about our favorite things? We'll get to know each other better that way."

Yuck. Holly grimaced. *The generation gap rears its ugly head.*

"I don't sing," Maggie said, sounding as hesitant as Holly.

Grace shook her head. "I don't mean we really sing. Just tell us about your personal 'Raindrops on roses.'"

"Oh. Well. Okay." Maggie stared out the window in thought for a moment. "I like bubble baths. Bubble baths, little yappy dogs, and sparkling jewelry. Holly, your turn."

All right, maybe this wasn't so lame, after all. Cheesy, but not overly lame. "Hmm . . . I'm gonna say *National Geographic* magazine. Shaper hair spray. Peregrine falcons."

"Aren't they extinct?" Grace asked.

"No. In fact, they were removed from the endangered species list in 1999. I saw one once during a trip to Canada. It was simply majestic."

"That sounds lovely," Maggie said.

Holly slowed as she approached an unfamiliar intersection. She decided to take a right. "Okay, Grace. What are your 'Whiskers on kittens'?"

"Grandbabies. Soup recipes." She paused, and a grin hovered around her lips as she added, "Black lace panties."

"Ooh-la-la!" Maggie exclaimed.

"Way to go, Grace," Holly added.

The activity continued for another five miles or so. Maggie had just included Hot Cherry Kiss nail polish among her favorite things when she smiled with delight and said, "Oh, look at that, girls. Look at the mama horse and her baby."

In a pasture off to their right, a spindly-legged foal gamboled around a calmly grazing mare. Holly pulled the car off the road and parked along the shoulder so the three women could watch the young horse at play against the crimson and gold backdrop of a springtime sunset.

Holly thumbed buttons and the windows rolled down, allowing the scents and sounds of the peaceful rural countryside to wash over them. Killing the ignition, she took what felt like her first completely easy breath since Justin turned her world upside down.

Maggie laughed softly. "Why, it's a picture postcard, isn't it? A carpet of bluebonnets. Magnolias in bloom. A beautiful sunset. All that's missing is a cowboy leaning on the split-rail fence."

"A cowboy wearing chaps," Grace agreed.

"And nothing else," Holly added.

All three women burst into a laugh that intensified when Grace added, "Except for a hat. He needs to wear a hat, too."

"But on his head," Maggie clarified. "Don't want to spoil the scenery. Now that would make a right fine post-card."

Her tone more animated than it had been all day, she relayed a story about the nude postcards she'd run across during a trip to New Orleans for a baseball tournament some years back. "It was just a regular little grocery store. I thought nothing about taking the boys in for candy and a Coke. Then, I heard my youngest boy Chase say, 'God Almighty, it's the sausage section.' 'Course, I immediately went over to chastise him about his blasphemous language and there they were—an entire rack of naked men postcards. Double-stamp size, if you get my drift. My face turned the color of Big Red soda pop, and that was before my boy John discovered the wind-up penises on feet and set one to jumping all over the counter. I thought I'd just die."

When Grace and Holly's giggles faded, she added, "When the team went to the movies that night, I snuck back to the store and bought eight penises. Gave 'em as Christmas gifts to the girls on the PTA board with me that year."

Once they all caught their breath, Holly said, "That's enough. My stomach hurts too much to laugh any more."

At that moment, the last little sliver of sun dipped below the horizon and the sky softened into shadowy shades of mauve, purple, and pink. Holly sighed. "I love Texas sunsets."

Grace reached over and patted her knee. "Thank you for sharing this one with us."

"Hear hear," Maggie added.

As a surprising sense of peace stole across her soul, Holly started her car and made a U-turn back toward Fort Worth. She switched on her headlights, then took one last look at the evening sky before focusing her attention on the road. Softly, she said, "You know what, ladies? Everything considered, today wasn't a total disaster, after all."

✻ four

Late Sunday afternoon, Grace sat surrounded by white on three sides while she typed on a laptop computer at a small round table just inside the main entrance to the Greystone Hotel's ballroom. The gowns—eighty-three of them—were those donated to Making Memories by local women and a surprising number of men during this weekend's sale.

While she typed names and addresses of the donors into Making Memories' database, Grace listened with idle attention to events taking place around her. At the check-out table just the other side of the rack of vintage gowns to the right she heard Fran Hansen advise a bride about a headpiece for the gown she'd chosen. At a nearby station, Maggie Prescott explained to another volunteer how to operate the clothes steamer. Near the dressing room door, a newspaper reporter interviewed a shopper for a follow-up article on the sale that would run in Monday's *Star-Telegram*. When the reporter asked the bride-to-be why she'd chosen a secondhand gown for her wedding, the young woman's response gave Grace goose bumps.

"My grandmother died of breast cancer two years ago," she said. "We were very close and I'll miss her dreadfully on my wedding day. When I heard about Making Memories, I knew right away I wanted to buy my gown from them. This way I get to help another breast cancer patient, and at the same time, feel like I'm sharing my special day with my nana."

It was the same sort of thing Holly's beau had tried to do, Grace knew. It was a lovely thought, but Holly wasn't ready for it.

"Yet," Grace said aloud as her gaze stole to the end of a nearby rack where Maggie Prescott's donated wedding gown hung. Maggie had said Holly loved her dress, that she thought it was the prettiest one at the sale. Maggie also didn't truly want to let the gown go, Grace could tell. If Grace had any disposable income whatsoever, she'd have bought the gown herself and put it away for the two of them to come to their senses. She'd thought about asking Fran to set the dress aside for a time, but upon reflection, she'd decided she didn't feel right about doing that. After all, the dress was lovely and would certainly sell quickly. The five hundred dollars that sale would bring to Making Memories would help send a family to Disney or buy a video camera to tape messages from a Stage IV mother to her children. Grace couldn't in good conscience interfere.

Grace pondered the problem of Maggie's wedding gown as she worked her way to the bottom of the donor list. She'd just begun typing Maggie's zip code when a familiar voice stopped her mid-stroke.

Holly Weeks spoke from the other side of the dress rack.

"Excuse me, Fran."

"Holly. How lovely to see you. I understood you weren't able to volunteer today."

Grace quit typing.

"To be honest," Holly replied, "I didn't intend to, but I realized a little while ago that I lost an earring yesterday. A gold hoop. It matches this one. Has anyone turned it in to you?"

Grace wanted to go say hello, but something in the young woman's voice gave her pause. She'd wait just a minute. Listen a little more. Thank goodness she wasn't morally opposed to eavesdropping.

"Oh, dear. I am so sorry, but no, we have had no jewelry of any kind turned in. That is such a beautiful earring."

"It was my mother's."

Oh no. An heirloom. Grace wondered if Holly had checked the rest room.

"Have you inquired at the front desk? I am certain the hotel has a Lost and Found."

"Yes. I struck out there, too. Maybe it'll turn up when the gowns are moved out of the ballroom. I'll hang around and help with breakdown if that's all right with you. It's not the most flattering reason for volunteering to help, I know, but . . ."

Fran laughed. "I never turn down a volunteer."

As the two women discussed where help was most needed at the time, Fran's cell phone rang. From the one-sided conversation that followed, Grace gathered a problem had developed regarding a wish Making Memories had granted to a Georgia woman who wanted to visit lighthouses along the Oregon coast. Fran discussed alternative lodging arrangements with her wish director, and immediately upon her finishing the call, her phone rang again. This time it was a local restaurant asking questions about the pizzas to be delivered during breakdown an hour later. Grace heard Fran say she'd need to ask the hotel liaison, then her voice faded as she walked away.

A shrill voice filled the void. "Who's in charge here? There's a problem with this gown and the girl in the dressing room said I'd have to talk to the woman in charge."

Holly said, "Fran is busy at the moment. Perhaps I can help?"

"My daughter wants this gown, but it has a tear in it, so I want you to deduct a hundred and fifty dollars."

Frowning, Grace pushed apart two of the wedding gowns on the rack separating her from the check-out table, trying to make a spot through which to peek at Holly and the skinflint without being seen. A bow on the bustle of an early nineties gown blocked her view of Holly, and she scowled at the fashion dinosaur. She was tempted to rip it off, but better sense prevailed. This might be some girl's dream dress. Grace shifted her chair instead.

The woman glaring at Holly was tall, fashionably thin, and dressed to the nines. She held a gown Grace recognized right away. She knew about the "tear." It was a tiny little quarter-inch slit on the train, probably made by a heel, and easily mended.

Grace rose and walked around her shield of white, intending to explain how a little iron-on tape would make the dress like new again, when the mother-of-the-bride continued to speak.

"Also, it's soiled along the edge of the train, so I want the veil and the slip for free."

Grace's chin dropped. The nerve of that woman.

Holly's voice dripped sugar as she briefly met Grace's gaze, then replied, "I'm sorry, but you will need to talk to Fran about that and she is busy right now on a phone call. I believe it has something to do with the wishes Making Memories is granting to terminally ill men and women with proceeds from this weekend's sale. You do know, don't you, that one hundred percent of the money raised from the 'Something Old, Something New' sale goes to fund wishes?"

Holly reached over to check the tag on the Demetrios Italian silk gown the woman had piled onto the check-out table. "What a lovely dress," Holly said. "Brand new, too. This is obviously one of the gowns donated by the manufacturer. You know, I believe this one retails for between eighteen hundred and two thousand dollars. Aren't you lucky to be getting it for the five ninety-nine price tag."

"It's soiled, I tell you," insisted the woman as Maggie abandoned the steamer and joined the tableau, her eyebrows lifted in a questioning arch. "I'm not paying over four hundred dollars for it."

"Mmm hmm. Won't it make you feel good to know that the money you spent was used to purchase . . . well, here, let me look at our list of wishes waiting to be granted." Holly lifted a sheet of paper from the table, a page Grace knew itemized pizza requests rather than wishes.

"It appears as if your purchase will pay for a video camera and VCR for an indigent young mother in Georgia. She wants to record herself reading children's books aloud so her two preschool children will still be able to

have their mother read to them after she dies. Oh, but
wait. Here it says the equipment costs over six hundred
dollars and if Making Memories discounts your brand
new designer gown, which is already reduced well over a
thousand dollars, we won't be able to afford both. Which
should we not buy, do you think? The camera or the
VCR? Oh, and by the way, your ring is simply beautiful. I
love canary diamonds. It's about two carats, isn't it?"

Maggie leaned over and spoke in Grace's ear. "That
girl is good."

By the time Fran finished her phone call and returned, Holly had completed the sale for full price and a
bonus. Maggie and Grace filled Fran in on the younger
woman's coup while Holly smirked over her victory.

Talk turned to the Making Memories organization itself, and Holly explained that she'd visited the foundation's website last night. She asked Fran about her
day-to-day work, then they spoke for a bit about the
wishes Making Memories had granted and those currently
waiting to be filled. It was only when Holly mentioned
how, in effect, when a person is diagnosed with breast cancer the entire family is diagnosed with cancer, that Grace
again heard the note of pain in Holly's voice.

Fran reached out and squeezed Holly's hand. "You lost
a family member?"

"My mom. It was thirteen years ago, but sometimes it
feels like yesterday."

Oh, Holly, Grace thought.

"Oh, Holly," Fran said. "She must have been young."

"Thirty-two."

Maggie elaborated. "Holly was only twelve."

"How terribly sad for you both." Sympathy and compassion filled Fran's expression. "A girl so needs her

mother at that time of life. Two of Making Memories' wish families include pre-teen daughters. Neither of the mothers are expected to live beyond Christmas. It's the saddest thing. I know how to relate to the women. I understand when they wish to talk or simply be silent. The children, the daughters especially, leave me at a loss. I do not know how to communicate with them. It breaks my heart. They break my heart. How does one deal with such a devastating loss at that age?"

"I made a list."

At Fran's curious look, Holly gave a little, embarrassed laugh, then explained about the Life List she'd mentioned during the brouhaha yesterday in the ladies' room. This time when she said that it contained thirty-two items, Grace made the connection between Holly's number of goals and the age her mother died. Had Holly chosen the number on purpose?

"What sort of goals are on your list?" Fran asked.

"Number twenty-five is 'I will win the Yard of the Month Award.' Number sixteen is 'I will teach an adult to read.' I've already checked that one off. Number eight is 'I will save a life.'"

"It sounds like an ambitious list," Fran said. "I love the idea of it."

Holly shrugged. "Don't be too impressed. Owning crotchless panties is on it, too."

Fran looked scandalized, and Grace barely held back a laugh. Maggie didn't even try. "Maybe I should make a list, too. Think of the fun I could have with it. I could use some fun."

Holly smiled crookedly, then pulled a gold hoop earring from her pocket and slipped it over the ring finger on her left hand. Looking at it, she continued, "I used it as an escape. Whenever my troubles got too heavy to bear, I'd dream about my list. I'd imagine myself skiing the Alps or diving a shipwreck. It helped me cope. You might want to pass the idea along to those daughters you mentioned, Fran."

The conversation was interrupted when a bride approached the table with a gown purchase. Moments later another half-dozen women waited in line, their arms full of white silk, organza, and lace. Grace and Holly pitched in to bag gowns and veils while Maggie helped Fran write receipts. When the rush was done, Fran glanced toward Holly and picked up where they'd left off. "Why don't *you* pass it along?"

"Pardon me?"

Fran offered a sensible, encouraging, you'll-be-ashamed-if-you-refuse-me smile. "I think it would be nice if you talked to the girls, if you told them about your list, how it helped you, and any other bits of advice you might have. You could talk to them from the position of having been in the trenches with them."

Grace thought it was a wonderful idea and she'd just opened her mouth to add her two cents when Holly backed away.

"Wait a minute," Holly protested. "I'm no counselor. No therapist. I'm certainly no expert on how to deal with a parent's death. I'm still messed up myself. I don't do cancer. I don't talk about it. I try not to even think about it. It's too hard."

Grace reached out and touched Holly's arm. "But you could be a friend who talks about female things. Makeup and boys and shoes. You could be a real-life Making Memories wish for those girls. You could give them a respite from their worries. I think it's a wonderful idea."

"No. It's not. Really." Holly's dark hair, tied in a youthful ponytail today, whipped back and forth as she shook her head.

Maggie tucked a pink pen behind one ear, then folded her arms. "It's a great idea and you know it. You know how to relate to youngsters that age. You're a middle-school teacher. Relating is your job."

"I teach math, not life skills. Believe me, I am the very last person who should volunteer for something like this."

"Nonsense," Fran said.

"I don't believe that," Grace scoffed.

"You should. Because I . . . oh, shoot." Holly raked her fingers through her hair. "I can't deal with this. I've got to . . . I'm just . . . oh, would you look at that?"

She gestured wildly toward the center of the ballroom. "That girl is dragging that long train behind her. Someone is going to step on it and it'll ruin the gown or somebody will get hurt."

She dashed away as if off to save the world rather than a particularly unattractive wedding dress.

Grace sighed as she watched Holly attempt to help a bride who obviously didn't want help. Maggie clucked her tongue. "Running away again. Something is going on there."

Grace agreed. "Holly acts like she's scared to death."

Maggie pursed her lips and thought for a moment. "A hotel employee mentioned to me a few minutes ago that they've set out chocolate cookies and drinks in the boardroom for volunteers. Let's get Holly to take a break with us. See if we can get her to spill."

Even as they made the decision, Holly returned. She addressed Fran, who now was busy with her calculator and receipt book, totaling the day's sales. "All right.

Here's the truth. I can't believe I'm being such a blabbermouth. First the list. Now this." She flung out her hands, gesturing toward the racks of wedding gowns. "I can't believe I'm in the middle of the fairyland of girl dreams, confessing my deepest and darkest."

She blew out a heavy breath. "I can't help those girls. I would be a terrible example. Teaching is one thing, but this is something entirely different. Believe me, those parents wouldn't want me around their daughters during such a vulnerable time."

"Why the heck not?" Maggie put her hands on her hips, her expression perplexed.

Holly shut her eyes, licked her lips, then faced her past. "When I was fifteen, a month after my mother's sister died, I attempted suicide."

Grace covered her mouth with her hands to hide her gasp. Maggie's eyes went wide and round. Fran gave Holly an encouraging smile.

"Daddy did everything he could. Sent me to a shrink, made sure I took my medicine." A smile flickered on her lips as she glanced at Grace and Maggie. "Took me on the best Saturday-Sunday drives.

"But nothing helped. I was thinking about trying again. Then one of my teachers started talking to me. Her mother had passed away recently and she said she understood what I was feeling. She talked to me, not about death and dying, but about girl stuff. Light stuff."

"Makeup and boys and shoes," Maggie said, repeating Grace's earlier words.

Holly nodded. "She got me to talk. By the time school let out for the summer, I was over the worst of it. She inspired me to become a teacher."

Gently, Fran asked, "So you will work with these girls?"

After a moment's hesitation, Holly again nodded. "Yes. I guess so. Except, I want to start out slow. I'm thinking we could exchange e-mails. See how it goes."

"Good idea." Fran found a note pad and a pen and asked Holly to write down the information she'd need.

When she was done, Holly straightened, obviously ready to beat a retreat. "The sale ends at four. It's quarter till now. Would it help if I headed for the dressing room and started boxing up veils?"

"Yes, thank you."

Fran explained how the veils and petticoats should be rolled and stored, and Holly headed off. Grace watched her go and realized the emotion filling her heart was a sense of maternal pride. The feeling surprised her. After all, she barely knew Holly. Still, something about the girl called to Grace, touched a place within her. She suspected it had something to do with the fact that Holly so obviously still missed her mother.

Maybe that was it. Maybe the connection Grace felt wasn't to Holly, but to the woman who couldn't be here to assist and advise her daughter as she navigated the maze of life. The notion made sense, considering. "I wonder what her name was," she mused.

"Who?" Fran asked.

"Holly's mother."

Holly's mother. The woman whose life the breast cancer dragon had extinguished way too young. The woman whose light, however, continued to shine. It shone in her bright, brave, empathetic daughter.

Grace knew just what to do. "Holly?" she called.

The young woman glanced over her shoulder. Grace

smiled tenderly and spoke the words Holly needed to hear. "Your mother would be so proud."

On Wednesday morning, Holly awoke slowly to the toasty sensation of sunshine on her face. Without opening her eyes, she grinned into her pillow. Sleeping late was one of the best things about this year's Spring Break.

She was trying hard to take note of all the things she enjoyed about her week off this month. She needed something to balance all the negatives that plagued her.

The smile faded. She and Justin had planned to go away this week. They'd had reservations at a B&B in the Hill Country. Holly had intended to spend the week working on number eighteen: *I will be a man's "Best He Ever Had."*

Instead, she'd spent her time on number twenty-seven: *I will read a thousand books simply for pleasure*. It was a worthy goal, but not nearly as much fun as the other.

She missed Justin so bad it made her stomach hurt.

Holly wondered if he'd taken off work as scheduled. She knew he wouldn't go to the Hill Country alone, but he might have gone somewhere else. He might have gone fishing. Justin liked to fish. Who knows, he might have gone up to his family's lake house at Lake Texoma for the week. He might be fishing with Mike Prescott. He might be catching a twelve-pound striper right this very minute, the same fish that was supposed to be destined for Holly's hook to fulfill number nine.

"Aaargh," she cried, burrowing her head in her pillow even as the phone beside her bed began to ring. She let it trill four times before picking up. "Hello?"

"Holly? It's Maggie. I just got a call from Grace and she's begging for our help. Are you busy this morning?"

Holly glanced at the stack of novels beside her bed. "My plans can wait."

"Wonderful. It's nine now. Can you be ready in half an hour? I'll pick you up on the way."

"On the way to where?"

"Silke's. A little boutique on Camp Bowie. We're meeting Grace there at ten. She wants help choosing her anniversary party dress."

"Oh, that sounds like fun. I'll be . . . Silke's?" Horror colored Holly's voice. "That's where Justin's mother took me to try on wedding gowns. That's where *Randall* works."

Maggie's tone imitated awe. "He is a god."

Holly's gaze landed on her stack of paperback novels. "Maybe I should skip this excursion, after all. If Grace has Randall's opinion, she won't need mine. I have a lot to do today and—"

"She wants very badly for you to join us. She asked me to make the request since this is your vacation and she didn't want to put you on the spot."

Randall. Ugh. "What if Justin's mother shows up?"

"I'll get rid of her. I promise. You can hide in the dressing room until I get the job done. Grace can sneak you cookies from the bakery next door."

Holly always had a difficult time saying no to sweets. At least that was the explanation she gave herself as, an hour later, she found herself exchanging small talk with the only man alive who'd put a tape measure to her breasts.

When Grace emerged from the dressing room in an ice blue beaded silk evening suit, Holly grasped the distraction like a lifeline. "That's beautiful. I love the color."

Randall directed Grace onto a carpet-covered plat-form in the center of the mirrored sitting area, then fixed and fussed and eventually shooed Grace back into the dressing room to change. The second dress was a simple black sheath with a jacket. Maggie adored it; Randall despised it. Holly feared they might break out into a fist-fight at any moment.

The debate raged for a dozen outfits and almost two hours. To Holly's surprise, she found herself weighing in with an opinion almost every time. However, the most important person in the decision-making process sank deeper into indecisiveness with every change of clothes.

"I give up," Grace wailed softly when Randall left the room in search of yet another outfit. "They're all pretty. They're all way too expensive. Maybe I should wear something I already have."

"To your golden anniversary party?" Maggie gasped, enacting a theatric faintness with a hand against her forehead. "I should say not."

"But Maggie—"

"No. Your fiftieth anniversary dress is second in importance only to your wedding dress."

"In that case, I *should* wear something from my closet. Ben and I were married at the courthouse. The dress I wore was six months old. I did have a pretty little head-piece with a veil." She paused, smiled wistfully, and added, "I always regretted not having a formal wedding."

For a moment, silence lay on the air like a delicate French lace. Holly felt a pang in her chest as she tried to swallow, longing for Justin.

Maggie sighed. "Our wedding was lovely. You saw my gown. I kept my veil. Actually, it was a hat. Very seventies. You wouldn't have expected it to go with the vintage gown, but somehow, it did."

Eyeing a stylishly turned out Maggie, Holly didn't doubt it for a moment. For today's shopping expedition, she'd dressed in basic, classic black that Randall had eyed with greedy attention. Holly glanced down at her own jeans and sneakers and winced.

"We married at Sacred Heart Church in Wichita Falls," Maggie continued. "We decorated the altar in votives and yellow roses. My colors were blue and yellow. Do girls even do colors anymore?"

Holly shrugged. She hadn't a clue. She worked hard to avoid weddings and their arrangements. She'd managed to make it to twenty-five without being a bridesmaid once—no easy feat, considering she'd been asked eight times.

Maggie giggled. "You know the worst thing about getting married in the seventies? The tuxes. To this day I can't believe I got Mike Prescott to wear a white tux and baby blue ruffled shirt."

"Oh, my," Grace said.

"He used to say that if I ever needed proof that he loved me, all I had to do was pull out our wedding pictures."

Seeing the sadness invade her eyes, Holly hastened to move the conversation along. "What did Ben wear to your wedding, Grace?"

Clasping thin hands, Grace gazed into the past. "His one and only suit. Navy blue. He looked so handsome."

Randall swept into the room with three more dresses for Grace, one of them an ivory silk. "Try that one next," Holly suggested. "It reminds me of a wedding gown."

"Why, you're right," Maggie agreed. "In fact, I saw something similar at the Making Memories sale."

Sadly, that particular dress didn't fit properly around Grace's hips and when Randall conferred with the shop's seamstress, she confirmed that this was not the anniversary dress for Grace.

Throughout the discussion, for once, Maggie remained silent. After Randall excused himself to make a phone call and just as Grace began to return to the dressing room, she piped up. "Why don't you buy a wedding gown. I sold a gown on Saturday to a woman who was celebrating her thirty-fifth. Fifty has so much more cachet. That's what you should do, Grace. Make a renewal of vows part of the party. You could finally have your formal wedding. Church, flowers, wedding cake. The works."

"Oh, that would be lovely." Grace's eyes lit with excitement, then suddenly dimmed. "I . . . can't do it."

"Why not?" Holly asked.

Grace's chin angled up, her jaw taking on a stubborn set. "Frankly, it's a personal matter and none of your concern. Now, I'd appreciate it if you dropped the subject."

She marched into the dressing room, then the door slammed shut behind her with a bang.

"Well." Maggie looked at Holly. "The woman does a good snit in addition to a sulk and a pout. Do you have a clue what just happened here?"

"I think you touched a nerve."

"Obviously. And Ben's Gracie showed us she has a temper. Last time I saw that much starch was when the Stay-Flo truck turned over on Airport Freeway."

When Grace returned a few minutes later she wore her own clothes and a contrite expression. "I apologize for my outburst. It was terribly rude of me. I hope you'll allow me to buy you lunch to make up for it."

Maggie slipped her arm through Grace's. "Honey, I never turn down a free lunch, although I insist on buying dessert."

"Good. Let's find Randall."

"I'm here, madam. Have you made your choice?"

Grace turned a pleading gaze on her two friends. "Which one? The blue? The salmon suit? The black one?"

"Well . . ." Maggie pursed her lips. "I think the blue—"

"None of them," Holly said, shoving to her feet, speaking with such certainty that it obviously took both Grace and Maggie aback. "She should have an ivory dress. This one was almost perfect. I think we should keep looking until we find one that *is* perfect."

Grace glanced nervously toward Randall. "But—"

He clucked his tongue and patted her hand. "Not to worry, Mrs. Hardeman. Your friend is right. You must continue to search. Might I suggest the Lemon Tree two blocks north? It's been a pleasure to help you. Miss Weeks. Mrs. Prescott."

"Thank you, Randall. You're a dear." Maggie flashed him her brightest smile. "By the way, I set aside a small stack of things I'd like. Charge them to my account and send them out to me, would you please?"

"It will be my pleasure."

On the way outside, Holly noted a shirt atop a small mountain of clothing and accessories piled high on a tapestry chair. It was the same shirt she'd seen Maggie admiring earlier. "Is *that* what you call a small stack?"

Maggie grinned. "I haven't been shopping in some time."

Grace suggested a small café in the hospital district.

They ordered salads to assuage guilt, then one piece of chocolate cake with three forks. They discussed their mutual love of chocolate while waiting for the dessert. Holly asked, "Have y'all tried the German chocolate cake at Colonial Cafeteria? This cake is good, but that's superb. We'll have to go there next time."

Maggie mentioned a chocolate torte served at a little Italian place up in Keller. The waitress who delivered their cake recommended the chocolate pie from a bakery over by Texas Christian University.

They each took a bite from a huge wedge of chocolate cake. Then, while an unsuspecting Grace smiled with pleasure, Maggie struck. "Now. Tell us why you vetoed my idea about a renewal of vows."

Grace's fork slipped from her hand and clattered to the floor.

"Maggie," Holly protested.

"Well, are we friends or acquaintances? I need clarification."

Annoyed, Holly slid a protective glance toward Grace. "What's the difference?"

"Acquaintances keep things light. Friends take it deeper."

After savoring another bite of cake, Maggie set down her fork and wiped her mouth with her yellow gingham napkin. "The fact is, ladies, I have lots of acquaintances, but very few friends. Actually, I don't know that I'd claim to have any true friends anymore. The two who qualified moved away, and while we still keep up, we've lost the intimacy that allows a girl to tell her deep dark secrets."

Grace nodded. "I've experienced a similar situation a time or two in my past."

Maggie continued, her tone serious. "I've done some

thinking since Saturday, and I realize I'm ready . . . I need . . . to make a friend or two. I need someone I can share my problems with. Someone I can talk to about Mike. It can't be my children—I won't put them in the middle despite the fact they've been ringing my phone like a fire alarm since the weekend. I don't have a sister and my mother is gone. My nail tech will do in a pinch, but I only see her every other week."

Holly sipped her iced tea, then attempted a nonchalant shrug. "If you need to talk to me about Mike, feel free. After all, you had a front row seat at the airing of my dirty laundry."

"But not mine," Grace said. She set down her fork. "I haven't told you anything of import, have I?"

"Maybe you have nothing to tell," Maggie said with a casual wave that conveyed the message she didn't believe it for a minute.

Grace responded with a rueful smile. "Oh, I have a secret or two I could share. But to be honest, it's been a pleasure for me to spend time with friends who don't know what it is. It's been a long time since I had the opportunity. I'd hoped it would last a bit longer."

"Oh." Maggie blinked in surprise. "Well, in that case . . . listen, sugar. Never mind. I'm not trying to force you into anything. That's the last thing I want to do. I was being selfish. I guess I just wanted a little reassurance that I can trust in this fledgling friendship of ours. At the moment, my brain isn't working well enough for me to trust my own judgment. It's because I'm too much like my mother, you see."

"Your mother?" Grace asked.

Interested, Holly leaned forward, silently encouraging.

"Yes, my mother. You see, for the most part she was a lovely woman. However, she had the biggest mouth south of the Red River. She'd tell total strangers that she was feeling poorly because she'd gotten her period that day. She wasn't shy about sharing the details of my personal body clock, either."

Holly stuck her fork into another bite of cake. "That embarrassed you."

"It mortified me. All my life, I've been afraid I'm going to grow up like her. And I am like her. I'm so like her it scares me. I keep hardly anything to myself. At least, I haven't up until the last few months when I've been so sad and not talking to anyone. Now after the scene with Mike on Saturday, I find I want to talk, but at the same time, I can't talk to just anybody. Not anymore. My thoughts and feelings are all jumbled. I don't even know why I'm sitting here saying all this. Never mind about any of it. I'll shut up now."

"Oh, sweetheart." Grace reached across the table and gave Maggie's hand a squeeze. "I understand. Truly, I do. You're at a crossroads in your life and it makes you vulnerable right now. Someone could easily take advantage of you. But your instincts are good ones, and it's right for you to listen to them. You want equality in your friendships."

"I want equality in my marriage," Maggie grumbled. "Lost that years ago."

"Well, I can't do anything about your marriage, but I can affect this friendship we're forming. I agree. We need to be on equal footing. I know hurtful things about you two and your men, so now I'm going to share a hurtful thing about me and Ben."

Grace took a fortifying bite of cake, set down her fork,

sipped her tea, then said, "Ben is making something that is already difficult for me almost impossible. I understand why he acts this way. Heaven knows, I love him so much I want this to be as easy on him as possible. But at the same time, I'm tired, so very tired of pretending. It saps my energy at a time when I need every resource. It would be so much easier if I had the freedom to speak from my heart about what I think and believe and how I feel. But that would make it worse for Ben and for the children, so I can't. On the other hand, why should I put his needs above my own, especially now? That I can't or don't or won't makes me angry. Very angry. And that wastes energy, too."

Defiantly, she lifted her chin, squared her shoulders, and took another bite of cake.

Holly and Maggie traded puzzled gazes. Maggie said, "You've lost me, Grace. What has Ben done?"

"He won't face reality, so that means I put on a happy face every day, pretending everything is fine when it's not. It's not."

"What are you pretending about?"

Turning her head, Grace gazed out the window. "I'm pretending I'm not scared when I'm frightened to the bone. I'm pretending I'm not in pain when every part of me hurts. I'm pretending that everything is going to be okay, when in my heart, I know that it won't."

"Grace, what's wrong?"

"When you suggested Ben and I renew our vows, I acted ugly because I was embarrassed. It was a wonderful idea and it was something I'd love to do. The fact is, we can't afford it. The Making Memories Foundation is paying the expenses of the party and I don't feel right about asking for more. I don't feel right about accepting party arrangements as it is. The treatments are working. Other families' needs are more immediate. My mistake was mentioning how much I wanted to bring my family together for a happy occasion in front of Fran."

"Wait a minute," Holly said, her heart beginning to thud. "Are you saying you are a Making Memories wish recipient?"

Grace met Maggie's gaze first, then Holly's. "Eight years ago, I was diagnosed with Stage II breast cancer. I had a double mastectomy, recovered well, and celebrated my five-year anniversary by taking a Caribbean cruise with my husband. I thought I was over the worst of it."

The blood seemed to drain from Holly's head. *No no no no no!* She wanted to shove to her feet and dash from the café, to run away from what she knew surely must be coming.

"Two years ago, it came back. The cancer had metastasized to my bones."

Maggie reached across the table to take Grace's hand.

Nausea rolled through Holly's stomach, and as the full implication of Grace's revelation hit her, she gasped and covered her mouth with her hands. Through her fingers, she breathed, "You're dying."

Then Grace did the most amazing thing. She laughed. "No, sweetheart. That's the whole point. I'm not dying, I'm *living*. As boldly and creatively and enthusiastically as I can manage for as long as God gives me."

Sobering, she added, "That, in a nutshell, is the problem. I'm trying to live, but my Ben is so hurt, so frightened, he can't see beyond the dying."

"And it's driving you crazy," Maggie said with sudden insight.

"Exactly. There's always an article to read, a new exercise to try, a new drug trial to investigate. He coddles me. He watches me like a hawk. Some mornings I wake up and he's lying there staring at me, his face so full of pain and fear it breaks my heart. It makes me feel guilty for being sick."

That particular sentiment pierced the cold fog that had gathered in Holly's heart. She shook her head. "No, you shouldn't feel guilty."

Grace waited until the waitress refilled their iced tea glasses. Then she squeezed lemon into her glass, plunked in a spoon, and stirred. Hard. "Nevertheless, I do feel guilty and that in turn makes me feel resentful toward Ben."

Maggie rearranged her napkin in her lap. "Looks to me like it's more than resentment. Sounds to me like you're nail-spittin' mad."

"I *am* angry." Grace drummed her fingers on the Formica tabletop. "I didn't get sick on purpose. I didn't want to have a recurrence. But I did. Now he has to learn to live with it. He has to let *me* live with it. I may have ten years left. I may have more than that. I may have twenty years left. And if I'm that lucky, if I'm that blessed, then by gosh, I don't want to spend the rest of my life dying!"

To Holly, the words seemed to reverberate through the café dining room. In reality, they only echoed through her mind. *I don't want to spend the rest of my life dying.*

It was, Holly realized, a profound thought. Something she might want to think about. Someday.

✻ five

Springtime weather in Fort Worth kept the timid on their toes. Thunderstorms blew in like clockwork, bringing fence-flattening winds, roof-battering hail, and sometimes that wickedest of storms, tornadoes. Three years ago, an April twister had ripped right through downtown, destroying buildings and businesses, livelihoods and lives. For the most part the city had recovered, but it would never forget. Especially on those spring afternoons when the air grew still and sticky and the sky turned mean.

However, most days from March through May, Fort Worth weather offered a glimpse of heaven. Warm without being hot, bright and breezy with the bluebonnets in bloom, these were days that lifted a heart, lightened a smile, and simply made a person feel good.

At least, that's what Maggie kept trying to tell herself. She figured if she said it often enough, the Black Mood

Devil that perched on her shoulder would eventually disappear.

But she wasn't counting on it.

She'd toted the demon-cloud around with her for months now, and when Mike moved out two weeks ago, it had set its pitchfork even deeper. She hadn't heard a word out of her husband since that day at the Greystone. Her boys were a different matter entirely.

They had taken their father's side in this fight. All four of them. For Maggie, it was the worst of betrayals.

They'd showed up en masse last night. Steven, her eldest, had done the talking. He'd sounded just like his dad.

"Condescending know-it-alls," she muttered as she slammed her car door shut in a parking garage downtown. "Try to tell me I'm acting poorly. Brats."

How dare they judge her? They didn't understand how she felt. Nobody understood. Shoot, Maggie didn't even understand.

They'd had the audacity to make an appointment for her with a therapist.

Maggie took aim at a small rock with her sneaker and sent it skidding across the concrete, the sound a lonely echo that suited her mood. Their interference really chapped her hide. So maybe she was having a bit of trouble adjusting. Maybe it wouldn't hurt to speak with a therapist again. But if she decided to do that, it would be her decision, not Mike's. Definitely not the boys'.

And if one of them brought up the state of her hormones again, she'd snatch them bald-headed.

She slammed her palm against the black button on the elevator. The doors opened immediately. For some reason, that gave Maggie a little surge of power. *You're losing it, girl.*

"Put it out of your mind," she told herself as she stepped into the elevator. Be Scarlett O'Hara and think about it tomorrow. Today was a day for play, and dang it, she intended to enjoy herself. Despite the fact that this year, as she strolled the white canvas tents of the Main Street Arts Festival, her husband wasn't at her side.

Curse the boat-buying runaway.

Maggie tried hard to improve her mood as she wandered from booth to booth admiring sculpture, pottery, and paintings on display. She managed a smile when a band struck up a Glenn Miller tune on the performance stage at Fourth and Main, and she laughed aloud when the little boy riding his father's shoulders in front of her decided he was finished with his ice cream cone and planted it in his daddy's hair.

Then she caught the scent of roasted corn—her all-time favorite street fair food—and the aroma triggered a pang of grief that pierced to the marrow. Last year Mike had teased her unmercifully when she'd asked him to purchase her a third ear of corn. They'd been happy and laughing like kids that day. It was only a week later that Maggie's mother fell ill and life as she'd known it began to unravel. In fact, the Main Street Arts Festival a year ago was the last time Maggie recalled truly having fun with Mike.

In recent years they had made the event a special retreat for the two of them. Each year they rented a hotel room downtown and made a weekend of it. The first afternoon, they would wander up Main Street from the courthouse toward the convention center at the south end. They'd nibble on ears of corn and spend an hour or so browsing the artists' offerings and listening to music before finally making their way to Alan MacCraken's booth. There, after much consideration and discussion, they would select that year's addition to their collection.

Alan was a woodcarver. He worked primarily in large pieces—his rockers were extraordinary—but every year he brought a selection of truly beautiful boxes made of glowing woods with intricate grains. Though Maggie wasn't a collector by nature, she wouldn't trade her boxes for the world. Not just because they were lovely, but because they represented a special time for her and Mike. After buying the box, they always returned to their room for afternoon lovemaking. It was a mini-honeymoon for them, an annual reaffirmation of their love and of their marriage.

Maggie kept her MacCraken boxes on display in the family room at home, where a glance invariably brought back memories of laughter and love—laughter and love that had been missing in their house of late.

"It's not all my fault, either," she grumbled, no matter what the men of her family said. "I should have had girls."

It was one of her greatest regrets, not having a daughter. Oh, she loved her boys. They were her life, which made their alliance with their father all the more hurtful. Nevertheless, she'd always wished for a little girl. She'd yearned to buy ruffles and lace, bobby socks and Mary Janes. She'd wanted long hair to French braid. She'd wanted to buy gold hoop earrings for her daughter, not a pair to split between her sons.

After Chase was born, Maggie had wanted to try one more time for a pink hospital nursery cap. Mike wouldn't hear of it. Four was enough, he'd declared. Maggie had always nursed a bit of resentment at that.

The flow of foot traffic in front of her bottlenecked,

and someone bumped into Maggie, jostling her thoughts back to the present. She checked her watch. Still an hour and a half before she was due to meet Grace and Holly at the Ashford. The thought of the upcoming meeting with her new friends and the manager of the luxurious new boutique hotel put a smile back on her face. Dabbling in this newfound friendship with Holly and Grace was just what she needed to drag her out of her funk. It gave her something to do, and Maggie needed that. Desperately. Thank God for a multitude of tasks.

Maggie had taken over planning Grace's anniversary party.

It had all started the day of their shopping expedition. Following her disclosure of her illness, Grace had thanked Maggie and Holly for helping her to look for a dress, ordered another refill of iced tea, then said, "One of the worst things about this disease is that I have been forced to learn to ask for help. I have always been a strong, energetic, capable person. I have taken care of myself—and others—for decades. It is very uncomfortable to be in a position of not being able to do for myself. I am not accustomed to asking for help. I am not good at it."

She paused and reached into her purse, withdrawing a small bottle of lotion. "This time it's a little easier because I think that helping me might help you, too, Maggie. You and Holly both. I think you could use a distraction in your lives right now."

Holly watched Grace rub lotion into her hands. The pleasing scent of roses teased her nose. "What do you need help with, Grace?"

"The reception. Making Memories is willing to make all

the arrangements, but they're based in Portland, and long-distance party planning is difficult and expensive. They don't know Dallas/Fort Worth vendors, and since I haven't planned a party since my daughter's wedding reception ten years ago, I don't know who to approach, either."

Finished with her lotion, she silently offered it to Holly and Maggie before adding, "For instance, I would be surprised if the florist we used was still in business. Half of our order was wrong. Liza was in tears when she saw daisies rather than roses at the altar."

"I'm good at party planning." Maggie creamed her hands, smiled at the scent, then reached into her purse. She drew out a small notebook, and flipped through the pages. "In Junior League circles, this little puppy is as valuable as the Dallas Cowboys' play book. Love the lotion, Grace. Where do you get it?"

"My sweet granddaughter makes it for me. All different fragrances. It's a hobby of hers. I could get you a bottle if you'd like."

"That would be lovely," Maggie declared.

Holly finally pulled herself out of the shock of Grace's news enough to say, "I can't plan a party. I only plan tailgate parties. And hardly any of those."

"But you are young and energetic. Some days my energy level lags, and you could be my boost. Plus, having your assistance would provide Ben some peace of mind, which would make life easier for me in that arena."

Holly agreed to help whenever her schedule allowed, though she warned the last half of the spring semester was a busy one for teachers as they prepared their classes for statewide standardized testing. They'd ended their lunch with a debate on musical selections the party guests would prefer.

When Maggie got home that afternoon, the first thing she did was to check her answering machine to see if she'd missed a call from Mike or the boys. The second was to call Making Memories and speak to their wish director, Anna Nelson, to make arrangements to personally fund Grace's wish—including a formal renewal of vows. Maggie had insisted on anonymity for the directed wish, of course. Grace would pitch a fit if she knew Maggie had involved herself in the financial end of things.

It was bad enough just trying to make the reception arrangements. The woman was so prickly about spending other people's money. Had it not been for Maggie's Junior League bargaining-with-the-vendors experience, she doubted Grace would have listened to a single suggestion about reception sites or caterers, never mind the fact she'd asked for Maggie's help in the first place.

The trick now was to pull off what would amount to a surprise wedding. Maggie had full confidence she could manage such a trick, however. She had always been a good schemer.

"Hi, Dad."

Holly stood at the kitchen window, gazing out into her backyard, portable phone against her ear.

"Sweetheart," her father said, delight in his voice. "I didn't expect to hear from you today. I thought you had plans to go downtown."

"I do. I just wanted to check in with you first." She hesitated, then said, "I dreamed about Mom last night."

He waited a beat. "Oh, really? A good dream?"

"Yeah. About that summer we planted tomatoes."

Jim Weeks laughed. "You mean the summer you planted *twenty-five* tomato plants? The summer your mom canned tomatoes, stewed tomatoes, made tomato sauce, tomato puree, tomato ice cream—"

"Ice cream? Oh, c'mon, Dad."

"Well, she made everything but that."

Holly giggled. "I remember giving away tomatoes to every house in the subdivision. Mr. Watson over on Augusta Street called me Tomato Toes because I dropped one on his driveway, then stepped on it. I was barefoot."

"You were always barefoot."

"Still am."

"Your mom was like that, too," he said, warm remembrance in his tone. "She kicked off her shoes the minute she walked into the house and only put them on when she had no other choice."

Holly's reflection in the window glass showed a wistful smile. She didn't remember that about her mom. "Why in the world did she let me plant twenty-five of them? She even helped me."

"Ah, I recall it as if it were yesterday." His voice brimmed with amusement. "When you and your mother came home from the nursery with her trunk loaded with tomato plants, I asked that exact question. I wasn't very pleased about it, to be honest. That little garden of yours totally messed up my mowing grid."

"Da-ad."

He chuckled. "Your mom smiled that mischievous smile of hers and told me you were a hardheaded little wench who argued your way into trouble. She said letting you have your way was a good way to teach you the price of excess. I believe you learned that lesson, too. Tomato Toes."

"Mama was good at teaching me life lessons, wasn't she?"

"She was the best."

Holly's teeth tugged at her bottom lip as she thought about Justin. What would her mom have to say about that situation? Of course, if her mom were here that situation wouldn't exist. Holly could marry Justin with a clear conscience.

"How are you doing, baby?" her father asked, jerking her back to the conversation.

"I'm fine," she lied.

"Have you talked to Justin?"

"No."

Not because he hadn't called. Her machine had half a dozen hang-ups on it, and Holly knew Justin had been the one who called. At least, that's what she liked to tell herself. "I'd better go, Dad, or I'll be late."

"Don't want that to happen. Tell your friends I said hello. I'd like to meet them sometime."

"Sure, Dad. You have a good afternoon."

"I plan to. Pretty spring day like this, I'm gonna take the Gray Swan out for a spin."

She'd opened her mouth to say good-bye when he added, "And Holly? This is a lovely memory you've given me this morning. I thank you for it."

A single tear rolled down Holly's cheek as she hung up the phone. Memories. To Holly, they felt more like tragedies than treasures. Memories of her mom. Memories of Justin.

Would memories be enough to sustain her? Somehow, she doubted it.

Grace was standing in line for a corn dog when she spied Maggie browsing in a booth half a block down the street. It was still an hour before they'd agreed to meet.

The younger woman must have had the same idea as Grace, to arrive early and enjoy the festival for a bit before their meeting with the hotel representative.

"Are you sure you want to eat that?" Ben asked as she handed over her tickets for the treat. "Lots of fat in a fried corn dog."

Grace wanted to snarl at him. Instead she smiled and said, "Yes, Ben, I truly do wish to eat one. I haven't had a corn dog in years."

He didn't say any more, but she could tell he wasn't happy about it. Of course, he hadn't been happy all morning, not since he realized she intended to do more than walk straight to the Ashford for the meeting.

Well, that's his problem, Grace thought with uncharacteristic ill will. He didn't need to be here to watch her, anyway. She'd wanted to drive herself into town but oh, no. Ben wouldn't hear of that. "Don't worry. I won't horn in on your time with the girls," he'd assured her.

No, but he'll horn in on my time with the ultimate fair food, she thought waspishly.

Then Grace looked at him, spied the concern in his eyes. Guilt melted through her like candle wax. She took one bite of the corn dog, then tossed the rest into a nearby garbage can and gave her husband's sleeve a tug and said, "Over there, Ben. It's Maggie."

She waved a hand and called her friend's name. A smile beamed across Maggie's face as she caught sight of Grace and returned her wave. Moments later, following an exchange of greetings, they continued their perusal of the artists' offerings.

Grace enjoyed the stroll. Her energy level was good today, and she enjoyed being among a crowd. It had been years since she and Ben had made it downtown for a festival. She had forgotten that events like this could be fun. When they stopped at a stained-glass booth and Ben found an angel for her collection that wasn't beyond their budget, the remnants of her resentment over the corn dog incident melted away.

The first rumble of trouble came when Ben tried to stop at the booth assigned to an artist named Alan Mac-Craken.

"Not on a bet," Maggie muttered, keeping her eyes front and center as she grabbed Ben's arm and tugged him right on by. When she continued to ramble on, Grace grew attentive to her words. "It doesn't matter. I don't want a wooden box this year. If anyone tried to give me one, I wouldn't accept it. Not that anyone would try to give me one. Anyone is too busy buffing up his boat."

Ah hah. Grace should have known. This had something to do with Mike.

"I think I'll look for a painting to buy. Maybe a shipwreck scene."

"Maggie? What's wrong?"

"Nothing's wrong. Everything is wonderful. It's a perfectly gorgeous day." With that, she burst into tears.

"Oh, no." Grace glanced worriedly toward Ben. "Here she goes again."

To Grace's surprise and Ben's relief, Maggie recovered fairly quickly. The chocolate-covered banana Ben rushed to buy helped. "I'm a sucker for sugar," she said, drying her eyes and accepting his offering. "I'm sorry. I just need something else to think about. Like your party. Listen, I've had a couple thoughts."

She rattled off some long, involved, and undoubtedly expensive notion about orchestras and tiered cakes, memory books and rose bouquets. She went on and on and on for a good five minutes until Grace's head started to spin.

Ben apparently reacted in a similar manner because he cut Maggie off in the middle of a sentence. "No. Absolutely not. That would be too much for Grace."

That's all it took to dissolve Grace's mellowed mood. She suspected that were she to glance at the plate glass window beside her, she'd see steam coming from her ears. "I'm not as fragile as a glass angel, Ben. I love your ideas, Maggie. I want to do them all."

"Gracie," her husband warned.

Maggie's eyes had gone round as funnel cakes. Everything inside of Grace tensed. She didn't want to cause a scene on a public street. She didn't want to cause a scene anywhere, especially so soon after Maggie's scene. But my oh my, she was getting tired of being treated like an invalid. She wasn't an invalid. Well, maybe by definition she was since she did have a disease, but she wasn't bedridden.

Ben continued to dig his hole deeper. "I agreed to this anniversary party only because you assured me you wouldn't overdo. If you're going to ignore my wishes, then—"

"It's *my* wish," she snapped. "My Making Memories wish. I'm the one who's dying."

He reared back as though she had slapped him.

Maggie winced, her gaze shifting between the two of them. "I'm sorry. I didn't mean to cause any trouble. Look, you just tell me what you want and I'll take care of all the details."

"No, Maggie." Grace shot her husband a fulminating look. "I want to help. I want to be part of planning my party."

A muscle worked in Ben's jaw. He wasn't ready to give in yet. He stared at Maggie. "My concern is that she'll overtire herself and not have resources available when she needs her strength."

"I'm not a child to be ordered about by an overprotective parent. I can judge my own strength or lack thereof."

He braced his hands on his hips and faced her. "You have gotten to be so stubborn."

The pain and frustration in his voice pierced her to the marrow. Poor Ben. This situation was so hard for him. Hadn't she often mused that being a patient's loved one was sometimes more difficult than being ill oneself?

She took a step toward him, placed her hand on his arm. "Isn't being stubborn a good thing, honey? Isn't stubbornness a sign of strength?"

His glare softened, then his mouth twisted in a rueful half-smile. "In that case, you should be able to tote the entire Dallas Cowboys football team around on your back."

Maggie grinned at his joke, then turned on the charm. "Ben, you should know something about me. If Grace is with me, she won't overdo. I can promise that. I'm delicate. I may be Southern, but I'm no steel magnolia. Except for when I'm shopping for shoes, and then I can go for hours. Still, I'm sitting down most of the time."

He let out a long, harsh sigh. "All right. I'll allow it. But Maggie, I'm taking you at your word. You keep an eye on her and don't let her wear herself out."

Grace traded looks with Maggie in silent communication. *See? See what I meant the other day? Constant coddling. He's driving me crazy.* Then, just as Grace dropped her head back to let out a silent scream, Ben added, "I love her so much."

"No need to say more, Ben." The gaze Maggie settled on Grace brimmed with understanding. "No need to say more."

Holly was late. She absolutely hated being late. It was one of her pet peeves. Her reputation at school for being the Tardy Slip Teacher was honestly earned.

Her phone call to her dad had delayed her only a little, but then she couldn't find her keys. Once she gave up the hunt and dragged out her extra set, she'd been ten minutes late leaving home. Then traffic was a mess, and she'd had trouble finding a parking space. She'd ended up in the high-dollar garage on Commerce Street, and she'd been lucky to find a spot there. Seemed like half the population of Fort Worth had decided to attend the Arts Festival today.

She arrived at the Ashford a full quarter hour late. The apologies spilled from her mouth the moment she spied her two friends seated on a small sofa, a dessert tray on the coffee table in front of them.

"Oh, hush." Maggie dismissed Holly's tardiness with a wave. "No harm done. Except to you, because we began sampling the fare without you and you missed out on the chocolate torte."

"Chocolate torte? Have you noticed that anytime the three of us get together, chocolate eventually becomes part of the equation?"

Grace slid the desserts toward Holly. "You have a problem with that?"

Choosing a petit four, Holly popped it into her mouth and grinned. "Not one little bit."

The hotel manager showed them around. The reception room was lovely, decorated in gold and silver and white. It had an intimate feel that Holly liked. When she mentioned it, she saw Maggie pull a small notebook from her purse and make a notation. Holly shot her a curious look, and Maggie blinked her lashes with an innocence Holly immediately found suspect.

"I can't plan a party without my notebook. I'd get kicked out of the Junior League. I've learned to write down every little thing."

They had some trouble with Grace, who kept tugging on Maggie's sleeve and fretting about costs. Finally, Maggie asked the manager to excuse them, then she launched into a long-winded explanation of how and why she could negotiate a rock-bottom rate. Grace's sensibilities were soothed. Holly didn't believe Maggie for a minute.

The woman was up to something and she intended to find out what. Her opportunity arrived when Grace wanted to call Ben and ask his opinion about the number of guests they might expect.

"Okay, so spill it."

"Spill what?"

"You are not going to get cheap prices because you're a Junior Leaguer and your husband's corporation does a lot of entertaining."

"Well, maybe not, but I do think it will help."

"What are you up to, Maggie Prescott?"

Maggie told Holly how she'd contacted the Making Memories Breast Cancer Foundation and arranged to pay for Grace's wish herself. She explained about the surprise "wedding" and touched on a few of her ideas.

"Sounds like an event more suited for royalty than the Hardemans."

Maggie drew herself up, affronted. "You doubt my taste?"

"No. I doubt the intelligence of going behind a friend's back."

"It's not going behind her back. It's a surprise party."

Holly pursed her lips. Maggie had a point there. Still, something about the entire enterprise troubled her. "Are you sure Grace will like it? Look how she worries about spending the foundation's money. Aren't you afraid she'll have a fit about spending yours?"

Maggie folded her arms. "Well, if so, she can just get glad in the same pair of pantyhose she gets mad in. It's my money and if I want to spend it on my friends, I will."

"But Maggie, this is such a special occasion. Are you certain you want to do anything that could spoil the day for her?"

"Holly, trust me. I won't spoil anything. I want to make it the best day of her life."

"Why? You hardly know her. Why does it matter so much to you?"

"Mike and I have money, Holly. What I spend on Grace's golden anniversary won't be a drop in our bucket. I can't do anything about her cancer, but I can make this wish of hers more than she dares to dream. I need to do this. Not just for her, but for me, too. I've taken care of other people nearly all my life. Right now, those other people don't seem to want to have anything to do with me. I need somebody to help."

"You need somebody to mother," Holly said, her eyes going soft with understanding.

"Yes. Yes, I do." Maggie flashed her a crooked grin. "Watch out or you'll be next."

"Hmm . . . in that case, I like my cars red and my vacations at a beach."

Maggie looped her arm through Holly's. Grace ambled across the lobby toward them. "So, will you tell on me or will you help me? I want you to help, Holly. I'll let you choose the flowers for the sanctuary."

"I'll help. And I'll keep your secret." Holly just hoped they were not making a really big mistake. "But I want to test the Ashford's chocolate torte before we go any further."

They finished their meeting and dawdled on the way to the garage where, it turned out, both Maggie and Holly were parked. Holly bought a beautiful wooden whirligig from a California artist. Grace found a leather wallet for Ben.

"Why don't I take you home instead of Maggie," Holly suggested to Grace. "I'm going by my dad's place and it's right on the way."

With travel arrangements settled, they returned to the garage. They exited the elevator on the second level, then made their way toward Holly's car. Grace and Maggie were in the middle of a heated debate on the best Cary Grant movie, so Holly didn't hurry them along upon reaching her Mustang. A couple minutes later, she wished she had.

A little girl's squeal echoed through the parking garage, a man's laughter on its heels. Maggie obviously noticed, too. She straightened and dropped her purse when the child giggled. "Uncle Mike, you're so silly."

"Uncle Mike?" Maggie muttered.

Holly felt as if she were watching a traffic accident in the process of happening. The man walking toward them was Mike Prescott. He carried a preschool girl on his shoulders and a pretty, petite woman in her late twenties or early thirties walked beside him. Smiled up at him. Clearly besotted.

The trio didn't notice Holly, Grace, and Maggie, whose face had now drained of all color. At least, they didn't notice them until Maggie stepped into their path and chirped out a bright, "Hello, Uncle Mike."

"Maggie." Dismay and what looked to Holly like guilt flashed across Mike Prescott's face.

Holly wanted to punch him in the nose. Maggie slashed him with her tongue.

"I've been meaning to call you about a few little problems." She ticked each item off on her fingers. "Let's see, the kitchen compactor is on the blink. Also, the commode in your bathroom is stopped up, and I think you must have taken the dog's pooper scooper with you when you left. Since these are all subjects . . . well . . . how do I say it? Dear to you? Close to your heart? Part of you? Yes, that's it. Since these subjects are all part of you, I wanted to have the opportunity to tell you about them to your face."

As she talked, he lifted the little girl from his shoulders and set her on the ground. His face turned as red as his wife's toenail polish. "Maggie—" he warned.

"That's all I have. Y'all enjoy your date." She finger waved and walked back onto the elevator. "Ta-ta."

"Ta-ta?" Holly muttered, scrambling with Grace onto the elevator just before the doors shut.

Maggie fell back against the wall, pale and trembling. "Oh spit. Oh spit. Oh spit."

They rode the elevator to the very top of the parking garage. When the doors opened, Maggie rushed outside, crossing to the waist-high concrete guardrail around the perimeter of the building. She turned her face into the breeze. "Oh spit. Oh spit. Oh spit."

Then she started to cry and Grace took her in her

arms, holding her, stroking her hair and crooning, "Cry it out, sweetheart. It's okay. Let it go."

Holly had a knot in her throat. She didn't know what to say to Maggie. How to act. Did she make excuses for the man? Cuss him out? At a loss, she patted her shoulder and made a totally inane observation. "I didn't know you had a dog."

"I don't," she wailed.

No dog? Then what was the pooper scooper comment all about?

Holly thought back over what Maggie had said. The answer came to her and she began to giggle. Grace glared at her, but Holly couldn't help it. "My God, Maggie. You are a true Southern woman. I'm so proud of you, and I am proud to be your friend."

Grace was now totally confused, but the words seemed to work on Maggie. Her tears dried and she stepped away from Grace. A hint of a smile played about her lips.

"I don't understand," Grace said.

Holly explained. "Think of what she said to him. The trash compactor. The commode. The pooper scooper. In that sweet Southern way of hers, Maggie just called her husband garbage and a piece of shit. Am I right?"

"Oh." Grace pursed her lips in thought, then nodded. "You go, girl."

six

m *aggie was a mess.*
    Oh, she'd put up a good front with the girls. She'd pulled herself together in under twenty minutes and had sent them home with a smile and a wave. They hadn't wanted to leave her, but she'd insisted. She'd needed to be alone.

In her contrary way, being alone meant returning to the crowds on Main Street. Now, despite the fact she shared the street with probably seventy-five thousand other people, she'd never felt more lonely in her life.

The good thing was she didn't need to worry about running into Mike again. He'd been leaving when she saw him, so the Arts Festival was the one place in Fort Worth where she could feel safe. If she ever felt safe again, that is.

Mike had a girlfriend. His girlfriend had a little girl. A little girl who wore hair bows and a sundress with watermelons and ruffles on it and called him Uncle Mike.

If she hadn't seen the proof of it with her very own eyes, she wouldn't have believed it. She'd considered the possibility, of course. Under the circumstances, she'd have been a fool if she hadn't. But up until an hour ago, she thought she knew the man. She'd have bet her most comfortable bra that Mike had never cheated on her.

She felt like such a fool.

She wandered the street for the better part of an hour and purchased three paintings, four sculptures, two pieces of furniture, and seven pairs of earrings, arranging to have everything except the earrings delivered the following week. All the shopping didn't make her feel better. In fact, it made her feel worthless. It reminded her how useless she was these days.

All she knew was how to be a wife and mother. Only now she had no one at home to be a wife to, no one to mother.

Heavens, she didn't want to go home. But she didn't want to stay here, either. She didn't want to shop anymore, she didn't want to listen to music. She didn't want to watch the dancers.

A voice—her mother's voice—sounded in her head. *Didn't. Didn't. Didn't. Didn't. Girl, what's the matter with you? Let's hear a "do" or two.*

"But that's the problem, Mama. Haven't really felt any 'dos' since you died."

Maggie did an about-face and headed once again for her car. As she approached Alan MacCraken's booth again, she pointedly turned her head away. That's when she spied the line of tables decorated with the banner: COOKS CHILDREN'S HOSPITAL. At the table farthest on the right, seated behind a sign saying HELP FIGHT CHILDHOOD DIABETES, Dr. Justin Skipworth handed a brochure to a young couple pushing twin two-year-old daughters in a stroller.

Holly's young man. She'd been thinking about him, wondering how he'd been doing in the wake of the Greystone contretemps. Wondering if he missed Holly as much as she obviously missed him.

Now she wondered if *he'd* had any dates with another woman.

This was her chance to find out. Besides, talking to Justin would delay her return to her empty house. Her empty life. Maggie couldn't ask for a better distraction.

Approaching the booth, Maggie smiled. "Hello. It's Justin, isn't it?"

"Yes, Justin Skipworth." He studied her for a moment, then offered a sheepish smile. "I'm sorry. I don't remember you."

Maggie clicked her tongue, shook her head, then gave an exaggerated sigh. "That's exactly what a woman loves to hear from a man."

When he winced, she laughed and added, "Don't worry. I'm teasing. I'm almost old enough to be your mother. Emphasis on the word 'almost.' However, it's the mom in me that would like a few moments to visit with you. Could you take a break from your duties here?"

"I suppose, but I don't know—"

"I'm a meddler as well as a mother. I'm Maggie Prescott. I had planned to call you next week, but I'd love to talk with you now if you can steal a few minutes. I was in the ladies' lounge with Holly at the Greystone that day."

"Oh." Light dawned in his expression. The brochure he held slipped from his fingers and fell back onto the table. "You're the lady in the antique wedding gown."

"Yes. Holly and I have become friends since then. She's not happy and I'd like to try and help her if I can."

Maggie watched a dozen different emotions play across his face before he made his excuses to his fellow booth workers, then stepped out from behind the table. "Where should we . . . ?"

"Somewhere more quiet, I think." Maggie jerked her chin toward the Tarrant County courthouse, half a block north of where they stood. "The side steps, perhaps. It's away from the music, but I enjoy the view."

They made get-to-know-each-other small talk as they purchased bottled water and ears of roasted corn at a concession booth, then walked the short distance to the courthouse. A rock band took the stage and cranked up their amplifiers, making conversation difficult, so Justin led the way around to the north side of the courthouse, which overlooked the wildflower-dotted banks of the slow-flowing Trinity River. He dusted off a place for them to sit on the stone steps. Maggie wished she'd worn jeans instead of her favorite floral sundress.

By unspoken agreement, they spent a few minutes savoring their snacks before tossing the cobs into a nearby trash can and getting down to business. Justin twisted the cap on his water bottle and swigged back a sip as if it were a bracing shot of whiskey. "How is she?"

Maggie licked salty butter from her fingers. "You don't know?"

He shook his head. "I haven't seen or spoken to her since that day at the Making Memories sale."

Maggie's heart sank. "That's what I was afraid of. She hasn't been exceptionally forthcoming with information about you. I tend to babble my business to anyone, but

Holly keeps her mouth zipped. She's not happy, I can tell that much."

Sipping her water, Maggie watched a flock of pigeons feast on breadcrumbs offered by a darling little red-headed boy. "One thing I do know. Holly loves you, Justin."

"She has a funny way of showing it." He sighed heavily. "I don't understand what happened. You were there. You saw it. Do you understand what happened?"

Recalling Holly's meltdown in the ladies' room, Maggie realized she had a fine line to walk. She wouldn't betray her friend's confidence, *but my heavens, these two seemed to be made for one another.* She wanted to help them find their way back together. Love was too precious to throw away. "I have my suspicions, but that's all they are."

"So what did she say?"

Maggie shook her head. "Sugar, the ladies' room is like a confessional and under the circumstances, I don't feel right betraying her confidence. What I will say is that I don't think we heard the whole story from her. It's my opinion that she thinks she's doing you a favor by turning you down."

"What? Doing me a favor. Is she crazy?" He scooped up a pair of small rocks from the step below him and chucked them one at a time toward the trunk of a nearby oak. "It's my mother, isn't it? The whole North Dallas society thing. She scared Holly off with that wedding gown shopping trip."

"Do you honestly think that?"

Again, a sigh. "No. Holly is stronger than that. But I don't know what to think."

Maggie reached behind her for another small stone.

Handing it to him, she said, "Talk to her, Justin. Get her to talk to you."

The rock hit the oak's trunk dead center. "How the hell am I supposed to do that? She never answers her phone."

"So you've called her?"

"Yeah. A time or two." He shrugged and stretched out his legs. "She never picks up, and I'll be damned if I'll talk to her machine."

Justin's long face made her want to reach over and hug him, but instead, she tried lightening the moment by patting his knee and teasing, "If you don't do something about that hound-dog expression, Doctor, we're liable to risk a leash law violation."

He looked at her with sad, golden-brown eyes. His mouth twitched, then he let out a low, mournful howl.

Maggie laughed, then gave in to the impulse to give him a hug. "You're a mess, too, Justin. As big a mess as me, I do believe, and that is saying a lot."

"How's that?"

"For one thing, my love life is in even worse trouble than yours."

"That's hard to believe."

"It's true. It's one of the reasons Holly and I bonded in the bathroom." Now it was Maggie's turn to offer a rueful smile. "She witnessed a scene between me and my husband that afternoon that gave yours a run for its money. She witnessed a repeat of a sort here today."

"Here? Holly's downtown?"

"Not anymore. She took our friend Grace home after the scene with my husband."

"Oh."

Justin pitched one more rock at the tree, then shot

her a curious look. Maggie could tell he wanted to ask about Mike. It was human nature to compare scars, wasn't it?

"I don't want to talk about my husband. I don't even want to think about him. To be perfectly honest, that's one of the reasons why I'm meddling."

The pigeons took flight, swooped over them. Maggie shielded her head with her hands until they were gone. "Justin, in your heart of hearts, why do you think Holly refused your proposal?"

He sighed heavily and leaned back, resting his weight on his elbows and stretching out his legs. He fastened his gaze on the leafy branches of a giant oak where a pair of mourning doves sat cooing side by side. "I honestly don't know. What does that say about our relationship? I've dated the woman for months. I thought I knew her, but obviously I misread her big time. My romantic proposal turned out to be a major disaster."

Romantic? He'd considered that romantic? What happened to candlelight and soft music? Maybe Holly had the right idea by refusing him, after all. "Why did you propose to her there, like that?"

"At the wedding gown sale, you mean?"

Maggie nodded.

Justin snorted with disgust. "I did it as a tribute to her mom. Her mother died of breast cancer. Holly talks about her a lot. They were very close. I thought she'd be pleased, that she'd feel like her mom was with her at such an important moment. Dumb idea, huh?"

Maggie winced. "It was a lovely thought, but in hindsight, I think you'd have been better served with candlelight and flowers."

"Yeah. I figured that one out myself." Justin rolled up

to a seated position, then clasped his hands between his knees. "I never thought she'd turn me down."

It wasn't the self-mocking tone of voice that caused Maggie concern so much as the hopelessness in his expression. Reaching out, she touched the younger man's arm and spoke from her heart, spoke from her experience. "Justin, don't give up on Holly. Don't forget that her problems, whatever they are, are real to her. Respect that, even if you don't always understand it. Don't forget that she's hurting and needs patience and support. She's been there for you when you needed her, hasn't she? If you really love her, how can you quit on her?"

"What?"

"Think about it, Justin. Try to figure out why she turned down your proposal."

"What do you think I've been doing for the past couple of weeks? All I do is think about it." He shot a heated scowl her way. "And I didn't say anything about quitting on her. Look, she cold-cocked me that day at the Greystone, but I recovered. It took a few days, but I called her. Of course, since she won't pick up the phone I might as well be calling Mars. Collect. I love Holly, but dammit, I'm human, too. This can't be all one-sided. She's got to make an effort, too. Every time she knocks me down, I'm a little slower getting up. Honestly, unless something changes, one day I'm afraid I won't get up at all."

"Or you'll go buy a boat," she muttered glumly.

"What?"

Maggie groaned and buried her head in her hands. She'd had this argument before a dozen times. With Mike. This was *their* argument. Mike's words were coming out of Justin's mouth. It was all getting too weird.

Needing a calming influence, Maggie reached for her purse and removed her lipstick and cosmetics mirror. She freshened the coral color on her lips, then returned her feminine armor to her bag. Slowly, she stood.

"I think her mom is the key to this situation. I think Holly is still grieving."

"Grieving? She isn't grieving. It's been thirteen years."

"Grief is as individual as a fingerprint, Doctor. I don't care if it's been thirteen days or thirteen years. Nobody has the right to say, 'Time's, up.'"

He held up his hands, palms out. "You're right. You're right about that. I just don't think you're right about Holly in this instance. She talks about her mom fairly often. She never tears up or anything. Sure, losing her mother was hurtful, but she's moved on. She's healed."

"Has she?" Maggie thought back to that day at the Greystone where Holly had cried *I don't want to die.* "What does she say about her mother's death?"

"Not much." Justin frowned. "Not anything, really. What I know about that I've learned from her father."

"You made it through medical school, Justin. You must have a brain in that head of yours. Use it. Figure out why she's scared."

"Scared?"

"Yes, scared. It's obvious as yellow on roasted corn. Figure out why, Justin, and you might just find the key to convincing her to marry you."

Maggie reached out a hand. "And in the meantime, since I'm in the process of becoming her friend, I think I'll do what I can to help."

Justin let her pull him to his feet. "Why? Why do you care? You hardly know her. You just met her two weeks ago."

"Ah, but it was a heckuva meeting." Maggie glanced in the general direction of the Greystone and shrugged. "I like Holly. Why shouldn't I care? Besides, in all honesty, helping her is going to help me just as much. I can use someone to mother for a little while."

"You think you can mother her into marrying me?" he asked with a grin.

"Maybe. Mother or scheme or manipulate. Sometimes the words are interchangeable."

Justin clucked his tongue and shook his head. "You are a piece of work, Maggie Prescott."

"Actually, I'm a mess. But I feel better than I did an hour ago, so I think I'll let you get back to your booth and I'll head out. I have places to go, men to meet."

"Men to meet?"

Maggie shrugged. She couldn't pinpoint exactly when the idea occurred to her, but it had been sometime during the past hour. What began as a whim had taken on substance as anger and the need for retribution seeped through her. "What's good for the gander and all of that. Say, do you know any nice men my age who might want to take me out?"

"You're married."

"So is my husband, but that doesn't seem to stop him from dating. You know, the more I think about the notion, the better I like it. We're separated, you see. Mike and I. Today I found out we're more separated than I had previously thought. Why shouldn't I see other men?"

Justin blew out a harsh breath. "You're dangerous, Maggie. I don't know if Holly should be hanging out with you. You'll give her ideas."

"I don't know about that. Holly appears to be pretty good about coming up with ideas of her own. Like the plan she'd made for the day you proposed. Now, that was an idea."

"Oh, yeah? What was it?"

Maggie tugged him down the stone steps. Maybe she shouldn't tell him, but he deserved to know what he was missing. "I have two words for you, Doctor. Storeroom sex."

Justin froze. His eyes widened momentarily, then narrowed when he grimaced. His voice raspy, he repeated, "Storeroom sex?"

"Something about crotchless panties, too." Pleased with his stunned expression, she reached out and patted his arm. "Don't whimper, sugar. It's not seemly for a medical doctor. Besides, I think she might have been kidding about the panties. Might have been a thong."

Sunday afternoon, Holly wheeled the lawn mower into the shed, then used the hem of her tee shirt to wipe the perspiration from her brow. Despite the pleasant temperature of the spring day, she'd managed to work up a sweat in the time it took to push the old mower over the three-quarters of an acre of green grass and pesky weeds.

Justin had tried to buy her a riding mower when the grass started growing this season, but she'd resisted. She already let her neighbor across the street show her up as it was. Mrs. Litty was fifty-seven and, as she was quick to point out, she still didn't use self-propelled equipment. While she didn't come right out and call her younger neighbor a wussy, Holly understood the implication.

Holly's home was in Richland Hills, an older suburb of Fort Worth located midway between downtown and D/FW airport. The town was a little pocket of rural surrounded by city, where modest homes sat on two-acre lots. In backyards, horses were as common as swimming pools. The homeowners were a mostly friendly mix of older residents who'd lived in their homes thirty years or more, and young families, many of whom had returned to the neighborhood in which they'd grown up.

Of course, friendly only went so far. Competition was fierce out here in the 'burbs, especially when it came to the beautification of their yards, and Holly hated to lose. Which was why she should make a run to the nursery for bedding plants. The rest of the neighbors had put in their annuals the weekend of the Greystone Hotel debacle. Her beds were still bare.

"Now there's a Freudian slip," she grumbled as she exited the garden shed. But she didn't want to think about the state of her bed.

So Holly turned her attention to her freshly shorn backyard. It did look better. She hadn't had the heart to do much more than put out her trash for pickup lately and she'd skipped her regular yard-work day last weekend. This morning as she'd left for church, her next-door neighbor, Mr. Philpot—aka Mr. Crankpot—had waved her down at the curb and put her on notice that he expected her to cut her grass today.

That was almost enough to make her get stubborn and wait another week. Since someone on the street was always having a set-to with Mr. Crankpot, the neighbors would have understood. But the Pokludas were having a graduation party for their nephew Friday night, so pride had won out over orneriness, and Holly had mowed her lawn.

Now she wished she'd stopped at the nursery for flowers on her way home. For the first time since her argument with Justin, she felt like doing something around the house.

Maybe that means I'm getting over him, the optimist in her suggested.

The realist gave a derisive snort. *Yeah. And maybe Mr. Crankpot will come plant your flowers for you, too.*

As Holly made her way around to the front of the house to set out the water sprinkler, the portable phone she'd set on the porch rang. Probably Cassie again.

Cassie Blankenship lived in Tomball, Texas, a suburb of Houston. A junior at Tomball High School, she was second chair clarinet in the band, played third base for the fast-pitch softball team, and had been elected secretary of the student council. She had an older brother, a younger sister, and a cat.

Her mom was a metastatic breast cancer patient and one of Making Memories' wish recipients. Since their week-long trip to Disney World last month, Cassie's mother had been sinking fast. Her personal goal was to make it until May twentieth, when Cassie had a date to the senior prom with her boyfriend, Mark.

Cassie and Holly had exchanged e-mails for three days before Holly broke down and called her. Since then they had talked at least once a day, sometimes more often than that. Cassie had proven to be a perfect fit for Holly's volunteer effort. The young woman didn't want to talk about her mom or cancer or dying any more than Holly wanted to talk about those things. She wanted to talk prom—her dress, her date, her up-do, her corsage, the limo. It was another escape to Disney World for the teenager, to Holly's way of thinking, and she was glad to provide a willing ear for Cassie.

Holly checked the caller ID window, a service added

just this morning, smiled, then picked up the receiver. "Hello, Daddy."

"Hello yourself, beautiful. I missed you yesterday on my drive. Wanna tag along with me on a Sunday drive next Saturday?"

"A Sunday drive sounds lovely. Where are you thinking of going?"

She hung up with a smile after she and her father had talked for a few minutes, making a date for three o'clock next Saturday afternoon. With her mind on their conversation, she didn't at first pay attention to the car driving slowly past her house. Only when it stopped at the curb in front of Mr. Philpot's house just on the other side of Holly's driveway did she give it a second glance.

The driver was a woman. The notion of the bachelor Mr. Crankpot having a ladyfriend gave her the first chuckle she'd had in days.

Then the woman got out of the car, removed something from the backseat, and walked around behind the Ford. Grace? Carrying purple petunias? Had they made plans she'd forgotten about?

"Good afternoon, Holly," Grace said as she approached, a nervous smile flitting on her lips. "I know it's rude of me to drop by like this, but . . ." She held the flat of flowers out to Holly. "I come bearing gifts. I hope you like petunias. I have a bottle of hand lotion for you, too, from my granddaughter. It's a vanilla scent this time."

Southern hospitality taught from the cradle made Holly's response automatic. She accepted the flowers saying, "I love petunias. Thank you. And don't be silly. You're welcome at my home anytime. Although I'm surprised you found me. I'm not listed in the phone book."

"Justin mentioned your address. He and Maggie had supper with Ben and me last night."

Holly almost dropped the plants. "My Justin? With Maggie? Maggie Prescott?"

Grace nodded, then gestured toward the flowers. "I brought a bag of potting soil, too, but I'll need help getting it out of the car. I've a difficult time carrying anything heavy."

Feeling numb from lips to toes, Holly followed Grace to her sky blue Ford. "What was Justin doing with Maggie Prescott?"

"Having supper." Grace turned to give her a shrewd look from eyes as blue as her car. "That's all it was. It was completely innocent and he only stayed so long because he was headed off to his gym and Maggie offered him use of her pool instead." Grace frowned and added, "No matter what her husband thinks.

"Now, are you up to planting these this afternoon? I came prepared in old clothes and I have my gloves and a trowel in the car."

Justin and Maggie having dinner together? Holly felt a clutch of pain that could have been heartburn, but wasn't. Maggie was a beautiful woman and Justin wasn't one to let an age difference bother him.

Then reason reasserted itself. No. He wouldn't. Justin would move on to another woman, but not this soon. He wasn't like Maggie's husband. Justin was a man of deep emotion. When he said he loved, he meant it. He wouldn't quit loving Holly so fast. He wouldn't just give up on her. Not without a fight.

That had been a pretty good fight in the ladies' room.

"Maybe in a bit, Grace," Holly said with a grim set to her mouth as she set the petunias beside her front flower bed. "First I'd really like to understand the reason behind your visit. What exactly brings you to my house?"

"Oh dear. Well . . . it's a rather long story."

Holly was not to be deterred. "I'm free the rest of the evening. Would you like to sit in the backyard or would you rather go inside?"

Grace smiled. "It's a wonderful afternoon. The backyard sounds perfect."

Holly showed the older woman to a patio set of wrought iron table and cushioned chairs, then offered her a choice of refreshment. Grace's reply sounded absent; her attention focused on the thousands of bearded iris blooms lining the perimeter of Holly's backyard. "Oh, Holly. Your flowers are magnificent."

"Through no effort of mine," Holly responded with a bittersweet smile. "I inherited this house from my aunt Janet and she put the bulbs in years ago. They were her favorite. I never see an iris that I don't think of her."

"That's lovely. What a nice way to be remembered."

As Holly's gaze trailed along the fence line, memories washed over her. "When she was dying, she asked us to move her bed so she could look out on the irises. It was December and the yard was ugly and the blooms were long gone. Aunt Janet said the memory of spring was stronger than winter's death, and that she could see those big purple blooms clear as day when she looked out the window."

"I've always hoped I'll go in the springtime. Time of new life, the Resurrection. Besides, nothing is sadder than standing at a grave site on a cold, blustery barren day."

Holly's eyes rounded. "Oh, I'm sorry. I didn't mean to bring up—"

"Don't fret. I don't have a problem talking about dying."

Well, I do. A lump of emotion formed in Holly's throat and she quickly excused herself to get their drinks. By the time she returned carrying a pitcher of tea and two ice-filled glasses, she'd changed into a clean shirt and wrestled her emotions under control. She poured the drinks, took her seat, and asked, "So what brings you to Richland Hills, Grace?"

"Maggie's in trouble."

"More than she knows if she starts messing with Justin," Holly grumbled in a halfhearted jest. The other part of her heart was completely serious.

"This has nothing to do with Justin."

"Then why was he at her house to begin with?"

Grace's sharp gaze was too aware. "Oh, just calm down a minute and let me tell the story."

Holly swallowed and offered what she knew must be a sickly smile. Grace took pity on her. Reaching over, she gave her hand a pat. "Apparently, after you and I left the festival, Maggie decided she didn't want to go home, so she stayed downtown. Justin was working a booth for the hospital and she ran into him. They talked and she ended up promising to make a large donation to his hospital's pediatric AIDS program. He came over to pick up the check. Ben and I were there because I had called to see how she was doing earlier and she broke down in terrible, hysterical tears. I needed to check on her after that. We all ended up staying for dinner, and when Justin said he'd missed his workout that morning, she offered him use of the pool. That's when the trouble started."

Holly took a bracing sip of tea and listened closely as Grace explained how Maggie's husband had come by the house to pick up some things he'd left behind only to find another man—a handsome, younger man—wearing Mike's swim trunks, dripping from his swim in Mike's pool. "It didn't sit well with Mike. That was obvious. Territorial male, and all that. Still, I think Mike would have left without any trouble except for the kiss."

"Kiss?" Holly's spine snapped straight.

"Yes. Just as Mike came sauntering into the kitchen, Justin paid Maggie a compliment on her cooking and she gave him a thank-you buss on the lips. She's a very demonstrative woman, I've come to realize. Anyway, to Mike's ears an innocent comment about Maggie's kiss being as sweet as her cake sounded nasty." She paused for a moment, then added, "It got physical, I'm afraid."

"Justin wasn't hurt," Holly said, her eyes widening with alarm.

"Not Justin. Maggie."

"What?"

"It happened so fast. The men were wrestling around, pushing and shoving, not throwing punches. Maggie launched herself into the middle of it, trying to break them apart."

Holly had no trouble visualizing the scene as Grace continued, "We never did figure out exactly what happened, but suddenly, Maggie was sitting in the middle of her patio with a hand covering her left eye. Someone's elbow got her."

"I bet Justin had a fit."

"I was quite impressed with his professionalism. Mike Prescott's reaction was the big surprise."

"Oh?"

"He grabbed a kitchen towel and went straight to the freezer and made an ice pack. He was so gentle with her,

Holly. Inept, but gentle. Maggie shouldn't have yelped like she did because then Justin announced he was a doctor and took over. Mike stomped off."

Holly could picture it easily. "What a disaster."

Grace sighed. "Mike loves her. I could see it in his face as plain as day."

"Then what the hell was he doing with that other woman?" Holly snapped.

"He claimed it was innocent."

"Yeah, right." She sneered. "*Uncle Mike.*"

"I think he told the truth. After seeing the look in his eyes last evening, I simply cannot believe he is cheating on Maggie. The problem is, she believes it and that's why she's going to get herself into trouble. Holly, Maggie claims she's going to start dating."

"Not Justin!"

"No, of course not Justin. Pay attention here. A twenty-five year marriage is self-destructing before our eyes. I can't stand by and watch it happen. We must do something."

"We?"

"The two of them have lost their way, and somebody should help them find it again. I think that somebody should be us."

"Us? As in you and me? Why? It's not our business. We hardly know them. I'm a teacher, for goodness' sake, not a marriage counselor. Besides, if anyone were to get involved in this, shouldn't it be their children?"

Grace shook her head. "They're caught in the middle, too close to the situation. They just get righteous and preach. No, Maggie and Mike need us, both of us. I can't manage by myself."

Jesus, would the guilt never stop?

Better she had run into the men's room than the ladies' room that day. Now Maggie wanted her to help Grace and Grace wanted her to help Maggie. Why in the world did they think she'd get mixed up in this soap opera?

Because it's not television. It's real life. Life and, in Grace's case, likely death.

"Why are you doing this?" Holly asked, the question bursting from her mouth like a geyser. "You have Stage IV cancer. Why waste the time you have on someone you hardly know?"

As soon as the words left her lips, Holly clamped her hands over her mouth. *Oh, God. How could I say something like that? How could I be so insensitive, so crass?* "I . . . I'm so sorry."

Grace simply smiled. "Why? It's a legitimate question. An understandable one, too. Holly, I've lived with cancer for eight years now. During that time, I have cried rivers of tears and been so depressed I thought the darkness might swallow me whole. I spent way too many days waiting to die."

Holly felt tears well up inside her, and she did her best to will them away.

Serenity showed in Grace's relaxed posture and faint smile as she gazed into the distance. "But somewhere along the way I began to realize that life is a gift, not a guarantee. I learned to be grateful for the moment and to have a keen appreciation for the enduring things in life. I discovered a new joy in watching a beautiful sunset, in sitting by a crackling fire while the cold winter wind blows a gale outside, in savoring the scent of cinnamon wafting from cookies baking in the oven. Most of all, I learned the value of love."

She reached across the table and took Holly's hand. "Sweetheart, if right this very minute an angel appeared in your kitchen and offered me perfect health if I'd give up the love of my family and friends, I'd have to tell her thanks, but no thanks. No treasure in life, not even good health, is greater than love. That's why I can't bear to see it wasted. That's why it's worth my time to do whatever I can to help Maggie and her man."

Giving Holly's hand a squeeze, she added, "I'll be more than happy to make a similar effort on your and Justin's behalf. Just say the word."

Holly couldn't fight any longer. "What do you want me to do?"

They spent half an hour discussing various possibilities, during which time Holly's insight into Grace's character grew. The quiet, sweet, and sometimes dotty exterior hid a terrier's heart. Once the woman got an idea in her mind, she wouldn't let it go. That particular characteristic probably served her well in her fight against disease. Holly could imagine Grace standing up in her oncologist's office and declaring his prognosis to be quite unacceptable and to find another one, thank-youverymuch.

Holly did manage to kill Grace's idea—derived from an old soap opera storyline—to lock Mike and Maggie in the cabin of his boat and not let them out again until they'd made love. She was less successful when Grace suggested they consider doing something to Mike Prescott's boat to delay his departure and give the pair more time to reconcile.

"After the brouhaha on Saturday, I suspect they're not ready to really talk with one another yet. They still have lots of anger and hurt between them. If he leaves town before they reach the point where they can communicate honestly and from the heart, I'm afraid they'll never find their way back together. That's why we might have to indulge in a bit of mischief with his boat. I got the idea listening to the oldies station coming home from Maggie's," Grace said. "Do you remember the song about the Sloop John B.?"

Holly nodded as the tune began swimming through her mind.

"I think the Kingston Trio recorded it," Grace continued. "Perhaps the Beach Boys, too, but I may be wrong. Anyway, the refrain says the singer wants to go home. It made me think of Mike. Then another line mentions hoisting the sails. The song stayed stuck in my brain all night long. I realized there must be a reason for it, and that reason came to me today. The song is the answer, Holly. You and I can heist his sails."

Holding her head, Holly groaned.

Her state of mind didn't improve much over the next few hours after Grace left. She kept hearing the sincerity in the other woman's voice as she talked about love, kept seeing an image of Justin's face everywhere she turned. She tried to summon up the energy to plant her flowers, but she simply wasn't in the mood. She was sitting on the front porch staring blindly into the night's shadows when the phone rang. Somehow, she just knew Maggie Prescott was on the other end of the line. Caller ID confirmed it.

"I give up," she muttered, yanking the receiver from the hook. "Hello, Maggie."

A pause, then, "How did you know it was me?"

"I'm clairvoyant."

"Really?"

"No."

"Well, spit. I could use a good seer."

"Kisser?" Holly screeched. "Did you say kisser?"

"No. I said 'seer.' As in sees into the future."

Holly massaged her forehead. "What do you want, Maggie?"

"I need help."

"In the famous words of Gomer Pyle, surprise, surprise, surprise."

"Pardon me?"

"I won't do anything if it has any reference whatsoever to anything nautical."

"Nautical? As in ships and the sea?"

"And mainsails. Exactly. So, do we have a deal?"

"Sure thing, sugar. Nautical themes aren't exactly high on my list these days, either. Which is a nice segue into my reason for calling. I want to make one."

"Make one what?"

"A list like yours."

"My Life List?"

"Uh huh. I'm beginning a new stage of my life, so I need to take stock of my dreams and aspirations and decide what I want to pursue. I'd like your help because you have experience at making a list, and you haven't had your head buried in PTA and Little League sand for the past twenty years. You might think of goals to pursue that I wouldn't."

Holly didn't know whether to feel flattered or annoyed. The Life List was her baby, after all. She wasn't certain how she felt about sharing it.

"Listen to what I have so far," Maggie instructed. "'I will date a man from every state in America.'"

"Jeeze Louise, Maggie." Holly grimaced and rubbed the back of her neck.

"I will spend—"

"Enough. All right. I'll help."

"Great. You can come over to my house and we'll plan—"

"No." Holly felt the need to gain a semblance of control. "My house. Tomorrow night. Five o'clock. I'll call Grace and get her over here, too. I stopped by the stationery store and picked up the invitation books. Grace needs to choose one so we can get them ordered."

"That's great. We'll do goal setting and party planning. I'll bring chocolate."

"Excellent. Only . . . Maggie?"

"Yes?"

"Bring your gardening gloves, too."

The moment Holly replaced the receiver, it began to ring again. Certain it was Maggie calling back, she grabbed it right up.

"Yes, Maggie?" she asked, giving a long, put-upon sigh.

"It's not Maggie," Justin said.

Holly almost dropped the phone. "Oh. I didn't . . ."

"Let the answering machine pick up."

"Actually I've had caller ID installed. I won't need to listen to hang-ups that way."

The line hummed distance between them before he asked, "Can I see you? Can we talk?"

Holly closed her eyes. "Justin, it's late. Tomorrow's a workday. I'm busy—"

"Sitting on your front porch. I see you. Let me come up."

For the first time, Holly focused on the cars parked along the street. Sure enough, Justin's sporty little Beemer was parked along the curb in front of Mr.

Crankpot's house. He sat on the hood, his cell phone pressed to his ear, his gaze pointed right at her.

Great. Oh just great. She wore a ratty old tee shirt and wind shorts, no makeup, and she needed to wash her hair. "I need to wash my hair."

"Lame one, Holly. I swallowed my pride and came to you. Now talk to me."

"I'm not responsible for your pride or your actions."

"True. But you should be polite to guests, even uninvited ones. That's how your mother raised you, isn't it?"

"Leave my mother out of this."

"That's just the thing, Holly. I don't know if that's possible."

Justin slipped off the hood of his car and started walking toward her. Instinctively, Holly scooted back a step, but she kept the phone pressed close to her ear.

"It's been suggested that your response to my marriage proposal might have been different had I gone for candlelight and soft music when I popped the question. I don't think I believe that. Recalling the look in your eyes, I think you'd have turned me down no matter what. Am I correct?"

Her stomach churned. She didn't want to do this. Not now. Not ever. "I told you from the first I didn't want to marry."

"Right. So answer this one question for me. Why?"

"Why?"

"Why don't you want to marry, Holly? Are you afraid of something?"

"Afraid?" She scooted back another step. Her mouth had gone dry as a forgotten backyard birdbath in July. "I'm not afraid."

He stood five feet from her now, his gaze locked upon

her. He continued to speak into the phone. "I think you are afraid, honey. I'm just not sure why."

Holly chose not to respond. Handy, since she couldn't speak past the knot in her throat.

"I asked myself what aspects of marriage might frighten you. Of course, I ruled out sex right away. And you like children, I know. You wouldn't be a teacher otherwise. I went over every aspect of our relationship in detail, trying to deduce what might be the problem. I came to suspect your attitude might have something to do with your mother."

"My mother?" She hit the off button on the telephone, then rolled to her feet.

"Yeah, your mom. You don't talk about her."

Now her breath was coming in shallow pants. "I talk about her all the time."

"About her life, but never about her death." Justin slipped his cell phone into his pocket. "I wouldn't even know you lost her to breast cancer if your father hadn't clued me in. Tell me, Holly. Did you see anyone after she died? A therapist?"

Be damned if she'd tell him about the suicide attempt. It was bad enough she'd spilled her guts to her women friends. She'd be totally humiliated if Justin learned of her weakness.

"It's not your business, Justin."

He looked away, his jaw set. His chest rose, then fell as he breathed deeply and visibly summoned control. He pinned her with a narrow-eyed gaze. "I disagree. You are my business."

"I'm not one of your patients."

"No, you're not," he snapped. "My patients are all younger than twelve. You only act like a child."

She faltered, swayed, his accusation piercing like an arrow. Damn him. She was giving him up for his own good. Couldn't he see that? She turned and made for the door.

"Wait, Holly. Stop." He bounded up the steps. "I'm sorry. That was uncalled for. I came here today to grovel, but frankly, I'm not very good at it. I haven't had enough experience with it."

"Arrogance keeps getting in the way."

"Yeah, well, I'm a doctor. What do you expect?"

He reached for her arm and Holly shuddered at his touch. A clamor of emotion assaulted her from within. She wanted him, yearned to be with him. Loved him too much to give in to her need.

"These last couple weeks have been lousy. Lonely. I know now more than ever how much I want to have you in my life. Deep in my heart, I believe you want the same thing."

Her pulse beat like a hummingbird's wings. Maybe she could still have something, if not everything. "You're ready to give up on the marriage idea?"

He shoved his hands into his back pockets. "No. No, I'm not. I love you. I want you for my wife. That hasn't changed. It won't change."

That does it, Holly thought. She might as well give up.

"I need for you to talk to me, Holly," he continued. "I need to understand what is keeping us apart. I didn't press you about it that day at the Greystone and that was a mistake. I truly believe that no problem is insurmountable if we work together to solve it. So please, honey. Tell me what it is. Tell me what you're afraid of."

"I'm not afraid!" she insisted, trying to convince him, convince herself.

"Is it your mom? Holly, are you worried you're going to get breast cancer like your mom?"

Dammit, Justin. It took all Holly's strength not to run inside and slam and lock the door. This was so difficult. She couldn't keep doing it. If he wouldn't compromise on the marriage issue, then she simply couldn't afford to see him anymore. The man was too stubborn, too convincing. Eventually, he might talk her around to his way, and that would be bad for both of them.

She'd have to do something, say something, that would put an end to their relationship once and for all.

Willing away the tears that threatened, she made herself face him and respond to his question. "I think at some point in time, every woman worries that she'll develop breast cancer, Doctor. I'm also aware that the average woman is at greater risk of developing heart disease than she is cancer."

Of course, Holly wasn't the average woman.

"You're exactly right. So tell me, am I totally off base here? Is the reason you won't marry me all mixed up in losing your mother so young and fearing the same thing will happen to you? If so, then we can fix it. I have statistics that will prove you're worrying unnecessarily."

Statistics. Right. He could take his statistics and shove them. "I thought your specialty was pediatrics, Dr. Skipworth. Not psychology."

"If it's not your mom, then what is it? Tell me, Holly. You owe me that much."

"Why are you doing this? Why are you making me hurt you? Can't you simply accept that I can't give you what you need? I can't love you anymore, Justin. I won't love you. Not anymore."

"Why, goddammit?"

Because you deserve so much more. You deserve to be happy.

But Holly didn't say it aloud. Instead, she hardened her heart, looked him straight in the eyes, and lied. "You're partially right. It is about my mom. She was an art history major and she planned to go to Rome to study for a year. When she met my dad, she gave up that dream. A part of her always regretted it. I promised myself I wouldn't do what she did. I didn't tell you because I didn't want to spoil the time we had."

"Tell me what?"

"I've been accepted into a Ph.D. program at Tulane. Right after the Hardemans' anniversary party, I'll be leaving Fort Worth."

🌸 seven

maggie eyed the fire ant mound rising like a miniature volcano from the clump of spring green weeds and winced. "Sugar, I am tickled pink that you've agreed to help me with my list, but I came over here for pizza and *planning*. Not planting. See, I forgot my gloves, and I find I'm just not in the mood to live dangerously."

"Dangerously?" Grace sat in the wrought iron lawn chair Holly had brought around to the front yard for her, then bent to pick up a six-pack of petunias.

"Yeah. 'Dangerously.' What else would you call digging in an ant-infested plot of dirt?"

"Gardening," Holly replied, her tone as dry as the soil caked on the bottom of her shoes. She tossed a pair of work gloves toward Maggie. "Don't fret. It's a dead hill. But if you're worried, you can start at the other end. I doubt you'll find anything there except for grubs, maybe a few slugs."

"Slugs!" Maggie wrinkled her nose and stepped back onto the front sidewalk. "I don't do slugs."

After a moment's pause, she added, "Not since Christmas, anyway."

Holly let out a snort of laughter. Grace's lips twitched at the corners as she gently freed a plant from its plastic tray. "Our next-door neighbor is a single lady. She wears a tee shirt when she mows her lawn that says 'Grow your own dope.'"

She waited until both Maggie and Holly expectantly met her gaze, then finished, "'Plant a man.'"

Maggie chuckled while Holly grinned and said, "A male-bashing joke from you, Grace? I'm shocked. What would Ben say?"

"He'd probably repeat one of the blonde jokes the guys tell at his work." Grace handed them each a garden trowel. "Start digging."

"Blonde jokes are so yesterday." Maggie gave her honey-colored hair a dramatic fling, then scanned the ground for bugs, worms, or any other nasties. Gingerly, she knelt and eased the tip of the trowel into the earth. When nothing wiggled, scurried, or oozed out, she dug deeper.

She hadn't dirtied her hands with earth in ages, and to her surprise, she found the task to be rather pleasant. The early evening air was balmy, the birds were singing, and someone in the neighborhood was grilling steak. She closed her eyes and lifted her nose into the heavy, rich scent. "Forget pizza. Let's go eat with them."

Holly sighed wistfully. "That's Mark Wilson. Sunday he smoked a brisket, and it was all I could do not to go knocking at his door like a beggar. And his wife bakes the absolute best brownies. I keep asking them to adopt me."

Grace nodded sagely. "A moist but chewy brownie is worth its weight in gold."

"Add pecans and I say it's gem quality," Maggie said.

With the first flat of flowers in the ground, Maggie stood and stretched. The sky above her was a bright, brilliant blue, empty and unending but for yellow thunderheads building off to the west. She shut her eyes, lifted her face to the sun, and drank in the warmth, searching for the peace Grace appeared to find in a Monday evening spent planting purple petunias with friends.

Instead, she thought of Mike, pictured him on the deck of his boat rubbing teak oil on a railing. Or suntan oil on his big-boobed bimbo. "I can almost smell the coconuts."

Holly rolled back on her heels, tipped up the bill of her baseball cap, and gave Maggie a curious look. "Coconut in brownies? Yew. Not for me."

She shook her head. She didn't want to explain. She didn't want to think about Mike, much less talk about him. "Suntan oil. I'm hungry. Why don't we call in the pizza now."

"Do you want to talk about your husband, Maggie?" Grace asked, her gaze knowing.

"Well, spit. Is everyone around here clairvoyant or am I that obvious?"

"You're that obvious." Holly drew back her arm, then stabbed her trowel into the ground. Standing, she stripped off her gloves saying, "You don't go five minutes without touching that shiner of yours and getting a sappy look on your face."

Maggie stopped herself, barely, from reaching up to press her black eye yet again. For some reason, she found the pain of the bruise strangely reassuring. "He called me today and asked how I was doing."

Holly led the way into the house, glancing back over her shoulder. "What did you tell him?"

"I didn't talk to him. I let the machine pick up."

"Why?"

Maggie shrugged. She didn't have an answer. She didn't know why she did anything these days. Or, to be more exact, why she *didn't* do much of anything these days.

She'd been bad enough during the months before Mike left her, but since then . . . well . . . some days she never got out of bed. The clouds hanging in her personal sky were dark, deep blue and purple, like her eye.

According to Mike, a couple doctors, and the National Mental Health Association website, Maggie was clinically depressed. She had a Zoloft prescription and a therapist, and she'd made an honest, though brief, effort with both. Neither seemed to make much difference. Actually, from her point of view, planning Grace's party had proved more beneficial than anything.

Which reminded her. "Did you check with Ben, Grace? Will you be free to shop florists on Saturday?"

"Yes." Talk turned to the anniversary party. As Maggie and Grace debated the wording of the invitations, Holly called in the pizza, then excused herself to wash up.

The older two women watched her leave, then after hearing a door close, Maggie observed, "That girl is downright allergic to anything that even hints at weddings, isn't she? We're a pair. She needs an antihistamine and I need an antidepressant."

"I need an anti-weary pill," Grace said with a sigh, leaning back in her chair. "All of a sudden I feel like I'm slogging my way through marshmallow cream. My get-up-and-go has got up and gone."

"I don't have any uppers, but I do have chocolate." Maggie gestured toward her purse. "Want to spoil your supper with a candy bar?"

Grace started to shake her head, then paused. "You know what? I think I'll take you up on that. I've learned not to wait for the things I want."

Maggie fished the Hershey bar from her purse and handed it over. "You seldom mention your illness. I'll be honest, Grace. I haven't quite known what to do or say to you about it, so basically, I haven't done or said anything. That's a ridiculous way to behave. So please, help me out here. Tell me how I can help you the most."

Grace reached across the table and squeezed her hand. "Maggie, I have a loving family and a circle of dear, dear friends who are always happy to run errands for me, drive me to the hospital, cook for me, and pray for me. I love them dearly, and their support is precious beyond words.

"What I haven't had, up until now, anyway," she continued, flashing a shy smile, "is a friend like you. A friend who lets me be normal, who gives me the opportunity to be connected to the world in ways that have nothing to do with cancer. Because my life has revolved around my disease for so long now, my family and friends see me as a cancer patient first, a woman second. You don't. That's so refreshing. It's such a gift you give to me."

"That's sort of embarrassing since I didn't have a clue I was doing anything."

"That doesn't lessen the value of what you've given."

Maggie considered the point for a moment, then smiled as satisfaction rolled through her. "That's nice. Thank you."

"You're very welcome."

"I have to tell you though, Grace, you've done me a similar good turn. Helping to plan your anniversary party perks me right up." She gingerly touched her eye. "And now I actually have some color to my life."

"I feel bad about that."

"Why? You weren't the one who hit me. Besides, it was worth a little black eye to see my husband wallowing in guilt. Even though I think the elbow that clipped me might have been Justin's."

Noting Grace's sympathetic expression, Maggie knew a twinge of discomfort. "I sound bitter, don't I? I don't like that. I don't want to do that. It's so cliché and I've always taken pride in being an individual. It's just that the thought of his having a bimbo makes me crazy."

"Are you certain that gal was his bimbo?" Holly asked as she strode into the kitchen, bringing the fragrance of vanilla skin lotion along with her. "I hear he denied it."

"Of course he denied it. He's a man. Men always try to lie their way out of trouble." She frowned down at the smudges of dirt on her jeans. Bitter honesty made her add, "The worst part of it is, I'm not blameless in the matter. I wasn't being a good wife to him."

"Don't," Grace snapped, as forceful as Maggie had ever heard her sound. "There is never any excuse for faithlessness."

Whoa. Maggie's brows arched. Had she pushed a button, or what?

The arrival of the pizza forestalled any inquiries Maggie might have made into the subject. Following a brief debate over whether to use paper or pottery, Grace set the table with pretty plates that matched the sunflower pattern on the glasses they'd been using. Holly directed Maggie to the napkins while she topped off their tea, then put a vase filled with a trio of purple irises in the center of the table.

As they took their seats, Maggie couldn't help but compare this meal with the last time she'd had pizza. John, her second eldest boy, had invited the entire family for supper to celebrate landing a new job. He'd set the pizzas on the coffee table in front of the hockey game on his wide screen TV and passed around paper towels to serve as plates. Not a one of the men in her family had seen anything wrong in it.

That had been the last time her whole family had gotten together. That was the last time she remembered truly having fun.

She took a bite of pizza and as the taste of pepperoni exploded in her mouth, Holly dropped a conversational bomb. "I think I'm going to move to Louisiana in August."

Grace swallowed the wrong way and had to take a sip of tea to quiet her cough. Maggie stared at Holly in amazement. "What?"

"I mentioned that Justin came by last night. He pressed me about marriage again and I told him I'd decided to pursue my Ph.D. I've been accepted at Tulane. I'll be leaving town right after Grace's party."

"Well." Maggie sat back in her seat. "When did this all happen?"

"At the same time the words went tripping off my tongue."

"You lied to him?" Grace asked.

"Yes and no. I applied to a number of programs last year before he and I started seeing each other, and continued the process mainly out of curiosity to see where I'd be accepted. But I realized after I said it that leaving here might be the best solution for both of us." She picked a pepperoni circle off her pizza slice. "After Maggie's encounter with Mike at the festival, I'm a basket case. You know, Justin very well could have been there, too. Everywhere I go, I worry I'll run into him. Every time I open the newspaper, I brace myself to see his photograph at some hospital fund-raiser or read his name in the society column. It's hard."

Maggie couldn't argue with her. After all, Holly might well have walked right past Justin at the festival, and Maggie was haunted by the same fears of unexpected meetings with Mike. In some ways, she'd be glad when he finally shipped his boat to the coast. Then she'd quit worrying about having a starring role in *Parking Garage Incident: The Sequel*.

Grace sipped her tea. "Do you *want* to go to pursue your doctorate, Holly?"

She sighed. "I love my job. Bonham Middle is a great place to teach." After swallowing another bite of pizza, she added, "My dad will have a fit."

Her non-answer had certainly answered the question for Maggie. "Sugar, don't take this wrong, but I'm not so certain this would be a good move for you. I don't believe it's ever a good idea to run from life, especially if a man somehow figures into the mix. Seems to me like that's just what you'd be doing."

Holly licked tomato sauce off her fingers. "You're one to talk. Excuse me, but aren't you the woman who admitted to staying in bed for two days last week?"

"That's why I feel free to advise you in this case. Although, come to think of it, I'd feel free to advise you in any case. I'm always free with advice."

Smiling, Grace said, "Yes, we noticed that about you."

"The question is, do you hear me?" Maggie reached across the table and took Holly's hand. "Sugar, what's really keeping you from marrying that adorable man?"

Holly got that deer-in-the-headlights look as she fiddled with her napkin. "I told you."

"You told us bits and pieces. Not enough to truly understand."

Holly rose from the table and paced her kitchen. "Maybe you don't need to understand. Maybe if you were the friends you claim to be, you wouldn't pester me about it."

"Maybe in order to be the true friends you deserve, we should encourage you to face difficult questions. Holly, I agree with Maggie. This idea of moving . . . it's one thing to move forward, another thing to run away."

"I'm not running away from Justin."

"You're running away from life."

Holly's chin went up, but quivered slightly. "That's not true. Life is running away from me."

"Oh, sugar." Maggie spied the tears in Holly's eyes, heard the desperation in her tone, and decided they'd probably pushed hard enough for now. "Just mull it over a bit before you make a final decision. Something as big as this deserves careful thought and consideration."

Hoping to lighten the mood, she gave her hair a toss. "Besides, personally, I'll be in big trouble if you go. I need you to be my dating consultant."

"Your what?" Holly's mouth gaped.

"My dating consultant. I have my first date next Saturday. It's been years since I've dated, and I let my *Cosmopolitan* subscription lapse years ago. I need someone to catch me up on the dos and don'ts of dating in the new millennium."

Grace shook her head. "You're not really going through with this."

"Sure I am. He's a nice man and I've known him for years."

"Who?" Holly sank into her seat. "Who is he?"

"His name is Max McNab. He cleans my pool."

"Oh, God." Holly sank back against her seat. "She has a date with the pool boy."

"He's not a boy," Maggie testily replied. "He's definitely a man—a responsible man who owns his own business, I'll have you know. For the record, I don't see what's wrong with a woman dating a younger man. Men do it all the time. My husband is doing it."

"How much younger is Mr. McNab?" Grace inquired.

Not quite meeting her friend's gaze, Maggie shrugged. "I don't know. Ten years, maybe twelve."

Holly buried her face in her hands. "If she says one word about the length of his hose I'm going to die."

"Oh, stop it. I'm not going to have sex with the man. I'm going rock climbing with him."

"What?" Holly and Grace asked simultaneously.

"Rock climbing. Out at Mineral Wells State Park. Bill takes climbing trips all over the country. He's going to teach me how to get started. It's something I've wanted to do for a long time now. It's going to be one of the items on my Life List. Item number one, in fact." She rose and crossed the room to where she'd left her purse. Digging a small notebook and a pen from inside, she returned to the table, opened it, and wrote:

maggie's life list
1. *I will go rock climbing in Arizona.*

"So, are y'all ready to help me figure out the rest of it?"

Holly set dessert—a chocolate ice cream-and-brownie sundae—and three spoons at the center of the table. "As long as you don't make sex with the pool boy one of the items, yeah. What else do you have in mind?"

"I just have a couple vague notions. Show us your list, Holly. Maybe that will give me some ideas."

They spent the next hour laughing and giggling as they offered up ideas and suggestions for Maggie's Life List while they cleaned up after dinner, then returned to the front flower beds to finish planting the petunias. Some of the suggestions were silly. Others, serious. All worth consideration.

"After all," Maggie said as she worked plant food into the soil, "collecting nail polish colors is as legitimate as collecting quarters."

By the time Ben arrived to escort Grace home, Maggie had settled on items one through three. "Rock climbing, touring the great churches of Europe, and winning a ribbon for my chocolate cake at the State Fair. I'm comfortable with those. For my number four, I still want to think a bit about the volunteer work. As much as I love my baby-rocking hours at Methodist Hospital, I'd like for whatever I add to be a different venue entirely."

"What about five?" Grace asked, eyeing the notes she'd taken during the discussion. "Have you made up your mind about it?"

Maggie glanced over Grace's shoulder at the rounded, regular writing on the yellow legal pad. She smiled. What was listed in the number five slot had come directly off Holly's list, her number twenty-one. "I will do something deliciously wicked," she read aloud. "Yes. Oh, yes. That one is definitely on my list. It's my number five. In fact, I have something already in mind for my number five."

"Not the pool boy," Holly groaned. "Please, tell me not the pool boy."

"No, not the pool boy." Maggie gave a sly smile. "But it does have something to do with water."

As was her habit, Holly remained in her classroom during lunch period on Friday to grade weekly tests. She had considered putting off the task until this evening just to give herself something to do, but she had a handful of students who regularly stopped by after school on Friday to get their scores. She didn't feel right about making them wait just because her social life had imploded.

She finished her first period exams and had started on the second when a knock sounded on her door. She glanced up to see one of her students from last year waving at her through the narrow rectangular window. Holly motioned for the girl to enter the classroom.

"Hi, Miss Weeks," Taylor Dodd said.

"Hello, Taylor. How's algebra going?"

"It's *so* hard," she said. "I'm doing terrible. I hate it." She gave her blond ponytail a dramatic toss, then sighed heavily.

Recalling the girl's tendency toward theatrics, Holly arched a skeptical brow. "What's your average?"

"Ninety-four."

"Ninety-four on a one hundred point scale. Have your parents grounded you yet?"

"No, of course not." The girl flashed a grin. "I'm office aide this week and I have a message for you from Mr. Thompson. He wants you to come to his office right away."

"Oh? Am I in trouble with the principal?"

Taylor's eyes rounded. "I don't know. Did you do something bad?"

Immediately, she thought of Justin. Holly shook her head. "I guess I'd better see what he wants. Please tell Mr. Thompson I'll be right there."

Holly slipped her shoes back on, rummaged in her desk drawer for her keys, and locked her classroom door behind her. With the children at lunch, the seventh-grade wing was relatively quiet, and her footsteps against the tile floor echoed off the walls as she made her way down the hallway.

She rounded the corner and turned onto the main corridor leading to the cafeteria and the school office. With her thoughts on why the principal had sent for her, she didn't notice the children holding the poster right outside the lunchroom until one of them called her name.

The sign was decorated in glitter and gold stars and read: CONGRATULATIONS, MISS WEEKS!

"What's this?" she asked as they motioned her into the cafeteria. Holly stopped abruptly as her eyes went wide. Her students—a boy and a girl from each of her six classes—were lined up on either side of the doorway, each child with a yellow rose in his hand. They quickly surrounded her, pressing the flowers upon her.

Holly laughed with delight as she collected golden buds, then abruptly fell silent in surprise as she heard Mr. Thompson announce, "Faculty and students, please join me in congratulating Bonham Middle School's Teacher of the Year, Miss Weeks!"

The cheers and applause brought tears to her eyes. The testimonials from her students made her laugh.

When the time came to return to her room for afternoon classes, she all but floated down the hall. It was the best day of her teaching career.

As she drove home, she wanted desperately to share the news with her best friend. Except, her best friend wasn't speaking to her anymore because she'd banished him from her life.

The grief in his expression when she sent him away would be burned on her mind forever.

That was three weeks ago now, and every day since she'd second-guessed herself, wondered if she'd said the right thing. Done the right thing. Justin's absence left a huge hole in her life. She missed making love with him, of course, but it was so much more than that. She missed his enthusiasm. She missed seeing his smile. She missed his stupid jokes and the heat of his body lying next to her as she slept. Most of all, she missed their daily talks when they shared the minutiae of everyday life and offered each other insight and opinion and support.

Justin would be so proud of the Teacher of the Year award. Middle-school teachers seldom had an opportunity for professional recognition, and Justin had complained about that in the past on her behalf. She imagined telling him about it. She could picture the light that would dawn in his eyes and the beam of his smile. He'd pick her up and whirl her around. Maybe do his "wah-hoo" noise of celebration. Then he'd kiss her, a big, smacking, you-are-such-a-WOMAN kiss. That would probably lead to sex, and celebration sex was always among their best. Come to think of it, had they ever had celebration sex because of her accomplishments?

No, it had always been Justin's accomplishments they'd celebrated. She'd tried to get him to make love after her first—and only—bungee jump, thus meeting goal number twelve on her Life List, but he'd gotten snippy about it. Justin did not like her doing anything the least bit risky.

And yet, he wanted her to marry him. What could be riskier than staking his future on her? Go figure.

At home, she changed clothes and tried not to reach for the phone. She held off by working in her yard until dark, then sitting down with a bowl of air-popped popcorn to watch a rented movie. Under the circumstances, her choice of romantic comedy was a poor one, and when the ending credits rolled on the TV screen, she cratered. She put her mind on hold and allowed her heart to take control.

Holly grabbed her purse and keys and dashed for the garage. She made the half-hour drive to Justin's house in just over twenty minutes, anticipation rising in her blood with every turn of the tires.

She didn't even know if he'd be home. She had no clue what his hospital schedule was this week. But she prayed he would be there. She needed to share her news. She needed to see him.

Oh, Justin. I've missed you so much.

Justin's home was a two-bedroom brick cottage in the hospital district of Fort Worth. Built in the 1930s, the house had been completely updated by the previous owner. It had charm and character and a small enough yard to give a busy doctor the pleasure of home maintenance with minimal commitment. The best feature of the cottage was its big front porch. Holly had spent many a night sitting on the porch swing necking with her fella.

Maybe he'd sit out here with her tonight. The setting

was lovely. Silver moonlight bathed the yard and the scent of roses drifted on the cool evening air. It was a perfect night for romance.

But you didn't come here for romance. You came for friendship. Remember that.

She noted the slight tremor in her hand as she pressed the doorbell. Her thoughts were in a whirl. Did he miss her, too? Would he be happy to see her? Would he slam the door in her face?

Surely not. She'd hurt him, angered him. But Justin wasn't the type to hold a grudge. Justin liked to move forward. He didn't stay mired in the past like Holly was wont to do. Of course, his past was a whole lot different than hers.

No matter what, he would be proud of her award. Holly knew that without a doubt. She knew in her heart that no matter what happened between them romantically, she could always count on Justin to be her friend. Her best friend.

As the bell's echo faded, she swayed sideways toward one of the long windows flanking the door. She tried to peer through the waves in the leaded glass for signs of life in the softly lit entry hall. Nothing. She couldn't hear anything, either.

"Come on, Justin. Be home." She cupped her hands around her eyes and leaned against the pane. Ah hah. Light in his study and in the hallway upstairs.

She rang the bell a second time, then saw movement on the staircase. She jerked back to stand innocently in front of the door and heard him call, "I'll be right there."

As the door swung open, he said, "Sorry we forgot the bag . . . Holly."

Pleasure flared in his eyes, but was quickly banked. He

was dressed in a tux, sans jacket, his tie looped around his neck, the ends dangling. The link on his left cuff was missing, his sleeve rolled midway up his forearm. She wondered why he was all dressed up. Some fund-raiser for the hospital, most likely. He looked so handsome he took her breath away.

"Holly," Justin repeated, his expression shifting to . . . what was that . . . dismay? "What are you doing here?"

So much for being happy to see me.

"Is something wrong?" he continued. "Is it your dad?"

Her throat tightened and she worked to force the words out. "No. Nothing's wrong."

Justin visibly relaxed, then seconds later abruptly straightened again. He glanced back over his shoulder. His dismay grew more pronounced. In fact, he appeared distinctly uncomfortable. "It's uh . . . late."

"I needed to . . ." *See you, touch you, love you.* ". . . to talk to you. I have something to tell you."

He stepped out onto the front porch, pulling the door shut behind him. Holly was taken aback by his action. He wasn't going to invite her in?

"Are you pregnant?"

Pregnant? Pregnant! Where did he come up with that? And was it hope in his voice? Or dread? Dread with a dash of panic. "No, I'm not pregnant."

He briefly closed his eyes. "The way you said you had something to tell me sounded serious."

Holly simply stared at him as she tried to understand her own response to his reaction.

"Look," he said, raking his fingers through his hair, a defensive note in his tone. "It's late. I thought maybe you were, too."

He abruptly shut his mouth. An eternity of silence

stretched between them, uncomfortable and awkward. She hadn't expected it to be like this. She wasn't exactly certain what she *had* expected, but certainly not this.

Stepping back, she fumbled for the car keys deep in a jeans pocket. Coming here had been a mistake. Thinking she could salvage their friendship had been a mistake. She couldn't tell Justin about her Teacher of the Year award. Not now. She should make up an excuse and go, but she couldn't quite make her feet move.

"Is this about your plans to move? Have you decided to leave town early or something? Have you come to say good-bye?" Justin folded his arms. Anger radiated off him in waves.

Tears stung her eyes and she blinked rapidly, shifting her stance so that her face fell into shadow. "No. That's not why I wanted to see you."

"If it's about that business over at Maggie's house, if Mike Prescott has tried to fill your head with his paranoid prattle—"

"No, Maggie and Grace told me what happened. I know Mike was acting stupid. You wouldn't start an affair with Maggie."

Justin grew unnaturally still; the force of his stare was palpable. In a deceptively soft voice, he asked, "How come you're so certain? She's a beautiful, sexy woman, and frankly, I like her very much."

Holly wrinkled her nose. "She's a beautiful, sexy, *married* woman, and I know your views about marriage vows. You won't be a party to cheating, even if they are separated."

Justin scowled but didn't respond. He couldn't argue with the truth.

Tension swirled in the rose-scented breeze. Holly

halfway expected to hear the crack of thunder, never mind that the night sky was free of clouds. She should turn around and leave right now. She knew it. Instead, she cleared her throat and tried again. "Justin, it's nothing serious. It's something to do with school. I had good news I wanted to share. If you have a few minutes, I'd like to tell you about it."

"I don't." His arms fell to his sides and he took half a step backward. "I don't have time tonight to listen. You should go, Holly."

He might as well have hit her with his fist. "Oh. All right."

Still reeling from the blow, fearing the tears would spill before she reached the safety of her car, she turned to leave. She was halfway down the front walk when the second gut-punch arrived in the form of a long white limousine that pulled up to the curb in front of her car and she heard Justin mutter, "Oh, shit."

The driver's door swung open. The chauffeur pushed a button and the trunk lid released with a click. He gave a little wave as he climbed from the car, walked around to the back, and removed something from the trunk.

Holly had to walk right past him to get to her car, so she couldn't help but notice the object he held in his hand. It was a small suitcase, an overnight bag. A floral overnight bag.

A woman's overnight bag.

"Excuse me," Justin said, pushing past Holly to meet the chauffeur at the curb. "Sorry for the trouble."

"No problem at all, Dr. Skipworth. I should have remembered Miss Larson had a bag in the trunk. Hope this didn't cause her too much inconvenience."

"No. No, not at all."

Holly's universe tilted. Miss Larson. Puffy Larson's daughter. Two-point-three kids.

Justin dug into his pocket for a bill, tipped the man, took the case, and turned around. At that point, Holly heard the snick of the front door opening behind her.

She really, really didn't want to look around and confirm what she already knew, but pride wouldn't let her run away. Taking a bracing breath, she turned and smiled. "Hello, Jenna."

She wore a little black dress, stiletto heels, sheer black stockings, and a smug smile.

Holly had to force herself not to glance down at her Bonham Middle School, Lady Falcon Basketball tee shirt, wind shorts, and flip-flops. At least she'd had a pedicure this past week. Otherwise she'd have felt completely naked.

"Why, Holly Weeks. We didn't expect to see you here tonight."

Obviously. A dozen different responses flashed through Holly's mind, ranging from caustic to catty to classy. She opted for the high road—even though doing so almost made her gag—and said, "That's a lovely dress you're wearing, Jenna. You look beautiful."

Squaring her shoulders, she turned to Justin and forced words through throat spasms. "I apologize for interrupting your evening."

"Holly, it's not what you . . ." Justin shifted his gaze away from hers, a muscle working in his jaw. He shoved his hands into his pockets, sighed heavily, then pinned her with a narrow-eyed stare. "You can't have it both ways."

Years of practice hiding her tears allowed her to answer him without breaking. "I know that. Now, if you'll excuse me, I have an early day tomorrow."

She flashed a quick, faked smile, then walked in calm, measured steps toward her car. Her knees felt as supportive as cotton candy. With blind luck she managed to insert the key into the lock on the first try. Once she'd made it safely inside the car, the tremble in her hand intensified. Metal clattered against metal as she tried to slip the key into the ignition. Finally, using both hands, she managed. As she fired the engine and put the car into gear, she glanced through her tears into her rearview mirror.

Oh, God. Justin. He stood watching her go, Jenna's overnight bag in his right hand. Jenna clung to his left. The yellow porch light illuminated her smile, a victorious testimony to orthodontia.

Holly waited until she'd turned the corner before gunning the gas. The sensation in her chest was a cross between severe acid reflux and a coronary.

Or maybe this was how a heart felt when it broke in two.

❊ eight

Before Grace opened her eyes Saturday morning, she knew she faced one of those days. Her stomach churned with nausea, her bones hurt, and fatigue lay upon her body like a leaden sheet. She could hardly summon the energy to get out of bed to go throw up.

Swallowing a moan, she rolled onto her side and opened her eyes.

Ben stood in the bathroom doorway, shaving cream spread across half his face, watching her. "You feel bad, don't you?"

This time, she couldn't deny it.

"Oh, sweetheart." His voice was gentle, the light in his eyes kind. He returned to the bathroom, washed the shaving foam from his face, then returned to their room, taking a seat on his side of the bed. "I have a little something I hope will cheer you up."

From beside his side of the bed, he lifted a pretty gift

bag with pink roses on it and stuffed with magenta tissue. Dangling from the string handle was a little paper angel. Grace smiled. Across the angel's robe, Ben had written: *I love you, Angel Gracie.*

She carefully untied the tag from the bag so she could save it. "Oh, hurry up, wouldya?" her husband growled, anticipation bright in his eyes.

She managed a laugh, pleasing them both, then peered into the gift bag. She spied white fluffy fur and sparkly gold satin. "A teddy bear angel, Ben?" she asked with delight, tugging the gift free.

It was the size of a newborn child, downy soft and cuddly. Sunshine beaming through the bedroom window picked up sparkles of multicolored glitter in the golden wings on his back and the halo around his head. "He's so cute. I love him."

"I thought you would. Kid across the street had one and it made me think of you. I couldn't remember the last time I gave you a stuffed animal. Decided it was overdue. Boy's mom told me where to get one."

Grace grabbed her husband's arm and pulled him toward her for a kiss. It had taken Ben upward of thirty years to learn how to buy gifts, but once he'd figured it out, he did it with style. In other words, he put some thought into it, which was all Grace truly desired. "Thank you, Ben. My little angel bear is excellent medicine."

His smug, satisfied smile slipped a little at the mention of medicine. He studied her closely. "It's worse than last time, isn't it?"

"Maybe a little." Actually, a lot, but Grace didn't like to complain. In her mind, that would be borrowing trouble.

For a person living with what was deemed a terminal

illness, she considered herself lucky to fare as well as she did. Most days she felt fine. Her energy level remained high and her pain level was no more than any other sixty-something woman could expect. But some days this elephant-in-the-room that was cancer got the better of her. Today the elephant had moved right into bed with her.

"I'll call Maggie and Holly for you," he said, standing up. "Their numbers are in the address book, right?"

Maggie and Holly? What . . . oh no. They'd planned another round of party-dress shopping today.

Grace wanted to scream with frustration. This was her own fault. She should have known not to schedule anything for the day following her monthly trip to the cancer clinic for her two-hour date with an IV drip. Never mind that the last three treatments had been side-effect free. She'd lived with breast cancer too long not to know to expect the unexpected.

"I hate to cancel on them," she told Ben.

"You can't go traipsing around from dress shop to dress shop today. It would be too much for you."

In this instance, she couldn't charge Ben with acting overprotectively. What he said was true. "I know. But I hate it, Ben. They've set aside the day for me."

"And you hate the idea of letting the elephant win."

"Can you blame me?"

His mouth quirked in a grin. "All the time, because it only makes me worry more. Then I tell myself that all your vinegar serves you well because it's fuel to fight that hairy old beast."

Grace gripped her husband's hand. Today the two of them were in balance, at peace. Today she needed him to take care of her as much as he needed to give care to her. She glanced at the clock. Seven A.M. Maggie was due to pick her up at ten. "Maybe we can give it an hour or so and see how I feel?"

He finger-combed her hair off her forehead. "Sure, honey. We'll give it an hour or so and see."

By nine, determination and meds had for the most part dealt with the nausea. The fatigue, however, had settled in to stay. As much as she hated to admit it, Grace knew she wasn't up to dress shopping today. Ben brought her the address book. She picked up the phone and dialed Maggie's number first.

Maggie answered on the second ring. " 'Mornin', Grace. You got your shoppin' shoes on?"

"Good morning, Maggie. I'm afraid that is why I'm calling. My shopping shoes seem to be pinching my toes a bit today."

Grace explained about the Aredia infusion and its occasional side effects. "I'm sorry, Maggie, but I'm afraid I don't have the energy for trying on dresses. I hate to cancel on you and Holly at the last minute."

"Oh, don't you spend a second fretting about it. Sounds to me like you already have all the bad feelings you need on your plate as it is. We'll shop for your dress another day. A time when you can truly enjoy it. There's no rush."

"I was so looking forward to it." Grace heard a shameful note of wistful self-pity in her tone and turned it to a more positive pitch. "Planning this party is the most fun I've had in years, and besides, I could use a dose of girl talk right now. It's better medicine than half the pills I take every day."

"I know exactly what you mean." Maggie's voice sounded as pensive as her own. "I'll trade my Zoloft for an hour with you and Holly anytime."

Reminded of Maggie's burden, Grace quickly took stock. "Maybe we don't have to cancel entirely. Would you want to go to lunch instead of shopping?"

"Are you up to that?"

"Yes, I think I am. I could use the distraction, to be honest, and besides, it doesn't take much more energy to ride in a car and sit at a restaurant table than it does to lie in bed. Maybe we could at least make more plans. I really enjoy the anticipation; it lets me live the excitement of the party many times."

"Hmm . . . that gives me an idea." Maggie sounded eager again. "So you're okay as long as it's riding and sitting and that's all?"

"Yes."

"Let me check into something. I'll call you right back."

Ten minutes later, the phone rang. As soon as Grace picked up, Maggie started talking. "Would you be comfortable in the car for an extra hour?"

Grace considered it. "Yes."

"Excellent. I'll be by at ten. Don't dress up. We're going out to the farm."

"The farm?"

Maggie's voice sparkled. "Mike's aunt lives up toward Bowie on the family cotton farm. She's a real sweetheart, plus—and this is why we're making a road trip—she makes the best peach cake you've ever tasted. If you like it as much as I expect you will, I want to ask her to bake the cake for the party."

They spoke for a few more minutes, then Maggie disconnected in order to call Holly and make certain she didn't object to the change in plans. At five minutes of ten, Maggie's silver Lexus whipped around the corner.

Watching from the kitchen window, Ben glanced over at Grace and winced. "She took that turn a little fast. Maybe this isn't such a good idea."

"Oh, hush." Grace leaned over to kiss her husband on his cheek. "You're just jealous you don't get to come with us."

Ben snorted. "Uh huh. Driving an hour to a hen party on a farm beats out playing a round of golf every time."

"Oh, go swing your five iron."

"I plan to," he shot back, grinning. Then his expression grew serious as he cupped her cheek and stared down into her eyes. "Are you certain you're up for this?"

"I am." She put firm certainty into the assurance. "It's just what the doctor ordered."

Ben bent down and gave her a tender kiss. "It gladdens my heart to see the sparkle back in your eyes. Have fun, honey. See you this evening."

Maggie bounded out of the car as Grace made her way down the front steps. Maggie wore tomato red capri pants, a rainbow-hued sleeveless cotton top, and sandals. Her hair was a half-shade more blond than it had been Thursday night, and her cat's-eye sunglasses sported rhinestone stars at the outer corners and concealed the remnants of her black eye.

"You remind me of an old-time movie star," Grace said by way of greeting.

"Yeah? Who?"

Grace considered it. "I'm not sure. A combination. Sexy Marilyn Monroe mixed with girl-next-door Doris Day."

Maggie beamed a smile. "I like that!"

She exchanged pleasantries with Ben, who cautioned Maggie to drive carefully and Grace not to overdo, and then they were off. Twenty minutes later, they pulled in front of Holly's house and Maggie beeped the horn. Holly opened her door and waved.

"Something's wrong," Grace said, as the young woman walked slowly toward the car, head down.

Maggie clucked her tongue. "I'm afraid you're right. Girl looks as low as a lawn mower set to scald. Look at that. Dressed entirely in navy blue. Not a speck of color on her."

Holly looked up and she winced. "No makeup, either."

Holly slipped into the backseat of the Lexus, peered over the top her black-lens sunglasses just long enough to meet Maggie and Grace's gaze, and said, "Good morning, ladies."

"My stars, sugar. Your eyes are as red as my britches. What's wrong?"

Holly turned her head to look out the window. "I'd just as soon not talk about it, if y'all don't mind."

Maggie and Grace shared a brief look of concern, then Grace said, "Whatever you want, honey. We're ready to listen if you change your mind."

Holly smiled her thanks, nodded, then sat quietly throughout the first half of the drive. Maggie and Grace discussed the anniversary plans, then their children. Maggie told a particularly amusing story involving her sons and a fund-raising car wash that turned into a mud fight and fines from the city.

Then, out of the blue, Holly spoke up. "Do you remember being thirteen?"

Grace frowned in concentration. "What's that, sixth grade?"

"Seventh. It's the grade I teach. My students, the girl

students, are constantly involved in friendship wars. I spend almost as much time dealing with the fallout of their battles as I do teaching math."

"Seventh grade." Maggie shuddered. "That's the year Lisa Lies-a-Lot Lehrman told Cheryl Norris that I'd kissed her boyfriend behind the school trash Dumpster so that Cheryl would run against me for secretary of the choir. Cheryl Norris never lost an election in her life—she's mayor of Phoenix now, I believe. Anyway, Cheryl won and I got ousted from the choir clique. It was the biggest social disaster of my life."

Grace shook her head. "How cruel of that girl to lie about you that way."

"You mean about the kiss?" Maggie paused long enough to honk her horn at the pickup that cut it too close when changing lanes. "Oh, that wasn't a lie. Lisa caught me red-lipped, so to speak. The problem was that earlier that day I saw her lyin' behind the bleachers letting Bill Watson feel her up. It was the second time I'd stumbled across that little scene, and I happened to mention the fact to a girl or two or three and . . . well . . . the nickname stuck." Maggie shrugged and added, "Thirteen is an ugly age for a girl."

Grace observed, "They haven't yet learned that female friendships will be the mainstays of their lives."

Holly tightened her seat belt. "I see it every year. Notes passed from one girl to another, secretly but at the same time obvious so that the outcast is sure to see it. Then the darting glances toward the poor girl, gasps and horror-filled giggles. The day before she had been liked, valued. Now she's the focus of their criticism and the butt of their jokes. Life changes in the blink of an eye."

Grace thought back to her daughter's junior high days. "It seemed like it was always worse in the spring right before school let out for the summer."

"Sexual stirrings," declared Maggie, her gaze flicking to the rearview mirror.

"That's probably part of it," Grace agreed. "Also, I think the herd mentality is strongest in girls at adolescence. What's the term they use? I can't remember. Chemo brain is acting up again. Something stress?"

"Peer pressure."

"That's it. They'll go along with behaviors they know aren't right in order to fit in with the group. That's what I saw with my daughter, anyway. Most girls that age need a bit more maturity before they are strong enough to stand against the crowd."

"I hurt for them," Holly said softly. "They're so raw with emotion. So riddled with contradiction. They need to be liked for themselves, but at the same time, they need to please. They long for attachment, but they desperately need to protect themselves from loss."

Maggie took her attention off the road long enough to shoot Grace a pointed look. "That's a curious thing to say. Why would they need to protect themselves from loss?"

"Friendships end," Holly said with a shrug. She then returned her attention to the scene outside her window, the wildflower-studded fields of north-central Texas.

The drive continued without further conversation. Maggie whistled softly beneath her breath while Grace tried to think of something to say to draw Holly out. The air of sadness hanging around her young friend was palpable, and it weighed on Grace's own state of mind. She closed her eyes, made use of the headrest. Exhaustion grabbed hold of her and squeezed.

Holly's softly spoken question drifted on the air like dandelion seeds. "Are we doomed to be thirteen all our lives?"

Maggie watched Grace lick icing from her fingers as she discussed possible cake toppers with Aunt Sadie. The peach cake had been a hit, just as she'd figured. Even sad-eyed Holly had swooned with delight when the flavor of that first rich, sinful bite exploded on her tongue.

Maggie felt like she'd hit a home run with the suggestion to visit the farm. Grace and Aunt Sadie were of an age with numerous similar interests. They'd bonded right away, and Maggie thought Grace looked a little perkier than she had earlier in the morning. A dose of Mike's warmhearted, gregarious aunt seemed to cure Holly of what ailed her, too. The retired teacher wasn't shy about expressing her opinions, and she and Holly had quite a debate about state-mandated standardized assessment testing. As for herself, Maggie needed nothing more than Aunt Sadie's comforting hug to make the drive worthwhile.

Even if she couldn't get away from memories of Mike in every room of the farmhouse.

Having decimated a second piece of cake and determined to stop the sinning, Maggie rose from her chair at the kitchen table and carried her plate to the sink. As she rinsed her dish, she glanced out the window and spied Holly seated on the back porch steps. She cuddled a red dachshund puppy in her lap, her fingers scratching the dog behind his ears. The tears on Holly's cheeks glistened in the sunlight.

Maggie's stomach sank. "She's crying."

Grace looked up from the photo album in her lap. "Holly?"

"Yes. Wasn't much of a walk. She hasn't been gone ten minutes." She turned off the faucet, then dried her hands on a tea towel. "I think I'll go talk to her. Leaving her alone doesn't appear to be helping anything. Something happened with Justin, I'll bet you money on it."

"I think you're right."

The screen door squeaked as Maggie opened it, then banged shut behind her. "Looks like you found a friend."

Holly lifted the dog and nuzzled his long floppy ears. "Actually, I lost one, Maggie. I lost my very best friend. And it happened when I wasn't looking."

Wood planks creaked as Maggie took a seat on the stoop. She stroked Holly's hair, tucking a stray strand back behind her ear. "Tell me about it, sugar."

"What are Grace and Sadie doing?"

"Poring over photo albums and scrapbooks. Sadie was showing her pictures of the cakes she's decorated, when they discovered they attended the same high school in Fort Worth. Sadie's always been a chronicler. They could be busy for hours. We have time. What happened with Justin that has you dragging your chin below your knees?"

Holly explained to Maggie about being named Teacher of the Year, how she'd wanted to share the news with her best friend, and whom she'd found at his house when she tried. "I was so worried about losing the lover, I never even thought about losing the friend. Somehow, losing the friend seems worse. Isn't that crazy?"

"No, it's not crazy at all." Maggie brushed off a spot on the stoop, then sat beside Holly. "I understand exactly. I was just about your age with a baby at home when Mike's company sent him to do some work on a dam in a remote part of Thailand. He was able to call home only three times during the four months he was away. I never missed him more. But as long as the nights stretched in my empty bed, Sunday afternoons were the worst."

She paused to scratch the puppy beneath his chin and make kissy noises. "Back in those days. Mike and I spent every Sunday afternoon up here at the farm. Aunt Sadie would watch the baby and Mike and I would work together on a list of chores she had ready for us. We worked so hard. We played a little. And we talked. We talked about everything under the sun. I knew everything there was to know about Mike Prescott in those days—his politics, his favorite books, his views on religion. His dreams."

She stretched out her legs, kicked off her sandals and wiggled her toes, then sighed heavily. "I couldn't tell you a title he's read in the past year to save my life."

"Y'all stopped coming to the farm?"

Maggie nodded. "When Mike went overseas, Sadie hired a helper. We'd come visit, of course, but it was never the same. We got busy with the kids. Busy with life."

The puppy in Holly's arms began to squirm and whine, and she set him on the ground. He gave two little puppy yips, then trotted off toward the barn.

Watching him go, Maggie gave a bittersweet smile. "Just like a man. You can hold them for so long, then they want to go exploring."

"Justin didn't want to go exploring. I sent him." Glumly, Holly added, "I just didn't expect him to make a discovery quite so soon."

"Yeah. It's a rotten feeling, knowing your man is off exploring."

"It's one of the worst feelings a woman can experience, in my opinion," Grace said. Maggie and Holly both looked over their shoulders in surprise as Grace opened the screen door and stepped outside. "Mind if I join you for a time? Sadie has gone up to her attic to look for something."

She carefully made her way down the porch steps and took a seat in the metal lawn chair, Aunt Sadie's "pea shelling" chair, just to the right of the kitchen stoop. "Ben had a bimbo once. Well, more than once, since the affair lasted three months. I didn't call her a bimbo. My term was 'paramour.' Which do you think is more insulting? I'm not certain I can decide."

Maggie couldn't believe what she was hearing. "Ben? Your fifty-year Ben?"

"Funny you should put it that way. I found out about the affair on his fiftieth birthday. She gave him a gift. A watch. The idiot forgot to take it off when he came home. Although, I've always thought, subconsciously, he wore it on purpose. The man couldn't handle the guilt. He wanted to get caught."

The emotions that rumbled through Maggie caught her by surprise. All three of them had been betrayed by their men. Wasn't that just a fine how-dee-doo. Were no men faithful? She recalled that moment in Holly's kitchen the other night when Grace had snapped that no-excuse-for-infidelity comment. She should have seen it then. Questions danced on her tongue like champagne bubbles. Answers seemed imperative to hear.

After all, Grace and Ben were still married. Maybe affairs didn't always murder marriages.

"What happened? Who was she? Did you have a clue beforehand?"

Graze gazed reflectively out toward the barn. "I knew things weren't right in our marriage long before he wore that watch home. He and I quit talking, quit doing much of anything together, and I let it go because Liza, our youngest, was in trouble. She'd married a young man who had developed a drinking problem, and she was trying to save him and her marriage. She needed her mom and all my energy was directed toward her. Then Ben's company announced a series of layoffs. For three months, he held on to his job, but on the final release, he got his pink slip."

She waited for a long moment before continuing. "I still didn't give him the attention he needed. I'm not excusing him, mind you, or condoning what he did, but I recognize that I contributed to our troubles. I wasn't there for him when he needed me. I left him vulnerable to someone who was."

Maggie shifted uncomfortably as Holly snorted with disgust. "The bimbo."

Grace nodded. "She set her cap for my Ben, never mind the fact he was a married man. We knew her from church and—"

"Church!" Maggie exclaimed.

"That's disgusting," Holly declared.

"Lots of sinnin' goin' on at St. Luke's. Believe me."

Maggie shifted position on the stoop. She truly didn't want to hear all the gory details; they hit too close to home right now. Yet, the reality that Ben and Grace had overcome their troubles dangled out in front of her like a carrot, and she wanted desperately to know the secret of their success.

Not that she wanted to patch things up with Mike. Oh, no. She was too angry. Furiously angry. Not just because of his Arts Festival date. Though she hadn't recognized it until now, Maggie suspected she'd been angry at Mike for a very long time.

Attempting to hurry the conversation along, she asked, "So how did you get from sinnin' to singing his praises? Since we're planning your golden wedding anniversary party, you obviously found a way."

"It wasn't easy. I was devastated when I found out. She was younger, of course. Not as young as our children, but close enough. Ben and I separated. He even filed for divorce."

"Oh." Maggie's stomach sank like a rock. "Tell me he didn't sail off to the Caribbean with her. I don't think I can do this anniversary party if he did."

"No, not that," Grace said with a chuckle.

"I can't believe you can laugh about it," Holly marveled. "I'm afraid I'd still be crying about it all these years later."

"Oh, I cried plenty of tears. An ocean of them. And I got angry and I grieved. Sometimes I wanted to murder him. Or her. Or him and her. Other times I was tempted to call her up and tell her she could have him for all I cared. I was forty-nine-years old and life as I had known it had vanished. I was miserable. Throw menopause into the mix and it only gets uglier."

Maggie shuddered at the thought. Propelling herself to her feet, she stepped down onto the grass. Her gaze trailed around the backyard, fixed on the blossoms of the magnolia tree standing halfway to the barn. In her mind's eye, she saw bunches of ripe yellow bananas instead of large, fragrant white blossoms.

Tropical fruit. Tropical women. Bikini bimbo or debutante, church lady or PTA-mom-with-cute-little-daughter-on-the-make, if Mike didn't have one already, it wouldn't be long. He liked sex too much.

She cleared her throat and asked, "How long were you apart?"

"Four and a half months. It seemed like four years."

"How did you get back together?"

Grace smiled at the memory. "He called and asked me for a date. I'll never forget it. I was just walking out the door to meet my lawyer for lunch when the phone rang. I debated letting it ring, but that's difficult for me."

"It's impossible for me," Maggie said. "I cannot ignore a ringing phone. That's why I always turn off the cellular when I'm driving. I don't want to crash into a tree when I'm fumbling around to answer it. Personally, I think it's a genetic thing."

"I don't have trouble with it," Holly said.

"We know," Maggie drawled.

Grace continued. "I thought we'd go to dinner and talk about the kids, the divorce, who would get what and all of that. Instead, he took me dancing. We hadn't been dancing in years. When he took me home, he parked at the curb. We sat in the car in the dark and talked, really talked, for the first time in forever. He told me he was sorry and that he'd been seeing a marriage counselor and that he'd like me to go with him. He told me he'd ended the affair and he didn't want a divorce. He asked for my forgiveness."

"So that was it? You kissed and made up?"

"Oh no. Repairing our marriage took a lot of time and effort. I had to understand that our marriage hadn't failed because of one major episode—his affair—but because of lots of little careless ones committed by the both of us. I had to learn that forgiveness was really a gift I gave to myself, more than to Ben. Once I figured that out, the rest of it came easier. Except the trust, that is. That was the most difficult thing to rebuild."

"So how did you do that?" Holly asked.

"Counseling helped, but what really healed the wound was time. That and getting cancer."

"What?" Maggie asked.

Holly's chin dropped in shock.

Grace nodded. "Following my third chemo treatment, my hair started falling out in clumps. I stood in the shower until the water ran cold, sobbing my eyes out. When I stepped out of the shower, Ben was standing at the bathroom sink. He'd shaved his head."

"How sweet," Holly said.

Maggie sniffed, unwilling to let the man completely off the hook for cheating on his wife.

"I realized I wasn't the least bit surprised. I'd known he'd be there for me. I'd known I could count on him. That's when I knew for certain and without a doubt that we'd make it. I trusted him. We had survived adultery and our marriage was stronger than ever. That knowledge gave me strength. Ben gave me strength. Then and every day since."

Holly asked, "Why have you told us all this?"

Grace gave them a Mona Lisa smile. "I thought maybe you needed to hear it. Maybe I needed to hear myself say it. As you know, I've been impatient with Ben of late. This morning he did something sweet—just a little something, mind you—and it reminded me of how lucky I am. How lucky we are."

"Are you saying Holly and I should overlook debutantes and bimbos?"

"Not at all. That's a choice that only the individual

can make. I just thought it was something you, my friends, should know under the circumstances."

Circumstances, Maggie knew, being Justin's and Mike's wandering eyes and maybe something else.

When Sadie appeared at the back door, a stack of scrapbooks in her hand, Grace rose from her seat and walked toward the stoop. Pausing, she took Holly's hand, then Maggie's. "I thought you should know about this because the two of you are working so very hard on my anniversary plans.

"I want you to know that this party is more than an event to mark the fiftieth year of our marriage. It is more than a celebration of love. It's a celebration of life. The happiness *and* the heartaches. You know that old saying about what doesn't kill you makes you stronger? Well, I am the perfect example of it. Ben's betrayal could have killed our partnership. It was as powerful and as destructive as the cancer. But in effect, it prepared us for the battle to come. We couldn't know that at the time, of course, which is the point I want to make to the two of you. I want you to think about that in the context of your own situations. I think it could help you."

Maggie and Holly sat silently for a time. Maggie mulled over Grace's revelation, tried to put it into context with her and Mike's situation. Similarities existed, but so, too, did differences. Mike denied cheating on her. Did she believe him?

Maggie simply couldn't say. Believing what she wanted to be true came harder, because she could be fooling herself.

A puff of breeze stirred the leaves of the tall cotton-wood tree that shaded the backyard and sent the swing made of rope and a weathered board swaying. The smell of freshly turned dirt drifted on the air and mixed with the kitchen scents of cinnamon and peaches to create that unique aroma that Maggie associated with family and the farm. She knew a sudden and now familiar soul-deep yearning for the past and the way life used to be. Before her boys grew up. Before Mike and she grew apart.

Back when who she was and what she did mattered. Hugging her knees, she tried to pinpoint exactly when she had lost herself—long before losing Mike.

✿ nine

holly tracked down the puppies to a shady spot beside an empty tin watering tub set inside the fence of an overgrown corral. Four of them cavorted under and around the legs of a sawhorse, tumbling, yipping, and yelping. Their antics distracted her and made her smile, quite an accomplishment on this particular day.

Holly leaned against the fence railing, soaking up sunshine, inhaling the scent of wild onion that drifted from a patch of greens alongside the barn. A flash of red to her right caught her eye and Holly turned her head to see Maggie strolling toward her.

"Aunt Sadie sent me to tell you fried chicken, mashed potatoes, coleslaw, and beans will be served on the back picnic table in ten minutes. I'm not the least bit hungry after two pieces of cake, but I know from personal experience with Aunt Sadie's fried chicken that I'll indulge until my seams are near to splitting. How 'bout you, sugar? Ready for lunch?"

"Yeah. Sure." Holly shrugged. "I don't know. I don't have much of an appetite."

"Still fretting about Justin?"

Holly rescued one of the puppies who'd scrambled to the top of a nearby hay bale and couldn't get down. "I keep thinking about Grace and Ben. How they made it. It's nice."

"Very nice," Maggie agreed.

"I keep coming back to the friendship thing. Sounds like that's when their marriage ran into trouble, when they stopped being friends. What about you and Mike, Maggie? Did you guys stop being friends before you stopped being lovers?"

Maggie rested her arms along the top fence rail. She stared at the bright red polish on her fingernails as she considered the question. "I guess we did, although if you had asked me a month ago, I would have denied it. Looking back, I realize we developed separate circles of friends. Mike had the people from work, and I had the bowheads."

"Bowheads?"

"The PTA moms. For a few years there, hair bows were quite the style for mothers of elementary school students. One of my boys made up the name and it stuck."

"Must run in the family. Did Lies-a-Lot Lehrman grow up to be a bowhead?"

"You betcha. PTA president. Wore a different bow every day for a year."

Holly bit the inside of her cheek to keep from laughing aloud.

"How about you? Do you and Justin have different circles of friends?"

"No. My friends have blended with his into one group." She whipped her head around and turned a wide-eyed gaze on Maggie. "I've lost them, too, haven't I? I didn't even realize. I've been holed up by myself and I haven't called anyone, but no one has called me, either. Why haven't they called? Any of them?"

She sighed heavily, her spirits sinking. Glumly, she muttered, "I don't have any friends anymore, do I? I might as well move off. No one will miss me."

"Why, Holly Weeks. If that's not the meanest thing you've ever said to me." Maggie shot to her feet. "What am I? And Grace? Chopped liver?"

"Oh, that sounded bad. I'm sorry. That's not what I meant." She threw her arm around Maggie's shoulders and gave her a squeeze. "You and Grace *are* my friends. Dear friends. Funny, isn't it, how fast that has come about."

"We're like soldiers. We've been through the Battle of the Bathroom together. Such a thing brings females together."

Holly's lips twitched with the faintest of smiles. "I think I'm very lucky to have you in my life. I don't know how I would have managed these past few weeks without you."

"That's better. I guess I won't have to beat you up, after all." Maggie returned Holly's hug, then said, "It's come along fast for me, too. My friendships usually begin somewhere other than ladies' rooms, and they develop slowly over lunches and shopping trips. We bonded in the bathroom and never looked back. We skipped right over being casual friends and went straight to being close friends, don't you agree?"

Holly pursed her lips, her expression turning thoughtful. Then she shook her head. "No, Maggie, I don't agree. From my point of view, we've gone beyond close. I think we're already to the necklace wearing stage."

"Necklace wearing stage?"

"I learned this from my students. There is a shop in the mall where my girls buy necklaces for their best friends. The pendants come in different sizes, but are usually hearts. They are broken in two pieces. One half says 'Best' and the other says 'Friends.'"

"I love it. That's just the sort of thing I missed, having only boys. I adore girl stuff like that. Tell me, do any of them break into threes?"

"Yes, I believe they do."

"Then we need necklaces. You, me, and Grace. What do you say?"

"I think it's a great idea. Although Grace might not agree. Her Best Friend heart pendant is split with Ben."

Maggie dismissed the notion with a wave. "But he's a guy. Isn't it a girl thing? They don't let guys in on a ritual like this, do they?"

"Not ordinarily, no. But twelve- and thirteen-year-old girls are at different places than we are when it comes to building friendships. Up until last night, I'd have given the other half of my Best Friend pendant to Justin. Before your trouble with Mike, you'd have given it to him."

Maggie pursed her lips and pondered. "No, I don't believe I would have. I haven't considered Mike Prescott to be my best friend for years."

"Really?"

"Surprises you, doesn't it? Makes you think that's a clear sign of when my marriage started going wrong. Isn't that what greeting card philosophy implies, that your spouse is always supposed to be your best friend? Well, I don't think that's necessarily so. I have a different theory when it comes to combining friends and lovers. It's something I've been thinking about these last few weeks. I think it all goes back to biology."

Holly's brows arched. "What do you mean?"

"I think there are times in our lives when friends are more important to us than lovers and vice versa. Think about it. When we're girls the ages of your students, who is more important to us? Not those knucklehead boys we're learning to flirt with. Our best friends are other girls because they can give us what we need at that point in our lives: trust and loyalty and compassion. Intimacy."

"Don't forget fickleness and cruelty," Holly said with a snort. "Middle-school girls love teaching those lessons."

"Yes, and those lessons help us later on, don't they? Now, I admit it all starts to change when our biological clock begins running things. Mind you, I'm talking in generalities here. I know not every woman feels that particular tick. However, I think that for the majority of women, when you strip away the veneer of civilization all the way down to the animal, the need to procreate is about as strong an instinct as we have. At that point, advances in medical science aside, we need a man to give us what we want."

"So it's good-bye girlfriends and hello honey?"

Maggie shrugged. "Isn't that the way it usually happens? Men are jealous souls and they don't like to share. More often than not, friendships suffer when a lover comes into the picture. But that's okay with us because at that point in our lives, we need our lovers more than we need our friends. So, is it any surprise that lovers become best friends?"

"Wait a minute." Holly waved away a fly that buzzed around her ankles. "I don't agree. You're making it sound like a friendship between a man and a woman is a second-class friendship. Also, women are just as jealous when it comes to their lover's friends. Need I say anything more than 'poker night'?"

"You're right. I'm not making myself clear. I'm not saying a lover's friendship is second class, I'm saying it's different. Sex makes it different, and in my opinion, not necessarily more intimate. But it's the friendship a woman needs while she's having her babies and making a home for them. You see, as long as a woman has young children, she is dependent on a man. She needs him for emotional and financial support. She needs him for—"

"Maggie!" Holly protested. "Have you checked the calendar lately? This is not 1950. Women have come a long way. We can support ourselves, thankyouverymuch. The last statistics I saw said there are more single mothers raising children in America today than married moms. That's reality."

"That's *hard* reality, Holly. Very hard reality. Raising my boys was the hardest job I ever had, the toughest one I can imagine. The most rewarding job I will ever have. Through it all, I shared the ups and downs of it with the one person who understood, my children's father. He didn't interfere with the job I was doing, but he supported me in it. Mike was the perfect best friend for me during those years. He cared. He was who I needed."

Maggie paused and cleared her throat. "I was who he needed, too. Mike was raised by old-fashioned parents in an old-fashioned family in an old-fashioned town. He needed to be the breadwinner. He needed to be the head of the household. Proud, stubborn, arrogant. He needed to be the boss and I let him. That's what he'd been taught. That's what made him Mike Prescott."

"So what happened?" Holly asked as the clang of a dinner bell drifted toward the corral.

Maggie pushed off the fence and gestured for Holly to follow her. Their shoes flattened ankle-high green grass as they forged a path toward the back of the house. "The boys grew up, grew independent. The dynamics of our family changed. They stood up to him, challenged him. Competed with him. Learned from him. Turned to him. Some days the testosterone in our house was so thick I worried I'd grow a beard. Mike loved it. I didn't. I felt left out and Mike had new friends. I wished my boys had all been born girls."

"You didn't really."

"No, I didn't really." Maggie drew a deep breath, then sighed heavily. "At the same time, I knew this was nature's way, the way God planned it. My kids loved me. Mike loved me. I shouldn't complain, but I did. I complained to Mary Nell Taylor, a woman my age who had her nails done the same time as me. Mary Nell complained to me about the way her mother kept telling her she was raising her kids wrong. We bonded. Grew to be best of friends. We told each other our true weight."

"Wow. Y'all *were* good friends."

Maggie nodded, then increased her pace to intercept Grace, who carried a big bowl of potato salad toward the yellow and white gingham tablecloth spread over the redwood picnic table. "A few months later, Mike and I were at a party and someone asked me who my best friend was," she continued. "She expected me to give the old Hallmark card reply: my dear husband, my best friend. Instead, I told the truth and said Mary Nell

Taylor. I'll never forget the scandalized look on that woman's face."

Holly detoured to the kitchen, then returned with a basket of rolls in one hand, a plate of chicken in the other. Sadie followed carrying the bowl of slaw. Holly picked up her conversation with Maggie where it had left off. "What was Mike's response?"

"He said he was surprised because he'd expected me to name our next-door neighbor. She and I walked every morning, but we were only social friends. It never occurred to Mike that I would have mentioned him."

Holly kicked at a clump of Johnsongrass. "Justin used to tell me I was his best friend."

"It's life stages, sugar. It's not that I loved Mike any less or that he quit loving me. Not then, anyway. Do you understand? It's a normal progression of a relationship. And as much as we love the men in our lives, it's my opinion that except during those years when a woman needs a man for the sake of her children, she'll benefit more from friendships with other women than friendships with men, be they sexual or platonic—if such a thing exists, which is a whole other issue. In general, for women, women make better friends than men."

"I just don't believe that."

"I do," Sadie said. "I read in *Good Housekeeping* that men usually name a woman—their wife, lover, sister—as their best friend. Maybe women are just better at friendship skills of listening, sharing. Men are taught by society to compete, not cooperate."

"That's a good point," Maggie observed.

Grace took a seat at the picnic table. "Ben is my soul mate, and I would be lost without him. I do consider him to be my dearest friend. But as much as I adore him and rely on him and confide in him, I need distance from him, too. Especially at this particular time in my life. Some things—my fear, my pain, my grief—I try to filter because when I open up, I double his burden."

"You shouldn't have to filter," Holly protested. "If the men in our lives love us, truly deeply love us, they should be the ports in our storms."

"Think it through, honey. Cancer is not my storm alone. Cancer is a storm for my family, and Ben is just as swept up in it as me. I am his port. I want to be his port. I want to shelter him and our children as best I can because I love them."

Maggie eyed Grace across a chicken leg. "But you still need someone to talk with when you're feeling low, right?"

"That's right. I'm not good in a support group. I need support, but I don't have it to offer in return because I use mine up dealing with my family. That's where a close woman friend or two," she added with a smile, "comes in. I need a girlfriend who will listen to my deepest fears and emotions and still have the objectivity to help me decide which icing to choose for my wedding anniversary cake."

"But why does this friend need to be a girlfriend?" Holly passed the potato salad to Sadie. "Why does gender enter into the question at all? I mean, I understand needing a friend in addition to a spouse. I understand the need to shelter your loved ones from pain. Plus, everybody needs somebody to complain to when a spouse does something stupid. But does that somebody necessarily need to be female? Guys can be just as supportive as girls, just as sensitive."

Maggie and Grace and even Sadie shot her skeptical looks.

"They can." Holly squared her shoulders and lifted her chin. "Justin could. He is. The man took me to the Making Memories wedding gown sale in memory of my mother. What could be more sensitive than that?"

Maggie licked her lips, then wiped them with her napkin. "Considering what happened, an argument could be made that it was a terribly insensitive act."

"She has a point, Maggie," Grace said. "Maybe it's something generational. Maybe people in her age group can be best friends with members of the opposite sex. What do you think, Sadie?"

"Maybe, but I've never seen it."

Maggie shot Holly a significant look. "You see, Holly, when it comes to friendship between men and women, sooner or later, sex gets in the way. I saw it in the movies. Cute show, remember? Billy Crystal says it to Meg Ryan."

Holly rolled her eyes, then stirred lemon into her tea. She waved her spoon in the air, punctuating her words as she declared, "That's not always true. I've had a number of guy friends I've never had sex with."

"But you *have* had guy friends whom you *did* have sex with, right? That's what proves my case. I've never had sex with my girlfriends."

"How reassuring," Grace said dryly.

Maggie laughed and used her spoon to swipe a glob of potato salad off Holly's plate. She popped it into her mouth, shut her eyes, and moaned with delight. "Sinful, Sadie. Simply sinful."

She licked the last vestiges of potato salad from the spoon. "Speaking of which, there was this gal who made a pass at me at a party once, although I didn't recognize that's what she was doing at the time. Mike had to explain it to me later." She paused, thinking back. A grin touched her lips. "He didn't know whether to be appalled or aroused."

"Puh-lease." A grin flitted at the edges of Holly's lips as she finished her chicken.

"Look at that smile," Grace observed. "That's what I like to see. Holly dear, you've been altogether too gloomy today."

"I agree." Maggie reached across the table and took Holly's hand. "Listen, sugar. As much as it pains me to admit it, I don't have all the answers. You may be right about the man/woman/friends thing. Maybe if I'd been a better friend to Mike he wouldn't have replaced me with a depth chart and a dinghy. Then again, maybe it was inevitable. I don't know. About the only thing I am certain of right now is that I'm awfully grateful that you and Grace have come into my life. If not for y'all, I'd probably be home in bed right now wallowing in self-pity, and that would be a crying shame. It's a beautiful day and there are puppies in the yard and another leg of Aunt Sadie's fried chicken on the plate for the savoring. It makes me happy inside. *Happy*. I haven't felt happy in months and months. Y'all have done that for me."

A wave of emotion rose inside Holly. She felt the pressure of tears build behind her eyes. Blinking rapidly, a tremulous smile hovering on her lips, she shrugged and said, "What are friends for?"

Then she leaned across the table, pressed a kiss against Maggie's cheek, and added, "Thank you."

Maggie flashed a grin, then quickly schooled it into a scowl. "Oh, spit. Was that a pass?"

"No, Maggie." Holly made a show of sighing and rolling her eyes. "I didn't use my tongue."

"All right," Grace said. "That's enough. Y'all are making Sadie and me uncomfortable."

"I'm not uncomfortable," Aunt Sadie piped up. "I've learned a lot about lesbians since I got Internet access here at the farm. Why, have you seen those pictures where—"

Maggie's chin dropped. "Aunt Sadie!"

She chuckled and eyed Grace and Holly. "Girl always has been gullible."

Maggie wrinkled her nose at her husband's aunt, then turned to Grace and changed the subject. "Did you decide on the cake?"

"Yes. I've never tasted a more delicious cake in my life."

"Me either. I've been to a dozen weddings in the past year and tasted cakes called things like White Chocolate Champagne, and Turtle Fudge, and Kahlúa Creme. Not a one of them melted in your mouth like Aunt Sadie's."

Holly asked, "What icing did you choose?"

Grace and Sadie shared a look. "That's still up in the air."

"If it were me, I'd choose the vanilla," Holly said. "That's the best vanilla icing I've ever tasted and I think it is the perfect complement to the flavor of the cake."

Maggie tugged a pencil and paper scrap from her pocket and made a note. Her tone casual, she asked, "What type of decoration do you prefer, Holly? Sugar flowers? Fresh flowers? A traditional bride and groom topper?"

The pain struck from out of nowhere. Subdued, Holly said, "I'm not getting married."

"I'm just talking hypothetically here. Personally I favor the traditional topper."

The words tumbled from Holly's mouth. "About a year ago I stopped in a little gift shop in the hospital district. They had a ceramic bride and groom, her in her wedding gown, him in his surgical scrubs. They also had one with the groom in a tux and the bride in scrubs."

Then she gave her head a shake. "Well, I don't guess it much matters what I'd put on top of a cake. Grace is the one who needs to make these decisions. What do you want, Grace?"

Pursing her lips, Grace stared at the table for a long moment in thought. "Peach cake, vanilla icing. Styled like the cake Sadie did for the Hallford wedding, with fresh flowers for a topper. Or maybe one flower. A perfect magnolia blossom."

"I adore magnolias," Holly said.

Having made her choice, Grace sat back in her chair, a self-satisfied smile on her face. Maggie lifted her chin regally and said, "My work here is done."

"That's handy timing because a truck just pulled into the drive." With studied casualness, Sadie added, "Did I mention that Mike was coming for lunch?"

Holly watched the color drain from Maggie's face. "Does he know I'm here?"

"I didn't tell him," Sadie assured her.

"He'll see my car. Maybe he'll just leave."

The sound of a diesel engine rumbled louder, joining with the crunch of gravel as a black Ford F350 rolled up beside the farmhouse. It came to a stop behind Maggie's Lexus. Her gaze on Maggie, Holly held her breath until abruptly, the engine died.

"Spit," Maggie muttered. She sent a panicked look toward Sadie. "I can't talk to him."

"It's time, Maggie," Grace said. "It's past time you talked to him."

Sadie added, "Privately. From what I understand, the two of you have not exchanged a word in private since he moved out."

"He told you that?"

"He alluded to it. Is it true?" When Maggie nodded, she clucked her tongue. "You get up right now and go meet him. Y'all talk on the front porch. Your friends and I need to get this food put away."

"But I don't . . . he won't . . ."

Sadie folded her arms and frowned sternly. "Margaret Ellen Prescott, you do as I say."

"Oh, all right." Maggie rose from the picnic table and dragged herself toward the house like a recalcitrant child. The screen door banged behind her just as Mike rounded the side of the house, walking toward them.

He stuck his hands into the back pockets of his jeans. "I didn't realize you'd invited other guests for dinner, Aunt Sadie. I wish you'd said something when you called."

"Don't be rude, Michael," his aunt snapped. "Say hello to Maggie's friends. I believe you've met Grace Hardeman and Holly Weeks?"

"We've not been formally introduced," Grace said with a smile.

Holly didn't smile. She refused to smile or offer her hand or do more than scowl at the man. Despite his aunt's admonitions, he appeared content to scowl right back at her. Sadie rolled her eyes and sighed. "Maggie's waiting on the front porch so the two of you can talk."

"I didn't come out here to talk with her. I came for fried chicken and chores."

"The chores will keep and so will the chicken. Now scat."

Mike Prescott did as he was told with almost as much enthusiasm as his wife, Holly thought.

Sadie lifted the platter of chicken, then motioned for Grace and Holly to follow as she hurried toward the house. "Come along up to the guest bedroom. It's the best place to eavesdrop on a conversation taking place on the porch. Acoustics are perfect. Something about the slope of the roof, my late husband used to say."

As she led them up the oak staircase to a bright room off the hallway, Grace glanced at Holly. "I don't think we should do this."

"Shush," Sadie said. Standing by the window, she made a two-fingered, come-along motion. Holly didn't hesitate. Grace and Maggie had become her friends after hearing her and Justin dust it up in the ladies' room. She knew without a doubt Maggie would listen in if the situation were reversed. Not that there seemed to be much to listen to. Downstairs, neither Mike nor Maggie were doing much talking.

Mike's voice sounded strained when he finally spoke. "Chase called yesterday. He made an A on that calculus test he was sweating."

"Yes, he called me, too. I'm thrilled for him. He studied so hard for that."

"Yeah."

Silence fell, stretched like a rubber band until Maggie said, "I talked to Lane, too. The company is sending him to Germany next month."

"Hmm . . ."

"I haven't talked to John or Steven," Maggie continued, hurt edging her voice.

Upstairs, Holly leaned toward the window. Maggie had mentioned that two of her sons remained fiercely angry with her over the split with Mike. The breach between them wounded her deeply.

"They're both fine. I'll . . . um . . . I'll be seeing them next week. They're meeting me in Galveston to see me off."

Holly couldn't see Maggie's reaction, couldn't hear it, but she sensed it. A fiery stab to the heart that stole her breath and weakened her knees. Grace must have sensed it, too, because she murmured, "Oh, Maggie."

Sadie shook her head. "That boy. I want to box his ears."

Maggie's voice trembled slightly as she asked, "When are you leaving?"

"I'm flying out to visit Lane tomorrow. I'll be gone a week." Mike expelled a heavy breath. "When I get back, I'm sending the *Second Wind* to the coast. I'll be leaving Fort Worth ten days from now."

Following an awkward silence, Mike added, "I was going to call you. Let you know."

Maggie's words dripped sugar. "How kind."

"Yeah," he snapped back. "I think so."

Upstairs, Grace shot Holly a significant look. "It's time."

Downstairs, the conversation died again, the quiet filled only by the chatter of a pair of mockingbirds perched on the eave. Finally, Maggie said brightly, "Well. My friends and I were getting ready to leave when you drove up, so we'd best get moving. I'll go tell them . . ."

As the screen door squeaked, Holly looked at Grace. "Let's get her out of here before she starts crying. She's not going to want him to see that."

Holly bounded downstairs, reaching the bottom as Maggie sailed into the house and headed for the kitchen. "I think we're about done here, don't you, Holly? Grace seems certain of her decision. Are she and Sadie out back?"

"Here I am." Grace's smile was both tender and concerned as she entered the kitchen. "Sadie stepped out to the porch."

Maggie nodded, her teeth tugging at her lower lip. "We're all decided on the cake, aren't we? We can leave? I don't want Holly to be late for her driving date with her dad, and of course, I must get ready for my date. Did I tell you we canceled rock climbing in favor of the symphony? I told you he's not a stereotypical pool man."

"I'm ready whenever your are, honey."

"If only I'd been ready twenty minutes ago," Maggie grumbled, tossing a brittle grin over her shoulder as she gathered her notebook from the kitchen table.

Compassion melted through Holly. She touched Maggie's arm. "Want me to go beat him up for you?"

"You sound like my boys," Maggie said with a laugh that quickly developed a hitch.

Seeing her friend's eyes go glassy with tears, Holly made quick work of handing Grace her purse and gathering her own backpack, then leading the way toward the front door. Sadie stood with Maggie's husband on the porch. Holly barely refrained from sticking her tongue out at Mike Prescott before turning to Sadie with genuine pleasure. She offered her thanks for a lovely morning, then stepped aside while Grace and Maggie said their good-byes. Mike, she noted, had walked to the far end of the porch, where he stood with his hands shoved into his pockets, gazing out toward the peach orchard.

Holly couldn't help herself. With lizard-like speed, she stuck out her tongue. Grace, sweetheart that she was, caught her at it, darted a glance around, then mimicked the action.

In a show of support, they flanked Maggie for the trip across the yard toward the car. Halfway there, Maggie surprised them both by halting abruptly. She pivoted, lifted her chin, and marched boldly back to the porch. Standing at the base of the weathered white steps, sunlight glinting off her golden hair, she propped one hand on her hip and looked up at her husband. "Mike? Would you answer one question for me before you leave town?"

He turned around. "I told you, Maggie. Cindy is only a friend. I'm not sleeping with her."

"That's not what I want to know. Well, I do want to know that, but it's not the question I intended to ask. I want to know, Mike, when did we stop being friends?"

He hesitated for only a moment. "July 8, 1996."

Maggie shook her head, her brow furrowed, her confusion evident. The sound of her husband's voice cut across the yard like a sharp, hot knife. "Chicago. The Raycom Industries national meeting. I gave the keynote. My first big public speech. I wanted you there with me, but you wouldn't come."

"I remember now. Steven had a track meet. The state championship."

"You thought it was more important to be with him than with me. I resented it and that made me feel about half an inch tall. What kind of a father resents his own son?"

"I didn't realize." Maggie clasped her hands in front of her, her eyes round and glassy with distress.

Holly glanced at Grace, angled her head toward the

car. She'd passed her comfort level of eavesdropping and she thought it time to give Mike and Maggie their privacy.

Grace, however, appeared rooted to her spot.

"You didn't say anything," Maggie continued. "Why didn't you tell me? I could have—"

"What?" Mike braced his hands on his hips, his narrow-eyed stare never leaving Maggie. "Disappointed our son by not being with him during what was then the biggest accomplishment of his life? I wanted you at that track meet, too. I wanted to be there. Did you ever stop to think how I felt when y'all called to tell me that his relay team won? That my son was state champ and I didn't get to see it because I was in Chicago busting my ass to make the money that paid for the damned shoes he wore to run in? Y'all were laughing and carrying on. So excited. Not a one of you said you wished I'd been there."

"But we did miss you, Mike."

"No, Maggie. You didn't. Not really. Because you were accustomed to my not being there. I seldom got to go to the track meets and the baseball games and the band contests. I had to work. Back then, I had a mortgage to pay. Car payments to make. Two thousand dollar trumpets to buy. Remember? We didn't always have money. By the time my machine patent paid off and I was able to meet our financial obligations without working sixty hour weeks, the boys were damn near grown. They wanted to do things with their friends, not their dad. Little League days were over. It pisses me off every time I think about it."

His eyes blazed blue fire. "My boys grew up, too, you know, Maggie. You're not the only one who's lost something. At least you got to enjoy having children around when we had them. I missed out on the biggest chunk of it. So next time you want to loll around in bed feeling sorry for yourself, you think about that."

She took two steps backward as if reeling from a blow. Wrapping her arms around her waist, she breathed, "I didn't know . . . you never told me." A cry caught in her voice as she added, "I thought you were happy doing what you wanted to do. Building yourself a career."

Mike's face contracted with anguish. He raked his finger through his hair, then rubbed the back of his neck. When he spoke again, the anger had disappeared from his voice. Weariness replaced it. "I wasn't unhappy. I liked my job. I was proud to provide for my family. It's just that sometimes . . . well . . . I was jealous of you. I felt left out. You were closer to the boys than I was. As long as you were at the state track meet and the ball games and recitals, everything was right with the world. And that's the way it should have been. You always were a damned good mother."

"But not so good a wife?" Maggie looked away from her husband, blinking away tears. "If I'd realized how you felt, I'd have come to Chicago, Mike."

"I know." The smile that briefly touched his mouth was the saddest thing Holly had ever seen. "But if I'd had to ask, then it wouldn't have meant as much to have you there."

"But—"

"Maggie, it's the same argument we used to have about me sending you flowers. You want them, but if you have to ask for them, they don't mean much. No, it was better all around that you attended the track meet."

"Better that I lost your friendship?" she asked, a shrill note to her voice. "Better that I lost your love?"

He sighed. "I loved you, Maggie. That didn't stop. I just couldn't count on you to be there for me. I couldn't count on you to be my friend, so I quit wanting to be yours. I quit caring as much."

Maggie swayed and Holly stepped closer, ready to offer her a hand should she need it. She looked as pale as Sadie's vanilla icing, and Holly halfway expected her to drop in a graceful Southern faint.

But Maggie showed the steel in her magnolia by keeping her spine straight, her chin up, and the quaver out of her voice as she said, "I'm sorry, Mike. Have a safe trip and enjoy your time with Steven and John."

She paused, looked him straight in the eyes, and spoke with sincerity as she added, "I hope you find what you are looking for out there."

The three women made the return drive to Fort Worth primarily in silence. Surprisingly, it was a soothing silence, the kind that comforted rather than disturbed. Halfway home, Maggie asked if they'd like to listen to music, and Grace selected a James Taylor CD. "My oldest boy gave me this album years ago. Of course, it wasn't an album. Albums were passé even then."

"Cassette tape?" Maggie asked.

"Eight-track."

Holly grinned. "Earlier this year the science teacher whose classroom is next to mine brought an eight-track player to show his students. You'd think it was dinosaur bones the way they reacted."

Soon the three of them were singing along to "Oh, Mexico" and "Walking Man." Holly could carry a tune, though she'd never been considered a good singer. Maggie's voice was throaty and sexy, but she couldn't hit a high note for beans.

Grace, on the other hand, sang like an angel. Hers was the kind of voice that seeped through a person's skin and sank into her bones. It was the kind of voice that filled a person's heart and touched her soul. It was the kind of voice that brought tears to Maggie's and Holly's eyes.

Especially when Grace crooned, "You've got a friend."

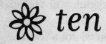 *ten*

*a*horn honked and *Holly glanced* first at her wall clock, then out the front window. The Gray Swan—with the top up, surprisingly enough—waited at her curb. She opened her front door and waved. "Be with you in a minute, Dad. I've got to find my shoes."

Holly grabbed her purse off the coffee table, then combed the house for her sneakers. She finally found them lodged behind the door in the dining room. Without stopping to put them on, she detoured through the kitchen to find her sunglasses, snatched up her keys, and headed out.

Holly looked forward to this afternoon with her dad. She could use a few light, playful hours following the trip out to Sadie Prescott's farm and last night's debacle at Justin's house.

Before she could guard against it, she wondered what the doctor was doing today. Was he working? Playing? Playing with Jenna Larson?

"Don't go there," Holly warned herself aloud as she locked her front door behind her.

The sidewalk felt warm beneath her bare feet, and the sensation suddenly brought to mind a long forgotten memory of a particular summer day. Holly had been about seven years old, maybe eight, and she was helping her mom put away groceries. Her dad was lying on his back on the kitchen floor, his head in the cabinet beneath the sink, a wrench in his hand. He wore a blue chambray shirt and faded blue jeans. He'd asked her mom something—Holly couldn't remember what—but she vividly recalled her mother's response: *It's hot enough to fry an egg on the driveway.*

At the time, Holly had been putting a carton of eggs into the fridge. What happened after that had been anything but pretty.

Laughing, Holly opened the passenger door. "Dad, do you remember that time—Justin?"

Holly backed up, checked the car. Yeah, it was her dad's car. Why was Justin driving the Gray Swan?

"Hi, Holly."

"Oh, God. Is something wrong with my dad?" He *never* let anyone else drive his car.

"Your dad is fine. I called him looking for you and he suggested I fill in as driver this afternoon."

Holly shook her head. She couldn't believe this. Justin. On a Saturday-Sunday drive. "No. This is our special time together. Dad wouldn't do that."

"I told him it was important. Please, come with me, Holly. Let me talk with you. I need to explain about last night."

Heaven help her, she wanted to know. She wanted to hear him say that Jenna meant nothing to him, that he didn't want two-point-three children who attended Montessori school. That he only wanted Holly, that he couldn't live without her, that he wanted to marry her and live happily ever after with her.

Jeeze Louise. Was she living in a fantasy world or what?

Nevertheless, Holly climbed into the car and shut the door.

They didn't speak as they drove through her neighborhood. Once on the highway, Justin headed west. "I thought we'd drive down toward Granbury, if that's all right with you. I heard you took a trip north toward Decatur earlier today. Somebody's farm?"

"Yes. A relative of Maggie Prescott. She's going to make the cake for Grace's golden anniversary party."

"That's nice. You've gotten chummy with those two lately, haven't you?"

"They're friends."

He nodded, drove in silence another few minutes, then said, "The range of ages between y'all makes for a rather unusual friendship, doesn't it? Don't get me wrong. I like Grace and Maggie very much. It's just sort of surprising to me that you'd befriend women twice and three times your age."

"You're adding extra years to both of them. No woman appreciates that." He also sounded almost . . . jealous. With the morning's discussion about friendship still fresh in her mind, Holly found herself encouraged by the notion. If Justin was jealous of her burgeoning friendship with Grace and Maggie, maybe having her for a friend still mattered to him. Maybe she hadn't lost her best friend, after all. He was here, wasn't he?

Because he was here, she made an effort to explain.

"I feel close to them. We have a strange sort of grandmother-mother-daughter thing going on, yet we're girlfriends, too. We have nothing in common and we're so much alike. They are interesting women, so much more so than women my age. Plus, they care about me. I know they truly care."

Justin glanced at her. "I care, too."

Sensing that this was his way of leading into the subject of the previous night, Holly waited rather than responding.

"I've never been a quitter. Whenever I've encountered roadblocks in my path, I've figured a way to go around them. But I've never encountered a roadblock quite like you before."

"How flattering," she said dryly.

"It's meant to be. I'm foundering here, Holly. I've never wanted anyone or anything as much as I want you."

"You have a strange way of showing it," she muttered, recalling the way Jenna had slipped her arm through Justin's the night before.

Justin shot her a quick scowl, then checked his rearview mirror, changed lanes, and took the next exit off the freeway. He pulled into a Wal-Mart parking lot, threw the car into park, and shut off the engine. "I'm angry that you'd quit on us."

"That's not fair."

"Fair? You have the nerve to talk to me about fair? Of all the—" He bit off his words and yanked open the car door. "Excuse me a minute."

He stalked around the car twice before climbing back inside. "I swore I wouldn't get mad. We never get anything settled because I get angry and end up storming off.

I'm not going to do that today. We're going to talk quietly and rationally and sensibly, like adults."

Holly stifled the urge to stick out her tongue.

"You threw me with your news about graduate school. Not that you'd want to go to graduate school, but that you'd leave Fort Worth to do it. That you'd leave me. Up until then, I figured we were simply going through a rough spot. I didn't . . . I don't want to accept that you could throw what we have away."

Me throw it away? Hah. She wasn't the one entertaining overnight-bag-bearing guests. With that thought uppermost in her mind, Holly couldn't stop her tongue. "So you threw it away instead? Is that what the date with Jenna was about?"

He had the grace to look abashed. "Maybe. I was hurt and reacting rather than acting. We both planned to attend the retirement party for a mutual friend, and when she asked me to escort her, I saw no reason to tell her no."

Of course he didn't. When did a man ever say no to sex?

"You hurt me, Holly. That afternoon at the Greystone just ripped my heart in two. After you turned me down and then wouldn't answer the phone, I was hurt and angry and frustrated and generally pissed off at the world. So when you came by my house and saw Jenna, I let you think it was something other than what it was. I wasn't going to sleep with her, Holly. Even before you showed up."

Yeah, right. Women always carry an overnight bag on their dates just in case they get lucky. Kinda like a man with a condom in his wallet.

"It offends me that you think I would."

He'd crossed the believability line with that one. She shot him a skeptical look.

"I'm not eighteen anymore," he said, offense ringing in his tone. "I don't want to nail every female that comes near."

Hah. She had him there. He'd tried to get her into bed from the first time they met. Holly folded her arms and turned her head away, staring out the window toward the outdoor lawn furniture on display in front of the store. Justin muttered a curse, got out of the car, and marched around it twice more.

"I offered her a bed—the guest bed—because she had an early flight out of D/FW this morning. Her new apartment is in Plano. It would have been silly for her to drive from my house, past the airport all the way to Plano, then back again."

Holly lifted her chin. "It's none of my business. We've broken up. You have the right to see anyone you want to see."

Justin grabbed the steering wheel in both hands, then banged his head on it as a truck pulled up beside them. A barrel-chested, beer-bellied man got out, shot a curious look their way, then barked out a command. "Stay, George. Keep an eye on things."

George proved to be an old, overweight boxer dog who hung his head out the driver's-side window and fastened his gaze on Holly, long strings of slobber dribbling from his mouth.

"Dammit, Holly. I love you."

A Wal-Mart parking lot. A drooling dog. The romance of the moment was beyond compare.

"I'm not quitting on this relationship. I won't quit."

In the truck, George started barking, loudly. He added

a couple of howls for good measure. Holly looked Justin straight in the eyes. "You don't have a choice. I'm moving away."

"Then I'll find a way to work around that. The only way you'll get me to quit on us, Holly, is if you give me a reason to believe I can't fix whatever's wrong. Of course, for you to do that, you'll need to tell me what's wrong."

Jeeze Louise, the man is stubborn. "Justin, we've gone over and over this."

"No, we haven't. You've never given me a straight answer."

This time, Holly got out and marched around the car, careful not to step too close to the pickup and barking, slobbering George.

On the first circuit, she stared down at her feet as she walked. On the second, she lifted her gaze and it was then, as she made the turn around the back of the car, that she spied the figure crumpled on the asphalt a dozen paces toward the store. George's owner. "Justin," she cried, rushing toward the fallen man. "Come quick. He's hurt."

He lay on his left side. His right hand clutched his chest. Holly knelt beside him. A heart attack, she guessed. She wondered if he carried nitroglycerine tablets. "Sir? Do you have medication I can give you? Nitroglycerine?"

"No," he panted. "George."

"We'll take care of him," Holly promised as Justin ran toward them, speaking into his cell phone.

"Paramedics are on the way."

As Justin arrived, the man slipped into unconsciousness. Justin immediately grabbed a box from the bed of a nearby truck and used it to elevate the patient's legs. With Holly's assistance, Justin started CPR.

The ambulance arrived quickly and within minutes departed with the patient. The small crowd that had congregated around them while they performed CPR dispersed, leaving Justin and Holly alone with the Gray Swan, a red Ford pickup, and George.

Holly leaned against the passenger door of her father's car, gazing at the anxious dog in dismay. Upon learning the patient's name and address from the driver's license in his wallet, Holly had tracked down his phone number and tried to reach his family. But no one answered and the message on the machine—"Hey, this is Ray. Leave a message." —didn't offer much hope that someone would be waiting at the suburban address to care for ol' George.

Instinctively, she turned to Justin. "What are we going to do?"

"The city animal shelter will take him. You can call back and leave the message on the machine. I'm sure he has family or friends who will check on things once they learn what's happened."

Holly was horrified at the thought of a beloved pet, accustomed to his home and owner, confused and alone in a cage. "No. We can't. I promised I'd take care of him."

Justin frowned and spoke in a familiar disapproving, stuffy tone. "You're not going to take him home."

Holly looked at the puddle on the parking lot beneath the truck's window. "No. I can't. I have to. Oh, no."

She closed her eyes. "But not in the Gray Swan. Dad would kill you."

"Me? Why would he kill me? You're the one wanting to rescue the dog."

"But you're the one he gave his keys to."

Justin winced. "You're not taking that dog home in this car."

"I know. I just said that. What we need to do is find someone who will . . . Maggie!"

Justin arched a brow.

"She doesn't live too far from here. Let me borrow your phone, Justin." Holly dialed the number, then said, "Maggie? I need your help."

Twenty minutes later, as Maggie whipped into the Wal-Mart parking lot driving her Lexus, Justin looked at Holly aghast. "This is a better solution? That's a sixty-five-thousand-dollar car, Holly. Better we had hot-wired the truck."

Justin made a soft, choking sound as Maggie climbed from the car. One glance at her friend told Holly why. She wore a bathrobe, furry pink slippers, and she had hot rollers in her hair. "My God, Maggie. What is on your face?"

"Mud mask. I've got a date tonight, remember? Now, I don't have much time. Where's that poor baby? Where's that sweet puppy George?" She spied him, knelt down in front of him, and cooed, "Oh, look at you. Aren't you a pretty pretty boy."

George took a long lap at her mud mask.

"No, no, no," Maggie said, giggling. "You ornery boxer boy." To Holly, she said, "I put a sheet down in the backseat. Help me get him loaded?"

George climbed into the backseat of the Lexus, made a circle around the buttery leather upholstery, then promptly jumped over the front seat to ride shotgun. Recognizing a lost cause, Holly sat in back. Waving at an unhappy Justin, she called, "Tell Dad I'll see him tomorrow."

Halfway to Maggie's house, she realized she'd successfully dodged Justin's question again. She wondered how many more reprieves she'd get. Reaching forward, she petted George's head. "Good dog."

Then George let loose with a particularly foul-smelling fart.

"Oh, you bad boy," Maggie moaned, hitting the electric window buttons. "Now I'll have to take another bath."

Her date was due to arrive in an hour.

Maggie suspected in an hour she'd be borderline certifiable.

"Why in heaven's name did I ever think this was a good idea?" she wailed as she stood in front of her lingerie chest, flinging a rainbow of panties and bras, slips and camisoles over her shoulder. Somewhere in one of the chest's eight drawers was a pair of pantyhose that did not have a run in them. Had to be.

"I'm certain I don't know," Holly drawled from her seat in one of the pair of wingback chairs that sat in front of the master bedroom fireplace. George sprawled in the other. "I've said this was a bad idea all along."

"I disagree," Grace observed. She reclined in Maggie's reading chair, a chaise lounge set in the bow window opposite the fireplace. With a cup of tea in her lap and an afghan draped across her legs, she'd been happy as a clam since Ben dropped her off in response to Maggie's request half an hour ago. "Maggie needs to do this right now. A bit of gentlemanly attention will help repair the damage done by seeing her husband with another woman."

"That's right," Maggie reminded herself. "If he's gonna date, I'm gonna date."

She needed the moral support. She needed the feminine advice. She couldn't make up her mind about what dress to wear, what shoes, what jewelry. The big question was her wedding ring. It didn't feel right to go out with another man while Mike's ring was on her finger, but she couldn't very well take it off. She and Mike were separated, not divorced. The ring belonged on her finger until the day her marriage officially ended. Then and only then would it be proper to take it off.

"What do people do with their rings from failed marriages?" she asked as she discovered a run in yet another pair of hose.

Holly shrugged. "I'll bet men throw their rings into their underwear drawer and never think of them again."

Grace sipped her tea. "I think it depends on a person's level of sentimentality. For some people, a diamond is a diamond is a diamond. They have no qualms about having stones reset in another piece of jewelry. For others, a wedding ring is a symbol of broken promises, and they're the ones who throw their rings off a bridge. I expect Holly is right where most people are concerned. I imagine most people tuck their rings away to collect dust in a jewelry box or drawer or bank vault."

"Half of all marriages end in divorce these days," Maggie mused. She discovered an unopened package of black pantyhose deep in the recesses of her slip drawer and held it aloft triumphantly. "Think of all those rocks lying around unused. It's a shame."

"What is a shame is the fact that George is drooling on your furniture. Do you have a bigger towel to lay across your chair, Maggie? You're going to regret it if your chair is ruined because you wouldn't put him outside."

"He's in a strange place and he's had a difficult day, seeing his master carried off in an ambulance. He needs company so he doesn't get depressed." Maggie brought out a bath sheet and rearranged George. "When was the last time you called the hospital, Holly?"

"Ten minutes ago while you were lost in the depths of your closet. I spoke with Mr. Hargrove's wife. He's still in intensive care but the doctors are cautiously optimistic. Her brother expects to be by here to collect George in half an hour. Twenty minutes, now."

Maggie glanced at the clock. "Oh, my. Look at the time."

She sat on the edge of her bed and ripped open the package of pantyhose. "Okay, I must make a final decision. Which dress?"

"The black one," Holly said.

"Gee, thanks. They're all black."

"Glad to help."

Grace said, "Actually, I'd like to see you in that red number you pulled out of your closet first. It has a certain flair."

"It's a slut dress." Holly shook her head. "Not appropriate for the symphony."

"Hmm . . . " Maggie tapped a hot red fingernail against her lip. "I would stand out in the crowd."

Holly gave an exasperated sigh. "It's a dress made to stand out on a street corner. You can't wear it, Maggie. Your date will take it as an invitation."

"Invitation?"

"For sex."

"No." Maggie's eyes rounded. "On the first date?"

"Surely not," Grace added.

Holly nodded sagely. "Trust me on this one, ladies. Maggie, you'd look like a million dollars in that red dress, but unless you want to personally check out the pool man's hose, you'd better stick to basic black."

Wow. Things had certainly changed since the last time she went through this process. Back then, boys were lucky to get a kiss at the end of the evening; forget anything more. Of course, back then she wore sweaters, high-rise pants, and penny loafers rather than a siren red dress.

Come to think of it, she had looked pretty good in those sweaters. Also, she did remember one instance where she'd let her date get past first base on the first date.

But she wasn't going out with Mike Prescott tonight.

"All right. I'll wear something else. But you pick it out for me, Holly. I can't choose." Maggie slipped off her robe and began the arduous process of pulling on her pantyhose. She wiggled, tugged, hopped, stretched, and bent. Red-faced, she finally settled the waistband into place.

"If a man were here right now, he'd consider that performance foreplay," Holly said, choosing two black dresses from the pile of seven. She held them up to Grace, who pointed at the one on the right.

"I keep expecting Jane Fonda to come out with an exercise tape: *Aerobic Pantyhose Dancing.*" Maggie accepted the dress from Holly and quickly slipped it on. After frowning at her image in the mirror, she turned gracefully before her friends.

"You look stunning," Grace told her with a smile.

"Not scared? I am scared. I'm frightened to death." Turning back to the cheval mirror, she twitched at her neckline and fluffed her hair. "What am I doing? I haven't been on a date in more than a quarter century. How am I supposed to act? What do I talk about? What do I do if he tries to kiss me?"

"You do whatever feels right, honey," Grace said. "Although I will add my caution to Holly's. Remember you are in charge."

"Sugar, I'm always in charge."

It was pure bravado, but it served Maggie well. She'd just slipped into her evening shoes when the doorbell rang. Her gaze flew to the clock. "He's early."

"Not too late to change your mind," Holly said.

"I'm not changing my mind." She glanced one more time into the mirror. "Maybe my dress, but not my mind."

Holly laughed. "You look gorgeous. C'mon, Grace. Let's get into position. Was it upstairs, third door on the right, Maggie?"

"The second door. That's the best place in the house for acoustics, then the balcony will give you a good view of the street."

"Aren't you afraid he'll see us?"

"If he's looking up at the balcony instead of me, then I don't want to go out with him after all."

The doorbell rang a second time as Maggie crossed the great room.

"Have fun," Grace called from upstairs. "We'll lock up when we leave."

"Make him keep his hands to himself," Holly added.

"I cannot believe I'm actually doing this," Maggie muttered. She pasted on a smile, then opened the door.

The man at the threshold wasn't Max. He was a stranger. A drop-dead gorgeous stranger, a cross between Harrison Ford and Mel Gibson. When he smiled, Maggie almost swallowed her tongue.

"I'm Jake Kendall. I'm here about a dog?"

"George."

"Yeah. Ol' Smelly himself."

"Come in, Mr. Kendall." She offered her hand. "I'm Maggie Prescott. George is such a sweetheart. Slobbery, but a sweetheart."

Ten minutes later, George and Jake had left the building, but not before Jake made a date with Maggie to walk the sweet, smelly thing Sunday afternoon.

"Jeeze Louise," Holly called from the top of the stairs. "Watch close, Grace. You're seeing a femme fatale in the making."

Grace smiled. "Actually, that's the standard Southern belle ringing."

"Oh, hush," Maggie said with false annoyance. Inside, she was giggling like a schoolgirl. When she opened the door to Max a short time later, Maggie's smile was genuine.

She had a lovely time on her date. The symphony was excellent as always and Max's company entertaining. They talked politics and literature, college football and laundry detergent preferences. At her front door at the end of the evening, he correctly read the panic in her eyes, thanked her for a lovely time, then gave her a friendly kiss on the cheek.

She floated inside. It was by far the most enjoyable evening she'd had in months. But when she shut the door behind her, kicked off her shoes, and set down her purse, the truth hit her like a fist.

Maggie was still alone.

Holly stood at Grace's kitchen sink filling a glass with tap water. The rich, full-bodied sound of Ben Hardeman's laughter drifted from the living room, nearly drowning out Grace's feminine chuckles, and Holly smiled at the sound.

She'd done a lot of that this week. Smiling. It had been a good week. Although Holly hadn't seen Justin, she'd talked with him on the phone every night. They avoided the touchy subjects like the two Ms—marriage and moving—choosing to center their conversations around his work and her students instead. The banter between them was almost as comfortable as it used to be, before the Making Memories wedding gown sale. She'd told him about being named Teacher of the Year and he'd sent her congratulatory flowers at school.

Classes this week had gone well, too. Her kids had scored high on one of the harder tests of the year. She'd had dinner with her dad one night and attended a neighborhood Crime Watch barbeque on another. Wednesday afternoon she'd accompanied Maggie to a florist where they ordered flowers for Grace's church for the renewal of vows. Plans for the big event were just about done—a good thing, in Holly's opinion, since Maggie's social life was taking up so much of her time now.

The woman had four dates this week. Four dates with four different men. Nice men, too. Not a one of them a loser. Holly didn't know how she did it. She had girl-friends in their twenties—attractive, outgoing, intelligent women—who couldn't get dates. Maggie decided to date for the first time in years and she immediately had men falling at her feet. It boggled the mind.

At least her reason for missing tonight's anniversary portrait sitting was a good one. Maggie's boys had called her this afternoon wanting to take her to dinner. Considering the tension between them of late, she'd been delighted. Holly hoped Maggie and her sons could smooth things over this evening because the rift with her boys troubled Maggie as much, if not more, than her estrangement from Mike. She'd said as much when she'd called Holly and asked if she'd fill in as photographer's helper at the Hardemans' tonight.

The portrait was something extra Maggie had arranged and she was specific about the shots she wanted: individual portraits, couple portraits, family portraits, father–sons, and mother–daughter. Holly needed to make certain the photographer covered the list, but primarily, her job was to soothe Grace's endless fretting about how much the photographs were costing Making Memories.

A noise behind her caused Holly to glance over her shoulder. The Hardemans' daughter Sally entered the kitchen. "How's it going in there?"

"Great. The photographer is wonderful. He set Mother right at ease. Not a mean feat, when it comes to having her picture taken."

"She doesn't like cameras?"

"She loves cameras, as long as she's the one behind the shutter. My mother is the snapshot queen; she has dozens and dozens of albums filled with pictures. The problem for us is that Mom's in only a few of them."

"Really?" Holly snapped her fingers. "We need to add single-use cameras to our list for guests to use to take snapshots during your parents' anniversary party. They make those cute little ones with wedding bells and ribbons on them. Your mom won't be able to hide from two hundred cameras."

Sally beamed. "What a wonderful gift for our family. That's a great idea. Mother will hate it when it happens, but she'll be so glad to have the pictures when the party is over."

Holly thought of Maggie's secret renewal-of-vows

plan. She was tempted to clue Sally in on the scheme, but since she didn't have a good sense of how Grace's daughter would react she decided to keep her mouth shut. Maggie would have a fit if Grace learned about the plan and put a premature kibosh to it.

"Your mom seems to be looking forward to the party."

"The party, the planning, has been the best thing to happen to my mother in a long time. For so long now, too long, Mom and Dad's lives have revolved around treatment and little else. The Making Memories gift has been a godsend for this family."

"I'm so glad the foundation was able to convince Grace to accept it. I understand it wasn't easy."

Sally snorted. "The woman is as stubborn as they come. Hardheaded and proud as can be. The stubbornness has served her well in her cancer fight, but the pride makes it difficult to help her."

"She's told Maggie and me that it's difficult for her to ask for help."

"It drives me crazy. My brothers and I would do anything for her. We want to help her, but she won't let us. Take this anniversary party, for instance. Before Making Memories stepped in, we wanted to host the party as part of our gift to them. You wouldn't believe the restrictions she placed on us."

Actually, Holly thought she probably would believe them.

"And Dad, I don't know how he manages day in and day out. She pushes him away and he pushes himself back. I don't think she understands how important it is to him to help her."

"And maybe he doesn't understand how much she needs to stand on her own."

"I know. I know that." Sally shook her head. "It's just so hard. People like to say that when a family member gets cancer, the entire family gets cancer and in a way, that's true. But when it comes to fighting the enemy, battling the cancer, we're powerless. We're not the surgeons who cut it out or the oncologists who poison it. All we can do is drive her to the doctor and pick up her medicine and hold her hand. When she won't let us do even that much, it makes a person feel, oh, I don't know the right word. Impotent, I guess. That makes you angry and then you feel guilty. Yet, I understand and Dad realizes that it's vitally important for her to be strong and independent. We all try to keep a balance, and sometimes we succeed, others we . . . well . . . trip a bit."

Seeing familiar pain in another daughter's expression, Holly was relieved when Grace's granddaughter Belle poked her head into the kitchen. "Mom. It's time to take the individual family pictures."

"I'll be right there, honey." Sally flashed an apologetic smile toward Holly. "I'm sorry. I shouldn't spout off like that. It's just that she's so happy in there tonight and it's so wonderful to see. Sometimes my emotions overflow."

"Please, don't apologize for your feelings. Women do that too much. It's one of my pet peeves. Your feelings are honest and they're yours."

Sally's smile stretched to a grin. "I see why my mother likes you so much. She told me you mentor a young girl who is losing her mother. I suspect you're excellent at it."

Embarrassed, Holly struggled for words. "I don't . . . I only . . ."

"Mom, come on," called Grace's granddaughter. "We're waiting."

"Saved by the Belle," Sally quipped with a twinkle in

her eyes. She checked her reflection in the chrome surface of the toaster, then finger-waved as she left the kitchen.

Knowing Maggie would expect a report, Holly waited for a few minutes, then followed. For the next twenty minutes, she watched the Hardeman family tease and joke with each other while the photographer made his way through Maggie's list.

"Great," the photographer said. "Two more to go. We're down to pets. Who has the cats?"

"They're in Nana's room," Belle said, scooting off her mother's lap as the front doorbell rang. "I'll get them."

Sally's husband headed for the door, wrestling his billfold out of his back pocket. "I'll get supper."

When the pictures were done, Holly joined the family for pizza. As the younger families began to take their leave, she picked up her backpack and prepared to go home. Grace said, "Oh. Must you leave? I'd hoped you'd be able to stay a bit and help me with something."

Other than grading today's quiz, Holly didn't have plans for the rest of the evening. She replaced her backpack on the counter. "I'm in no rush. I expect Cassie Blankenship to call, but she has my cell number."

"How is she doing?"

Holly frowned. "It's difficult to say. Our phone conversation is a Cancer Free zone. She seldom mentions her mom. She said she'd call today after she gets home from the salon. She's trying out hairstyles for the prom. So, my friend, what can I help you with?"

"I've been working on my Life List. I want to get your opinion."

Holly's stomach sank. She wished she'd never mentioned her Life List to Maggie and Grace. For some reason, both women thought they needed Holly to check off on the items they chose to include. No matter how often she explained that the list signified her friends' own personal goals, both Grace and Maggie used her as a sounding board for their ideas. To be honest, Holly rather enjoyed listening to Maggie's outrageous ideas. So far they'd been silly things. The woman never failed to be entertaining.

Grace, on the other hand, tended to be more serious. The last Holly had heard, Grace had three items on her list: to reconcile with an old friend with whom she'd had a falling-out years ago, to do an act of charity every day, and to bake with her grandchildren at least once a week.

Each item said so much about Grace and the kind of person she was. Caring. Compassionate. Filled with love. Family-centered. What bothered Holly about Grace's list, why she resisted discussing it, was her sense that Grace was using her list to put her affairs in order.

"I've decided on my goal number four," Grace said.

Holly braced herself to hear something along the lines of *I will put name stickers on my angel collection indicating who I want each piece to go to once I'm gone.*

"I want to copy you and your number twenty-one."

Surprised, Holly mentally ran through her list. "Wicked? You want to be deliciously wicked?"

"I don't want to *be* deliciously wicked," Grace chastised. "That's not what your twenty-one says. I want to *do* something deliciously wicked."

A slow smile spread across Holly's face. "What do you have in mind?"

"I'm not sure. I have an idea or two, but it's not something I've spent a lot of time thinking about in the past. I hoped you might have some suggestions."

"Hmm . . . should I be flattered or insulted?" Holly asked with a laugh.

"Flattered. Definitely flattered." Grace opened her pantry and removed a plastic cake carrier. "It's German chocolate. I hid it from my family. I thought a discussion like this deserved chocolate."

"Grace, I adore the way you think."

She cut the first slice just as the doorbell rang. "Ben, will you get that, please?"

Moments later, Maggie Prescott stood in the kitchen doorway. Her eyes were red and tears ran in mascara-stained streaks down her cheeks. Her bottom lip trembled as she said, "Hi, y'all. Got a tissue? Guess I should've shopped for waterproof mascara, after all."

"Oh, Maggie." Grace rose from the table.

Holly rushed toward her friend. "What's happened?"

"My babies. They hate me." She wiped her eyes with the back of her hand. "My babies hate me."

As Maggie buried her head in her hands and sobbed, Holly cast a pleading look toward Grace. Ben stuck his head in the door and waggled his eyebrows. Grace shook her head, then put her arm around Maggie's waist and steered her toward the kitchen table as Ben made himself scarce. Knowing Maggie, Holly grabbed a box of tissues off the counter and shoved one into her friend's hand.

"Put the kettle on, would you, Holly?"

"I can't believe they hate me," Maggie wailed.

Grace pulled a chair away from the table. "Sit down, dear, and tell us what happened."

"It's Mike. Of course, it's Mike. Who else would be so cruel as to turn my boys against me?" Maggie melted into her seat, then wiped her eyes, blew her nose, and started sobbing all over again.

In the midst of a déjà vu moment, Holly wondered how many boxes of tissues Grace had in the house. "Maggie. What happened?"

"He called last night. Jake Randall took me on a picnic and I slipped in the mud so I was in the shower when Mike called and Jake told him that's where I was and Mike took it wrong and he called the boys and asked what the hell is your mother doing and they think I'm a slut and it's not me it's their dad and they won't listen to me because they are just like him and I'm so angry at them. I am angry at all of them."

That was just the start. For the next half hour while drinking two cups of tea and devouring three pieces of cake, Maggie rambled and vented and wailed and wept. The story that emerged both stirred Holly's ire and broke her heart. She didn't know what to say to offer Maggie comfort.

Grace managed to sum up the situation eloquently. "In this moment, I am reminded of an old saying. Men have only two faults." She patted Maggie's hand. "Everything they say . . ."

Holly and Maggie finished it with her, ". . . and everything they do."

The resulting laughter lightened the mood and Maggie's consumption of tissues slowed considerably. "I'm so glad I came over here. Y'all have made me feel so much better. I just knew you would."

Holly licked chocolate icing off her fork. "I wish we could do more. Would it help any if Grace or I talked to your sons, tried to explain your position?"

"You mean those thick-headed, dim-witted, lame-brained boys I've devoted my life to? Thank you, but no. I'm not even certain I'll talk to them again myself." Maggie wrinkled her nose. "Now, let's change the subject. How did the portrait sitting go?"

"Oh, it was wonderful," Grace said. Enthusiasm lit her eyes and colored her voice as she described the activities of the evening. Talk turned to the anniversary party and the three women spent the next half hour discussing details and making plans for the coming weekend. They declared the task of finding the perfect dress for Grace to be the first priority.

At ten o'clock, Holly called it an evening, reminding the others that tomorrow was a workday for her. Maggie, too, decided to take her leave, and since her car was parked in the driveway behind Holly's, she backed out of the driveway first.

As Holly waited on Maggie, Grace approached her car. Eyes gleaming, she knocked on the driver's-side window. Holly thumbed the button and the window lowered.

"It's time, Holly. Remember my idea? I know just what I need to do to accomplish number four on my Life List. Why don't you come with me. It'll qualify as your number twenty-one. It'll be a two-for-one deal."

In the face of Grace's excitement, Holly didn't know whether to nod or run. "I'm almost afraid to ask. What wicked action do you have in mind?"

"Nothing as exciting as sex in a storeroom, I'm afraid," she said with a devilish grin. "Still, it qualifies and I think it'll help Maggie's morale. How about it, Holly? Want to help me heist Mike Prescott's sails?"

✿ eleven

moonlight spilled across the placid surface of Lake Texoma as the weekend died away, fading into the tranquil peace of a Monday morning. On the hillside surrounding the marina, air conditioners droned, while from down on the water came the occasional squeak of Styrofoam dock supports and lap of gentle waves. Drooping strings of yellow dock lights joined halogen lamps perched atop wooden poles to provide pockets of illumination amid the shadows. The night was sleepy, silent, and, Holly thought, more than a little scary.

What else could she expect when arriving with vandalism on her mind?

"I can't believe I'm doing this," she muttered, as she tucked her hair beneath the baseball cap Grace brought for purposes of disguise. "I'm a teacher, a role model for children. Nowhere on my Life List does it say anything about committing a felony."

"Oh, hush." Wearing a stylish ash blond wig from her chemo days, Grace keyed open the trunk of her six-year-old Ford and gestured toward the bag of supplies they'd purchased at the twenty-four-hour Wal-Mart half an hour earlier. "You remind me of my youngest granddaughter. Child whines more than a Skil saw."

"I'm not whining." Holly retrieved the sack from Grace's arm, wincing as the cans inside clinked together. "I'm expressing legitimate reservations. We could get into real trouble for this."

Grace shut the trunk with a quiet snick. "Maybe. But we're not going to get caught, and even if we did, Texas is a community property state. The boat is still half Maggie's. If she says we acted at her behest, who's to say we'd be in any trouble at all?"

"But we're not acting at her behest, and if she knew what we are up to she might just tell us to jump off a dock."

"Balderdash."

Holly swallowed a laugh. "Balderdash, Grace? Getting a bit spicy with the language, aren't you?"

"Put a sock in it, Weeks."

That response stopped Holly in her tracks, causing her tennis shoes to slide across the gravel. Loudly.

"Hush! You're going to ruin this before it ever gets started."

Yeah, that's the idea. But Grace Hardeman, criminal-in-the-making, would not be denied. The woman was a terrier. A terrier with gray hair, a Madonna smile, hot pink sneakers, and breast cancer. How the hell was Holly supposed to argue with her?

Ben Hardeman had proved to be no help. When he drove Grace to Holly's home in the middle of the night, she had asked him to talk some sense into his wife. "This is an idiotic idea," Holly had said. "Never mind the criminality of it. She has no business doing mischief like this. You've got to stop her."

The man just laughed. Laughed! "Holly, Holly, Holly. Don't you know me well enough by now to know I've tried? Anything short of locking her in the closet wouldn't stop her. Look at her. My Gracie is sparkling. Even if I could change her mind, which I don't believe is possible, I'm not about to attempt anything that might douse her light."

"But this is the silliest scheme."

"Yes, and I think we have your Life List to thank, don't we?"

That, Holly hated to say, was one of the reasons she had such reservations about the entire idea. For the first time, she understood how Justin must have felt about the bungee jumping. Her list was also the reason why she'd agreed to accompany Grace. She felt responsible. This wasn't at all the way she'd intended to satisfy her number twenty-one.

At that point, Ben had given her a hug. "Don't worry. As Grace loves to tell me and as I'm slowly beginning to understand, it's her life. Whether we like it or not, you and I and everyone else needs to let her live it the way she wants."

Thinking about it now as a fishy scent drifted on the night air, Holly muttered, "Somehow I don't think the local law is going to listen to that argument when we're caught in the act of committing a felony."

"Felony, shmelony. We're doing a little redecorating, that's all. Besides, aren't you the one who put 'Do Something Wicked' on her to-do list first?"

"Wicked, yes. Criminal, no. I can't believe I let you talk me into this. What if there's a night watchman? What if they have guard dogs? What if someone lives on his boat and he gets up in the middle of the night to pee and he sees us?"

"If someone lives on his boat, he has a bathroom, a head, and he's not likely to do his business off the bow of his boat. As to the watchman and the dogs, I checked into it and it's not a problem."

Which didn't say the dogs and watchman didn't exist, Holly noted. Glumly, she said, "If we get caught, I'll lose my job. It'll make the paper, you just watch. I can see it now. 'Teacher of the Year Given the Boot Due to a Boat.'"

"Or how about 'Big Mouth Causes Murder at Lake Texoma—and We Don't Mean Big Mouth Bass.' Now *be quiet!*"

Grace led the way down the hill toward the Grandpappy Point marina, where soft security lighting illuminated hundreds of boats floating peacefully in their slips. Holly anxiously scanned the mix of sailboats and motorboats for signs of life. Doing this at all showed a definite lack of intelligence. Doing it in good weather was insane. Three o'clock in the morning or not, somebody was likely to see them.

"Why did I ever open my mouth about my list," Holly grumbled beneath her breath. Louder, she mocked, "How about a bit of not-so-petty larceny? What's a little vandalism to a half-million-dollar boat? Five to ten at the Big House, that's what."

Grace glanced over her shoulder. "I don't think it cost that much. He bought it used, remember, plus he did some refurbishing."

"Like that makes a difference." Holly lifted her eyes to the night sky and sighed.

Ahead of her, Grace stopped in front of a numbered slip, pulled a small flashlight from her pocket, switched it on, and checked a small scrap of paper in her hand. A faint click carried to Holly as the light blinked off, then Grace said, "This should be it. I'll check the stern and confirm this is the *Second Wind*, just to make sure, then we can get to work. Which color do you want to use, Holly? Pink or red?"

She wanted to use her feet. To run away. "Pink." The lighter color seemed like the lesser crime.

Grace slapped a paintbrush onto Holly's palm. She envisioned allowing it to drop off her hand and onto the dock where it might slip into the crack between two boards and fall into the lake with a gentle splash.

Then Holly remembered the anguish on Maggie's face as she stood in the doorway of Grace's kitchen Friday night and the hurt that had flashed in her eyes when that little girl called Maggie's husband Uncle Mike. Her grip tightened around the brush handle.

As Grace handed her a can of paint, Holly's gaze strayed toward Mike Prescott's boat. From out of nowhere, she recalled the light of pain in Mike Prescott's eyes as he watched his wife climb into her car to leave that day out at his aunt's farm. The hurt wasn't all one-sided.

Holly wondered what an observer would have seen in hers and Justin's expressions when she turned down his proposal, when she saw him with Jenna Larson.

"It's the *Second Wind*, all right," Grace said. "The mercury vapor security lights are brighter than I expected, but if we remain in the shadows as much as possible, I think we'll be all right.

Holly exhaled a heavy breath. Her emotions rocked like the boat beneath her feet as she climbed the boarding ladder and stepped onto the *Second Wind*. Silently, she helped Grace aboard. She had tried hard not to think about Jenna. Doing so gave her a sour feeling in her stomach and queasiness wasn't the best thing to bring aboard a boat. She believed Justin's protestation of innocence. That wasn't the problem. The problem was that the problem hadn't changed. Jenna Larson would still make a perfect wife for Justin. Holly would still be a perfectly terrible choice for him. She and Justin might be talking again, friends again, but the underlying situation hadn't changed one little bit.

Justin wanted to marry and start a family. Holly didn't dare marry and have children.

That truth broke Holly's heart.

Justin might be back in her life for now as her friend, but it wouldn't, couldn't, remain that way forever. Someday he'd find a wife and their friendship would never be the same.

The thought of Jenna as that wife scraped her heart raw. And in the meantime, Holly would remember that smug smile on Jenna Larson's face until the day she died.

"Whatever happened to the church lady?" she asked in a conversational tone as she followed Grace along the starboard side of the yacht.

"Not so loud," Grace cautioned in a whisper. "Let's get to work. Quietly, though. Remember that water carries sound. What church lady?"

"The woman who went after Ben."

"Oh." Grace used the chrome railing for balance as she stepped toward the bow. She set her Wal-M sack on the deck. "She married the choir d moved to Montana. Get to work, Holly. Let's not waste time."

Holly cupped her hands around her eyes and attempted to peer through the boat's tinted windows. Not surprisingly, she couldn't see a thing.

"What are you looking for?" Grace asked as she pulled a can from her plastic sack. "Do you expect to find evidence that Maggie is right and Mike does have a paramour?"

"No. I'm not going to jimmy the lock and look inside." Holly reluctantly accepted the can of pink paint from the older woman. "Besides, I believe him. I don't think that woman he was with at the Arts Festival is his mistress. If he were guilty, he wouldn't have sicced his boys on their mom when he learned about her stepping out. That was the action of a righteous man."

"And a hurt one. You have a point. Nevertheless, he acted unfairly by involving the children and it hurt Maggie deeply. I firmly believe that marital troubles should be kept between a man and wife. If your hunch is correct and Mike is not guilty of infidelity, then Maggie has complicated the situation by dating."

"To put it mildly."

"At least she's doing something again, getting out among the living again. That's a good sign, even if her actions are motivated by retribution rather than a desire to create a new life for herself."

"I wish Mike would see that," Holly said. "I think he loves her, Grace. Did you see the look on his face that day at Sadie's farmhouse? I think he's as torn up as she is this trouble. But running out on her, or I should say from her, doesn't solve anything."

actly right, Holly my friend." Grace Holly met her gaze before firing her zinger. "Which is why I hope you'll reconsider your notion to move away from Fort Worth."

"Ouch." Holly winced.

Grace chuckled. "Get to work, dear, or day will break before we're done."

Taking the warning seriously, Holly knelt in the *Second Wind's* bow pulpit, dipped her brush, and got down to business. She didn't want to be anywhere near Lake Texoma when Mike Prescott arrived at the marina.

She doubted he'd be happy to find pink and red hearts painted all over his half-million-dollar boat.

In the end, she couldn't blame Grace for the fate that befell them. Holly was the one who got wrapped up in the creative process and lost track of time. If she hadn't insisted on painting hearts on the windows of the flybridge, they'd have been long gone before trouble arrived.

As it was, she had one hand on the wheel, the other wielding a paintbrush, when the voice spoke from out of the shadows on the dock. "Ladies, you're under arrest."

The ringing of the phone in the middle of the night was every mother's nightmare. Even as her eyelids struggled open, even as her mind registered what had awakened her, Maggie's thoughts flew to her children. Her heart began to pound.

Red numerals glowed four forty-five as she lunged for the phone on the bedside table. Her voice croaked, "Hello?"

"Michael Prescott, please," requested an official-sounding voice.

Oh, God.

Maggie spoke in a rush. "He's not here. This is Mrs. Prescott. Is this about one of my boys?"

A lifetime ticked by during the slight pause before he spoke again. "No ma'am. I'm calling in regard to a fifty-foot Viking yacht registered in your husband's name. I'm Captain Marv Hobbs of the Pottsboro Police Department. We apprehended two suspects in the act of vandalizing a boat named the *Second Wind*."

The *Second Wind*. Maggie sat up straight. Every time she heard that name it chapped her butt.

"Look, Captain, that is my husband's toy and he's not in town at the moment. Since I personally don't care if the boat floats or not, I'd just as soon get back to sleep. He can take care of this—"

"Excuse me, Mrs. Prescott, but the vandals claim to know you." His voice rose in disbelief. "The women claim to have your permission to . . . decorate . . . the property."

Maggie reached over and turned on the light. "Would you repeat that, please?"

"Yes, ma'am. Two women, a Miss Holly Weeks and Mrs.—"

"Grace Hardeman," Maggie interrupted, relaxing against her pillows, her lips beginning to twitch with a smile.

"Yes, Hardeman. A patrol officer apprehended them earlier this morning aboard the *Second Wind*."

"You mentioned something about decorating?"

The captain's voice sounded pained. "It's difficult for me to call it that, ma'am, though that's what those two claim. 'Defacement' is the better word, in my opinion. She's a beautiful boat. Or she was."

"Just spit it out, Captain." Maggie was grinning widely now. She wiggled back into her goose down pillows, getting comfortable.

"They painted her with graffiti, Mrs. Prescott. Pink and red hearts. All over the hull."

A laugh burst from her throat. She slapped a hand over her mouth and tried to turn it into a cough. Pink and red hearts. My oh my, she couldn't wait to get a look at that.

The captain continued. "We caught 'em red-handed. Crazy thing is, the older woman claims they were working for you. That they had your permission to be aboard and to . . . to . . . commit that atrocity. I don't believe it, of course. We caught them perpetrating a malicious act in the middle of the night. They were even in disguise. The older lady wore a wig."

"Really? What color?"

"Pardon me?"

"What color wig?"

"Um . . . blond. The younger one was in a baseball cap."

Grace as a blonde, hmm? Maggie wanted to see that, too.

"You need not come down to the station, ma'am," he said. "Just confirm that they're lying and I'll take it from there."

I just bet he would. "Something tells me you're a sailor, Captain Hobbs."

"No ma'am. I run a bass boat." Fatigue colored his tone as he added, "Now about those charges?"

Maggie let the silence stretch as she imagined the look on her husband's face when he got his first glimpse at the pink and red hearts on his dreamboat. Gosh, she hoped she wasn't asleep. It'd be terrible if this were only a dream.

"Ms. Prescott . . ." the police captain said. He paused

for a moment as if searching for just the right words. "I can't imagine any man . . . well . . . the *Second Wind*, she's something special. It's ridiculous to think your husband—"

"That yacht is half mine, sir. I can decorate it as I wish. Now, I have a question for you. If I were to tell you Holly and Grace are telling the truth, that they were aboard with my permission, and that I happen to like pink and red hearts very much, would you release them immediately?"

His sigh was loud and long and filled with disbelief. "I'd have no choice."

"I see. Well, that brings up a problem. No matter what permission I did or did not give my friends, they never should have visited such an isolated spot in the middle of the night. Two women alone out at the lake like that? It was foolish. Dangerous, even."

"I won't argue with you."

"You know, if they were my kids, I'd leave them in jail for a little while. Just to teach them a lesson. Then I'd send their father down to bail them out."

He sighed again and Maggie thought she heard him mutter something about dad-blamed modern women. "Mrs. Prescott, are you pressing charges against Ms. Weeks and Mrs. Hardeman?"

"Well, Captain Hobbs, I can't rightly say. I need to think about it a bit. Search my memory for what I said and didn't say. I'll get back to you shortly. All right?"

He muttered and grumbled and eventually growled a good-bye. Maggie let out a giggle that turned into an honest-to-goodness, roll-around-the-bed bout of laughter. Pink and red hearts. Sounds like they turned it into the Love Boat. What had possessed them?

The answer came to Maggie on a sigh. Friendship. That's what possessed them. Though she wasn't exactly certain of their thought processes, she knew without a doubt they did it out of friendship. "And in that case, one good turn deserves another."

Maggie climbed out of bed and padded to the study, where she pulled a Fort Worth phone book from a shelf. The first number she called was already on speed dial. Ben Hardeman answered on the first ring.

The second call she made was taken by an answering service. Ten minutes later, her phone rang. Grinning, she lifted the receiver. "Hello?"

"Maggie? Justin. What the hell is going on?"

🌼 twelve

"*I'm gonna get fired*," Holly moaned. Seated on the end of her bunk in the Pottsboro city jail, she buried her face in her hands. "I'm going to lose my job, then my car, then my house, and I'll end up living under an overpass picking up aluminum cans off the highway median to sell so I can buy food."

"Oh, Holly, don't be such a drama queen." Grace inspected the bunk for dirt, then took a seat opposite Holly. "You're not going to lose anything. Maggie will take care of everything, just you wait."

"Wait till when? They fit us with orange jumpsuits? Orange is not my color, Grace. It makes me look sallow. I don't want to spend ten-to-twenty looking sallow."

Grace responded to Holly's misery with a laugh. Not surprising, since the woman was laughing at everything tonight. When the officer flashed his light in her face, she'd raised her hands, said "oops," then giggled. When he'd cuffed her wrists behind her back and put his hand on her head to guide her into the patrol car's backseat, she'd chuckled with delight. The capper had come when he'd lifted the radio mike and reported the apprehension of two criminal-mischief suspects. Grace had let out a joyful chortle and said, "Oh, this being wicked is fun, isn't it? I've never been arrested before."

Then she'd launched into a series of questions about procedure, asking them with such excited interest that before long, the policeman started casting puzzled glances into the rearview mirror.

Grace had actually pouted when Captain Hobbs said they wouldn't be fingerprinted right away and maybe not at all, depending on how their story checked out with the owner of the *Second Wind*.

"I don't understand you, Grace." Holly looked around the barren cell with disgust. "You're actually enjoying this!"

"Why shouldn't I? Nothing bad is going to happen to us and I feel like I've stepped onto the set of Mayberry. Don't you think the captain looks like Andy Griffith? A young Andy. When Opie was still a boy." She patted her hair and grinned. "Tell me I look younger than Aunt Bee."

Exasperated, Holly shook her head. "This isn't a TV show. It's real life. This is a real jail. We're gonna need real lawyers."

"Poppycock. Don't be such a worrywart. And a spoilsport, too, for that matter. You, as much as anyone, should understand. Aren't you the one who invented the Life List?"

That damned list. "As far as I recall, spending time in jail isn't on it."

"Maybe it should be. This entire adventure has certainly made me feel alive. Don't be such a fuddy-duddy."

"I can't believe this. The last time I took a personal day from work was in December so I could go Christmas shopping. I thought *that* was bad. How can I explain jail time to my principal?"

The door leading to the outer offices opened. An officer escorted Ben Hardeman inside. "Ben!" Grace exclaimed. "You're here. How did you find out? I didn't call. I've been asking when we get our phone call, but no one is telling us anything. Who called you?"

Instead of answering, he folded his arms, sighed, and frowned at his wife. "Gracie, we raised two children. Never once did I get called down to the police station in the middle of the night to bail one of them out of jail. Just what do you have to say for yourself?"

She cocked her hip and flashed him a downright wicked smile. "I've changed my mind about handcuffs. Take me home, handsome."

"Oh, God." Holly massaged her forehead. "That's more information than I needed, Aunt Bee."

"Aunt Bee?" Ben asked, leaning against the metal cell bars and smiling indulgently at his jailbird bride.

The woman simply laughed. A vivacious, excited, full-of-life laugh. "It was so exciting, Ben. My heart never pounded so fast as it did when Captain Hobbs flashed that light on my face. I could see the gun in his hand. He had it pointed right at us! It was a good thing I was sitting down, otherwise I'd have fallen. I went weak in the knees and shook like a tree in a gale, Ben."

At least Ben Hardeman has the grace to grimace at that, Holly thought.

He cleared his throat. "I'd just as soon not hear about any guns, honey. In fact, you might want to keep the most exciting stuff to yourself. I was pretty worried tonight, and well, a man my age needs to watch the stress and take care of his heart. Wouldn't want an attack to take me out before our anniversary."

"Oh, pooh." Grace shot him a false scowl. "You and Holly make a fine pair of sticks-in-the-mud. Now hush and let me tell you about the handcuffs."

Ben chuckled and reached through the bars to take his wife's hand. "Tell me about the handcuffs."

Grace told her story, relaying the events of the night with a voice that bubbled like champagne. She laughed and she giggled and she babbled. She lit up the jail cell, a live wire who brightened the entire office and even had the lawmen grinning in reaction.

A *live wire*, Holly thought. *Alive*.

Alive. Alive. Alive. The word throbbed in her head like a mantra. The scene around her altered, sharpened, but at the same time, somehow pulled away. Holly felt insulated and apart. She was an observer, not a participant, and what she saw confused her.

Was this a natural result of an adrenaline rush combined with lack of sleep and paint fumes? Somehow, Holly didn't think so. Somehow, she sensed that if she could only understand this moment, a lot of other moments might fall into place, too.

Grace Hardeman was dying, but she was laughing and her husband was laughing. Mama had never laughed when she was dying. Holly's dad had never laughed.

An officer unlocked the cell door, telling Grace the captain had agreed to her request to be fingerprinted. Delighted with the news, Grace pressed a kiss to Ben's cheek as she passed. He chuckled and watched her leave with warm eyes.

"How can you bear it?"

He turned to meet her gaze. "What?"

"How can you bear the thought of losing her?"

Ben's eyes narrowed and he stared at her hard. Abruptly, his gaze softened. "How old are you, Holly?"

"Twenty-five."

"Twenty-five, hmm? Old enough to learn a thing or two if you're smart enough to do it. It took me longer, a lot longer, and I had to make some really stupid mistakes first."

He dragged his hand down his bristled jaw. "Gracie and I have had our ups and downs. Our life together has been a mix of lemons and lemonade. But Grace is now and always will be a good-time memory for me. She tells me I'm the same for her. We've worked hard to make it that way. It's important to us both that whichever of us goes first, the other has as few regrets as possible. That's what will kill you. Believe you me. I have regrets. One big fat colossal regret in particular."

The church lady, Holly suspected.

"You see, Holly, it's not the memories that crush your soul, it's the regrets."

Holly grew totally still as Ben's words echoed in her mind. *It's not the memories that crush your soul, it's the regrets.*

Not memories, regrets.

She felt as if she were swaying on the edge of a tall cliff.

Desperately, she tried to step back. "But she has metastatic cancer. She's more than likely terminal. How do you live with that?"

"Honey, we're all terminal. We just don't know the iming." Smiling wryly, Ben rubbed the back of his neck.

"In that respect, you could say Gracie is luckier than most because she figured out not to waste the time she has. That's more than most of us do."

That, Holly understood. Her Life List was all about not wasting time, wasting life.

Ben continued, "Would I rather she didn't have cancer? Of course. Would I trade places with her if possible? Damn straight I would. But that's not possible. That's not our life. Before she left the house for this little adventure of yours, she gave me a hug. Her hair brushed my neck. Tickled me. Now, to the uninitiated, that's a normal occurrence. But I felt that tickle clear to the bone. You want to know why?"

Solemnly, Holly nodded.

"It's not because she has hair now after having gone without for a while. It's because it's different. The texture is different. The color is different. But it tickles my neck just like her other hair did. You see, Holly, Grace is different now. So am I. We've gone beyond the couple we used to be and moved into something different, something new. It has its ups and downs, true; but I honestly think it's something better. This is our life and we're living it without regrets. If I outlive my Gracie, that will be my memory. Never my regret."

A band of emotion constricted Holly's chest and burned in her throat. She wrapped her arms around herself and rocked slowly, slightly, back and forth.

Movement in the doorway brought her back. She looked up expecting to see Grace. Instead, she spied the perfectly-powdered-coiffed-and-costumed-despite-the-earliness-of-the-hour Mrs. Maggie Prescott. But she wasn't by herself.

Justin stood with her.

*   *   *

He didn't drive her straight home. He wanted to see the boat.

Holly sat in the passenger seat of Justin's pickup and tried to work up some saliva as they traveled the winding lakeside road that would take them to the harbor. She didn't have much luck. Her mouth was dry as beef jerky.

The morning sky was bright with thin wisps of clouds clinging to the color of a pink dawn, strings of pale cotton candy stretched against a springtime blue. Pink like half the hearts slashed over the lovely lines of the *Second Wind*. Holly sneaked a peek at Justin's profile. He wore his stuffy expression. They hadn't exchanged a dozen words since leaving the jail.

Shrinking against the seat, Holly wished for Maggie, who had filled the silence with her chatter earlier. She had pranced into the jailhouse, a queen come to review her troops. Her scepter was her tennis racquet; her regal robe a white cotton sweater tied stylishly around her shoulders. Her crown was the smile on her face—bright and brilliant as any jewel under the sun. Her long, tanned legs beneath the flirty white tennis skirt suited a movie queen more than a blooded Royal.

The captain and his men all but dropped to their knees in a bow.

Maggie charmed the men with little more than a bat of the eyelashes and a few "sugars" and shortly, Grace and Holly had been free to go.

Exiting the jailhouse with bubbly Grace and sparkling Maggie, Holly had felt like a flat Dr Pepper.

Maggie had detoured by the marina on her way to jail to see the results of their handiwork. To say she was delighted would be an understatement. Once out of hearing of the lawmen, she'd laughed with evil glee and demanded all the gory details. Grace had been delighted to provide them. Toward the end of Grace's recitation, Maggie had burst into tears at the notion that her friends had cared enough to wreak vengeance on her behalf.

Throughout the friends' leave-taking, Justin stood silent and impassive, his expression impossible for Holly to read. Maggie had called him to come give Holly a ride home, of course. She'd called both Justin and Ben. Her excuse was a crock—a breakfast tennis date that she simply couldn't be late for. Holly didn't believe it for a moment. Maggie was simply trying her hand at matchmaking.

Since she and Grace were guilty of the same effort, Holly didn't feel she could protest.

Justin pulled his truck into the parking lot at Grandpappy Point. "Which one is it?"

Holly pointed toward the dock farthest to the right. "It's slip eighty-five. Three or four boats from the end." Aware of the understatement, she finished, "You can't miss it."

When Holly made no move to get out of the car, he hesitated. "Aren't you coming with me?"

She shook her head. The last thing she wanted was to get a look at last night's work in daylight.

The crunch of tires against gravel had her nervously looking around. It would be just her luck for Mike Prescott to drive up. Instead of Maggie's husband, she saw Grace step down from Ben's truck. She gave Holly a cheerful wave before getting into her own car, left at the marina following the arrests, to follow her husband home.

"I rode out here with Grace. She could have taken me back," she grumbled. "I didn't need Justin."

But she did need Justin and that was exactly the problem.

When he returned to the car, he was whistling "Row, Row, Row Your Boat." He didn't say a word, simply started the car and made a U-turn out of the parking lot. He continued to whistle softly, the sound of which began to grate on Holly's nerves within half a mile. Gradually she quit being nervous and began to stew.

Who does Justin Skipworth think he is, anyway? Never mind that Maggie called him. He's not responsible for me. We're not married. We're not dating. We're barely even friends anymore. High-handed man. Thinks he's always in charge. Has a God complex, so stereotypical of doctors.

Holly spent the rest of the drive conjuring up memories of every time Justin acted in an overbearing way, and by the time they arrived at her house, she'd managed to work herself into a decent froth. She had the passenger door open before he'd brought the vehicle to a halt at her curb.

Leaping out, she slammed it hard. "Thanks for the ride."

She darted for her front door, hoping, praying, she'd hear sounds of his leaving. Instead, he continued that damned whistling as he strolled up her walk. "Sure, Holly, I'd love a cup of coffee," he said, smoothly taking her key ring from her hand and slipping the house key into the lock. "Thank you for asking."

She bared her teeth and growled at him. The blasted man laughed—laughed!—as he sauntered inside her house.

"I'm out of coffee."

"Oh? Then I'll scrounge up something else. What ⸱ do you have to be at work?"

"I'm taking a personal day."

"That's handy." He walked into the kitchen and over to the ceramic canister set. He lifted the lid of the third largest and peered inside. "Why, this is shaping up to be my lucky day. You do have coffee. Looks like you were mistaken, Holly."

"Help yourself. I need to grab a shower. I know you probably should be getting to work yourself, so just pull the door shut behind you when you leave."

The resumption of that dad-blasted whistle was his only reply. Holly fled to her bedroom, hoping her luck would change and he'd be gone by the time she'd showered and shampooed.

Once locked safely behind the bathroom door, she changed her mind about the shower and ran a hot bath instead. She flipped on the radio to a classical music station, pinned up her hair, added coconut-scented bath oil to the tub, then stripped off her clothes and sank into the water with a sigh. She leaned back, closed her eyes, and willed herself to relax.

It worked. She awoke to cold water and a crick in her neck. After a moment's confusion, the events of the night came roaring back. "Justin," she murmured, her gaze going unerringly toward the door.

She rose from the bath and reached for a fluffy blue towel. Drying herself, she checked the watch lying on the vanity. Two hours? No wonder her fingers and toes had shriveled like prunes.

Confident that Justin would be stethoscope-deep in ear infections and toddler snot by now, she flung her towel over her shoulder and padded naked into her bedroom.

He lay stretched out on her bed, his feet bare, the

sleeves of his sky blue dress shirt rolled halfway up his forearms. His briefcase lay open on the floor. He had a stack of files spread across her midnight blue sheets and he was reading from a report as he spoke into Holly's phone, ". . . set up an appointment for her with Dr. Marks. I'm concerned about those protein levels."

"What are you still doing here?" Holly demanded, yanking the towel from her shoulder and holding it in front of her.

Without glancing toward her, he held up an index finger signaling her to hush and continued his conversation.

At that, Holly saw red. She was tempted to hold up a finger herself, only not her index finger. Instead, she retaliated by clearing her throat, dropping her towel, and sauntering forward in a slow, hip-rolling walk to her dresser. She mentally marked one up for her side when, with a groan in his voice, he said into the phone, "I think it breast we go ahead with the tests."

For good measure, Holly took her time choosing her underwear.

"Witch," Justin said as he disconnected.

Holly simply smiled as she pulled on a tee shirt and jeans. She caught a glimpse of herself in the mirror and was pleased to discover that outwardly, she appeared calm. Inside, she was a bucket of nerves. Justin hadn't hung around for two hours on a workday just to make phone calls. Justin had something to say to her.

And Holly, underneath her panic and her fear and her insecurities, wanted to listen. Only not in her bedroom. "I'm going to make an omelet. Would you like one?"

He sat up. "That sounds great. Thank you."

The two had shared the familiar task dozens of times,

so without discussion, Justin chopped onions and green peppers while Holly blended eggs and milk. She added a pinch of salt to the eggs, then asked, "Ham?"

"Just cheese for me, please."

Justin set the table and poured juice and coffee. He grabbed a pair of scissors from her junk drawer and stepped outside for a moment, returning with an iris. He slipped the flower into a bud vase and placed it in the middle of the table.

If Holly had any doubts before, she knew better now. By putting a flower on the table, Justin had turned this ordinary breakfast into an Occasion. Just what kind of occasion was yet to be seen.

He waited until they both were seated. As Holly spread her napkin on her lap, he took his first bite. "Mmm. Great as always. I've missed our omelets." He paused, looked her straight in the eyes, and said, "I've missed *you*, Holly."

That wasn't such a bad start. He could have said gee, he really enjoyed their phone conversations last week but Jenna Larson adds pineapple to her omelets and they're really good. Holly took a bite of her eggs, savored the flavorful blend of cheddar cheese, onions, and green pepper, and tried to decide on a response. She swallowed, sipped her juice, and settled on, "I've missed you, too."

Justin briefly closed his eyes. The tension she'd sensed hovering around him eased. Holly continued to eat her breakfast, surprised her nervousness didn't make her eggs taste like dry grits. In fact, the omelet was delicious, the best food she'd tasted in weeks.

Maybe Holly wasn't as nervous as she thought. Maybe she was enjoying the moment. Justin was back in her house. Back in her kitchen. Back where he belonged. And he didn't appear in any hurry to leave.

She knew she should insist he go.

She couldn't force the words from her lips.

They finished their breakfast making small talk, and Holly began to hope that maybe nothing more would be said, that they could pick up where they'd left off and sweep the problem of marriage beneath the rug where it belonged.

She suspected she wouldn't be that lucky. So when the table was cleared and the dishes rinsed and in the dishwasher, she wasn't too surprised when Justin touched her arm and said, "It's a pretty morning. Let's go out back. I've been doing some thinking, a lot of thinking, and I think it's time we talked."

"Justin, I really don't—"

"Please?"

Holly knew when to surrender with dignity. "All right."

Their destination was a shady spot beneath a pecan tree and the wooden glider crafted by a group of Mennonites down in the Texas Hill Country. Justin had bought it for Holly for her birthday, and they'd passed many an hour sitting in it, slowly swinging back and forth while conversing on matters both great and small.

Something told Holly they wouldn't be debating the superiority of blue snow cones over orange ones this morning.

Justin sat beside her. He took her hand in his and she left it there.

A few minutes passed in peaceful silence. Holly steeped herself in the pleasure of the moment: the warmth of the sun on her face, the chatter of the squirrels in the pecan tree, the familiar-and-oh-so-missed scent of the man she loved. It was heaven. Pure heaven. *Worth spending a night in jail for*, she told herself with a grin.

Justin lifted her hand, brought it to his mouth, and pressed a sweet kiss against her palm. "Honey, it's time. I need to talk about our situation. I need an answer to the question I asked on our aborted Saturday-Sunday drive."

When Holly failed to speak up, he continued. "I'm a good doctor and a damned fine diagnostician, but I obviously misread the symptoms in our case. Talk to me, baby. Help me understand. Why won't you marry me?"

"Oh, Justin." Her heart wrenched. How could she tell him? What words would possibly convey the feelings she herself didn't entirely understand?

Yet, she wanted to try to explain. She wanted him to know. Justin was a smart guy. Maybe he'd understand the parts of it that Holly couldn't. "You know what? I want to tell you. I do. It's a surprise even to me. But it's hard. I don't have words for all of it."

"Then give me what words you can, love."

She laced her fingers through his and gave his hand a squeeze. "For most of my life, I've felt like I've been floating down a river in a boat. I have no oars, no paddles, and I've been drawn into treacherous rapids. The current is fast and it's rough and it's rolling. Up ahead, I hear the roar of a waterfall. I've tried paddling away from destruction by hand but it makes no difference. I've tried baling out to swim, but I can't get out of the boat. Every day, every hour, every minute draws me closer to that godawful roar.

"I'm on that river to stay, Justin. No matter how badly I want off, I know there is no way to avoid going over the waterfall. That's why I've always said I can't marry you. I love you too much."

Briefly, he closed his eyes. "I needed to hear those words. I didn't realize until now just how much. As long as you love me and I love you, we can work this out."

"Dammit, Justin. Didn't you listen? I cannot bear the thought of sucking you down into the river with me."

"I heard that part, too. I'm not sure I understand the metaphor." His smile was tender as he reached up and gently tucked a stray strand of hair behind her ear. "What does the waterfall symbolize, honey?"

This was so hard. In her head, Holly knew her fears weren't entirely rational. In her heart, she heard the inevitable, threatening roar of the waterfall. What words would make Justin understand? He was the most pragmatic man she'd ever known. He would wield his medical knowledge like a scalpel in an effort to slice her beliefs to ribbons. He'd fume with frustration when none of it made a difference because her life, her future, was preordained.

Something strange happened. Holly heard voices in her head. Two voices. Grace and Maggie, each whispering in an ear: *But what if you're wrong?*

For a moment, Holly went still. Everything inside her froze. She didn't even breathe. *What if I'm wrong? What if I'm not doomed by bad genetics?*

Her palms grew damp and her pulse started to pound and her mind began to swirl like a slow-moving eddy. Holly thought of Grace, of her serenity and strength in the face of her disease. She thought of Maggie, of how she worked to reclaim her positive attitude in the midst of personal despair. She thought of Ben Hardeman and the truth in his voice when he said it wasn't the memories that crushed a soul, but the regrets. She thought of her dad and their Saturday-Sunday drives.

Some great universal truth lay buried in that flotsam, just beyond her reach. If only she could figure out what it was.

"Sweetheart, tell me about the waterfall."

She turned her head and looked at Justin. Stared deep into his eyes. In their golden brown depths, she found compassion, encouragement, and love. So much love.

It gave her strength.

"The waterfall is cancer. Breast cancer." Holly took a deep, bracing breath. "It's death."

Justin nodded. "And you think you're going over the falls."

"Yes. My mother died at age thirty-two. Her mother and two of her sisters have all died young from breast cancer. I have my mother's eyes, her smile, her hair. Her hips. In another few years, I'll have her cancer, too. If we married, you would be just like my dad. One day you would wake up and I wouldn't be there anymore. It was awful, Justin. My dad was such a mess for so long. Losing Mom all but destroyed him. He's never recovered from loving and losing her. I don't want that for you. Maybe if you weren't so much like him, I wouldn't worry about you as much. But you are like him and that's one of the reasons I love you so much."

"Oh, Holly." Justin kissed the back of her hand. "That's why you turned me down?"

"Yes. This is my destiny, Justin, but it need not be yours. It's why I told you from the beginning I wouldn't get serious. I had good intentions, but I wasn't strong enough. I fell in love with you and I couldn't bear to let you go. I talked myself into thinking we could go along the way we were. Then you proposed and . . ." Holly shrugged.

"Ah, hell, Holly. For a mathematician, you don't know jack about statistics. Don't you know that—"

She hushed him by placing her index finger against his lips. "What I know, what I've recently come to realize, is that it probably wasn't fair of me to make the decision for you."

"Damned right it wasn't." He sighed, loud and long. He shoved to his feet, then stalked away for five steps before halting abruptly. Turning around, he marched back. "I'm sorry. You've finally opened up to me and that's good. I know I should remain calm and be understanding, but the fact is I'm annoyed as hell."

This came as no surprise to Holly. She'd known he wouldn't like what she had to say. But he'd wanted honesty. Wanted revelations. It reminded her of the old adage about watching what you wished for because you just might get it.

"How could you do that to me?" he demanded. "To us? Have you that little faith in me? Do you really think I'm the kind of jerk who would turn tail and run if you got sick?"

"No, I don't think that at all. I think you're the kind of man who would stick right by my side throughout the whole thing and probably suffer more than I. You're so much like my dad, Justin. You're already taking Saturday-Sunday drives, although it's my opinion that a Jeep suits you better than a rebuilt sports car."

He muttered a curse beneath his breath, then sank back into his seat and sulked. Holly eyed his hands, his talented, healing hands, and said, "I've seen firsthand how much he suffered. I heard him those nights when he broke down and sobbed, cursing God for taking her, asking why it couldn't have been him instead. He wanted to die, Justin. I heard him say it more than once. I don't want to put you through that. I don't want you to suffer the same way, too. And you would, Justin. That's the kind of person you are."

He raked his fingers through his hair and grimaced. "Maggie told me to figure out why you turned me down. You wouldn't believe some of the wild ideas I came up with. This one . . . shoot, Holly. You should have known better."

He looked her straight in the eyes. "I'm a doctor in love with a woman who has a strong family history of breast cancer. You think I didn't consider this possibility months ago? You think I didn't investigate current research? You think I didn't spend some time thinking about it, weighing the risks, deciding what was right for me? I went into our relationship with my eyes wide open, Holly."

"Did you really?" Holly didn't know how she felt about that. It was one thing for her to decide she wasn't good enough for Justin. Had he reached a similar conclusion . . . well . . . that would have been something else entirely. "Why didn't you say anything about your concerns?"

"I did. At least, I attempted to on any number of occasions. Each time, you dodged the subject like a pro. Goddammit, Holly. You're a brick wall when it comes to your mother's disease. I couldn't even tell if you realized you might be high-risk."

"High-risk. That's me," she said bitterly. "Me and my mutant gene."

Justin winced. "So you've confirmed it? You've been tested?"

She turned her head away. "No."

"No?"

"No!"

"All right, then. But you have gone for risk counseling."

"No."

Scowling now, he visibly summoned his patience. "You've talked to your doctor about your risks?"

She shook her head.

"You've researched it yourself, then. Books. Medical journals. The Internet."

Holly didn't want to see the incredulous stare that went with his tone. She turned away. "I don't need to do special research, Justin. A woman picks up plenty of information during the daily course of life. Newspapers, television, magazines do plenty of breast cancer awareness stories, especially during October. I know what I need to know, and I don't like to think about it. I'd rather spend my time thinking about ways to live, not how I'm going to die."

Frustration bubbled over. "I can't believe this. In medical school they told us patients sometimes react this way. That some patients prefer to bury their heads in the sand and hide from reality. That a percentage of patients would rather run away from the truth than seek ways to help themselves. But I have to tell you, Holly, I never figured you for cowardice. Not Miz Bungee Jumper. Not Miz Skydiver."

His charge stung, but Holly ignored it. It seemed the safest thing to do at the moment. She simply wasn't ready to check her reflection for a yellow stripe down her back.

"Why?" she wondered aloud, her gaze lifted toward

the sky. "Why does everyone insist on throwing my Life List in my face today?"

"Oh, baby." Justin visibly relaxed. He pulled her, resisting, into his arms. "How can you be so brave and so filled with fear at the same time? Did any of those articles or TV segments mention the fact that sharing a family history of breast cancer does not mean you're fated to develop the disease yourself? That even if your mother did have one of the BRCA gene mutations, odds are only fifty-fifty that she passed it along to you? Did a twenty-second public service spot during Breast Cancer Awareness Month happen to explain how your chance of developing the disease may be no worse than that of the average American woman?" When she didn't respond, he gave her a little shake. "Well, did it?"

Holly ceased her struggles. "Is that the truth?"

"Yes. I would never lie about something so important."

Holly realized that. The information put a new spin on a perception she'd held for years. A fifty-fifty chance. "Well, of course. Simple statistics. I should have known. I'm a math teacher."

"Exactly."

Her mind spun. Absorbing the implications of this new information would take time. In the end, would it change anything? Holly didn't know, not yet. Was half the risk acceptable?

As she rested her head against his shoulder, deep within her, hope sparked to life. She wondered if that tiny flame could withstand the dampening onslaught of her fears.

She had so many fears.

"When my mother died, I wanted to die, too. I miss her every day of my life."

"I'm sure you do. You loved her. I know if I lost you, I'd miss you until the day I died. I'd remember you and mourn you, but, honey, I'd move forward. That's what you need to do now. I understand that as an adolescent, as a teenager, you probably needed to insulate yourself from the whole idea of breast cancer. You're an adult now. You need to quit running away and face your fears. That's the only way you'll conquer them. Right now, they're conquering you."

Holly was tired of people accusing her of running away. *Then maybe you should stop doing it*, whispered a voice in her mind.

She blinked. It was true. Justin's thinly veiled accusations were correct. "You think I should get tested?"

"I can't make that decision for you. That's something only you can choose. What I do strongly believe, both as a physician and as the man who loves you, is that you need to educate yourself about breast cancer and your risk factors. Your true risk, not your perceived risk."

"But I don't want to know about it," she whined.

"Then you'll always be afraid."

Jeeze Louise. The man was right. "I hate it when you're right."

"I know." He patted her hand. "It's why you're always in a bad mood. I'm always right."

She opened her mouth to protest, but he wasn't through. "Something else I want you to think about, Holly. Don't take this the wrong way, but have you ever considered the notion that in addition to protecting my heart, you're also trying to protect your own?"

"What do you mean?"

"Life comes without guarantees. I could get hit by a truck on my way home, and you could be the one mourning me. Maybe part of the problem here is that you're unable to make a commitment out of fear of losing someone else whom you love."

She pulled back. "What? Did you give up pediatrics to become a shrink? That's a terrible thing to say."

His smile was wry. "Honey, we're all gonna die. It's a question of when. I'm simply suggesting—"

"I don't want to hear your suggestions."

"All right."

They passed a moment in silence. Holly kept the glider swinging with a push of her foot against the ground. "Grace's husband said the same thing. About dying being a question of when for everyone."

"Smart man."

It's not the memories that crush your soul, it's the regrets. "Yeah, very smart."

"Holly?"

"Hmm?"

He took her hands in his, squeezed them tight. "Let's take this back to your waterfall metaphor. We all have a waterfall. Every one of us. But what if your waterfall is a long way away?"

Sudden tears swelled in her eyes. She blinked them back.

"Think about it, Holly. What if you've reached a bend in that river of yours where the current has slowed? Picture it. See that scruffy old oak tree growing alongside the riverbank?"

She closed her eyes and nodded.

"That tree is me. I have deep roots and strong branches, and one of them hangs low to the water. It's close enough that you could pull yourself to safety. If you reached up for it. Reached out to me."

Tenderly, he cupped her face in his hands. "Do it, honey. Pull yourself from the current. You can count on me to shelter you, to support you. My wood is strong; I won't crack. I'll give you footholds to the sky. Marry me, Holly. Be my wife."

Yearning melted through her. "Oh, Justin, you're breaking my heart. I'm too afraid to tell you yes, but I don't want to say no. I really, really don't want to say no."

His hands fell away from her and he put some space between them. Solemnly, he asked, "What do you need, Holly?"

"A shrink."

He smiled tenderly. "No shame in that. Do you want me to get you a name?"

She sighed. Actually, she'd already had a therapist. About a year ago, she'd seen a doctor twice before chickening out on showing up a third time. "I think what I need is a library card and a few hours on the Internet. I need answers. You're right, Justin. I need to learn not to be afraid."

"Afraid? You?" He showed her a crooked smile. "The woman who bungee jumps for fun? Who wants to jump from a perfectly good airplane just for the hell of it?"

"But I *am* afraid. Marriage frightens me, but the thought of living without you scares me just as much. The idea of dying with regrets rather than memories chills me to the bone."

"Then don't let it happen. No regrets. That much you can control. Marry me, Holly. We'll make those memories together."

She wanted to say yes. With every fiber of her being she wanted to say yes. But she couldn't. Not now.

Not yet.

"Maybe you could get me a name. Not a therapist, but a genetic testing center. It wouldn't hurt anything for me to look into getting tested, would it? Looking into something isn't a commitment to go through with it."

His smile warmed her clear to the bone. "I'll get that name tomorrow."

✳ *thirteen*

*t*he repeated ringing of her doorbell wrenched Maggie from the oblivion of her afternoon nap. Sluggish, mushy-headed, and weary to the bone, she lifted her head off the couch pillow and peered at the clock on the VCR. Red numerals reading twelve o'clock flashed on and off and didn't come close to telling her the time. Following a power outage two weeks ago, the clock needed to be reset but Maggie hadn't a clue how to go about it. The men in her house had always taken care of such tasks.

Ring. Ring. Knock. Knock. Knock. "All right, already," she called, rolling off the couch. Must be UPS. The driver for her neighborhood had always been heavy-fisted.

Maggie was almost afraid to see what he had for her today. One night last week, unable to sleep and feeling desperate around three A.M., she'd gone a bit crazy and tried something she'd never done before. With her TV remote in one hand and a phone in the other, knowing her Visa number by heart, she'd spent almost an hour surfing the home shopping channels, ordering whatever product happened to appeal at the moment. Afterward, she didn't have a clue as to what she had bought. So far she'd received a carrot juicer, a set of red silk sheets, and a metal detector. No telling what would show up today.

Padding barefoot toward her front door, she passed the grandfather clock in the entry hall. Ten minutes to two. She'd stretched out on the couch just before the noon news. Her fifteen-minute power nap had turned into a two-hour siesta. Funny how often that happened these days.

Of course, today she had an excuse to sleep. She'd been up since before dawn, hadn't she? And upon her return home, she'd spent an hour in the pool swimming laps. She'd earned her two hours of sleep. Still, it was a good thing she'd taken her nap inside instead of by the pool. She'd be burned to a crisp by now.

Thinking about sunburned skin made her realize she was about to answer the door wearing only her swimsuit. The white tank suit was flattering and comfortable, but she never wore it in public because the top part wasn't lined and her nipples showed through the Lycra. That was more than she was comfortable showing the UPS driver, so she detoured into the front bathroom, grabbed a towel, and draped it over her shoulders.

Knock knock knock.

"Just set it down and go," she grumbled, a little worried as to why he didn't do just that. What had she purchased that required a signature? Diamonds? A vague recollection of a sparkling bangle bracelet left her wincing as she opened the door.

Oh, spit. Mike.

At first glance, he appeared calm and collected, a weekend boater in khaki shorts, golf shirt, and deck shoes. Taking a second, closer look Maggie noted the gleam in his eyes, the aggressive jut of his chin, the drum of fingers against his thigh. A sailor spoiling for a fight.

"What . . . I thought . . . you're back in town early." She swallowed hard. She wasn't ready. Not now, like this. The confrontation about the boat was supposed to be fun. She'd had it all planned, imagined it all the way home from Lake Texoma. He'd be ranting and raving and she'd calmly buff her fingernails until suddenly, he'd fall silent. He'd rake his fingers through his hair, tremble a little, then tell her it was all a mistake, that he didn't really want to leave her and sail off to St. Thomas with a woman half Maggie's age. He'd tell her he loved her, he'd always loved her, and he would love her until the day he died. Then, big, strong, proud Mike Prescott would fall to his knees and beg for her forgiveness.

That's how this was supposed to happen. Instead, he'd caught her napping. Literally. And after getting a good look at him, she didn't think he'd hit his knees begging anytime soon. "Why are you at the front door? Why didn't you use your key?"

"Because I don't live here anymore," he snapped. "That would be trespassing. Same as if somebody boarded the *Second Wind* without permission."

As always, the name of that dad-blasted boat stirred her anger. She was tempted to shut the door in his face. Instead, she turned and walked away, leaving him to follow, or not, whatever he chose. In that moment, Maggie honestly didn't care.

Seconds later, Mike slammed the front door shut. From the inside.

Ordinarily, she and Mike conducted their arguments in their bedroom and that's where he headed first thing. For today's event, Maggie decided a new venue was in order. She padded to the kitchen, where she opened the refrigerator door and browsed, finally choosing carrot sticks for her snack. Opening the plastic container, she stuck a carrot into her mouth before setting the plastic box on the counter behind her. Next, she bent over to peer into the back of the fridge in search of the ranch dressing.

She caught Mike staring at her butt when she straightened and turned around. Then his gaze fell to her breasts and his mouth settled into a grim line. "Are you alone?"

Beneath the transparent Lycra, Maggie's nipples drew into tight little beads. *Oh, great. Just wonderful.* Wasn't this just what she needed? One little lusty look and her headlights went on for the first time in months. "Alone?"

"No boyfriend around?"

It took her a moment to make sense of what he was asking, but when she did, her temper flared. She considered shooting a stream of salad dressing at his face. "No. I gave them all the afternoon off. They need rest to keep up their strength."

"Bitch."

Maggie blinked as the word sank into her like a knife. In all their years together, Mike had never, ever used that sort of language with her. That he would now offered a clear signal of just how far their marriage had sunk.

Defeat rolled over her. She closed her eyes and sighed. "Fine. Let's get this over with. What is it you want to say?"

Mike, it seemed, wasn't in the mood to cut to the chase. "I returned to Texas today and discovered my home had been vandalized in my absence. I called the cops to report the crime. I thought kids had done it. Imagine my surprise when I learned that the responsible party was not a gang of teenage hoodlums, but my wife. My wife who had told the police she'd decided to redecorate *our* boat."

Feeling vulnerable, Maggie casually reached up to readjust the towel.

"Why did you do it, Maggie?" he asked, his tone soft and menacing as he stepped toward her. "Was it fun, Maggie?"

Brazenly, she lifted her chin and exaggerated her natural drawl. "All that black and white. You know that particular color scheme has never appealed to me. It cried out for color."

Mike stopped mere inches away. He reached for a carrot stick and she smelled his aftershave. Eternity. Oh, my. Eternity was her favorite.

"I read the police report. It was a good plan. I bet you enjoyed putting it together." He dipped the carrot into the dressing. "Did your girlfriends have a good time with the spray paint? Bet you hated to miss that part."

"I think Holly used a paintbrush, rather than spray paint," Maggie murmured as he held the carrot stick up to her. He had a strange look in his eyes, a gleam she couldn't read. She'd known this man for more than half her life and knew him better than anyone else in the world, but she didn't have a clue what he was thinking now.

It unsettled her. Challenged her. Maggie thought she should probably crunch the carrot he offered, snap it in two with gusto. Instead, instinctively, she licked away the dressing with one, two, three slow strokes.

Mike made a quiet groan. "Damn you."

Now she recognized the gleam in his eyes. Sexual, predatory. A look she hadn't seen in months. Years, even. His gaze slipped lower, fastened on her chest. He reached up and yanked away the shielding towel.

That was it. The unmistakable signal. Her husband, the one who was leaving her and sailing off to coral reef lagoons and sugar-sand beaches, wanted to have sex with her.

Maggie knew better than to use the words "make love."

Mike was angry. He knew she'd been dating. Knew she'd brought another man into their house. Maybe wondered—needlessly, of course—if she'd taken one into their bed.

No, love would have nothing to do with this. This was about a male staking claim to what he still considered his.

Her eyes drifted closed. She wanted to let him. Heaven help her, but she wanted to be with her husband, even with all this anger, this tension, swirling between them. For the first time in months, she wanted bursting skyrockets and moving earth. She wanted passion. She wanted Mike.

A wicked voice whispered in her head, *And if you do it and it's good, maybe he won't go.*

His finger lifted, traced the outline of the aureole clearly visible through her swimsuit. "You're still my wife."

It was so much more than a statement of fact. It was a claim and a question and, in a reassuring way, a promise. Maggie answered from her heart. "Yes."

He kissed her, then backed her up against the refrigerator and assaulted her mouth. It was rough. It was wild. It was wonderful. He scooped her up into his arms and carried her out of the kitchen and through the house toward their bed.

As she clung to him, the familiar halls tilted to a new angle of view. Maggie was dizzy with need as he settled her onto the mattress and stripped off her swimsuit, hungry with a desire she'd thought lost to her forever. She welcomed him with an enthusiasm that for too long had existed only as a memory. She was a bold and demanding lover, a wanton. She made him moan, made him beg. And Mike returned the favors.

Finally, she collapsed atop him, slick and sated and straining for breath. She attempted to shift her body and roll beside him, but he wrapped his arms around her and refused to let her move.

That was fine by Maggie. She was happy where she was. Though Mike had been the one to leave the house and take up residence on a boat, she felt like she'd been the one who'd come home.

They lay in silence together and Maggie steeped in the soothing comfort of simply being held. She'd always adored post-coital cuddling and counted herself lucky that Mike didn't skimp in that department. Once he caught his breath, he rolled onto his side, keeping her tucked tight against him. He would doze now for a few minutes, she knew, but he wouldn't turn her loose. These were the familiar, intimate patterns of lovemaking. When he awakened, they'd talk.

They had a lot of talking to do, Maggie admitted. Serious issues with which to deal. They'd hurt one another, inflicted serious damage to their marriage. Pessimistically, she wondered if they'd ever again enjoy an anniversary in the wake of the disastrous twenty-fifth.

As Mike let out a soft snore, Maggie's thoughts drifted. The past few weeks had been hard. The estrangement from her boys had all but ripped her heart in two. Maybe she could fix that now. The thought made her smile and burrow closer to Mike.

Mike. It felt so good to have him back in their bed. Living by herself had been pure misery, a lesson in true, bone-deep loneliness. Shoot, she'd only *thought* she'd been lonely when Chase went off to school. That had been a picnic compared to this. She'd never before felt so . . . empty.

Her experiment in dating had offered little relief. In truth, she'd disliked herself during the entire process. Not that she'd done anything of which she should be ashamed, because she hadn't. Mike had written the rules, after all.

But she didn't want to think about that. Not here, not now.

She snuggled against Mike, the heat of him warming a place within her that had been cold for too long. She'd withdrawn, from Mike, from life. She could recognize that now. In hindsight, she found it rather amazing, since she wasn't at all one of those people who thrived on being alone.

Thank God for Grace and Holly. Her new friends had kept her sane and steady in recent weeks. If not for those two, she might never have left the house. Imagine her home shopping network bills in that case.

She shuddered at the thought. Mike gave her arm a sleepy pat and Maggie smiled. Her thoughts continued to drift. She wondered how Holly made out with Justin this morning. Hopefully, Maggie's decision to call him had been a good one. Ben certainly had been happy to receive her call. He'd been worried. She'd heard it in his tone. Then his reaction to learning that his wife was in jail had been priceless. After being reassured that his wife was all right—happy, in fact—he'd laughed. Just let loose a loud, delighted guffaw.

He loves his Gracie, Maggie thought wistfully. It was clear in everything he did, as was the love Grace felt for him in return. Now there was a marriage that proved adversity could be overcome. They'd walked through the fire and survived.

Maggie could look at them and feel better about her own marriage. She and Mike didn't have infidelity to deal with. He hadn't taken his dating any farther than she had. She was positively certain of that. She knew her husband. He wouldn't be sleeping beside her now if he'd been sleeping with someone else.

No, today had been a turning point for them. Maggie felt more optimistic than she had in months.

Then Mike opened his eyes and his mouth and ruined it. "Whose bright idea was it to paint my boat?"

A pinprick of irritability burst the bubble of her contentment. Reconciliation sex required an "I love you" or two in her book. That, and an "I missed you." An "I'm sorry for being a jerk" wouldn't have been bad. Instead, the first thing out of his mouth was a comment about that stupid boat.

"I bet it wasn't you. Pink hearts aren't your style."

No. She'd have set the blasted thing on fire. "Actually," she drawled, "I knew nothing about the new paint job for your boat until after the fact. If they'd asked me, I'd have told them to use something else because a little acetone will clear the paint right off the gel-coat. They don't know that. The girls haven't any experience with boats."

"Wait a minute." Mike rolled away and sat up. He narrowed his gaze. "You weren't in on this?"

So much for cuddling and tender words of love. "No."

"It wasn't an idea you cooked up to keep me from leaving?"

Unease spidered up her spine. The edge in his voice warned her this was no casual question, so Maggie took a moment to consider her response. She'd learned long ago to choose her words carefully in any disagreement she'd had with Mike. He was easily offended and quick to go on the attack.

"Maggie? Answer me."

She sat up, clutching the sheet to her breast as she met his ice-edged stare. Her irritability cranked up to annoyance. So much for afterglow.

It didn't seem right that Mike didn't carefully consider his words, too. He always said whatever he wanted to say. No tempering to keep peace in the family. No filtering to maintain the balance. Just straight-from-the-gut honesty no matter what.

It made his failure to speak a word of love in the afterglow of their first lovemaking in months all the more hurtful.

Maggie lifted her chin. Maybe it was time to give him a dose of gut honesty right back. If he didn't temper his words, why should she? After all, she needn't worry about keeping peace in her household anymore. Her household had changed. Priorities had changed. She'd changed. Or at least, she was changing.

She opened her mouth and spoke the bald truth. "I wasn't trying to keep you here. I was furious at you for siccing the boys on me. This was all Grace and Holly's idea. While I'm not entirely certain about their motives, I think it was an act of retribution on my behalf. I know it was an act of friendship in support of me."

For a long moment, he didn't move. Didn't twitch, didn't blink, didn't even seem to breathe. Then abruptly, he muttered a curse and threw back the covers. Climbing out of bed, he snarled, "I need a shower. Do you mind?"

She felt like kicking his bare butt. Instead, she cattily gestured toward their bathroom. "Be my *guest*."

She waited until she heard him step into the shower to scramble from the bed. Finding underwear, shorts, and a shirt, she fled for another bathroom. Maggie didn't know she was crying until she spied the streak of tears on her cheeks as she passed the mirror in the hallway.

What had just happened? How had they gone from intimacy to estrangement in a few short sentences?

What was going to happen now?

In a torment of self-recrimination, she quickly bathed and dressed. Needing something to do with her hands, she returned to the kitchen and began emptying the dishwasher. She put away the glasses first, then the silverware. She'd taken the first plate from the rack when Mike entered the kitchen.

He'd changed clothes, pulling on jeans and a blue chambray shirt he'd left behind when he moved out. His expression was troubled.

That bothered Maggie worse than anger would have. She didn't judge it to be a good sign at all.

He dragged his hand down across his jaw. "Maggie, I'm sorry. I think it was probably insensitive of me to get up and take a shower like that."

Probably insensitive. The man was a genius.

"I didn't mean . . . well . . . I wanted to think. About the boat."

Maggie set the plate on the counter. Hard. *That sorry boat.*

"I thought about it, and you must have said something," he continued. "They wouldn't have done their mischief if you hadn't said something that would make them think you would approve of their prank."

She slammed the silverware drawer shut. "I might have said something about taking a hammer to the stern. I truly hate the name you gave it."

"*Second Wind?*" he replied in a flabbergasted tone. "What's wrong with *Second Wind?*"

She straightened her spine, squared her shoulders, to tell him exactly what she thought. "It feels like a dig at me. When a person needs their second wind, that means their first one has died. I'm not dead, Mike. I'm not old and dried up. I resent the implication that I am."

She pulled a dinner plate from the dishwasher, banged it onto the counter, then reached for a second.

"That's crazy, Maggie," he said, dismissing her point with a wave of his hand. "You're being stupid."

Maggie stared down at the dinner plate she held, one of the set of Franciscan he'd given her for Christmas two years ago. Echoes from twenty-five years of marriage rippled through her mind. *You're being stupid. Don't be stupid, Maggie. That's just stupid.*

Maggie deliberately opened her hand. The plate crashed to the tile floor and shattered like her control.

"Don't. No more, Mike." Emotion churning, she whirled on him. "You don't live here anymore. I've listened to you talk that way to me for twenty-five years, but never again. You are not going to come into my house and call me stupid!"

"What? I didn't call you stupid." He lifted his shocked gaze from the shards of pottery. "I said what you *said* was stupid. That's different."

"Not to me, it's not." And Maggie hated it. She always had. How many times had he said something like that to her? Too many to count, that's for sure. Little digs. Mean-spirited jokes. Often it was the tone of voice that grated, rather than the words. They were mild insults, veiled put-downs. Never cruel, but always irritating. Her husband, putting his wife in her place.

But in the interest of maintaining the peace and keeping the balance, she'd let him do it. She'd swallowed her protests and learned to ignore the undermining cuts. But she'd always heard them. Each time and every time for twenty-five years.

"It's not different to me," she repeated, feeling herself grow taller, "and since you're speaking to me, I'm the one who matters. Or should matter. I'm not stupid. My opinions and my feelings are just as valid as yours. When you decree that something I say is stupid, you might as well be calling *me* stupid. I won't tolerate that. Not anymore. You don't talk that way to your colleagues. You don't say such things to your children. Why should it be okay to say it to me?"

For a moment, it stopped him cold. "Shit, Maggie. I guess I didn't think I needed to watch my every word with my very own wife!"

"Maybe you should have watched your words closer

with me than with anyone else. You should have respected me more than anyone else. I was your wife, your partner. Not your servant, your whipping boy. Not somebody to put down to make yourself feel better."

He looked at her as though she had grown two heads. Instead, Maggie thought, she'd grown a backbone.

Standing in the middle of her kitchen, Maggie experienced a moment of clarity so brilliant it was almost blinding. She didn't have to ignore put-downs anymore. She didn't have to swallow anything she didn't want to. *I'm no longer protecting a nest. It's empty. I don't need him anymore.*

He no longer has all the power.

It was the first time the thought had ever occurred to her.

Her anger abruptly disappeared. She looked around for a dish towel because her palms had suddenly started to sweat.

Mike blew out a hard sigh, then walked over to the kitchen table and pulled out a chair. He looked like he'd taken a blow. When he finally spoke, she plainly heard bewilderment in his tone. "Do you really feel that way? That I treated you like a servant?"

Maggie started to automatically answer yes, but then she paused and considered the question. Not, for a change, because she wanted to choose her words carefully in order to keep the peace, but to make certain she answered the question honestly.

"Sometimes, you did. Not all the time, or even most of the time. I don't think I'd have put up with it if you had. At least, I hope I wouldn't have."

"I loved you, Maggie. I always loved you. I always tried to show you. I tried to make you happy."

Maggie's heart broke just a little. He didn't understand, which wasn't surprising since she didn't exactly understand herself. "I know that, Mike. I'm not saying I wasn't happy because for the most part, I was. You know I loved you and I loved being a mom to the boys. I just have all this . . . I don't know . . . anger, I guess."

"Anger? Why?"

"Because you had all the power."

Abruptly, he shoved to his feet. "That's bullshit."

"No, it's not." Maggie's pulse sped up and her mouth went dry. "Our entire married life, you have controlled me."

He snorted. "I wish."

"It's true." She was on a roll now, feeling the fire of the righteous. "You controlled the purse strings, you controlled our social lives. You controlled our sex life."

"Now you're pissing me off."

"It's the truth. And I think that deep down inside myself, I'm pissed off and I've been pissed off for a long, long time."

His eyes went round as bottle caps. Maggie never used that word. She thought it was tacky. But now, as never before, it fit. "You had all the power in our family, and I didn't fight it because I knew that while we were creating a home and raising a family, it was better for everyone if I didn't rock the boat. But I harbored resentments about it, Mike. I started out as your equal. My grades were just as good as yours, my professional prospects just as bright. I had dreams."

"Oh, I see where you're headed with this. It's about Steven, isn't it? You had everything going for you and then I got you pregnant."

She shook her head. "*We* got me pregnant. We were both responsible. I've never thought otherwise."

"But you're still mad because we had Steven and you had to quit school."

"It's not that simple. I've never regretted having Steven. How could I? I've loved him since the day I realized he was growing inside me. But you have to admit, having a child when we did changed my life more than it changed yours. That day out at the farm you talked about envying the time I had with the kids. Did it never occur to you that I might have liked to walk around a bit in your shoes, too? That's part of why I'm angry, Mike. You never thought about that, did you? Except for missing the occasional track meet, you had it pretty good. You had the family, but not the responsibility of the family."

"Not the responsibility! Hell, Maggie. I was the sole financial support of the family, of five other people. *That* is real responsibility."

"As opposed to what? Taking care of sick children? Nurturing them? Seeing that their needs were met? Teaching them to be good, honest, respectful citizens? Oh, but I didn't do a very good job of that, did I? One word from their father, the man who moved out on their mother, aka Uncle Mike, and they suddenly think it's okay to call their mom a whore."

He did that cracking his knuckles thing like he often did when angry and frustrated. "They didn't say that."

"Everything but." At the memory, temper roared through Maggie. "I don't know what exactly you said to them, Mike Prescott, but it was wrong. It was wrong and mean and vicious and cruel. I don't know if I can ever forgive you for it."

"What is this?" he exploded. "Are you having a hot flash?"

It was Mike's good luck she'd already emptied the silverware from the dishwasher or she might have thrown a knife at him. "Get out, Mike. Now."

"Gladly. I got what I came here for. No need to stick around this house or this city or this state. I'm outta here, Maggie. Today. Pink and red hearts and all."

In shock at the new cruelty, Maggie stood gaping at his back as he walked out. Again. Moments later, the front door slammed shut behind him.

Maggie stood barefoot in the kitchen with her pottery, her heart, and her marriage lying shattered on the floor around her. "Well," she said, testing her voice, her ability to breathe. "That was fun."

She kicked at a four-inch piece of pottery. It sailed across the floor and banged against the baseboard, leaving a scratch in both the wood and her big toe. As she stared down at the tiny pearls of blood beading on her skin, the door opened and Mike marched back inside and stomped across the tile.

"I bought the boat months ago. It was supposed to be your anniversary gift. I'd planned for us to take a trip together. I meant it as *our* second wind, not mine. Our second wind for our second half of life."

Numb, she watched him stride out. This time, the door shut gently behind him.

For a long moment, Maggie waited, braced, listening, but this time, he didn't return. At some point her jaw began to hurt and she consciously unclenched her teeth. With deliberate calm, she pulled the trash can from beneath the sink, then removed the two remaining plates and three cereal bowls from the dishwasher. One by one, she threw them at the hard tile floor. They broke with a sadly satisfying crunch.

The phone rang just as she retrieved the broom from the utility closet, followed almost immediately by the chime of the doorbell. She grabbed the portable phone's receiver on her way toward the front of the house. "Hello?"

It was Grace talking a mile a minute about Holly and a decision and a girls' night out on Tuesday. She finally finished by saying, "You'll come, honey. Won't you?"

Maggie frowned, realizing she'd only caught about every third word of her friend's soliloquy. *Come where?* "Um, sure. But Grace—"

"Wonderful. We'll pick you up at seven. See you then. 'Bye now."

" 'Bye," Maggie replied as the doorbell rang again. Her heart began to race. Mike? No, he wouldn't ring the bell. Not now. Would he? Maybe. She yanked open the door. "Mike, I—"

"Afternoon, Mrs. Prescott," said the UPS driver as he held out his electronic clipboard. "Can I get you to sign for these, please?"

He gestured toward the small mountain of packages at his feet. Maggie counted, then let out a groan. Eighteen.

She stood in the doorway until the driver climbed into his big brown truck and roared off. Only then did she reach down and lift the top package off the stack. What would this one be? Jewelry? A small appliance? An item of apparel that probably wouldn't fit?

The return address read Maguire's. "Maguire's," she murmured, searching her memory. "Maguire's."

When it came to her, she let out a rather desperate giggle. She tore off the packing tape and yanked open the box. She sank down onto her front porch like a Halloween scarecrow and laughed until she cried.

Inside the box, white Styrofoam worms cradled a brown plastic bottle with a label that read: Maguire's No. 45.

Boat polish.

Holly and Grace had just exited the freeway on their way to Maggie's house when Justin called Holly's cell. She pulled into the same Wal-Mart parking lot where she'd encountered George the Drooling Boxer while talking with her darling doctor.

When she answered, Justin told her the patient who had him worried, a four-year-old asthmatic girl now battling pneumonia, was showing improvement, but that he thought he'd bunk down at the hospital tonight just in case. They exchanged teasing endearments, then Holly hung up, smiling.

"You're getting married, aren't you?" Grace asked. "That's what this big decision of yours is."

"What makes you think that?"

"Your cat-'n'-cream smile. Something happened when Justin took you home on Sunday, didn't it?"

Holly's grin turned wistful. "Something happened, but no, Grace, we're not engaged."

"Then you made love, didn't you? The first time since he asked you to marry him at the Making Memories wedding gown sale."

"Grace," Holly protested, embarrassed despite the fact this woman already knew details about her sex life like the fact she'd intended to make love with Justin in a storage closet at the Greystone Hotel.

"Am I wrong?"

"Just look at the scenery, would you?"

Grace laughed, but thankfully quit her pestering as they drove the rest of the way to Maggie's.

Maggie's home was a stately, three-story red brick manse built on a two-acre wooded lot, larger than the suburban norm. White begonias bordered the winding brick walk that led up to a front porch where big clay pots flanked the carved oak double doors.

They were halfway up that walk when the door opened wide and Maggie appeared wearing loose fitting white capris, an oversize cotton candy pink shirt belted at the waist, and a truly ugly pair of shoes. Shocked because this was the first fashion crime Holly had seen Maggie commit, Holly lifted her wide-eyed gaze to Maggie's face. Immediately, she saw that her friend's eyes were too bright, her smile too lively. Something was seriously wrong.

Holly and Grace shared a concerned look as Maggie greeted them in a voice brimming with false cheer. "Hi, girls. I'm so glad you're here. Y'all come on inside and let's visit a little before we go."

Inside, Maggie led them to a pretty, glassed-in garden room that overlooked the backyard pool. "Oh, honey, your yard is beautiful," Grace declared. "I didn't notice the magnolia trees before. Look at all the blossoms. The perfume in your backyard must be divine."

"It's nice."

Holly didn't look at the trees, her attention having been captured by the dessert buffet set up against one wall. "Maggie? Are you having a party?"

"I always serve refreshments to guests."

Holly quickly counted. "Fifteen desserts, Maggie?"

She shrugged. "They're all chocolate."

"Oh, my," Grace said, her eyes rounding at the sight.

"That's it." Holly pulled a padded chair away from the wrought iron table and gestured for Maggie to sit. "Tell us what's wrong."

"Wrong? Nothing's wrong." Maggie ignored Holly's unsubtle demand and handed her a dessert plate instead. "I recommend the torte. I'm a bit disappointed in the butterscotch brownies. Thank goodness I ordered three different kinds. It'd be terrible not to have a decent brownie to offer."

Holly shot a pointed look toward the dessert table, then at Maggie's feet and her pink, purple, and orange shoes. "If your taste in chocolate can in any way be compared to your taste in your footwear, I believe I'll pass."

Grace frowned. "I don't recall anyone mentioning bowling."

Maggie winced and wiggled her toes. "They are awful, aren't they? I don't know what possessed me to order bowling shoes. I have a pair in red, blue, and yellow, too."

While Holly tried to smother a grimace, Grace asked, "Do you bowl?"

"Not since third grade when my Girl Scout troop took lessons."

Generously, Grace said, "I remember reading a year or so ago that bowling shoes were a fashion fad for teenagers and young adults. People actually stole rental shoes from bowling alleys. It became such a problem they hired extra security to watch departing feet."

"Yew." Maggie wrinkled her nose. "I refuse to do rental shoes. I raised four boys, and I know from personal experience that Lysol cannot work miracles."

The three women studied Maggie's feet. Holly shook her head. "Those shoes are definitely not you, Maggie."

Like a perpetual motion machine, Maggie touched up flower arrangements and rearranged forks. "I know."

"Why are you wearing them? Why don't you just take them back?"

"Send them back. I ordered them from QVC or HSN or one of those networks, but I'm not going to send them back and I am going to wear them because Mike would totally, positively hate them."

Ah hah, thought Holly. *Now we are getting somewhere.*

"Is he back?" Grace asked. "Has he seen the boat? In hindsight, I admit I've had doubts about the appropriateness of our actions. I'm not certain what got into me. I was caught up in the fervor of the moment. Please, Maggie. Tell me we didn't make things worse for you."

"No, you didn't make it worse. Yes, Mike saw the boat. He came by and we . . . fought . . . and I really don't want to talk about it."

"Oh, dear." Grace reached blindly for chocolate, seizing a truffle. "I should never have tried to be wicked. It obviously backfired and I'm a terrible friend."

When Maggie laughed, Holly concluded she'd just seen her friend's first honest reaction since they'd arrived.

"Sugar, you're a wonderful friend. The best. I'm glad y'all painted that stupid ol' boat, not only because it was darned funny, but because it gave Mike and me the opportunity to air out our differences. We needed to do that, and now I need to think but I don't want to do it now. Right now, I want to sample one of those sweets and go shopping. That is where we're going, right? I have to confess I was a bit distracted when Grace called the other day."

Holly shared a look with Grace before saying, "Actually, we asked if you wanted to try that new coffeehouse downtown because Grace had heard they serve a selection of chocolate desserts."

"Oh." Maggie glanced at the buffet and winced. "Now I know where my idea came from."

"It doesn't matter. We can go anywhere, do anything, as long as it's quiet. Mainly, we wanted to get together because Holly has something she wants to discuss with us. Maggie, are you certain I didn't make things worse for you?"

"Positive." Maggie patted Grace's hand. "Now, what would y'all think about just staying here? I have peace and quiet and plenty of chocolate. Plus, if we get our talking done, I could use some help opening packages that have stacked up on me the past few days."

"Here sounds great," Holly said, eyeing the fudge. Good thing she'd run an extra mile this morning in anticipation of tonight's decadence. Hanging with these women could be hard on the waistline. "The privacy will be nice, in fact. The things I need to talk about are personal, and I'd just as soon not have strangers overhear."

"Personal?" Maggie repeated.

Holly fumbled for a way to get started. What had sounded like a good idea on Sunday was less appealing now. Grace must have sensed her discomfort, because she chirped up, "I thought she was going to tell us she'd finally agreed to marry Justin, but she says no. Now I suspect that the two of them made love."

Maggie folded her arms, sat back in her chair, and studied the younger woman. "I suspect you're right, Grace. Now that I look, it's written all over her. The sparkle, the glow. Justin took her home and tucked her in and she's as happy as a clam. I'm going to take credit. I knew it was right to call him and send him up to Lake Texoma. You were ready. So, was it delicious?"

"I'm not going to talk about it." Holly paused, then added, "He was an animal."

Grace choked on her tea. Maggie sighed. Holly burst out in a laugh that carried a twinge of hysteria. "Oh, y'all. I told him why I can't marry him. I told him all of it. We talked about it for a long time."

"*It*, Holly? What is *it*?"

She took a deep breath and told them. Neither Grace nor Maggie appeared surprised to hear of the fears she harbored. In fact, she suspected her tale only confirmed their suspicions.

She did manage to surprise them, however, when she got to the heart of the matter and brought up the idea of genetic testing. "Justin says the majority of daughters of breast cancer patients overestimate their risk."

"He's right," Grace said. "This is a question I researched on my daughter's behalf. Somebody published a study that found among women of all ages with a first-degree relative with cancer—"

Maggie interrupted. "What's a first-degree relative?"

"A mother or sister or daughter," Holly replied.

"—eighty percent estimate their lifetime risk to be fifty percent or higher. The fact is that the lifetime risk for that group is about one in eight, which is the average risk for women in the general population."

"So Holly's risk is no higher than mine?"

"Well, no," Holly answered. "Possibly, but I don't know that. I haven't been tested and I'm not certain I want to be. That's the big decision I have to make, and I'm looking for advice from the two of you."

"Grace I understand, but why me?" Maggie asked. "You could fit what I know about genetic testing on the tip of a mascara brush. It seems to me that Justin's the one to give you guidance in this. He's the doctor, after all."

"But he's a man."

Maggie sighed heavily. "Now that is a definite drawback."

"What I meant is that no matter how hard he tries, he'll never be able to understand completely the emotional implications of this entire question. Add to that the fact that he has a vested interest in whatever I decide and . . . well . . . I need my girlfriends for this one. I just need to talk it out, to decide what to do. I don't want to make the wrong decision."

"Oh dear." Grace took a slice of torte and a chair. "I don't believe it's a question of right or wrong decisions. This is a difficult subject. It's a highly personal journey and only you can decide what information you need as you travel. I learned that in facing this question with my daughter."

"So she's had testing done?"

"No. We don't have a family history extensive enough to warrant it. However, in researching the question, I discovered no easy answers exist when it comes to gene testing for breast cancer."

"Why not?" Maggie asked. "If a simple blood test could tell me whether or not I'm destined to get it, I think I'd want to have it done."

"It's not a simple blood test, for one thing. It's a very complex, very expensive blood test that is most likely to be inconclusive and uninformative for Holly."

"But must she have conclusive results? Wouldn't any scrap of information be helpful to her? Like they say, information is power. Holly needs every particle of power she can muster at this point in her life to deal with her fears. That's all she has now. Fears, not facts."

"You've just made my point for me. Testing won't provide facts, just probabilities."

"Probabilities are better than nothing, aren't they? Especially if, like Justin said, she's already overestimating hers."

"The implications of those probabilities are so complicated, so controversial, and so potentially life-changing that in this case, information might well do Holly more harm than good." Grace sighed and toyed with her fork, not eating. "For someone who claims to know nothing about the subject, Maggie, you are doing a fine job of presenting a pro-testing argument."

She turned to Holly. "What is it you would hope to get out of testing? What will you do with the results? You won't be able to trust a negative result."

"Are you certain about that?"

"Yes, honey. I am. My family researched this question within the last year. The only way to get a negative result you can feel certain about is to belong to a family in which the mutation has been identified in others who have tested positive for it. That's not possible in Holly's case, since her mother and aunts have already passed on."

"Oh. Well, there goes my hope of marrying Justin without bringing a guilty conscience to the altar with me."

"A guilty conscience? Why would you have a guilty conscience?"

"I know what it's like to watch somebody writhe in pain for weeks on end and to be helpless to do anything to stop it. I won't do that to those I love. I refuse to."

Nodding, Grace put down the scrolled silver fork. "Okay, with that in mind, let's address the matter at hand. Why would you get tested at all? If you can't trust a negative result, why would you want to know you tested positive? How do you think you would react? Would you do anything different? Would you change how you manage your health?"

"Manage my health?" Holly winced. "I can't say I actually do that. I've always felt why bother to do breast self-exams when I'm a walking time bomb."

For a moment, her confession left her two friends speechless, until Maggie declared, "That's nonsense. I can't believe you'd be that foolhardy with your health."

"You should be ashamed of yourself," Grace added.

Holly didn't know what to say. Hers was a response based upon emotion, not rationale, and she didn't know how to explain it. Instead, she tried to defend. "There's not a lot of health management involved for someone my age. I do see my gynecologist once a year."

Maggie snorted. "Just to get your birth control prescription refilled, I'll bet."

Rather than admit that Maggie was right, Holly addressed Grace's other questions. "As far as how I'd feel if I tested positive . . . well . . . I don't know. I don't think I'd be any more afraid than I am now. In fact, it might be a relief to have it confirmed."

"Would you take better care of yourself?" Maggie demanded. "Do those self-exams? Follow a low-fat diet? Exercise? Have mammograms?" She glanced at Grace. "Is she old enough to have mammograms?"

"At twenty-five? Ordinarily, no. However, I think with someone with her family history they do start them young."

"Great," Holly said. "So even if I don't carry a genetic time bomb, the doctors can do me in with radiation."

"Oh, you and your attitude make me so mad. Say you're right. Say you're bound to get it. That doesn't mean you have to die from it, you know. Breast cancer is beatable, especially if you catch it early."

"This is what your Life List is all about, isn't it, Holly?" Grace asked with insight. "They're not so much goals to achieve as things to do before you die. My stars, I never realized what a negative outlook you have."

Testy now, Holly snapped, "It's not negative. It's realistic."

"It's bull ca-ca," Maggie said. "Have you talked to a counselor about any of this?"

"I've spent years in therapy."

"Not a shrink. A breast person. Somebody who specializes in situations like yours. There must be someone like that out there."

"A genetics counselor," Grace said. "Genetics counseling isn't counseling about stress or anxiety, or therapy in a traditional sense. Instead, it explores the issues we've talked about here tonight. Things like making sure you understand your genuine risks of inheriting a genetic mutation and what you can do to minimize those risks. It helps you to thoroughly think through what you would do or feel if you have a mutation and what you would feel if you don't. A genetic counselor also touches on areas like social and job discrimination, privacy issues, and family relationship issues."

"That sounds exactly like what you need, Holly." Maggie stood still for the first time since they arrived. "You've never spoken with a genetics counselor before?"

"I didn't know such a person existed."

Maggie looked at Grace. "Where do we go to get her one?"

"Actually," Holly said, "now that you mention it, I think I read something about counseling in the paperwork Justin gave me about the testing program he recommends. Seems like you go through counseling before they do the blood work."

Grace nodded. "That's good. I'm very relieved to hear that. I know when Sally and I looked into it, some commercial labs didn't require counseling as part of the process. I think that's awful. Just because the technology exists doesn't mean we should use it indiscriminately. People cannot make good decisions without good information."

"I thought you said there weren't good or bad decisions."

"I said right or wrong. That's different from good and bad. Although, maybe 'decision' is not the right word in this case. Maybe what Holly faces is more of a process. She has information to gather, options available to her to learn about that hopefully will empower her."

"Empowerment. Now there's a word I like."

"Oh, me too." Standing at the buffet, Maggie sank her fork into a slice of triple chocolate cake. "I need some of that myself. Although, I did make a stab at it on Sunday. Mike came over and we had sex, then I threw him out of the house."

"What?" Grace and Holly shouted simultaneously.

"It'll keep. Let's finish talking about Holly first."

"I'm done," Holly hastened to say. "I've decided. I have an appointment next week and I'm going to keep it. I'll talk to the counselor and then decide yea or nay on testing. So, Maggie. Tell us what happened."

"I should have known it wasn't UPS. They don't deliver on Sunday."

❀ fourteen

Justin and Holly didn't speak as they exited Simmons Cancer Center in Dallas. Justin handed the parking ticket to the valet and while they waited for their car, he clasped Holly's hand. She returned his grip, hard. He was her anchor, her source of strength. She'd have been lost had he not come with her today.

Her thoughts swirled like cotton candy around a paper cone. So much information to process. So many decisions to be made.

She and Justin had just spent an hour and a half with a risk assessment counselor, this after having spent a considerable amount of time prior to the meeting developing a medical family tree and recording lifestyle information. Her brain was full of percentages and statistics, but one undeniable, unsurprising fact came through loud and clear.

She was considered high-risk.

Uh, duh. You've known that since you were twelve years old.

Yeah, but now it was official. The computer models said so. That nice, compassionate genetic counselor had spoken the words aloud. Most telling of all, her risk assessment level was high enough so that her health insurance company would pay for the testing.

The valet pulled up in front of them with Justin's truck and they climbed inside, still not speaking. Holly wondered what was going on in his mind. She wondered if anything he'd heard in the conference room had *changed* his mind. No, she wouldn't torment herself with negative thinking.

She cleared her throat. "There's a park bench across the street near the pond with the fountain. It's a pretty day. Would you want to sit there with me for a while?"

His quick glance and a smile reassured her. "I'd love to."

He drove to the city park, leaving the truck in the parking lot nearest the pond. They walked hand in hand toward the graceful wrought iron and wood park bench on the grassy verge and sat down. A small flock of sparrows scattered at their approach and Holly shaded her eyes to watch them swoop and sail off into the pale blue sky. "Flying away does tend to appeal at times."

"You think so?" Justin tucked her closer against his side. "Where would you like to go?"

She closed her eyes and sighed. "Tahiti. Banff. Hearne."

"Hearne?"

"Hearne, Texas. South of Waco on Highway Six. The Dixie Café serves the best chicken fried steak with cream gravy in Texas."

"Ah. Health food."

"Did you catch that one graphic the counselor showed us? About diet and exercise?"

He spoke in his Dr. Stuffy voice. "A low-fat diet and regular exercise can significantly lower your risk of developing many diseases, not just breast cancer."

"Still, if four hours of exercise a week can lower a woman's risk of developing breast cancer by forty percent, I'd be a fool not to get up and move. It's something I can do. A way to be proactive."

He nodded. "A way to take some control."

Holly closed her eyes and listened to the soothing sound of the fountain. "What do you think I should do?"

Without hesitation, he said, "Exercise. And marry me."

Something inside Holly eased as she grinned. Not that she'd honestly expected Justin to abandon her, but reassurance was nice. "You know what I mean."

"Ah, honey." He brought her hand up to his mouth and kissed her knuckles. "As much as I love you . . . as much as I'd love to take this burden off your shoulders . . . I can't make this decision for you. It wouldn't be right. It's your life, your health."

"You're afraid I'll blame you in the future."

"Sure. Once we're married, I imagine I'll provide you plenty of opportunities to lay blame at my feet. Why start early?"

"Jus-tin," she chastised.

"Hol-ly," he mocked.

She smiled. "The counselor was nice, wasn't she?"

"I was impressed. Good presentation of the data. The visual aids helped simplify complex subject matter."

"Even I understood it, and I went into this entire business knowing nothing."

"I won't mention how crazy that makes me every time I think about it," Justin said. "Or how irresponsible it is for you to have ignored screening of any kind up until this point."

Holly rolled her eyes. "I appreciate your reticence."

"I'm the epitome of reserve."

"Or something."

He grinned, leaned over, and planted a quick, hard kiss against her mouth. Holly sighed.

She reached into her bag and pulled out the stack of papers and pamphlets the counselor had given her. She flipped through the pages until she found the personalized flow charts of steps to take should she test positive or negative.

"I really don't see why I need to test. Look, the procedure they recommend in either case is almost identical."

"True."

"And despite their assurances, can I truly count on my results remaining private? I could face discrimination for insurance or employment. No matter what laws are passed, you know it happens."

"Yes."

"What if the results did come back positive and instead of helping me cope, it made matters worse. I couldn't unlearn the facts."

"No, you couldn't." He paused for a moment, then said, "When will you schedule the test?"

Holly's heart swelled. Justin knew her so well. "I'm tempted to do it as soon as they'll let me, but I'm going to be deliberate about this. Give myself time to be certain of my decision. I may even wait until next fall so I'll be working during the three week wait. I think the waiting for results might be the hardest part of the process."

"It often is."

Holly sighed. "This might be a mistake, but I honestly don't think so. What I've learned in the past few weeks since I started researching has helped. Maybe I'm slowly coming to realize—in my heart, not just in my head—that if I get breast cancer, my experience need not be like my mother's or my aunt's. I don't have to die."

Justin shoved to his feet, threw out his arms, lifted his face toward the sky, and shouted. "Hallelujah!"

"Oh, sit down." Glancing around, she tugged on his khakis. Maybe he didn't have a stuffy side, after all.

He had a tender smile on his face as he looped his arm over her shoulders and pulled her tight against him. "You don't know how good it is to hear you say that, sweetheart. What finally got through to you? The statistics? The visual aids?"

"Grace."

Justin pulled back to look at her, the question in his gaze.

"Before I got to know Grace, my perception of disease came from my experience with my mom and with my aunts. Anytime I heard so much as a whisper about cancer, I buried my head in the sand. Grace didn't give me a chance to hide. She's a special woman, Justin. She's strong and she's vital and she's so courageous—and she's Stage IV. Look how well she's living. That gives me so much hope."

"It should. Things change so fast. Every week a new paper says the opposite of what was said six months ago. Treatment is very different now than it was when your mom and her sisters were diagnosed. Grace's medical management is much different. Honey, you're already much better off than your mother was. Like the counselor pointed out, now that you've been named high-risk, you qualify for all the high-tech screening. You could join a research study and contribute toward finding new treatment methods or cures. Would that count for anything on your Life List?"

It warmed her that he'd thought about her Life List. She'd shown it to him only a couple of weeks ago and as this question indicated, he'd quickly grasped its importance. Holly considered the inquiry. "Taking a real stretch, maybe number eight."

"What is number eight?"

" 'I will save a life.' "

"That's no stretch at all, honey. Contributing to research may lead to saving thousands of lives. You could give number eight double checks."

The mention of her list led Holly's thoughts in another direction and her gaze trailed back to Justin's truck. Most men stocked their tool boxes with tools. Justin's ordinarily contained three toys to every tool. "Do you still keep kites in your tool box?"

"Sure. I know you enjoy flying kites."

Number fourteen required her to fly a kite in every month of the year. Up till now, she had about half the year accounted for. June, however, remained a "to do."

"The wind is perfect today and this is a great spot. No power lines to snare them. Do you have time?"

"I cleared my calendar except for evening rounds. What color do you want? I know I have red, blue, and pink bat kites. My big super-sailor cloth one tore last time I used it."

"Pink, please."

"I thought you hated pink."

"I did. That whole pink ribbon thing and breast cancer awareness turned me off. But I'm coming around. Fran Hansen gave me a little pink ribbon pin to wear. Think I should start wearing it, don't you?"

"I love you, Holly Weeks."

She gave him a quick kiss. "Go get my kite, Dr. Delicious. I can't think about this anymore. I'm in the mood to play."

Play is exactly what they did. They had a height competition, a trick competition, and a fastest-in-the-air competition. They laughed and cheered, jeered and complained depending on the outcome. Eventually, Justin declared Holly the overall winner, and he rolled his blue kite in. Holly stood watching the pink plastic wings soar, humming beneath her breath, and smiling. Filled with peace.

Justin moved behind her, wrapped his arms around her. Supported the reel of string. Holly leaned against him and yearned to remain that way forever, sheltered in his loving, supportive arms. The possibility that it might not happen added a cloud to her blue sky. "How will you deal with it, Justin?"

"Hmm?"

"If I'm BRCA-positive. How will you feel?"

He pressed a kiss against her hair. "I'll be there for you. That won't change."

"How can you be certain?" She thought it was the most important question she would ever ask Justin. "If I'm positive, there's a fifty percent chance I'll pass my altered gene to our children."

She felt his muscles grow stiff. His grip on her arm tightened, then heedless of the kite, he whirled her around to face him. He gazed deeply, intensely into her eyes. Captured by the fierceness of his stare, Holly allowed the kite string to slip from her hand. The pink kite sailed free.

"What?" she asked.

His voice was raspy, rough. "Our children? Are you saying you'll marry me, Holly?"

Oh. Oh, dear. She hadn't meant . . . she hadn't realized. "Justin, I'm sorry. That's not what I meant."

His arms dropped and he turned away. Walked a few endless steps away.

Holly felt horrible. She'd hurt him. One more time, she'd hurt him. Why did he put up with her? He stood facing the pond and the shooting fountain, his hands shoved into his back pants pockets. "Justin? Please. I'm trying. I truly am. These issues . . . these questions . . . are too important to ignore. After what I've learned today, I would be irresponsible even to think about marrying you unless you can accept the reality that your children might be at risk if I am their mother."

"Dammit, Holly."

"That's even if I could have children. If the ovarian specialist doesn't want to yank out my ovaries immediately."

"Now you're being foolish." He swung around and glared at her. "You have no history of ovarian cancer in your family."

"But if I'm BRCA-positive, my risk is higher. You heard her say that, didn't you? I know the risk is higher with BRCA1 than with BRCA2, but you can't ignore it. She said some women who test positive do choose to attempt to avoid the Big C by pre-need surgeries."

Holly repeated the clinical terms to help make her point. "Prophylactic oophorectomies and mastectomies. How would you deal with that, Justin? Having a wife with no breasts or ovaries?"

"Dammit," he snapped. "You are determined to look at this in the worst possible light, aren't you?"

"See, we have a difference of opinion right from the first."

An ache grabbed at her heart. "To me, the worst possible light is dying. That you would rank my loss of feminine attributes at the top of the scale answers my question, doesn't it."

"That's not what I meant and you know it."

She shrugged and folded her arms across the hollow in her stomach. He stomped toward her, planted his feet in front of her, and folded his arms, too. "Listen to me, Holly Elizabeth Weeks. I'm trying not to take this too personally, because I know you're vulnerable at a time like this. I don't mind repeating myself, but I need you to listen. Will you do that for me? Will you listen?"

She nodded.

"I love you. I love your sparkle and your wit and your determination. I love your compassion. I love your tenderness with young children. I love the way you inspire your students to try their best. I love the respect you show your father. I love the little snore you make when you're deeply asleep. I love your competitiveness. I love the way you stick to your guns. I love your intelligence. I love the thickness of your hair and the color of your eyes. I love your smile."

His voice deepened. "And yes, I love your breasts. I love to touch them and feel them and taste them. I love the way your toes curl when I draw your nipples into my mouth and suck them. Would I miss your breasts if they were gone? Yes. Would I grieve for the children we could not make were you to make the choice to have your ovaries removed? Deeply. Would I worry about how premature menopause would affect you both physically and emotionally? Of course. Would I still think you are beautiful if they take your breasts? Yes. Would I still love you if they take your breasts?" His voice broke like a teenager's. "Goddamn right I would and shame on you if you think I'm so shallow I wouldn't."

Holly swayed and he reached out and clutched her arm. "I love you, Holly. I love you with your breasts or without them. I love you with your ovaries or without them. I will love you if you are BRCA-positive or if we never learn your genetic disposition. I will love you whether you choose to deal with your risk with conservative screening management or chemo prevention or radical surgery. I want you to be my wife no matter how this situation plays out. I love you, Holly. I want a life with you for as long as God allows, be it a month or a year or fifty years like Grace and Ben. I won't give up on you. No matter what the future brings, I want to share mine with you."

The tears that slowly filled her eyes during his impassioned speech overflowed and spilled slowly down her face. He took her hands in his, held them tight, placed them deliberately against his heart. "Marry me, Holly. Be my wife. Be my life."

"Oh, Justin. I want to say yes. You don't know how badly I want to say yes."

"Then open your mouth and spit it out."

"I . . . I . . ." She fumbled in her pants pocket for a tissue. He handed her his handkerchief. "Do you believe what I just said?"

"Yes. I do."

"Good answer. That's all you really need to know how to say. Now let's match that answer up with the right questions."

He waited, intent, silently urging her on.

She gazed up into his eyes, drawn into emotions so deep she thought she could drown. The words he wanted to hear and she wanted to say formed on her tongue and froze. Something, some inner intelligence or insecurity, she couldn't tell which, held them back.

"Holly?"

"You don't know how much I needed to hear that. It helps. Truly, it does. But for me to commit to a future with you or with anyone right now . . . it just wouldn't be right. I need, I think we both need, facts in hand before we make permanent decisions."

He sighed and grimaced as if he'd tasted something bad. "Your lack of faith in me hurts, Holly. What will it take to convince you I mean what I say?"

"I believe you mean it. Now."

His face seemed to age before her eyes. "But you can't trust me to mean it a month from now or a year from now."

Grief for them both wrung her insides. "Please, Justin. I've come a long way in the past few weeks. Grant me that. Now I'm asking for a little more time. For both of us."

He shoved his hands into his pants pockets and rocked back and forth on his heels. "I guess I'm afraid if you test positive, you'll tell me no."

"I'm afraid if I test positive, I'll tell you yes, but for the wrong reasons."

"As long as you love me, any reason is good enough for me."

"Oh, Justin." Holly touched his shoulder. "I don't mean to hurt you."

"I know. It's hard on a man's pride though, Holly."

"I know."

He sighed heavily. "All right. I'll give you your time, but I won't ask you again. Next time, you have to ask. One more rejection and I doubt my self-esteem could recover."

Holly rolled her eyes at that. The doctor's self-esteem was strong as garlic.

A mockingbird's song drifted on the gentle breeze and the flock of sparrows returned, circling the pond and its fountain before alighting on green grass. Holly hooked her arm through his. "If we were going to a high school reunion this summer, think we'd win the prize for most paranoid pair?"

His mouth twitched with a grin that didn't reach his eyes. "Undoubtedly."

"Think counseling could help? Couples counseling?" As he shot her a look of surprise, she continued, "It might be good for us to talk to someone with a different perspective—a neutral perspective—who can help us both sort out our feelings and our needs. It might help us to avoid problems down the road."

"I'll talk to anybody, anytime, if you think it'll help. Especially if you keep using phrases like 'down the road.' It gives me hope." He pressed her arm against his side. "You want to set something up or shall I?"

"I'll do it. I thought we could try the marriage prep program at church."

"This is sounding better and better to me all the time."

Justin wrapped her in his arms and pulled her tight against him. "In fact, I think that preparation needs to start right away," he said as he nuzzled her neck. "There's a hotel just up the street. How about it, honey? Wanna practice being married?"

*　　*　　*

Grace suspected something was up. Ben had acted downright peculiar this morning, fixing her breakfast, picking out a sweater for her to wear, then dithering on and on about which pair of shoes she should choose for today's shopping trip. As if she wouldn't know to don comfortable shoes to go hunting for the perfect anniversary dress.

Plus, he'd hovered. He repeatedly quizzed her about her energy level and shot her assessing looks at least a dozen times. It was driving her crazy, especially since he'd been better of late, almost casual in his care. In fact, ever since that day in the coffee shop when she spouted off to Maggie and Holly about Ben's patronizing ways, he'd hardly gotten on her nerves at all.

Grace acknowledged that much of the change might lie in how she perceived him rather than in how he acted, but still, this much attention was ridiculous. What was the matter with the man?

She got her first inkling when Maggie and Holly arrived to pick her up. In a bright white limousine.

"What in the world?" she marveled as a uniformed driver opened the car door and her friends unfolded from inside.

"Morning, friends," Maggie said. "Isn't it a simply gorgeous day? Grace, I had the silliest dream last night. I dreamed you wore a leisure suit to your anniversary party."

"What's a leisure suit?" Holly asked.

"Oh, my, sugar. Thanks for making me feel like Methuselah. Leisure suits were *the* men's fashion mistake of the seventies."

"Why would Grace wear a man's suit to her anniversary party?"

"I don't know. Neither do I know why she served her

guests watermelon. Enough of dreams. Let's get on to fantasy. Grace, are you ready?"

Grace eyed the limo and tried to ignore the flutter of excitement inside her. She'd never ridden in one before. "Ready for what?"

Maggie gestured to the car with a flourish. "To go shopping."

"Is something wrong with your car? Holly or I could take our car."

"Not to this shop, we can't," Holly murmured.

Maggie grinned and walked up to Ben and kissed him on the cheek. "Thanks for helping with this, sugar. I promise we'll take good care of her."

Grace's gaze flew up to meet her husband's sheepish one. "Take care of me?"

"I want you to have your special dress, Gracie. We all want that. Maggie suggested a way to make it happen and it seemed like a good idea, so I went along with it. I hope you'll be gracious about it."

Gracious? Now why would he feel the need to provide that particular warning? "What have you done, Ben Hardeman?"

"Oh, don't get snitty. All he did was pack a bag." Maggie glanced toward Ben. "You did remember to include the girdle, I hope."

"It's in there."

"My underwear? The two of you are discussing my underwear now?"

"It'll be fine, Grace," Holly assured. "I promise. But you need to kiss your husband and get into the car or we'll be late."

"Late? Late for what? Where are we going?"

Her friends and her husband shared a look. Maggie

said, "Holly and I are volunteering at the Making Memories wedding gown sale this weekend, and we thought it'd be worth the effort to see if that dress we admired at the Fort Worth sale is still on the racks."

A Making Memories sale? Back in town so soon? "I haven't heard any promotion about the sale."

"They haven't exactly come back to town," Ben said as he leaned down to plant an enthusiastic kiss on Grace's mouth. "Not our town anyway. Have fun, Gracie. I'll see you tomorrow."

"Tomorrow?"

Her husband caught the chauffeur's gaze and gestured toward the oleander bush at the end of the driveway where, Grace noticed for the first time, her overnight bag sat. "Where are we going?"

Maggie ushered her toward the car. "The Making Memories sale. Just like I told you."

"Where is the wedding gown sale?"

Busy taking their seats, neither Maggie nor Holly responded. Grace finally got her answer when Ben leaned into the car and fastened her seat belt as if she were a toddler in a car seat. "If y'all have any extra time and get a chance to run by Busch Stadium, I'd sure like a Mark McGwire tee shirt."

Grace, knowledgeable about baseball after living with a true fan for almost fifty years, gasped. "Busch Stadium? St. Louis? We're going to St. Louis?"

"And buy snow globes of the arch for the grandkids, too."

She was speechless as the limo pulled away from her house. In fact, she didn't find her voice until they were halfway to the airport. Summoning control, she quietly asked, "Would one of you please explain?"

Maggie pulled an emery board from her purse and began filing her nails. "Now sugar, no need for conniptions. I was talking with Fran Hansen about a directed wish I've decided to grant to a young mother who wants to take her children to the Grand Canyon, and she mentioned they were extremely short on volunteer workers at this weekend's sale."

"But a last minute plane ticket like this, they're so expensive."

"Don't you worry about that. I have oodles of frequent flier miles and we're all gonna share my hotel suite and by buying your dress from Making Memories you'll be supporting the foundation."

Grace frowned. "I can't accept—"

Holly reached over and clasped Grace's hand. "Please, Grace. She needs this. It's been a bad week."

Immediately, Grace's self-concern vanished. "Oh, honey. What happened?"

"The boys are being their father's sons. John came by the other day and things seemed to be better between us. Then I asked him to be my date to your party. He started crying, Grace. My big, handsome, grown-up boy sat down on my sofa and cried like he did when he was five. I feel so bad. I really want to get away from it, at least for a day or two. When Fran told me how desperate she was for helpers, this excursion seemed like the perfect answer. Say it's okay, Grace. Please?"

"Just don't do it again. You're a doll, but I don't like surprises."

Grace's brows arched upon taking her seat in first class, another new experience for her, but she didn't comment. Maggie and Holly were giggling like schoolgirls and she hated to spoil their mood. Especially since they probably wouldn't understand her objection to their doing something nice for her.

Grace wasn't certain she understood her feelings herself. She'd always been an independent person. And proud. Too proud, maybe. That characteristic had served her well during most of her life and proved helpful while fighting her disease. Pride and independence walked hand in hand with strength, in Grace's opinion. *Heaven knows, a woman needs all the strength she can get while fighting for her life.*

However, that same strength and pride and independence made it difficult to ask for help, to accept the charity of others. Limo rides and first-class tickets were lovely. It pleased her to know her friends thought enough of her to go out of their way like this. But at the same time, she found the experience humbling. Almost humiliating. She'd always paid her way in life, and now, because of insurance premiums and pharmaceutical co-pays and disallowed claims, every penny she and Ben scraped together was marked to pay one bill or another.

Poor Ben. He was the one who should be sitting here in first class taking a trip just for fun. He'd given up so much for her over the past eight years. He should be enjoying this treat instead of her. *I'll get by Busch Stadium to get him his tee shirt if I have to walk.*

From her seat across the aisle, Maggie said something to a male flight attendant that made him burst out laughing. Holly looked at Grace and shook her head. "The woman is a natural-born flirt."

A brokenhearted flirt, Grace thought. She was worried about Maggie. Her laughs were too brittle, her smiles too false. If Mike Prescott were to wander down the aisle of this airplane at the moment, Grace would be hard-pressed not to fling her ginger ale into the man's face.

In the relatively short time she'd known them, Grace had come to love Maggie, and Holly, too, as if they were her own. They were Friends with a capital F, better in some ways than family. Grace felt blessed to have them in her life, even if they did act a bit high-handed in arranging shopping trips.

At some point, Grace needed to sit down and talk with them about it. Even if their hearts were in the right place, they needed to understand she couldn't, wouldn't, accept more . . . charity. That's exactly what this trip was. Frequent flier miles were just like money, after all. Donated frequent flier miles were gold to the Making Memories Foundation, providing tickets for Disney World wishes and the like. And a hotel suite? If Maggie had made this trip alone, she wouldn't rent an entire suite for a night. "On second thought, maybe she would."

"I'm sorry, Grace," Holly said. "Did you say something?"

"No. Just mumbling to myself. I think I'll try to take a little nap. This is shaping up to be a very busy day."

A little after noon, they arrived at the wedding gown sale. Rather than being located in a hotel ballroom, today's event was being hosted by the St. Louis Junior League in a beautiful room at their facility. The moment Fran Hansen spied them, her eyes lit up like twin searchlights. "Grace. Maggie. Holly. It's so wonderful of you to come."

She gave them quick hugs, threw volunteer tee shirts their way, and told them where to get to work. "We're here to shop, too, Fran," Maggie cautioned as she tugged on the bright pink shirt. "Grace needs to find her dress."

Fran nodded. "I went through the gowns last night

after setup and pulled out the suits and other dresses I thought would be appropriate. Grace has her own reserved rack and of course, she's welcome to shop whenever she wants."

They went right to work, naturally falling into the assignments they'd had at the Fort Worth sale. Grace noticed Maggie in a huddle with Fran a time or two throughout the afternoon and she felt a shimmer of unease, wondering what mischief her friend was cooking up now.

Sales were brisk and the women kept busy until Maggie convinced Grace to break for a soft drink during a midafternoon lull. Cokes in hand, they took seats in the restaurant and debated the day's most obnoxious mother of the bride until Holly strode into the room, raving.

"Maggie? Have you looked at the vintage racks?"

"Yes. I helped the sweetest girl find a vintage gown not twenty minutes ago."

"Did you go through the size eights?"

"No. She was a sixteen."

"So you haven't seen it. It's still there. I cannot believe it's still there."

"What are you talking about?"

"Your wedding gown. It hasn't sold yet. It's the most beautiful gown on the racks and I can't believe these silly girls are too clueless to see that. They're so busy shopping for strapless dresses to show off their buff bodies that they look right past the beauty and workmanship and romance of a gown like yours."

She grabbed an apple from a basket set out for volunteers, took a bite, and plopped down into the seat beside Maggie. Grace debated whether or not to mention the fact that the dress likely hadn't sold due to her own actions.

During the Making Memories sale in Fort Worth, she had asked Fran to set the gown aside. Though Maggie had donated the gown in good faith, Grace believed she'd acted precipitously, out of emotion rather than true desire. Maggie would come to regret the impulsive act as soon as she resumed thinking with her head rather than her heart. It would be such a shame if the gown were gone by then.

Maggie said, "Don't feel offended on my behalf. I know why the gown hasn't sold. Last time I called Fran, I asked if anyone had purchased my dress and if she had a name and address so I could send the bride a note of good wishes and fill her in on the history of the gown. Well, Fran got to looking and eventually found it on a rack of gowns needing to be mended. Today's sale is the first time it's been out for girls to look at."

Not for long if Grace had anything to say about it. First thing she'd do upon finishing this break would be to fetch Maggie's dress from the vintage rack and hide it among the dresses reserved for her. Ten minutes later, that's exactly what she did.

A steady stream of shoppers kept them busy throughout the afternoon. At about two-thirty, one of the local volunteers drove Grace to the nearby hotel so she could check into their room and rest for an hour or so. She returned to the Junior League facility shortly after five to find Maggie ringing up the sale for the day's final purchase.

"It's a record, Grace," Fran Hansen told her as she tallied up the take. "Thirty-one thousand dollars today. That's at least six wishes we can grant. This is awesome."

Holly said, "After all the media coverage Making Memories received today, I expect we'll have a bigger crowd tomorrow."

Maggie closed and locked the door behind the delighted bride, her mother, and the oversize bag containing a wedding gown, slip, and veil. Moments later she opened it again so that a quartet of shoppers who'd been dallying in the dressing room were able to leave. "Is that everyone?"

"I think so," Holly responded.

"Excellent. Grace, are you ready to shop?"

While in her hotel room Grace had removed the girdle from her suitcase that Ben had so helpfully packed. Now she reached into her handbag and waved it about with a flourish. "Aye aye, Captain."

"Shall we adjourn to the dressing room, then, ladies? Holly, you want to grab Grace's rack from the storage room where we left it?"

Holly had spent the final hour of the sale cleaning up the dressing room, so only a handful of gowns remained on the "go back" rack. Fran saw to those while Maggie brought in a vegetable tray with assorted dips she'd ordered from the restaurant. "A waitress is right behind me with water and soft drinks, coffee, and cookies. I thought a little snack might be in order to tide us over to dinner. I've ordered a bottle of champagne, and some sparkling cider, too, for those of us who shouldn't mix alcohol with our meds."

Maggie placed the tray on a table set against the wall, then grabbed a poofy bit of lace from one of the veil racks that stretched down the center of the room. Plopping it on her head, she grabbed a carrot stick and sprawled in one of two upholstered chairs they had commandeered from the entry hall.

"All right, party girl," she said, flourishing her carrot stick like a baton. "It's time to strip."

"Maggie," Holly protested. "Have some sensitivity.

Grace might not feel comfortable undressing in front of us. We're not at Silke's Boutique with its private dressing rooms, you know. That's why I set up a screen for her."

"That's all right, Holly." Grace pulled off her pink volunteer tee shirt, then began unbuttoning the white blouse she wore beneath it. "Actually, I used to be much more modest than I am now. Before my surgery, I'd have been hard-pressed to undress in front of a group of women, but having a mastectomy changed that. Doctors, nurses, technicians, curious friends and family. Why, in the past eight years, I've had more people look at my chest than a Playboy centerfold."

Maggie, Holly, and Fran chuckled at that as Grace slipped off her blouse to reveal a plain, functional pocket bra. "This is my favorite bra. It's new. I like the silhouette it gives my body. Combine it with the extra-super-put-your-rear-in-a-vise girdle, and I think I look pretty good for an old broad."

"Sugar, you look great," Maggie said, hopping up to rifle through the rack of gowns. "If there were a Mrs. Golden Anniversary Beauty Pageant you'd win it hands down. My oh my, these dresses are lovely. Randall at Silke's would have a jealous fit if he saw these. You know what? I think we need a system. How about we start with the suits, then work our way toward the shorter dresses, then the longer gowns? That way we'll . . . hey, this is my dress. What's it doing on Grace's rack?"

"I put it there."

Maggie's face lit up. "You want to wear my gown? Really?"

"Not exactly." Grace managed to turn her back to Holly without being obvious, then she waggled her brows in warning.

"It's a wedding gown—a beautiful, fabulous, wonderful wedding gown—not an anniversary party dress. After Holly mentioned it, I hunted it up. I've thought about the story you told of the Belgian lace and your grandfather and World War Two. I wanted to get a look at it again. Then I got to thinking about all the dreams this wedding gown represents. Your grandparents', yours, Mike's, the person's who made this lovely lovely lace. We've said it before, I know, but it bears repeating. A wedding gown is much more than simply a dress."

Grace hung Maggie's wedding gown on the end of the rack and spread out the train. "Look at this, girls. Think about it. In the sisterhood of women, the words 'My wedding gown' speak to much more than a dress. They're subtext, a code of communication that arises from deep within the feminine soul and goes far beyond satin, lace, beading, and embroidery."

"I like the sound of it, but I'm afraid I'm not following you one bit," Maggie said, her gaze shifting away from the gown.

"It's a bit off the wall, I know, but I've been mulling this over for some time. Don't think about the dress per se; think of the symbol. The dress a woman chooses to wear on her wedding day is an outward symbol of the very essence of being female. Whether it's white satin, lace, and a long flowing train or denim jeans and a tee shirt, the outfit a woman chooses to wear while repeating her wedding vows will always and forever symbolize her at one of her most powerful moments."

"That's true." Holly walked around Maggie's gown, her expression filled with wistful admiration. "No one is more powerful than a bride on her wedding day."

Maggie snorted. "It's all downhill from there."

Grace pretended not to hear. "The gown the bride wears represents her femininity, her sexual allure, her maternal might. It's her aspirations, wishes, and desires. It's hopes and dreams and a place for memories to cling."

"Oh, stop it," Maggie said. "You're going to make me cry and that's not why I've come here." She pulled a classically styled skirt and jacket in ivory silk from the rack. "Here. Let's start with this, shall we? Grace has at least thirty dresses to try. Maybe more. This will take some time. Speaking of time, did y'all get in on that debate between the bride and her mother about planning the wedding around the football game?"

"No. I missed that," Holly said.

"Apparently the couple plans to marry in the fall and the bride's father is a huge Notre Dame fan. He's afraid a two P.M. wedding will interfere with kick-off, and he's threatening to pull his financial support if they won't schedule events around the game."

"Jeeze Louise," muttered Holly. "I'm a big college football fan, but that's going way too far for me."

The mood in the dressing room lightened after that. The women joked and made small talk as Grace worked her way through the suits. She found two that she liked and she set those aside. A third had definite possibilities, but the zipper was stuck. Grace glanced up. Fran sat by the doorway mending the hem of a lovely designer gown that had been donated earlier that morning. Holly stood beside the rack of gowns, her expression thoughtful as she gently fingered the lace. Maggie was touching up her lipstick. "Maggie, would you help me with this, please?"

"I'd be happy to, sugar."

It took some thread picking and bottom wiggling, but the zipper finally slid upward. It was then that Grace decided to send up a test balloon. "Holly, would you please do me a favor now?"

"Sure thing." She flashed a perky smile. "What can I do?"

"I want you to try on Maggie's dress."

Holly froze. "What?"

"I want you to see what it looks like on you."

"But . . . I can't . . . I don't . . ."

Maggie's head snapped up. "Of course you can. Trying on a dress is no commitment to anything. Honest. I want to see how my dress looks on you, too."

Holly eyed the nothing of a veil Maggie had yet to remove and grinned. "Okay, but only if you play dress-up, too."

"It's a deal." Flashing a grin, Maggie headed for the dressing room door. "I know just where I'm going to start, too."

Maggie made a beeline for the sales floor and returned moments later with a dress Grace had noticed back in Fort Worth. She pilfered through the small mountain of slips, then exclaimed, "Ah hah! Here it is."

"A hoop skirt, Maggie?"

"I'm a Southern belle. I've wanted to wear one of these ever since I was ten years old and on vacation and we toured an antebellum home in Vicksburg, Mississippi."

In a flash, she stripped off her clothes.

"I didn't realize Southern belles wore thong underwear," Holly observed.

"I made the switch just recently, but I think I'm going to like it. Seems like my panties always ended up there anyway, so I thought why fight it? Zip me?"

"Turn around." Holly grabbed hold of the zipper and

gave it a tug. "Suck it in, Scarlett. This may not be a sixteen-inch waist, but it's not too far from it."

It was a painstaking process, but she finally managed to get the gown zipped. When she was done and stepped away, Grace said, "Oh, Maggie. Aren't you beautiful. Scarlett O'Hara has nothing on you. You are a true magnolia of the South."

"Fiddle-dee-dee. You are so kind, Mrs. Hardeman." Maggie waved an imaginary fan.

"She's a pink magnolia," Holly observed wryly. "We better get her out of that dress before she faints from oxygen deprivation."

"Fiddle-dee-dee," Maggie repeated. "I'll have you know pink magnolias don't faint . . . but I might burst into bloom if you don't hurry with that zipper."

Having finished her mending, Fran used a small pair of scissors to snip a thread, then stood. "There's another hoop skirt gown out there in a larger size. Do you want to try that one?"

"Oh, I do," Maggie enthused. "That would be fun. First, though, it's Holly's turn. Get nekid, girl. I want to see you in my dress."

"It won't fit me," Holly complained as she tugged off her Making Memories volunteer tee shirt. "I'm a good three inches shorter than Maggie."

"Three?" Maggie eyed her up and down with a measuring look. "Uh uh. More like five. But being short won't be a problem here. It's no big deal to cut it down."

" 'Short?' "

A mulish light entered Holly's eyes and Grace hastened to intercede. "Of course, since we're just playing dress-up, it doesn't matter if the dress fits or not."

The bickering continued while Maggie helped Holly

into the dress. It was only when she'd been buttoned, snapped, and zipped and turned to face the mirror that conversation in the dressing room died.

"Oh, Holly," Maggie said, her eyes going wide.

Grace steepled her hands over her mouth. "It's perfect for you."

Silently, Holly stared at her reflection. Her eyes grew glassy with tears.

"Buy it," Maggie whispered, a rasp in her voice.

Holly sucked in two deep breaths. "I can't."

Grace watched her young friend and felt her heart twist. "Sure you can, darling. You're a magnolia, too, you know."

"A Southern belle?" she asked with a laugh. "I hardly think so."

"I know so. Not a wimpy Southern belle, though, and just as strong, just as pink, as our own Maggie Scarlett."

"Wait a minute. This dress isn't too tight?"

" 'As God is my witness . . .' " Maggie quoted *Gone With the Wind* as she reached for a carrot stick. "Sugar."

"Work with me here, Holly." Grace fluffed the wedding gown's train. "You live in an established part of town. Do you have many magnolia trees in your neighborhood?"

"Yes, we have quite a few, actually."

"How many have pink blooms?"

"Hmm . . . only one I can think of. It's in Mr. Crankpot's backyard. He's very proud of it."

"As well he should be. It's the same in my neighborhood. White magnolias outnumber pink magnolias twenty to one. They're just as soft and fragrant as their cream-colored counterparts, but their color sets them apart from the crowd. Pink magnolias are special. Pink magnolias have strength. They have character."

"Hah. If I'm a pink magnolia, then I'm afraid I have root rot."

"Poppycock. Your roots are just fine. Still a little shallow, perhaps, but you're a young sprout. I like this metaphor, Grace. I have only one problem with it. If Holly and I qualify, then you do, too. It seems only fitting. Remember the subject of the painting in the ladies' room back at the Greystone where we first met? Pink magnolias. I think it's a sign. We'll have our own special club, just the three of us. For now, anyway. We can be the founding members of the Pink Magnolia Club."

"Sounds a lot more interesting than Junior League," Grace observed.

Maggie nodded. "I could buy us our own clubhouse in Fort Worth and we could host Making Memories wedding gown sales there. We'll decorate the building in accents of pink. Pink is the breast cancer color, so it's symbolic in that respect, also. We wouldn't want to make everything pink, of course. I don't know a single man who is at ease standing on a cotton candy–colored carpet, and we want men to be comfortable in the Pink Magnolia Club, too."

"Jeeze Louise. Stop. The Pink Magnolia Club? It sounds like a cocktail lounge. Quick, somebody call the paramedics. I think oxygen deprivation ruined Maggie's mind."

"All right. Be that way. Just remember one thing for me, would you?"

"What's that?"

"I know my horticulture, sugar. Magnolias are considered to be long-life-span trees."

❁ fifteen

*t*he women took a break from the dressing room when the cleaning crew arrived to vacuum and dust. When they returned and Maggie took a good look at the rack of reserved dresses Grace had yet to try, she began to get a bit worried. She'd been so certain Grace would find her dream dress here, but she'd already worked her way through half of them and so far, nothing was perfect. The anniversary party was only six weeks away. What if none of these gowns worked? This entire trip would have been a great waste of time.

Well, except for the fact that Fran had needed their help. They'd done a good job today. Maybe they should consider today's volunteer work the first official act of the Pink Magnolia Club. That way, if Grace didn't find her dress, Maggie wouldn't feel like such a failure.

Yeah. And maybe cats would bark, too.

From deep within her, a truth welled up and burst

from her mouth without warning. "I've got to fix myself, girls, or I won't deserve to be a Pink Magnolia."

Grace's and Holly's heads swiveled in unison and they stared at her in shock. "What?" Holly asked.

"I think I've gone a little bit crazy the past few weeks. If I don't do something to help myself, next thing you know I'll be renting dates off the Home Shopping Network."

"Do they do that?" Grace asked.

"I don't know. It doesn't matter. That's not the point." She paused, licked her lips, then added, "I seem to be out of control."

Holly's brows rose in alarm. "Maggie, you haven't gone to bed with any of those guys you've been seeing."

"No. It's not that. I don't want to do that. Not now, anyway. Who knows, though, it might be next. I could turn into a slut."

"We'd have to kick you out of the club in that case," Holly drawled.

"I don't deserve to be in the club now. I'm not a strong woman. What strong woman orders a dozen jeweled dog collars when she doesn't even own a pet?" She paused, pursed her lips. "I wonder how ol' George is doing. Maybe he could use a new collar. Although what I ordered is probably too prissy for a boxer dog."

Holly hung up the dress she had selected for Grace to try next. "Why the sudden streak of insecurity, Maggie? This isn't like you."

"Grace hasn't found a dress yet."

Holly simply stared at her. Bewilderment furrowed her brow. "I'm starting to worry about you."

"That's what I've been trying to tell you. I'm worried about me, too." She dropped her gaze, noticed the rings on her left hand. She wondered where Mike was at this very moment. Who he was with. What he was thinking. Had he thought of her at all? Did he miss her at all? "I never did decide what to do about my wedding rings. They haven't seemed to bother the fellas I've dated."

"Which tells you something about the fellas," Holly observed.

Maggie couldn't argue with that. "Maybe it's time I stopped wearing them."

Grace and Holly shared a significant look. Grace asked, "What feels right to you?"

"I don't know. What would I do with them?"

Holly shrugged. "A teacher I work with removed the diamond and melted down the gold and had a pendant made."

"I wouldn't like that. Talk about having your ex hanging around your neck all the time." She shuddered.

"Honey, are you all right? We don't need to do this anymore. Maybe we should go on back to the hotel now. We can start again tomorrow."

"Do you feel bad, Grace?"

"I'm fine. I thought maybe you . . ."

"I'm fine, too. Just being silly. Pay me no mind. Must be hormones. That's what Mike always said when I got a little goofy. Here, let me help you with this next dress."

Grace had finally worked her way through to the floor-length gowns. Maggie could tell her friend didn't expect to find the perfect dress in this bunch, but then, she didn't know how appropriate a more traditional wedding gown would be.

Grace stepped into a slim-skirted Italian silk, and Maggie tugged the zipper up. The overhead light reflected off the facets in her wedding ring, causing the diamonds to sparkle. "Diamonds and dreams," she murmured. "You know, girls, a woman's wedding ring is just as symbolic as a woman's wedding dress. Maybe more. A gown may symbolize feminine power, but the ring . . . ah . . . the ring represents her dreams. Maybe dreams are the most powerful force of all."

She stepped away from Grace to find both her friends looking at her with wonder. "That's a profound thought, Maggie," Holly said.

"Don't say that like you're surprised." Maggie grinned, then sobered as she studied the two-carat stone set in platinum. "So what do I do with my rings now that my dreams are dust?"

"Don't do anything until you're divorced, for one thing," Holly said. "Don't give away your rings like you gave away your gown."

Maggie shrugged. "Maybe Fran would have a use for them. She could resell them and use the money for wishes just like she does the gowns."

Grace gasped.

Holly gaped. "You're brilliant. That's a great idea."

"You think so?"

"I do," Fran said from the dressing room doorway, excitement shimmering in her voice. "I think it's a super idea. Oh, my. Think of the money we could raise for Making Memories. It's a perfect supplement to our wedding gown sales."

"I can see a few problems with it," Maggie said. "Security troubles, primarily. You couldn't sell them like you do the gowns. You'd be begging to be robbed. No, you'd need a different system, but I'm sure you could devise something that would work. You'll need an appraiser on board, of course. However, I don't think you'll have trouble collecting rings. I know I'd much rather give you my wedding set than hide it in my panty drawer."

"You do it for me, Maggie," Fran said. "You devise a plan I can present to my board. You're the perfect person for this job. You've done such a great job planning Grace's anniversary party. Please say you'll help?"

"Just like that?" Maggie asked, amazed.

"'Just like that' is the only way I get anything done," Fran replied with a laugh.

"Do it." Holly slipped an arm around her waist. "It's just what you need, Maggie, and the job suits you perfectly. You do like your sparkles, after all."

"True," Maggie mused. Excitement sparked to life within her.

Grace nodded. "I agree with Holly and Fran. This is exactly the challenge you need, honey. It'll be so good for you. It's a very worthwhile project, and I believe that building a program from scratch like this, why, it's like a new baby. A new baby to put in your nest to nurture."

"My empty nest," Maggie said absently while her mind raced. Ideas bloomed. Plans began to form. So caught up in the moment was she that it took her a moment to notice the change in the atmosphere of the room. Finally, belatedly, she spied the delight in Holly's eyes, the approval in Fran's expression. She heard the wonder in Grace's soft whisper, "Oh, my."

The dress was a knee-length, ivory Italian silk with a matching beaded jacket. Modest, elegant, with timeless lines and classic appeal, it could have been made with Grace in mind.

Then Fran said, "I can just picture Grace walking down the aisle of that church. It's the perfect dress for the ceremony."

In a cold, quiet voice, Grace asked, "What ceremony?"

"Uh oh," Holly murmured as tension slowly swept through the room.

Grace held herself like a queen, her back straight, shoulders squared. A pretty Bavarian crystal crown hung on the wedding veil rack behind her, and Holly was tempted to pin it to Grace's hair to complete the look. A stronger temptation was to bolt for the door, saying "I told you so" as she passed Maggie, leaving her to deal with the fallout.

And it looked to be a lot of fallout.

"*What ceremony?*"

Holly watched Maggie draw a deep breath, then leap from the proverbial plane. "Well, shoot. You weren't supposed to find out. We've planned a surprise for you. It's going to be wonderful, Grace. You deserve so much."

"Tell. Me. What. You've. Done."

Maggie shot Holly a beseeching look, but she kept her mouth zipped. This was Maggie's idea, Maggie's plan. Hadn't Holly tried to warn her? Hadn't Maggie dismissed Holly's caution with a sweep of her hand? To Holly's way of thinking, Maggie had earned the sharp side of Grace's tongue. Up to a point, anyway, for Holly simply couldn't see Grace taking her anger too far.

Maggie walked to the center rack and began straightening the veils. "We wanted your fiftieth wedding anniversary party to be everything you dreamed of and more. It's your Making Memories wish, sugar, and we wanted it to be something everyone will remember for years and years to come."

"What ceremony!"

"Oh, Grace. You're going to love this." Maggie flashed her a nervous smile. "You and Ben are scheduled to renew your vows at St. Stephens. Reverend Banks will preside. It will be a traditional wedding service, the formal wedding you never had. I can't wait for you to see your little granddaughter dressed up as a flower girl. Your daughter is your matron of honor. She has chosen a flattering gown in the prettiest shade of pink. Magnolia pink, in fact. I decided just today we need to add magnolia blossoms to the floral arrangements. I'll do that as soon as I get home. Your sons drew straws to see who gets to walk you down the aisle. I don't remember who won, though. I'd have to check my book. Ben and Sally chose the music, but now that the surprise is out, you might as well look over everything and see what adjustments you'd like to make."

"Who is paying for all this?"

Holly held her breath as Maggie darted a look toward Fran. She stepped forward and said, "The arrangements are all part of your Making Memories wish."

"How much has it cost?"

"Cost? Oh, I couldn't say."

"Do I need to call the foundation's wish director and ask her? She's the one who makes the arrangements, right?"

"Ordinarily, yes. But in this case—"

"In this case what?"

Fran darted a glance toward Maggie. "It's different."

"How?"

"Well . . . um . . . it's a directed wish."

"Which means?"

"The funds to pay for your wish are not coming from wedding gown sales. A donor chose your wish to grant. She's paying for everything."

Grace stood silent and still, taking it all in. Holly started to breathe again. Maybe this wouldn't cause a big stink, after all.

She thought too soon. Eyes blazing, Grace whirled on Maggie. Her hand flew out and she slapped Maggie's cheek. "How dare you!"

Oh, no. Holly gasped and covered her mouth with her hands.

Maggie fell back a step, her hand against her cheek. She blinked rapidly, fighting back tears that were clearly due to emotional rather than physical pain. "Grace . . . I—"

"Don't try to deny it. I know it's you. Maggie Moneybags. Maggie the Manager. You've done it all, haven't you? Your money is paying for everything. Never mind what I wanted, you knew best."

The bitterness in her voice caught even Holly by surprise. Maggie looked like she was about to faint. Fran had her head bowed and she rubbed her temples with her fingertips.

"Please, Grace," Maggie tried again. "Give me a chance to explain."

"Why should I?" She tore off the jacket, yanked down the zipper on the dress, and shrugged out of it. "Will explaining change a thing? From the very first you knew how I felt about accepting charity from Making Memories."

She threw the dress at Maggie.

"Now, Grace," Fran scolded. "It's not charity."

"No? Let's see. Someone else is paying for something for me because I can't afford to do it. I call that charity."

"It's a gift," Maggie snapped, clutching the dress to her chest. "And dad-gummit, Grace, you are not being very gracious about accepting it."

"Maggie's right, Grace," Fran hastened to say. "It is a gift. She called me right after the Fort Worth sale asking to grant your wish."

"See? That proves my point." Grace's voice was a full octave higher than normal. "She didn't even know me then. She wasn't giving me a gift, she was giving me charity. And I don't want it. I don't need it. I'll have a backyard barbeque just liked I'd planned from the beginning. You can take your wedding gowns and flower arrangements and organists and . . . and . . . stick 'em in peach cake."

With a last glance around, she stomped toward the door.

"Hold on," Holly said, stepping in front of her. Panic fluttered in her chest. "Just wait a minute, Grace. Don't you think you might be overreacting just a tad here?"

"Oh, so you're on her side, too. I should have known. Three is always a difficult number in a friendship because two gang up and take sides against one. It was that way when I was growing up. It was that way with my daughters. I should have expected it."

"I'm not on anyone's side. You're not being fair."

"Fair? You want to talk about fair? Going behind a friend's back, lying to her, are acts of fairness?"

"It was a surprise. We were trying to do something nice."

"And I know why." Tears spilled from Grace's eyes and she vibrated with emotion. "I know why. You think I'm dying. You've done all this because you think I'm dying. You've been my friends because I'm *dying*!"

The word echoed in the sudden silence.

Chin held high and voice regally chilly, Grace said, "Excuse me. I need to run by the baseball stadium while I'm in town."

Grace left them standing like statues. Fran sent Maggie and Holly a worried look, then raced after Grace.

Holly whirled on Maggie and said the first thing that came to her mind. "I told you this was a bad idea."

Temper sparked in Maggie's eyes. "Thank you very much. That's just what I needed to hear. 'I told you so.' That really solves the problem, doesn't it." She stomped across the room to where her purse lay on a table.

"Well, it's true. I warned you from the beginning that she wouldn't like it. She doesn't want to be treated special. It plays upon all her fears. You wouldn't have done all this if she weren't sick."

"But she *is* sick." Maggie fished a giant-size bag of M&M's from the depths of her handbag.

"Not with us, she's not. That's why we're her friends."

"Aha." Maggie ripped open the candy bag with a flourish. "So I have to *lie* to be her friend? Excuse me, but isn't that what her complaint is?"

"Don't yell at me about it."

"Well, she's not here to yell at." Maggie took a handful of M&M's, then offered the bag to Holly. "I'm frustrated. She agreed to be a Making Memories wish recipient, so I shouldn't get hammered for granting it. I wouldn't have gotten to know her otherwise. You know, Holly, I don't appreciate your holier-than-thou attitude. I could use some support here. Grace is spittin' mad and all I tried to do was help." Hurt colored her tone as she lowered her voice and grumbled, "I can't believe she called me names. Moneybags. Maggie the Manager. That's so rude."

"If the Ferragamo fits," Holly muttered, popping green and yellow pieces of candy into her mouth.

Maggie scowled, swallowed, and said, "Excuse me? What did you say?"

"I said if the shoe fits. It's not always easy for a person with normal resources to pal around with someone who spreads money like dirt. As far as being a manager, you can't deny you have control issues."

Maggie's back snapped straight. She grabbed the candy bag from Holly. "Control issues?"

"Yes, control issues. You try to control everything, Maggie. Speaking from a teacher's perspective, I'll bet you were the PTA mom from hell."

"I resent that. I was a good mother to my sons. My job was to teach them and nurture them and make them feel safe. I taught them values and gave them guidance. I instilled them with self-confidence and self-esteem. They've grown into fine young men. Men to be proud of. I did a good job." She tossed a half-dozen M&M's into her mouth at once.

Holly curled a lip. "Yeah? I guess that's why none of them are talking to you now."

Maggie gasped, choked on her candy. Holly hit her once on the back, then stepped away. She felt a shimmer of shame at the cruelty of her words, but the look on Grace's face, the pain in her voice, had boiled all Holly's insecurities to the surface.

Grace was afraid.

Holly hadn't realized that, not until just now, and it shook her to the core. The strength. The confidence. It was all assumed, an act, just an illusion. Grace was faking it and that made her whole hissy fit about lying downright hypocritical.

Maggie wasn't one to let an attack go unchallenged. Once she found her tongue, she wielded it like a weapon. "At least I have children. I'm not too afraid to live my life. You and your Life List, that's such a joke. You're

gonna ski black diamond mountains and dive underwater wrecks, but you're too scared to risk everyday living. Maybe I am too controlling on occasion, but at least
I know what control is. You've given yours away."

Holly's spine snapped straight. "I have not."

"Oh? Right. You're basing decisions today on whether
or not you might have your boobs cut off in ten years.
Now that's command-and-control thinking. Good thing
you're not in the military. I'd worry about our country."

"No wonder Mike left you."

Maggie stepped back, lips pinched in a blanched face.
She threw down the bag of M&M's. Round, colored can-
dies rolled across the floor. "I think we're done here.
Don't you?" Maggie strode toward the door. "The limo
will take you to the airport. I'm going to run a few errands before the flight back."

In the empty dressing room, Holly stared at the two
wedding gowns lying crumpled on the floor. Crumpled
gowns. Crumpled dreams.

Crumpled friendships.

And they still had the long flight home. Holly shuddered at the thought and quoted Bette Davis. "Fasten
your seat belts. It's going to be a bumpy night."

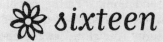

sixteen

maggie walked into her living room and kicked off her Jimmy Choo pumps. She checked her watch and calculated she had an hour to kill before she needed to leave for the hairdresser for her quarterly session with a streaking cap.

It was the one bit of pampering she completely despised. Throughout most of her life, she'd taken great pride in being a natural blonde. Then one morning three years ago, she'd looked into the mirror and saw something worse than the gray other women her age were beginning to see. Maggie saw dull. Faded, flat, washed-out blond. Lifeless blond. She'd rushed to the hairdresser that very afternoon.

She wasn't actually due for a color touch-up for another two weeks, but tomorrow she was scheduled to speak at a chamber of commerce meeting about Making Memories' new Diamonds for Dreams program and she wanted to look her best.

Upon returning home from the debacle in St. Louis—
which had concluded with a truly tense plane ride home,
seated between a scowling Holly to her right and a steaming Grace on her left—a lonely Maggie had jumped feet
first into getting her idea up and running. Putting her Junior League experience to work, she had labored around
the clock meeting with security specialists, jewelry ap-
praisers, and marketing people to develop a business plan.
Now the program was ready to be launched.

Maggie had not felt such a sense of accomplishment
in years. She hadn't ordered anything off the shopping
network for the past two weeks.

That reminded her of the stack of packages waiting in
the dining room to be opened. Now would be a good
time to tackle that task. If she worked steadily, she might
get through half of them before she left for the beauty
shop.

Picking up her shoes, Maggie walked to her bedroom,
where she changed out of her business suit into shorts
and a cotton blouse. With a mind to the job before her,
all the paper and cardboard and packing, she pumped a
bottle of lotion on the bathroom vanity and slicked up
her hands. The pleasing fragrance of lilacs drifted over
her, and she was reminded that this particular bottle had
been another gift from Grace and her granddaughter.

Sadness melted through her and she consciously shifted
the direction of her thoughts. She'd wear her red power
suit to the luncheon, she decided. Black pumps. Clear nail
polish and understated jewelry. She'd be the consummate
professional, no PTA bowhead, and the audience would
take her seriously. Respect her and her ideas.

Mike had regularly attended chamber meetings like
the one taking place tomorrow. What would he think if

he were in the audience? He'd be proud of her, she bet. If they were still together, she'd want him to be there.

Just like he wanted you to be in the audience for his keynote at that Chicago conference, only you chose the track meet instead.

"Oh hush," she grumbled aloud to the voice in her head. She'd been hearing way too much from her conscience of late. Ever since Holly had called her everything but a controlling bee-witch, she'd been defending herself from herself a dozen times per day.

Maggie marched into the dining room and ripped open the first package she laid hands on. A set of embroidered golf towels. Oh, joy. No one in her family played golf. Maybe she'd send them to John. He could use them to wash his car. Or maybe he would pass them on to Mike. He could use them to polish the teak on his boat.

"The *Second Wind*," she muttered softly. Funny, but the name didn't bug her as much as it once had. As ironic as it was, the past few weeks Maggie felt like she'd gotten a second wind herself.

Putting together the Diamonds for Dreams program had proven to be just the ticket to pull her from her doldrums. She felt useful for the first time in months. Taking an idea from conception to implementation was rewarding in a way she'd never before experienced. This must be similar to what Mike felt in his professional life every time he designed something new.

In a way, that put the two of them on an equal footing. Maggie smiled ruefully at the thought and reached for another package. She'd yearned for a sense of equality for years, and now that she could legitimately lay claim to it, he wasn't around to see.

He'd be happy for her, though. She knew that. Mike wasn't competitive that way. He never begrudged another's success. *No, he just didn't like it when you dated.*

"He dated, too," she grumbled as she shoved aside foam packing worms to reveal a set of bar glasses etched with the letter P. Lifting one from the box, she frowned at it as a treacherous little thought snuck in. *You can't blame him. You were a total witch to live with.*

Sighing, Maggie wondered if the neighborhood Presbyterian church might have a use for the glasses. She certainly didn't.

She checked her watch, then reached for a fourth package just as the doorbell rang. She peeked out the dining room window and groaned. An overnight delivery truck waited at the curb.

Maggie opened the door to a too-familiar face. "Hi, Gary. I'd hoped I'd seen the last of you for a while."

He grinned. "Mrs. Prescott, you wound me. I haven't been here for three days. I'd hoped you'd missed me."

"Don't take it personally, sugar. I say that to all my deliverymen. Now, what do you have for me?"

Signing for the package, she waved Gary off and closed the door behind him. Moseying back to the dining room, she picked at the shipping tape bonding the envelope flap, finally ripping it away. The small padded envelope contained a black velvet ring box and a note. Curious, she read the note first.

Dear Mrs. Prescott,

I have enjoyed working with you these past weeks to develop a security plan for your Diamonds for Dreams project. You are doing a very fine thing.

Enclosed, please find my donation to your cause. These rings belonged to myself and my late wife, Sarah, who lost her fight with breast cancer three years ago. We had been married seventeen years.

Thank you for providing me with this opportunity to honor my beloved wife.

> Sincerely,
> Jack Harris
> Lumas Security

The diamond was a one-carat emerald cut, the matching his-and-her wedding bands simple gold rings. Maggie looked at them and burst into tears. These were the first donations to Making Memories' Diamonds for Dreams program.

"It's going to work," she spoke aloud, her words echoing in her empty house. "It's going to be a success."

She wanted to call someone, share the news. She rushed to the phone and automatically dialed a number. "Cody and Prescott Engineering," came the operator's voice.

Oh, shoot. She'd called Mike's office. "Sorry. Wrong number."

She slammed down the phone, thought for a moment, then dialed the Making Memories Foundation office. Fran wasn't in.

Maggie hung up, then paced the kitchen. Who could she call? Who else would appreciate her news? Not the boys, certainly. She'd love to call Grace or Holly, but she couldn't very well do that when they weren't speaking to her.

Mike was the one she really wanted to tell. Mike.

Her traitorous gaze drifted back toward the phone.

"Oh, you couldn't reach him even if you tried," sh scolded. "He's gone. He's sailing the ocean blue. He's ou of touch." Even as she said it, Maggie walked to th phone and dialed his cell number.

Darned if the man didn't answer, sounding distracte and impersonal. "Hello?"

"Uh, Mike?"

Following a dead silence, he asked, "Maggie?"

"Yeah. Um. It's me. Hi."

"Are the boys all right?"

"Oh, yes. I'm sorry. The boys are fine. As far as know, anyway. They're not why I called."

Silence stretched. Eventually, she figured out h wasn't going to fill it. "Can you talk, Mike? Is this a goo time?"

Again, he paused. "I guess."

"Good." Maggie wound the phone cord around he finger and wished she'd used the portable to call. "You'r not going to sail out of the cell's reach anytime soon?"

"I'm moored."

She wanted desperately to ask where, but a note in hi voice warned her not to do it. "Are you enjoying you trip?"

"What's this about, Maggie?"

She was quiet for a moment, searching for words. "I'v done something really neat, Mike, and I wanted to tel you about it."

When he coughed, Maggie couldn't tell if it was rea or fake. He excused himself to get a glass of water, an she waited impatiently, gripping the handset hard, won dering if someone was with him. She didn't take a goo breath until he returned and said, "Okay. I'll listen."

Her back against the yellow-striped wallpaper, Maggi

slid down the wall and sat on the floor. This would be easier if he didn't sound so removed from her. Nervous, she began to tell her husband about her idea.

At first, she rattled on a bit, but when he started interrupting her with questions that indicated interest, she settled down. The awkward pauses disappeared and the strain stretching across the line eased. Eventually, Maggie forgot about the tension and trouble between them, and simply spoke with Mike, the man to whom she'd been married for twenty-five years.

Hearing admiration at her accomplishment in his tone, she puffed up with pride. The conversation continued for almost an hour. Only when the topic turned personal did the uneasiness return. Maggie wished she'd never asked him where he was moored.

Mike cleared his throat. "I'm still on my way to the Caribbean."

"Oh." It told her nothing she wanted to know, not his location or whether he was traveling alone or with a young and supple companion. She didn't want to delve any deeper because she feared he'd end the conversation. She wondered if he might feel similarly when he quickly changed the subject.

"So what do your new friends think about Diamonds for Dreams?"

Leave it to Mike to choose a sore spot. "I haven't told them about it. We've had a . . . well . . . I guess you could call it a falling-out."

"Oh? Over what? Did the young one try to poach on your dates?"

Great. Just great. Maggie closed her eyes. This conversation was sliding downhill fast—and yet, to her surprise, she didn't want to hang up. Didn't want to give up.

"We had a big fight because I planned a surprise party fo
Grace."

Maggie told Mike about the vow renewal debacle and
her row with Holly. To her utter shock and surprise, he
rose to her defense. "Your heart was in the right place
and they shouldn't be so judgmental. Not if they're true
friends."

His words warmed her, filled a place within her that
had felt empty for too long. At the same time, it stripped
her down to honesty's bare bones. "They have a point,
Mike, and you know that too well. I've recognized that
about myself. Finally. I do like to be in control."

"You're a leader, Maggie."

She blinked, taken aback. It was a far cry from calling
her stupid.

"That's a nice way to say it," she said finally, a slow
smile spreading across her face. She unwrapped the
phone cord from around her finger, then entrapped it
again. "I appreciate your support. The fact is I'm a control nut who freaked out when she couldn't control the
passage of time. My boys grew up and I couldn't stop it.
felt useless and I took it all out on you. I wasn't a good
wife to you after Mother died, Mike, and I'm sorry fo
that."

The telephone line hummed a one-note tune withou
words. Maggie held her breath, her mouth dry, though
she wasn't quite certain why.

Finally, Mike said, "I need to go now."

Maggie's heart sank below her stomach. "Oh. Okay."

"Um, thanks for calling."

"Thanks for listening."

"Yeah. Well. 'Bye."

" 'Bye."

Maggie climbed to her feet, but didn't hang up the phone. Neither did he. "Mike?"

Click.

She sighed heavily and hung up the phone. It rang almost immediately and she grabbed it, her heart pounding. "Hello?"

"Mrs. Prescott? This is Prestige Salon. You are late for your two o'clock and Maurice asked me to call and see if you still wanted color this afternoon."

"My roots." Maggie groaned. "I'm so sorry. Tell Maurice I'll be down in ten minutes."

She made it in eight and blew into the salon streaming heartfelt apologies. She patronized Prestige Salon because they made it a point to run on time, and she felt terrible about causing her hairdresser to run late. "Skip the cut if you need to make up time, sugar, and just do the color. I'm so sorry."

He rubbed the bridge of her nose with his thumb. "Don't fret, love. You'll get wrinkles. You've never before been late to an appointment, and I was worried."

"It's been a rough day."

"Sit in my chair and relax. I'll give you a quick neck and shoulder massage before we get started."

After his magic fingers loosened the knots in her neck, he smoothed the streak cap on her head and tied it beneath her chin. He then selected a hook from his implement drawer and began plucking strands of hair through the cap's small holes. Despite his gentle touch, Maggie got tears in her eyes. Though she tried to blame them on a tender scalp, she knew they more likely resulted from a broken heart.

Maurice had pulled hair through the cap on half her head when Maggie's cell phone rang. Her breath caught. Mike?

"Hello?"

"Maggie? It's Holly."

The call caught her totally by surprise and for a moment, she couldn't respond. Then the bitterness, the loneliness, of the past weeks welled up inside her and emerged in her words. "Well, if it's not Miss Pretend-to-Be-a-Friend."

"Save it for later. Justin just called. He's making afternoon rounds at Harris and he told me. Maggie, Grace has been admitted to the hospital."

Holly's hands trembled as she worked the buttons on her shirt. She'd been changing out of her work clothes when Justin called and she'd placed the call to Maggie while standing in only a pink bra and panties.

The sound of Maggie's hello had been welcome to her ears, and she'd felt an immediate sense of relief. But instead of comfort and support, Holly heard snotty remarks from her former friend. The fact she'd been dressed in underwear at the time somehow made it worse. Embarrassed, she retreated into snotty thoughts of her own.

Fashion-plate Prescott had probably answered the phone wearing her little black dress and diamond earrings while drinking a martini before her date took her to the symphony. Never mind that Maggie didn't drink and the Fort Worth Symphony wasn't performing tonight.

"Of course, if she wants to go to the symphony, all she needs to do is whip out her checkbook. She can rent out Bass Performance Hall and hire the musicians for a night."

Holly fumed about Maggie while she pulled on socks and tied her sneakers. Her mutters continued while she grabbed up her keys and dashed for the door.

Deep inside, Holly sensed she focused on Maggie as a coping mechanism. She'd heard the defensiveness in the woman's voice, and despite all her faults, Maggie wasn't ordinarily catty. But if thinking tacky thoughts about Maggie Prescott helped to get her through the next few minutes and hours, then she'd just be tacky. Holly didn't care about being fair at the moment. She needed something, anything, to help her to avoid worrying about Grace. Otherwise, it might not be safe for her to drive.

She backed her car out of her driveway and gunned the gas past Mr. Crankpot's house. As she braked at the stop sign at the corner and waited for traffic to ease, her gaze fell upon a row of beaded irises in the yard across the street. The blooms were all gone, the leaves wilting toward brown. Holly burst into tears.

"Grace is going to die," she moaned.

All Holly's doubts, her insecurities, her fears came rushing toward her like a West Texas dust storm. Grace would die. Ben and her children and her grandchildren would be devastated. They'd never recover.

Grace admitted to the hospital. Why? Holly's fingers drummed the steering wheel. What catastrophe had put her there? The possibilities were endless. Had she a reaction to her meds? Had her cancer spread from her bones? Had she broken a bone, a hip? Had her pain become unmanageable?

"Oh, Grace." Holly reached beneath her seat for the tissues she kept stored there. She tossed the box into the passenger seat beside her, grabbed one, wiped her eyes and blew her nose.

Grace in the hospital. Was she there for the duration? Had she gone there to die? That's what Holly's mom had done. She'd lain in her bed and suffered and screamed.

Holly had heard the screams in her nightmares for years afterward. She still heard them.

"I don't want Grace to die." The spoken words were pure prayer. "Especially not like that."

It wasn't fair. Grace didn't deserve this. She was too good a woman. Stubborn, but good. She should live to a ripe old age. She should see her grandchildren grown and happy. She should complete her Life List. She should—

Holly braked hard at a red light. "Jeeze Louise. Her anniversary."

The big day was only two weeks away. Two weeks. Oh, no. Poor Grace. Poor Ben. Their golden anniversary. Why did this have to happen now? Not three weeks from now? Hadn't she heard dozens of stories about terminal patients who outlived their doctors' prognosis because they wanted to reach a certain anniversary or attend a special event? What happened here? How could Grace falter two weeks—two weeks!—before the Big Event?

"Oh, God. Is this Maggie and my fault?" Holly's shoe slipped off the accelerator. Had they completely ruined the Making Memories wish for Grace, taken all the pleasure out of it, caused her to falter in her goal to live past the big day?

Tears streamed down Holly's face. She'd never forgive herself.

These thoughts and others just as bleak continued to roll through Holly's head as she took the hospital exit off the freeway. The red brick building rose twelve stories against the pale blue sky and she frowned at the sight of it, debating where to park. Would it be faster to try the emergency room first or should she head straight for the patient information desk in the lobby?

Dang it, she should have quizzed Justin more when he called. Since he'd been in his hurried, harried doctor mode, he'd told her only that he'd run into Ben in the hallway. Grace had been admitted and Justin thought Holly would want to know. His news had shocked her, sent her reeling. The dozens of questions now tumbling around her brain hadn't occurred until after he'd hung up.

It occurred to her that Justin might have hurried off the phone on purpose. Maybe he hadn't wanted to be the one to reveal how bad Grace's condition really was.

Holly's stomach was in knots as she parked her car and hurried through the hospital's front doors. She stopped at the patient information desk. "Mrs. Grace Hardeman, please? I'm told she's been admitted, but I don't know where to look—"

"Room 563. Use the central elevators and turn left."

"Thanks." Holly dashed for the bank of elevators and punched the up button hard. As the doors opened and the elevator began to ascend, it occurred to her that Grace might not want to see her. Maybe she hated Holly now. Or if Grace was willing to forgive and forget, Ben might feel differently.

With that thought lying heavy on her heart, she exited the elevator and followed the signs leading to Room 563. Outside her destination, she wiped sweaty hands on her pants, then knocked.

"Come in," Grace called.

At least she was still alive. Holly pushed open the heavy door, walked inside, then stopped in her tracks and gasped. Every visible inch of Grace's skin was red and inflamed. What in the world happened to her?

"Why, Holly. This is a surprise."

"Justin called me. Grace. Oh, Grace." Holly stepped toward the bed and began to babble. "I'm so sorry about everything. I feel so bad about everything. I wish I could fix everything."

Grace's brows arched. "And everything would be . . . ?"

Holly fumbled for a reply. "I just . . . I don't . . . I want to be your friend, Grace. I just want to be your friend."

Her answering smile lifted a shadow from Holly's heart. "I've missed you, honey. I'm sorry we quarreled."

"Oh, me too." Holly blinked back tears, but couldn't keep the horror from her voice when she asked, "Grace. Your skin. Are you in terrible pain?"

Her friend grimaced. "Oh, it's awful. I don't ever recall being this uncomfortable, not even during chemo when I was nauseated all the time. Logic tells me that was worse, but time dulls the memory. Whereas this nonsense today is impossible to ignore." She thumbed a button on the rail and the bed shifted her into a sitting position. "Look at this."

She flipped back the sheet, revealing her legs. Holly covered her mouth with her hand. The hospital gown hit her mid-thigh. From there to the tip of her toes, Grace's skin was one bright reddish-pink rash.

Oh my God. Is this what skin cancer looks like?

"This shouldn't be happening. This is so awful. Where's Ben? Where are your children? Why are you going through this alone?"

Grace grimaced as she shifted uncomfortably in her bed. "Ben's gone down to the cafeteria for coffee with your Justin. We haven't told the children. I especially don't want my granddaughter to know about this. Not until it's over."

"Until it's over?" Holly slumped into the guest chair. She could hold back her tears no longer. "Until it's over? Grace, how can you say that!"

She buried her head in her hands and sobbed.

"Holly, what is it?"

"I don't want you to die! I love you and I'm ashamed because even as I worry about how Ben will manage, worry about your children and grandchildren and their grief, I'm also thinking about me. You're dying and I'm worrying about myself. How's that for being selfish?"

She wiped her eyes, determined to be stronger for Grace. "I thought I was finally learning to deal with all of this. After our trip to St. Louis, I made a decision, Grace. A big one. I wanted to call you and talk to you about it, but after our quarrel . . . well . . . I decided to wait until I got the results. Now I wish I'd called. I wish . . . oh, Grace."

"What results, honey?"

"I had the test, Grace. I have an appointment tomorrow with the genetics counselor to review the results. I'm okay with it. At least, I thought I was okay with it. I've even been looking at bridal magazines. The mother of one of my students is a florist and I actually asked her about bridal bouquets. But now . . . seeing you here . . . like this . . . I don't see how—"

"Holly, wait. You don't under—"

"I should have known I was borrowing trouble. I'm not getting married. I can't get married. Nothing has changed." She fumbled in her purse for a tissue and blew her nose. "Maggie was right. I have no control over my life. I won't allow Justin to share my nightmare. I won't marry him."

Hearing a sound from the doorway, she looked up.

Ben entered the room holding a steaming cup of coffee in each hand.

Behind him stood Justin. Anguish flashed across his face before his expression abruptly went cold. Blank. Without saying a word, he turned where he stood and left.

Ben tossed Holly a chastising look as he handed his wife a cup of coffee. Shaking his head, he followed Justin out the door.

Silence descended in their wake. Holly eyed the kidney-shaped plastic barf bowl and wondered if she'd need to use it. Her stomach churned like a Texas tornado.

Grace sipped half her coffee before she spoke. "You really chap my hide, Holly Weeks. Which, I might mention, only compounds the current problem."

"What do you mean?"

"So much is itching me. Where do I start?" She sighed heavily. "You *should* be ashamed. It offends me to hear you talk that way. Do you know what I would give to have my health like you do? Do you know how much I wish I had your energy, your possibilities, your future? How dare you waste it. How dare you!"

Grace sat up straight. "Do you think you are the only one who is afraid? I'm the one with metastatic breast cancer. I'm the one who, barring a miracle, will most likely die of this disease. I have every right to be afraid and sometimes I am. Sometimes I'm terrified. But I've never, ever, allowed that fear to make me a victim. Shame on you for letting it win."

"But—"

"Hush. I'm not done with you. I know your mother's death was wrenching to the young girl you were. I know it's difficult to live with the knowledge that you might carry a bad gene. But my stars, girl, you must get a grip on yourself. Life is short, whether we live to be twenty-five or ninety-five. You owe it to those who love you to live every minute of it. You owe it to your mother's memory. How many items are on your Life List?"

The unexpected question blanked Holly's mind. "Uh, thirty-two."

"Then you need to make it thirty-three. You need one more line that says 'I will die knowing I have lived.' And right before you take your final breath, I expect you to pick up that little gold pen of yours and check the damn thing off!"

While Holly fumbled for a response to Grace's cursing, a wild-eyed, wilder-haired figure burst into the room. "I got here as fast as I could," Maggie gasped.

Jeeze Louise. And Holly had thought Maggie looked strange that day in the Wal-Mart parking lot. This was the first time Holly had seen a frosting cap worn in public. The clear plastic ties hung undone, brushing her shoulders. Strands of blond hair had been pulled through the cap on only half of her head. She wore jeans and a yellow polka dot blouse and carried a brown accordion file and a cute, Kate Spade yellow polka dot bag.

Holly smiled for the first time in over an hour. For a pretty woman, Maggie Prescott displayed very little vanity. Bossiness, however, remained in plentiful supply.

"I've made a list of specialists, Grace." She nodded toward the file. "They're ranked in order of reputation. I have phone numbers and contact names, but I haven't talked to a soul. This is entirely your decision. I'm here to help you if you'd like, but I won't do a thing unless you okay it first. I also have names for those to speak with regarding insurance concerns. Oh, and I've included names of hotels near the medical centers and the different discount programs they offer for patient families."

She handed the file to Grace and in doing so, took her first good look at Grace's skin. "Good gracious, sugar. Look at you. Where in the world have you been gardening? The poison ivy nursery?"

Grace held out her arms and grimaced. "Isn't it awful? My sweet granddaughter whipped up a new fragrance in lotion for me and it turns out I'm horribly allergic to it. I used it for the first time after my bath this morning and broke out in hives from head to toe."

"Hives?" Holly squeaked. "This is hives?"

"You poor thing," Maggie said.

"It's not some vile form of skin cancer?"

Grace leveled her a chastising look. "You never even asked, Holly. You simply assumed."

"They put you in the hospital for hives? Because of skin lotion?"

"I recently began a new medication and this reaction concerns my doctors, even though I'm personally certain the lotion caused the trouble." She gestured toward the IV bag hanging beside her bed. "They're giving me an antidote of sorts that requires careful administration. Something to do with my immune system. That's why they're keeping me. I'm happy to be here, though, because the itching has almost stopped. It was driving me crazy."

Maggie shot Holly a glare. "I was led to believe you'd . . . um . . . suffered a setback."

"Yes, well. Who was it that said 'Reports of my death have been greatly exaggerated'?"

"Mark Twain." Holly scuffed the toe of her sneaker

against the tile floor. "Maggie, take that ridiculous cap off your head."

"Cap? Oh. Oops." Maggie winced as she whipped off the frosting cap and finger-combed her hair. "I forgot. I was in a hurry to leave."

Grace thumbed through the file Maggie had given her, reading aloud the tab. " 'Grace's Cancer File'?"

"I like to keep organized." Maggie's smile was sheepish. "Thank goodness you don't need all that information. I'll take the file home with me if you'd like. You might not want it cluttering up your house."

"There must be a hundred pages in here."

"Closer to two hundred, I think." Maggie pulled the room's second guest chair up close to the bed. Taking her seat, she leaned forward, speaking earnestly. "Grace, I know this looks like a lot. I want you to know I didn't look into this because I think you're fixing to . . . to . . . expire. I'm just a believer in the adage that information is power and I want you to have access to everything you need to make the best decisions possible for the treatment of your disease."

"Maggie, this is the nicest gesture of friendship I have ever received."

As Maggie visibly relaxed, Grace's gaze fell to her lap. Holly saw her swallow hard. Then, looking up, she addressed them both. "I apologize for what happened in St. Louis. I overreacted. I know your hearts were in the right place, and I acted the ungracious, ungrateful witch."

"No, Grace," Holly protested. "We shouldn't have gone behind your back that way."

"Perhaps, but it was lovely that you did. Earlier, Holly, I scolded you for allowing yourself to be ruled by fear. Well, I need to practice what I preach. You see, I'm so afraid of being afraid. Sounds silly, doesn't it? But it's the truth. When I first learned my disease had metastasized I was crippled by fear. Hearing that diagnosis the second time . . ." Her voice trailed off; she shut her eyes and shuddered.

Maggie reached out and took her hand.

"I wasted my days waiting to die," Grace continued. "It was an ugly way to live and it took counseling and convincing by my health care providers that death was more than a few days away. But the fear is always lurking in the shadows. As silly as it sounds, the fear frightens me more than the cancer. That's what I was reacting to in St. Louis. When I think others believe I am dying, that old monster starts emerging from the darkness."

"I understand," Maggie said. "Believe me, I understand. Since Chase went off to school, I've been motivated by fear. Or maybe I should say *un*motivated by fear, since I couldn't drag myself out of bed some days. I've been afraid to live my life, too. Because it's a different life from the one I've been living for the past twenty-five years and I didn't know how I'd manage. I was afraid that since I wasn't a stay-at-home mom anymore, I wasn't anything. When I first met you guys, I think I knew that in my head, but I didn't know it in my heart. In my heart, I was still so afraid. That's what made me so . . . so . . . what's the word?"

"Dictatorial?" Grace offered with a smile.

"Domineering," Holly suggested dryly.

"Oh, you girls." Maggie grabbed a tissue from the box on Grace's bedside table and dabbed at her eyes. "Mean. I was mean."

"No," Grace said, shaking her head. "You weren't mean."

Maggie's and Holly's gazes met and held. Silently they acknowledged that a few moments of mean had occurred, but those had happened after Grace left. They'd also been reciprocal.

Maggie sighed heavily. "I've done a lot of thinking since St. Louis. I've been trying to work up the nerve to call you both and apologize. To you, Grace, for barging ahead with my plans when I knew you'd rather me leave it alone. And to you, too, Holly. I said some awful things. Friends don't speak that way to one another and I'm very sorry. I've missed you two."

"You're wrong, Maggie." Holly drummed her fingers on her knee as the other two women sent her a look of shocked surprise. "Friends do speak that way to one another. True friends do, because they're honest with one another. Now, they might manage it with less snarkiness than we indulged in, but they tell the truth. That's what we did. Seems to me, it did us each good to hear what the other had to say. I know without a doubt my life has been emptier since St. Louis. I'm so very sorry for hurting you both, and I dearly hope you'll forgive me. But for my part, I'm glad you said what you said. I know I can trust you to be honest. That's important to me, especially now when I have such a big decision to make."

"About Justin?" Maggie asked.

Holly nodded. Grace let out a snort of disgust. "You'd better be careful, girl, or Justin just might make the decision for you." She looked at Maggie. "Holly was in the middle of one of her panic attacks earlier when Justin arrived to hear her declare that she couldn't marry him."

"Oh, Holly." Maggie rolled her eyes. "Men do not have unlimited patience. Believe me. I know. You shouldn't string the poor man along any longer, sugar. It's not fair to either of you."

Holly opened her mouth to defend herself, to explain how her fears for Grace had awakened her own, but then she realized she had no defense at all. Maggie and Grace were right. "When it comes to allowing fear to run our lives, I figure I win hands down. I intend to settle things with Justin once and for all. I've been waiting until after tomorrow."

"Tomorrow?"

"She gets her genetic test results tomorrow."

"Oh. Wow." Maggie leaped up, circling the bed to hug Holly. "Who's going with you? Justin?"

"No. He doesn't know I've been tested. I'm going alone."

"Oh, you can't do that. I'll come with you. What time is your appointment? We could go in my car if you— Oh, wait. I'm doing it again, aren't I? Well, shoot. I'm sorry. Um . . . would you like some company tomorrow, sugar?"

Holly laughed and gave Maggie a quick hug. "Thank you, but this is something I need to do by myself. I had to argue with the counselor to get her to okay it. They ordinarily want you to have someone with you."

"For a reason," Grace scolded.

"Don't ask me why I must do it this way because I can't explain it. I just know it. Deep in my bones, I know it. Support me on this?"

Grace reached up and maternally tucked a stray curl behind Holly's ears. "Of course we will, won't we, Maggie?"

"Sure." Maggie pursed her lips as she eyed the rash on Grace's arm. "What new fragrance did your granddaughter put in her lotion, Grace?"

"Oh, you'll like this. She heard me telling Sally about the floral arrangements for the party. When she heard me prattle on about how much I adore the fragrance, she special-ordered the essential oil in order to make the lotion."

It took Holly a moment to put it together, but when she did, she started to laugh. "Magnolia? Magnolia-scented lotion gave you hives?"

Grace nodded and held out her reddened hands with a flourish. "Guess that makes me a charter member of the club now, hmm?"

"Sugar," Maggie said. "That makes you president!"

❀ seventeen

Saturday morning, Holly arrived at her dad's house to find him out front watering the lawn. "Hey, handsome. Wanna go for a Saturday-Sunday drive?"

Twenty minutes later, they drove off in the Gray Swan, the top down, the picnic basket Holly had prepared sitting on the backseat. "This is the nicest surprise, honey. When I called yesterday, you sounded like a drive with your old man was the last thing you wanted."

"I'm sorry. Yesterday was a bit of challenge and it took me a little while to figure out that a Saturday-Sunday drive with my dad was exactly what I need to cheer myself up."

"Is something wrong, baby?"

They rode for two more blocks before she answered. "Daddy, do you still miss Mama?"

"Every day of my life."

His answer made her next question even more difficult. "Do you ever think you'd have been better off if you'd never married her?"

"Holly Elizabeth Weeks. What sort of question is that?"

"A fair one, I think. You've been widowed thirteen years, Dad, and as far as I know, you've never been involved with another woman."

He grimaced, glancing in the side mirror. "Well, you don't know everything."

Holly arched her brows.

"I've seen a few women since your mother died, Holly."

"You have? You never mentioned it to me."

"I'm entitled to some privacy, aren't I?"

Holly was intrigued. "This from the man who passed out a questionnaire to every boy I dated?" She quoted. "'In fifty words or less, what does DON'T TOUCH MY DAUGHTER mean to you?'"

He scowled. "That's different."

Holly didn't think so, but that wasn't the conversation she wanted to pursue right now. "So who were these ladies? Anyone I know? Where did you meet them? Did marriage ever come up?"

He braked the car to a stop at a red light, then turned to her. "Why the third degree? You have something to tell me? Something about you and Justin, maybe?"

"No. Well, sort of. Maybe. I'm trying to get something straight in my mind. Dad, why didn't you remarry?"

His brow furrowed. "Maybe I should pull off the road if we're going to have a conversation like this."

Softly, Holly said, "It's important to me, Daddy."

Jim Weeks sighed. "The answer is simple. I haven't remarried because I haven't fallen in love again."

"Why?"

"Why? I don't know. I just haven't. I haven't found the right person."

"Do you think you haven't found her because you're not really looking? Maybe you were so wounded when you lost Mama that you unconsciously built walls around your heart to protect it. Maybe it's better to live alone than to risk love and lose again."

Her dad scratched his Saturday stubble. "Nope, you're definitely wrong there. Losing your mom was the worst thing that ever happened to me, true. But loving her was the best. The joy of loving her has the pain of losing her outdistanced by a West Texas mile. Not only did I get you out of the bargain, I had fourteen years of true happiness, fourteen years' worth of precious memories I'll carry with me until the day I die."

"Memories, not regrets," Holly murmured, thinking of Ben Hardeman.

Her dad took her hand and squeezed it. "That's right. I could go on for hours, but I'm not certain what you're looking for from me. I don't know what's going on in your mind, Sunshine. I gave up that exercise the day you came home from the mall with a nose ring."

"That was a joke, Dad. It was a clip-on."

"Whatever. Holly, what's this about?"

"I want you to take me somewhere, Daddy. I need you to show me the way."

"All right. Where we going?"

"The cemetery. I haven't been there since the funeral. I want to visit Mama's grave and I need you to show me the way."

A pleased smile bloomed slowly across her father's face. "I'll be happy to show you, Sunshine. Very happy."

Twenty minutes later he parked the car in a tree-shaded lane in Riverside Cemetery. His car door squeaked as he opened it and prepared to get out. "She's just down this row. Near the rose bushes. Remember how she liked roses?"

Holly remained in her seat looking straight ahead, staring not at the emerald grass and bed of pink begonias, but into the past. Back to the days before her mother fell ill. Back to the days of laughter. Her father opened the passenger door. "Holly?"

She took his hand and left the car. They walked past three graves before she stopped. "Dad? Could I . . . would you mind . . . I think I'd like to do this by myself."

Surprise flashed across his expression. "Sure, honey. Whatever you need. I'll listen to the car radio. The Rangers are playing a day game."

Holly kissed him on the cheek, then continued past the small bronze rectangles until she reached the one that read *Elizabeth M. Weeks, Beloved wife and mother.*

Holly twirled the yellow rose her dad had purchased in the cemetery's flower shop and swallowed hard against a knot of emotion threatening to block her throat. She bent down and slipped the flower into the brass urn built into the grave marker, then drew a deep breath and exhaled in a rush.

"Hi, Mama."

Minutes dragged past. The summer sun beat down upon Holly and perspiration beaded on her skin, trickled down between her breasts. She plucked at her shirt. "I hate wearing a bra in summer. They're so hot. I can't go without, though. I'm not flat-chested anymore. Took me a long time to get boobs, but once I got them . . . well . . . I'm stacked, Mama. Just like you were. I have Daddy's eyes and his hair color, but I have your boobs. Lucky me, huh?"

The slightest of breezes whispered through the leaves of a giant old pecan tree standing nearby. From somewhere off to her left, Holly heard the slam of a car door. A woman about Maggie's age helped an elderly woman make her way toward a section of graves bordered by a hedge of Indian hawthorn.

"What am I babbling about? This is the very first time I visit this place and I spend my time whining about my boobs and the heat. If my friend Maggie were here with me now, she'd tell me I'm being insensitive, complaining about boobs here, under these circumstances. She's a good woman, Mama, and she means well, but she doesn't understand. I hope she never does."

A monarch butterfly fluttered in dips and loops before coming to rest on the E on the grave marker. Watching its black and gold wings open, then close, Holly took it as a sign.

The butterfly was a symbol of resurrection, of new life emerging from the darkness. *Appropriate*, Holly thought, *under the circumstances*.

"It's different with my friend Grace. She probably would understand how I'm feeling. You'd like her, Mama. You'd like both Grace and Maggie. They've been good friends to me. Like mothers, after a fashion." Holly slipped her backpack-purse off her shoulder, dropped it on the ground, then sat cross-legged beside it.

Holly gazed around, breathed in the peace. Funny, but she'd expected a cemetery to be an uneasy place. "Daddy picked a nice spot here. I guess I'm an awful daughter for never having visited before now. I've been afraid, Mama. Not of the cemetery, but of facing you. Facing . . . life.

Funny place to come to face life, isn't it? I'm just as contrary as always. Daddy says I get that from you. I have your contrariness, your cleavage."

She closed her eyes and said it. "Your mutant gene."

Holly had tested positive for the BRCA2 gene mutation.

"I haven't told anyone. I won't tell Dad. He's already lost one of us. I don't want him to worry himself sick that he'll lose the other, too. You see, I'm not entirely pessimistic. Even with the altered gene, it's still not a sure thing I'll get breast cancer, Mama. It's not a hundred percent. Like the counselor told me, everybody has damaged genes. I just know what mine is. I may not be able to beat the Big C entirely, but I can sure as heck beat it back with a stick.

"I'm glad I had the test done. I know I'm a candidate for all the high-tech stuff—special screening, clinical trials, chemoprevention. Surgery if I want it. Medical science has come so far in the years you've been gone. They've learned tons since the mid-nineties when the BRCA gene mutations were identified in the research lab. I think I've finally realized that I don't have to die. What I have to do now is try and figure out how to live."

Holly unbuckled the flap of her backpack, reached into its depths, and fished out her smooth leather wallet. Opening it, she reached into that special spot between her driver's license and her Discover card and removed the rectangle of paper. "This is my Life List, Mama. I began it the day of your funeral, and I refined it over the years. It has thirty-two items on it, because that's how old you were when you died."

Again, she extended her hand into her backpack. This time she pulled out her special gold pen. Unfolding the paper, she perused her list. "I've done okay. Checked off quite a few items. Could probably mark through a few more right now. Take number one, for instance. I'm always kind to telemarketers. Everyone has a job to do and they are people, too."

Holly checked off number one. Going down the list, she marked through number six: *I will have a friend who makes me laugh and one who lets me cry*; number fifteen: *I will own glasses that match, a good set of wrenches, and a pair of crotchless panties*; and after a moment's consideration, number eighteen: *I will be a man's "Best He Ever Had."*

I have confidence Justin would concur, she mused.

Gracefully, Holly rose to her feet. She tucked her pen into her pants pocket and held the sheet of paper in both hands. "My Life List," she said. "I thought if I did all these things, I would be Living with a capital L. But I was wrong. What I've come to realize, what my friends helped me to see, is that this is no Life List. This is a list of things to do before I die. It's a death list. A dying list. I've been spending so much time trying to Live—capital L—that I never learned to live. Well, I'm done with that, Mama. I'm ready, finally ready, to starting living my life. The first thing I'm going to do is this."

Holly ripped her Life List in two. Then in four. Then in eighths. She ripped it over and over again until her Life List was no more than confetti. She threw the pieces up into the air to scatter on the breeze. Laughing, she whirled around.

"Girl, have you lost your mind?" her father called.

She looked around to see him standing a dozen yards away. Out of earshot, thank goodness. "No, Daddy, I haven't lost my mind. Although, I feel as if I've lost ten pounds."

"Don't start that. I swear, you are just like your mother, whining about your weight. What is it about women and weight, anyway?"

They stood beside Elizabeth Weeks's grave for another ten minutes, chatting and reminiscing. Laughing. Then Holly returned to the car, leaving her father to his own private thoughts in the place his beloved wife had been laid to rest. As she walked away, she heard him say, "She turned out good, didn't she, Lizzie?"

Her heart warmed and the smile stayed on her face as she approached the Gray Swan. Waiting for her dad, she rapped the tip of her gold pen against the dashboard and hummed the old Helen Reddy song "I Am Woman."

Her dad sauntered back to the car and climbed in, saying, "Where next, pumpkin?"

"Let's do an all-right-turn day and see where that takes us, okay?"

"Sounds good to me."

He started the motor, but just before he put the car into gear, Holly stopped him by placing her hand on his arm. "Wait, Dad. Before we go, do you happen to have any paper with you? I need to write myself a note."

"Look in the glove box. There's a small spiral where I keep gas mileage notes."

She found it, ripped out a sheet, then with her special pen wrote a title:

My Living List
First and Last Item: I will die knowing I have lived.

She folded the slip of paper and tucked it into her wallet in a new special place, between the photos she carried of the men in her life: her dad and Dr. Justin Skipworth.

"You need to be home any certain time?" her father asked.

"As long as I'm home by four, that'll be fine. I have a date tonight with a handsome doctor."

She couldn't think of a better way to start living.

Maggie cracked open the bride's dressing room door and peeked out into the church. "He stood me up," she grumbled. "The most important date I've had in twenty-five years, and he stands me up. I can't believe it."

"Oh hush," Holly said. "Today isn't about you, Maggie Prescott."

"I know that. It's just that nothing is turning out like I'd planned. That's difficult for me."

Holly walked over and gave Maggie's arm a comforting pat. "Everything is lovely, Maggie. Don't worry. The church is beautiful. The reception room looks divine. Grace is happy as a clam."

Maggie sniffed. "I still think she could have let us help her get dressed."

"Quit being such a baby. It's only right Sally helps her, and the room is exceptionally small."

"She could have dressed in here with us. She didn't have to use the lavatory."

"Maggie, what's going on? You're . . . oh . . . you're nervous, aren't you?"

"Of course I'm nervous. This is the most important event I've ever planned. I want everything to be perfect and it's certainly not starting out that way. Grace hasn't let us see what she is wearing and the ribbons on her bouquet are white instead of ivory and I've already ruined one pair of pantyhose and I only brought one spare and I'm going to be alone at this party today and while being alone isn't a problem for me because I've learned I'm okay with it, I didn't want to be alone today and I don't like it!" She grabbed a tissue from the box just as a knock sounded on the door.

"Don't start the waterworks, Maggie. Please. You'll ruin your makeup and your eyes will be all red and Grace will worry."

"You're right." Maggie paused, took a deep, bracing breath, and with determination, shook off her tears. Then she answered the door and time stood still.

Mike.

"Sorry I'm late. My flight was delayed."

Maggie couldn't speak. He looked tall and tanned and so handsome that he took her breath away. *I've missed you, Mike Prescott.* Finally, she found her voice. "I'm so very glad you were able to make it at all. Thank you for coming."

"Thanks for inviting me." He hesitated, then said, "You look great, Maggie."

She beamed and preened, smoothing the skirt of her pale pink sundress. "Thanks. You'll see a lot of pink around here today. Grace has decided it's her favorite color."

"You always were pretty in pink."

Maggie wanted to kiss him. She wanted to throw her arms around him and kiss his socks off. And maybe more. Now was not the time, however. They still had issues to cover, plenty to settle between them. But his acceptance of her invitation to the Hardemans' anniversary party was a start. A very nice start.

Maggie was greatly encouraged.

"We're still getting dressed in here or I'd ask you in."

She smiled sheepishly as she showed him the hole in her stocking at the ankle. "If you want to take a seat, I'll join you just before the ceremony begins."

"All right. Good. Well, I'll see you in a few minutes,, then."

Maggie shut the door, then leaned against it, swallowing a squeal of pleasure but allowing her smile full rein.

"*Mike* is your date?" Holly demanded. "I thought he was on a boat in the Caribbean."

"He was. He flew back for me."

"So you're back together? Why didn't you say something?"

"We're not back together. We're talking about it."

"Talking is good," came Grace's voice.

Maggie and Holly turned as she glided out of the lavatory into the dressing room. Holly clasped her hands in front of her mouth. "Oh, Grace, you're gorgeous."

Maggie clapped with delight. "It's the Making Memories dress. The one from St. Louis."

Grace nodded. "It's perfect. I may be stubborn, but I'm not stupid. It wouldn't do for me to wear anything else. The week after our trip, I called Fran and asked her to send it. This and one other."

She unzipped a garment bag hanging on the clothes rack and removed a familiar dress, a vintage wedding gown made of slipper satin and Belgian lace. Maggie's wedding gown. "I didn't feel right about letting it sell to anyone else. Maggie, you have given me so much. Please accept my gift to you in return."

"On one condition," Maggie said through teary eyes. "Holly must promise me she'll borrow it if the need arises. Which I suspect will happen in the very near future."

With reverence, Holly trailed a finger across the aged slipper satin and Belgian lace. "It's the most beautiful wedding gown in the world."

Maggie and Grace leaned forward anxiously. Maggie asked, "So you'll wear it?"

Holly nibbled at her lower lip, then smiled a Mona Lisa smile. She checked her watch. "It's almost time. Maggie, we'd better find our seats."

"Holly!" Grace and Maggie both protested.

Laughing, she opened the door. Grace and Ben's son, resplendent in his tux, stood just outside, his hand raised to knock. "Come on in. She's ready."

Holly finger-waved a teasing good-bye, took a step from the room, then stopped and looked back over her shoulder. "Congratulations, Grace. You are an inspiration and I'm proud to be sharing this day with you."

No one spoke for a moment after she left, then Maggie sighed with mock frustration. "So, was that a yes or a no?"

Grace laughed. "I think it was a definite maybe."

Nodding, Maggie lifted Grace's bouquet from a florist's box on the dressing table. "Now be careful with this," she said, handing it over. "I still think it was a mistake to use magnolias."

"Quit being such a worrywart. The doctor said the flower itself won't bother me, and in my opinion, nothing else would do."

"If you turn into a pink magnolia and clash with your peach cake, don't blame it on me." Maggie kissed Grace's cheek and whispered, "Happy anniversary, sugar. I hope this day is all you dreamed it would be."

She dabbed at tears as she hurried down the aisle, then slid in next to Mike and offered a loving grin. He leaned toward her, brushed a quick, gentle kiss across her lips, then tucked her arm through his.

Maggie settled back to watch the ceremony, for the first time looking forward to the second half of her life.

Grace stood beside her son at the back of the church, gazing toward the altar where Ben waited, flanked by their children and grandchildren. Time seemed to stop as her heart overflowed.

What a gift she'd been given, this life of hers.

She'd had fifty years with Ben Hardeman. Fifty years. It was hard to imagine that so much time had passed. Gazing up the aisle toward the weathered, wrinkled man, she recalled the freckle-faced boy who'd thrown baseballs at milk bottles to win a figurine for her at the county fair on their first date. She'd always said she fell in love with him the moment he'd handed her the pink chalk cherub.

They'd had their ups and downs, of course. Some downs lower than others. She had a photograph hanging in her kitchen of a bubbling mountain stream bordered by fir trees and pines and pretty columbines. The caption beneath the photo quoted Carl Perkins. "If it weren't for the rocks in its bed, the stream would have no song."

It was, Grace thought, a good analogy for life. Her personal life stream had lots of little rocks, a few logs, and a couple of humongous boulders along the way. As water rushed over and around the obstacles, it created that wonderful, exciting music of life well lived. Between the white water, life drifted in placid pools of peace, its song soothing and restful and welcome until rocks appeared to stir up the froth once again.

Rocks would reappear. Of that she had no doubt. One big boulder in particular lay in wait before her.

But today wasn't a day to think about endings. Today as a day to think about love and life and living well. he'd been so blessed.

Ben. Her children. Grace's gaze drifted toward her aughter, then to each of her sons. Babies had been the reatest joy of her life. Her children had fulfilled her, iven her life purpose, enriched it and anchored it and :nt it soaring. Nothing she'd done in her sixty-seven ears was as important as raising her children. Each of hem had turned out fine, too. Better than fine. Oh, ire. A time or two her kids had been rocks in her ream, but they'd all made it through the rapids to-ether without getting too terribly soaked.

And her grandbabies. They were pure pleasure. They vere her reward for fighting the fight for the past eight ears.

Her youngest grandson, seven-year-old Sean, saw her ratching him and waved. In the second row from the ont, Maggie followed the path of Sean's gaze and added wave of her own.

Grace smiled. Husband, family, and friends. Dear iends. Friends who brought humor and variety to her vorld, who supported her during those troubling, rocky imes. Dear friends who enriched her life.

If her stream went dry today, Grace would go knowing he'd taken her own advice. She would die knowing she ad lived. In the meantime, she wasn't wasting a minute.

Grace had *Living* to do.

The big band sounds of Glenn Miller and Tommy Dorsey drifted on the air at the Ashford Hotel. Hot anapés sizzled in buffet trays, the aroma a pleasing blend f spices, meat, and fresh-baked pastry. Uniformed wait-ers carrying trays of crystal champagne flutes mingled with the guests. At the far end of the room, a small crowd gathered in front of a laptop computer to watch the PowerPoint presentation of old family photographs the Hardemans' grandson had put together as his gift to his papa and nana.

Holly primped in the ladies' room. She freshened her makeup, reapplied her lipstick, and rubbed cream perfume on pulse points at her wrists and the base of her neck. She wanted to look her best, needed it to boost her confidence. Justin was acting stiff and stuffy toward her.

He was still sulking about what he overheard her say in Grace's room at the hospital that day. Holly suspected being surrounded by wedding paraphernalia exacerbated the problem. She returned to the reception and cast her gaze about, searching for Justin. Maggie and Mike stood near the front of the room admiring his aunt's peach cake. While Holly watched, he reached out and took his wife's hand. Maggie glanced up at him and smiled.

Holly sighed with satisfaction and continued to survey the room. Meeting Grace's gaze, she grinned and waved. Her friend was laughing, beaming, surrounded by her family and friends. Holly had never seen a woman look so happy.

Then, Holly found him. Dressed in his dark blue suit, a white shirt, and a sky blue tie, Justin leaned casually against the painted white wall, his arms crossed, an unreadable expression on his face. He waited for Holly to come to him.

"Will you dance with me?" she asked.

He nodded but didn't speak, leading her onto the dance floor. Holly went into his arms like she was com-

ng home. They danced to "Moonlight Serenade" in si-
ence.

When the band segued into "Stardust," she asked,
"What's the matter, Justin?"

"This is more difficult than I expected it to be."

"What is?"

He closed his eyes and shook his head. "Never mind."

Holly did mind. She'd made him unhappy and she
had to fix it. Thank goodness she had a plan.

So much had changed since the day he first asked her
to marry him. She was no longer the woman who'd sauntered up Main Street toward the Greystone Hotel, her
Life List in her purse, the love in her heart overshad-
owed by despair. She had changed. The fear was gone.
Now, the time had come to prove it to the man she
loved.

"Justin, did you mean what you said that day we saw
the genetics counselor?"

"I said a lot that day, but yeah. I meant what I said.
Don't worry, Holly. I told you I won't ask you to marry
me again, and I meant it."

"That isn't what I'm talking about. I mean the part
about the test results. That you'll love me and want me
no matter what the tests reveal."

He stopped mid-step. "Have you finally made up your
mind? Are you going to have the test?"

"Answer my question first. Did you mean it when you
said you'd love me whether I'm positive or negative or
have surgery or not?"

"Of course I meant that!"

"I thought so."

"Holly, I—"

She shushed him with an index finger against his lips.

"Maggie told me she let slip what I had planned that da[y] at the Greystone."

He blinked, obviously taken aback by the change i[n] direction of their conversation. "Storeroom sex an[d] crotchless panties."

Grinning, she dipped her hand into her neckline an[d] pulled out the key she'd carried nestled between he[r] breasts since bribing the maintenance worker earlier tha[t] morning. She swung it back and forth in front of Justin['s] face. "I had set a goal to do something deliciousl[y] wicked. Now I simply want to live."

"Is that a key to . . . ?"

"I checked it out. The Ashford's storeroom is nice[r] than the Greystone's."

He missed a step. "Oh, God."

The band played the refrain of "Taking a Chance o[n] Love" as Justin's hand slid from Holly's waist south[.] "What about the rest of it?"

"The rest?

"The panties."

"Now, sweetheart, I don't want to spoil the surprise."

He groaned and pulled her closer, burying his fac[e] against her hair. "Witch."

Joy bubbled up inside Holly, overflowing her heart[.] Laughing, she pulled away, took both his hands in hers[.] "I'm not afraid anymore."

In the periphery of her vision, she spied Maggie an[d] Grace, standing beside each other, watching her. Cheer-ing her on.

Then her focus narrowed to Justin. Only Justin. H[e] was her world, her strength, her future. Her love. "I'[m] asking."

"Hmm . . . ?"

"I love you, Justin Skipworth. Will you marry me?"

"Holly," he breathed out in a long, relieved sigh. His chocolate brown eyes warmed with pleasure and his mouth curved to a satisfied grin. "Jeeze Louise, woman. I thought you'd never ask."

Dear Readers,

I hope you have enjoyed the hours you've spent with Grace, Maggie, and Holly. Writing this book has been a labor of love for me, primarily because I've seen firsthand the wonderful work done by the Making Memories Breast Cancer Foundation.

Grace's fiftieth wedding anniversary party is a fictional example of the kinds of wishes Making Memories fulfills for metastatic breast cancer patients. Actual wishes granted have ranged from Disney World trips to computers to a video camera for a dying young mother to use to record bedtime stories for her preschool children. Maggie's Diamonds for Dreams program is being launched even as I write this. The story she tells about her World War II–era wedding gown is based on the tale relayed to me by Cecilia Greenstein when she donated her mother's dress at the Making Memories wedding gown sale in St. Louis. I thought it was one of the most beautiful gowns I had ever seen and in fact, I later purchased it as a keepsake, much to my husband's chagrin. (Closet space is at a premium in my house.)

In researching this novel, I traveled to Making Memories' headquarters in Oregon, where I learned about the organization's day-to-day operations. I visited the warehouse where the foundation stores most of its ten thousand wedding gowns, helped open boxes of arriving donations, and met many of the volunteers who work with Making Memories' founder, Fran Hansen.

Much of my time, however, was spent reading the letters—thousands of them—that have been included with the donated dresses. I found myself laughing over them and crying over them, sometimes both at the same time. I read messages of hope and courage, of healing and humor and faith and despair. I read letters from brides whose marriages ended shortly after they were begun and letters from brides who had celebrated their golden wedding anniversary. I also found letters from brides who had purchased their gowns from Making Memories. One was from a daughter whose mother had donated her own wedding dress in memory of a breast cancer victim, not knowing her daughter hoped to wear it when she married. The daughter bought back the gown and wore it as a surprise for her mom. The foundation has given this family a truly wonderful memory.

Through these letters, I came to see the very real and human emotions that are part of the Making Memories tale. I tried to bring those worries and fears, dreams and desires to Grace, Holly, and Maggie in *The Pink Magnolia Club*.

Since that first trip to Oregon, I have become very involved with the Making Memories Breast Cancer Foundation. My fourteen-year-old daughter, Caitlin, and I work as many wedding gown sales as we can manage. I most enjoy volunteering at the donation table. Caitlin prefers returning gowns to the racks from the dressing room. Easier to pick out her favorite that way, she tells her dad as he shudders at the thought of his baby as a bride. We've had some lovely mother-daughter times at the sales. We've made some very special memories together.

That, you see, is what it's all about.

Here's wishing each of you makes a special memory with someone you love today.

Geralyn Dawson
November 2001

acknowledgments

I want to thank Linda Robinson, genetic counselor at the University of Texas Southwestern Medical Center, for her time, interest, and expertise. My thanks to the women of the Yahoo Breast Cancer Club, who patiently answered my questions and offered such valuable insight, and also to Susan Friedman and the "previvors" of FORCE, *www.facingourrisk.org*, for sharing your fears and feelings. You helped me breathe life into this story and I'm exceedingly grateful. And as always, special thanks to Sharon Rowe, Pat Cody, and Mary Dickerson, critique partners and friends. I love you all dearly.

I wouldn't have been able to write this book without the support of two very special women, my agent, Denise Marcil, and my editor, Caroline Tolley. You heard my passion for this story and believed in me, and that means so very much. You're my champions and I thank you from the bottom of my heart.

Finally, my thanks to Fran Hansen, founder of the Making Memories Breast Cancer Foundation. Fran, Oprah had it right. You truly are an angel.

For more information about the Making Memories Breast Cancer Foundation, please visit its website at www.makingmemories.org.

Wedding rings, wedding gowns, and cash donations may be sent to:

Making Memories Breast Cancer Foundation
12708 SE Stephens St.
Portland, OR 97233

Information on how to become a Making Memories wish recipient can be obtained through the website or by contacting:

Making Memories Breast Cancer Foundation
Anna Nelson, Wish Director
232 S. Cole St.
Molalla, OR 97038

Those interested in purchasing a wedding dress from Making Memories should check the website to see when a gown sale is coming to your area.

Readers can write to Geralyn via her website at www.GeralynDawson.com.

WIN A HANDMADE QUILT!

Enter
The Pink Magnolia Club
Sweepstakes!

To enter, go to **www.simonsayslove.com**, follow the instructions
to send an e-postcard of *The Pink Magnolia Club* to a friend,
and you will automatically be entered in a sweepstakes to win a
one-of-a-kind Making Memories Wedding Gown Quilt!

This stunning work of art is a queen-sized, thirty-five square
quilt with a subtle Southern theme in hues ranging
from soft golden candlelight to bright bridal white, with the
centerpiece a Southern Belle embroidered in metallic
gold thread. Incorporating materials from twelve different
donated wedding gowns, including organza, bridal satin,
taffeta, antique satin, cotton brocade, beads, sequins,
and dozens of different laces, the Making Memories
Wedding Gown Quilt is a special keepsake to be treasured
always. Designed and created by Zeta Moore of
Benton City, Washington, this quilt was donated by the
Making Memories Breast Cancer Foundation.
See exclusive photos of the quilt at www.simonsayslove.com!

The Pink Magnolia Club Sweepstakes ends
on November 1, 2002, so hurry and enter today!

Also available from

GERALYN DAWSON

The Bad Luck Wedding Night
Sizzle All Day
Simmer All Night
The Kissing Stars
The Bad Luck Wedding Cake
The Wedding Ransom
The Wedding Raffle

SONNET
BOOKS

Published by
POCKET BOOKS

2352-03